Andrei LIVADNY

The Crystal Sphere

Thank you FOR yo
and inspiRA
They mean so much
Andrei Livadny.

The Neuro

BOOK ONE

MAGIC DOME BOOKS

The Crystal Sphere
The Neuro, Book # 1

Published by Magic Dome Books, 2017

ISBN: 978-80-88231-23-3

TABLE OF CONTENTS:

CHAPTER ONE

A THUNDERSTORM raged over the metropolis. The thin strip of electrostatic car wipers was struggling under the torrents of rain pelting the windshield.

My ancient Rover held the road well. The squat outlines of deserted neighborhoods whizzed past. The disabled autopilot flashed an anxious red light on the dashboard.

I loved it. The road softly flew past. It was already dark. Flashes of lightning illuminated the urbanscape. Earlier that day, the city had been melting in its own heat, making the expected evening weather change all the more welcome.

Gradually, the tension began to release me. The stuffy office, the bullying boss, even the realization of the fact that my own life was flashing uselessly past didn't feel as oppressive any longer. Another couple of miles, and everything would be different.

I touched the communicator to activate it and sent a voice message,

"Hi Christa, I'll be online in about twenty minutes. Don't be late. We have an instance to do, remember?"

A bolt of lightning raked at the unfinished power substation building, digging into its latticework pylons and exploding in cascades of sparks. It looked both beautiful and spooky.

Network connection temporarily unavailable

Only a year ago, this used to be the asshole of the world. Now the whole area was already consumed by the advancing metropolis. The little town I'd grown up in was already in line for demolition, deep foundation pits gaping along both sides of the road.

I'd been offered several relocation choices. I hadn't decided on any of them yet. I was playing for time. Tonight I might know. Once we completed the quest, I'd have a serious conversation with Christa. We'd been together for almost six months. We'd been a party, I mean, doing a complex non-linear plot line which was impossible to complete solo. We had twenty-four hours to do one final dungeon.

And then what? Would we just disband? Was it the time to go our own ways?

As I pondered over all of this, I hadn't even noticed the last mile flying past. A dilapidated nine-story building filled my headlights, its façade darkened with time. They weren't going to tear it down quite yet. Normally, big developers have little patience for stubborn tenants like myself — and they'd been on my case for a good ten days already. All because of Christa and the quest which had a strict deadline. Moving house really didn't fit into my immediate plans.

Well, look for yourself. I had a nine-till-five job in the office. I couldn't very easily quit, either, considering I'd just taken out a loan to upgrade some equipment I used. Plus my bank refused to accept Middle Earth in-game currency! They'd told me, in as many words, that this legendary virtual world was rapidly becoming defunct, losing users by the minute. So they'd offered me an ultimatum: either I joined Crystal Sphere — the Infosystems Corporation's latest baby — or I'd have to use my real-world wage as security.

I parked up by my front door. They'd already disconnected the elevator. Never mind. I could use some exercise.

The steel door of my apartment creaked, as

old as everything else was here. My parents' furniture and choice of design didn't look like much, that's for sure. Still, these modest quarters housed some of the latest cutting-edge gaming equipment.

A U-shaped console occupied the room's center.

"Activation," I said, heading for the kitchen.

The fridge was empty but I wasn't that interested in food at the moment. I grabbed an energy drink and used it to wash down an upper.

Tomorrow I might have a proper meal. Why not? I could invite Christa to a café. A restaurant I couldn't afford, but still we needed to meet up, have a chat and celebrate. She lived somewhere nearby: we'd mentioned our respective providers once, discovering we used the same company which meant we were almost neighbors.

I didn't give a damn about unwritten real-life meeting etiquette. Both Christa and I were responsible adults. It was probably true what they said these days about the latest technologies steering humanity toward extinction. Meaning, all relationships were rapidly becoming virtual. I disagreed entirely. My own parents had met online, and that was a fact.

A familiar beep awoke me from my musings. The system had booted up. I finished off my drink, stripped down and changed into an elastic suit studded with emulators — a real beauty.

Welcome to my world where a run-of-the-mill office rat was about to transform into a level-124 warrior!

Three interlinked curved monitor screens with a built-in holographic 3D function glowed invitingly at the center of the room.

I slumped into the seat and connected my suit's optic cables to the console.

Reality faded into the background of my mind.

* * *

MIDDLE EARTH. LOGIN

At first, the virtual world appeared on the screens as a 2D picture. Then it expanded, acquiring depth, and enveloped me, surrounding me with high-density holograms.

For a few more seconds I still could make out the outlines of my apartment; then they too disappeared. Tactile emulators kicked in. My hand got caught on a bramble. A thorn pierced my skin. The quiet rustle of the apartment's environment generator was drowned out by the whisper of leaves. Earthly forest smells wafted in my face. A beetle buzzed past, the sound quickly dying away in the thick shadows.

The immersion levels were unbelievable. This was as far as the latest gaming technologies could possibly take you. Science just couldn't improve on this no matter how hard they tried.

I was alone. Christa was late. This wasn't like her at all.

I looked around me, taking in the small forest glade. The entrance to the dungeon was still sealed with shimmering magic symbols. A scared rabbit scampered past. The ferns next to a mossy cliff swayed.

A mob?

Well, what do you think?

A Werewolf, level 105, the system informed me.

My peripheral eyesight blurred, framed with a smudged crimson line as combat mode kicked in. The Fury points counter quivered, gaining momentum. Fury points could only be generated in combat in order to perform various combos. They could also be used by certain unique creative abilities only available in combat mode.

The werewolf howled and leaped out of the shadows into the moonlight. This was a strong and sinewy veteran. His gray hair bristled. His eyes glowed; his jaws emitted a long low growl.

He wasn't much for me level-wise. He didn't offer much XP but could do a nasty job on my armor. He had this ability called Fire Claw.

But still... better that than nothing at all. I took cover behind my battered full-length shield which received the first hits. It worked! My Fury bar soared to half way up. The shield's Durability plummeted, but the mob's Energy had its limits too. He leaped back, his flanks heaving. Now was the time to counterattack.

I let go of the shield. As it thumped onto the rocks, I whipped out my two single-handed swords, stripping the werewolf of half his Life, and rolled back to the safety of the mossy cliff, picking up the shield on my way — it could still take another couple of hits.

I parried again, building up my Fury count. I could use every point of it later tonight. We were looking at a long, hard session.

With a ripping sound, the mob broke through my defenses. His fiery claws dug deep into the rock, stripping the moss away and leaving deep scores in the stone. I recoiled just in time, diving aside, then moved swiftly behind him.

By then, his Life bar was barely glowing: I'd had a Bleed debuff cast over both my swords. After another whack from me, the werewolf convulsed on the ground, wheezing.

Now I had to act double quick. I had a dozen seconds at the most.

I always kept a special sharp-edged crystal in a quick access slot. Ripping off the glove, I laid it in my hand, then activated my unique ability, available only to players of my class starting at level 100.

My Fury bar plummeted as the energy I'd accumulated during the fight was now being channeled into the transparent crystal. Bright red lights flickered, casting their glow over my face. The tips of my fingers prickled.

You've received an item: Crystal of Fury

Phew. I'd done it. All that practice had finally brought some results. The ability had a two-hour cooldown.

The precious stone I'd just created could be used in two different ways. I could either install it into my weapon slot or use it in combat when the going got really tough to retrieve its energy, maxing out my Fury count.

Weapons with dedicated slots were in fact quite rare. You needed an experienced bladesmith to make one. If you tried to build it yourself, the result could be what you least expected — useless or even harmful — courtesy of Lady Luck.

With this one, I had five Crystals of Fury — and still I had a gut feeling I might need each and every one of them tonight. The quest chain that Christa and I had been completing over the last six months was obliged to culminate in the mother of all battles. Whom with, I didn't yet know. Those who'd done this dungeon before us had been remarkably secretive about it.

In the meantime, the werewolf stopped convulsing. The combat mode switched off automatically. I cast a look around, searching for any more mobs, and decided to check the monster for any loot. One never knew, he might drop something worth my while.

A familiar popping sound filled the air.

"Hi, Christa. You're late," I picked up the werewolf's heart — a rare ingredient used in alchemy — and turned round only to see a new system message,

Christa, a level 128 Sorceress, has left your group!

You no longer belong to any players association.

I froze in dumb surprise, watching as interference distorted her face. Her name tag modified, then disappeared.

I was facing a strange woman. This new avatar had nothing to do with Christa even though lots of little details of her clothing and gear were screaming her name. Like the runic bracelet on her wrist. This was a relic item you could neither lose, sell, nor give away. These kinds of items never parted from the player. She'd gotten it off the last dungeon boss we'd smoked. I could still remember her eyes shining with pleasure as she'd read its stats.

I pulled myself together. "What's going on?"

"Just finalizing a few things," she replied coldly.

"Christa, this is the final instance! If you've decided to go solo or join a clan, be my guest, I'm not staying in your way! But we need to close this quest!"

"I'm not Christa. I'm not interested in her commitments," she quipped, apparently about to log out.

"Wait! Can't you explain?"

The sorceress turned round and looked me over. With a sigh, she acquiesced. "I've just bought this account."

"Why?" I asked mechanically. That wasn't what I was thinking about. Christa had been successfully leveling up for the last two years, point by grueling point. Why would she want to sell her account? I knew how precious she was about her online identity. Oh no: I could smell a rat from where I stood.

"You're not a newsy person, are you?" she

asked indifferently. "There's an action about to be launched in Crystal Sphere. The game developers have made it possible to transfer other fantasy game accounts there. Unfortunately, they cut your levels down but you do get to keep all your gear, skills and abilities. As you level up, they become available to you again. Clear enough?"

She must have misunderstood my hesitation as she added, "Look it up. I'm off now. Too many things to do."

With another popping sound, she disappeared.

* * *

For a while, I sat by the cliff looking up into the starry sky as I tried to digest what had just happened.

So the final dungeon wasn't meant to be. Six months of gaming down the drain. Apart from the levels gained, that is.

Christa! Why, or why would you do such a thing? You should have told me! Why would you sell your own account, of all things?

I just couldn't wrap my head around it. Only last night we'd been busy making plans for the future. Whatever could have happened in the last twelve hours?

I had no idea what to do. Anger and

desperation were marring my judgment.

Couldn't she have waited another twenty-four hours? We'd invested so much time, effort and money into doing this particular plot line! We'd had high hopes about this final dungeon — and what for? No, no, no. I shouldn't be thinking like that. Something must have happened to her. Christa couldn't have done this to me.

Then again, why not? What did I really know about her?

Still, why would she sell out?

The most logical answer would be: she needed money really badly. A lot of it, too.

I stood up and looked around me. Pointlessly I touched the slab of rock barring the entrance to the dungeon and ran my fingers over the familiar sequence of magic symbols that opened it.

You can't enter a dungeon on your own, the system reported.

* * *

LOGOUT

The residual pine scent from the environment generator still lingered in my room. The holographic screens had already switched off. A single search result filled the monitors:

Crystal Sphere opens doors to all fantasy game characters!

We've created a unique boundless game world which has a place for everyone.

Are you reluctant to part with your old online identity? We're prepared to accommodate you! Our abilities allow us to support any race or class as well as any relevant development branches. Hurry! The Crystal Sphere knows no clans or clan wars. You just might become the first legend of this brave new world!

Warning: account transfers will entail a 5:1 drop in levels. But not to worry: all your skills will be safe, waiting to be unblocked as you level up your character.

Now it was starting to make sense. That's why my bank had refused me a loan secured by Middle Earth currency: they must have gotten wind about the upcoming merge. It looked like this Crystal Sphere might assimilate all pre-existing game projects. At the same time, in this clanless new world of unclaimed resources and territories, nobody needed a steady flow of high-level players: therefore the level nip.

The offer was almost too hard to resist. You couldn't argue with that. Lots of folks out there would love to join a new world while preserving their old avatars. Others, however, wouldn't have minded changing their char without having to level a new one up from scratch. For that reason, the prices on leveled-up accounts must have soared.

This explained a lot. Still, I had this anxious itch. Over these last six months, I thought I'd known Christa well. I'd believed we had more in common than just team play. Now she was gone. She could be in trouble and still I couldn't help! How was I supposed to find her in a city where every neighborhood had a population of over a million?

Wait a sec... there was one other option. And I just might try it while the scent was still fresh!

In my time, I too had sold a few chars that I'd leveled in other worlds. So I knew exactly the right person to turn to. The middleman in every such deal was obliged to record the vendor's IP address. I could still find her!

Afraid of losing heart, I quickly scrolled through my nanocomp contact list until I found the right one and texted him.

After five minutes, I received a reply,

I might help. 1000 credits, by bank transfer.

For me, that was a lot of money. I still had to move house.

Of course! How could I have forgotten! Once I moved, I'd lose all trace of Christa. Then I'd never find out whatever had happened to her.

Agreed. Give me the bank account number.

* * *

What made me do it, might you ask? There's no clear-cut answer to that. It's just that I sensed this void in my heart that was filled with anxiety, for want of a better feeling. That's exactly what happens when you don't know what to do — you just don't seem to be able to think of any positive scenarios, brooding over all sorts of horror stories instead.

It was already two in the morning when I stopped by the doors of a capsule apartment located on Floor 207 of a supertower. That's exactly the kind of automated dwelling I'd be looking at myself very soon.

No idea what I'd been thinking of. I'd bought a pizza on my way and pulled my Dad's old baseball cap over my eyes, deciding to pretend I was a delivery guy who'd got the wrong door. This was the best thing I could come up with. You could call me a small-town guy, I suppose.

Only when I touched the front door sensor,

did I remember that all supertower deliveries were done by pneumatic capsules.

"Who's there?" a quiet voice asked, quivering. Had she been crying?!

"Pizza delivery," I managed. "Did you order?"

"No, I didn't," the intercom sobbed. "Go away."

"I've got your address in the book."

"Okay, then," the door slid soundlessly aside.

I stepped into a small room typical of those new transformable dwellings of today.

Christa?

My heart clenched. She sat in a deep soft chair at a console identical to mine. Her tear-streaked face was pale and drawn. The bank of monitors still showed the familiar clearing next to the dungeon entrance, complete with the dead werewolf.

"Just leave it there on the table-" she halted. "Alex? Why are you here? I've done everything to avoid this! Aren't you mad at me?"

"Why did you sell your account?" I demanded.

"I didn't want us to meet in real life," she wiped her tears. "I could see it coming. I didn't want to explain. So now, please, forgive me and just go! Can't you see you're hurting me?"

"What the hell's going on?"

"I've got ANM," tears poured down her cheeks. "So please just leave me. Do you want me to call the police?"

"I don't think so," I laid the wretched pizza onto the table and stepped toward her. "We need to talk. You really think I'm gonna leave you?"

* * *

I left the police station about half past three in the morning.

I stopped on the sidewalk, my breathing deep and uneven.

The ANM. The virus which had infested every city five years ago. None had been able to explain the nature of its genetic mutation. There was no proven cure.

How long a sufferer would live depended on lots of things. Many had managed to get back to their feet and even lead a normal life. Christa's body, however, had proven not as strong. She was fading away — and she knew it, too. For her, virtual reality had become her last refuge, the only way to escape the horror of her life.

I walked to the car. Why hadn't she told me anything? That way I wouldn't have insisted on meeting her in real life. We could have switched to the Crystal Sphere together.

Too late. Christa had second-guessed my intentions and done everything to antagonize me, unwilling to hurt either of us. She must have thought I'd be angry enough with her to simply forget her once and for all after this dungeon incident. She probably thought I'd be so mad I'd never want to see her again.

I got in the car. I wasn't in the best of moods. The storm had long ended. The traffic was non-existent at this early hour.

I had to go home and give it a good think. I didn't give a shit about my having been cautioned by the police. I wasn't going to leave Christa alone — even though I had very little idea how I could possibly help her. We might not even be able to play like we used to before. She wouldn't be able to. She'd know that I knew.

I put my foot down, trying to release the pressure. The gray ribbon of the tarmac whooshed beneath the wheels. The disabled auto pilot kept flashing its little red light.

Finally, the intersection. I took the first right turn into a spiraling slipway, then straight on again, this time heading for my own home.

Tufts of mist drifted over the highway. The terrain to its both sides was free from its usual concrete shell, the earth of the freshly-dug foundation pits oozing moisture.

I would come up with something. I knew I

would.

The piercing warning of the proximity gage made me jump. A giant construction robot was slowly emerging onto the highway. Mechanically I wrenched on the steering wheel. The Rover's bumper exploded in a cascade of plastic fragments as it rammed a flimsy construction site barrier.

The gray misty dawn span before my eyes as earth and sky swapped places. My chest and stomach went cold. Finally, the airbags kicked in. A crushing blow and the screeching of the car's crumpling bodywork... then darkness.

* * *

They were taking me somewhere on a gurney.

Through the pain and haze of the heavy medication I could hear voices; I even managed to understand what they were saying.

"He's one lucky motherfucker."

"Sure. Did you see the height of that pit? It's a miracle he survived at all."

"I saw his car. It was on the news. A ball of steel. It took the rescue team an hour to cut him free."

I couldn't feel my body — neither my legs nor my arms. I must be in a really bad way. The pain in my chest kept coming back despite all the medication they kept pumping into me.

A blinding light assaulted my eyes. The air smelled of antiseptics.

"Right, let's move him. On the count of three. One... two..."

Darkness came back.

This time it didn't hurt, as if they'd separated my mind from my body.

Voices resonated in the background. A man and a woman. I couldn't help trying to work out what they were saying.

"You think you could bring him round for a short while?"

"Why?" the woman's voice rang with contempt.

"I'd like to speak to him."

"You can't. It's too dangerous. He's too weak after the surgery. And he needs to survive a lot more of them."

"Who's paying for his treatment?"

"What do you mean, who? The insurance."

"They have a certain limit, don't they?"

"They do," she admitted reluctantly. "They pay for the intensive care and minimal aftercare. His bank has already contacted us. It's complicated."

"You call this humane? You drag this guy back from the dead, pump him full of drugs and patch him up — all this just to throw him back out onto the street?"

"Well, I'm sorry! In case you didn't notice, we're still fighting for his life. The rest, at the moment, is academic."

"It's not. We all know what's gonna happen. He'll leave your charitable institution a cripple, only to spend a few more years in his own personal hell!"

"What are you implying? Speak up! I agreed to see you but I'm afraid both my time and my patience are limited."

"I'd like you to bring him round. I need him to be able to make conscious decisions."

"Absolutely not. In any case, what do *you* care? You're just some corporation making computer games!"

"That's exactly what I need to talk about. Not with you — with him."

* * *

Life had lost its meaning.

Darkness kept swallowing me, time after time. I'd resurface only to taste pain and return, submerging deep into my black stupor. So it lasted until the blinding light came on again.

"Good. There are reflexes. The medication is working. He's coming round."

"How much time do I have?"

"Ten minutes. Possibly, more. It depends."

"Thanks. Could you please leave us alone for a bit?"

"No, but-"

"Please. I insist. Don't make me pull any more strings."

"I hope not. That's the only thing you seem to know how to do!"

The door slammed.

I heard the sound of steel chair legs being dragged across the tiled floor. Someone set it by my bed, then slumped into it.

Whoever he was, his aftershave left a lot to be desired. Gradually, his outline loomed through the blur surrounding me. I could only make out a lab coat draped over the man's casual clothes.

* * *

"Nice to meet you, Alex. I'm Sergei Borisov. I'm here representing Infosystems Corporation. As your doctor has told me, we don't have much time. I suggest we move directly to business. Do you remember what happened to you? The accident?"

"Why?" I croaked. "Is it so bad?"

"Not at all!" he said cheerfully. For some reason, his faked optimism made my pain subside. I prepared to hear him out. I could use a ray of hope.

"We could pick up your medical bills."

"What's the catch? Spit it out."

"If you wish. Would you like to know the real state of your affairs?" he avoided the direct answer, apparently wanting to pump up the gloom first. "You have multiple spinal damage, not to mention all the other fractures and injuries you suffered."

I began drifting away again. A machine at the head of the intensive care capsule beeped an anxious warning.

I waited, but no medical staff came running. Apparently, the man's string-pulling techniques were strong enough to make sure no one disrupted our conversation.

The machine beeped again. My head began to clear, a new bumper dose of medication preventing me from fainting.

"Alex, you shouldn't worry so much about it. It's in your own interests to stay lucid until this conversation is over."

"What's the catch?" I repeated, barely moving my lips.

"We possess a whole bunch of unique new technologies. We might use them to help you."

"Sorry... I don't see what games have got to do with healthcare... even cutting-edge ones..."

Ignoring my skepticism, he reached into his breast pocket, producing a tiny microchip sealed in plastic.

"What... is it?"

"This is the future of gaming. The neuroimplant. It's comprised of artificial neuronets. Once you're plugged into it, you won't need all those holographic screens, scent generators, tactile sensors... This tiny little thing processes all game events, uploading the result directly into the player's brain. Can't you see? This device provides full immersion into cyberspace. It would allow us to live there just as we do here, experiencing the whole range of sensations — even those unknown to human beings!"

Holy shit. And I used to consider my home system the latest technological breakthrough!

"They're yet to be tested on human beings," he added.

"Sorry... this is revolutionary.... the mind boggles... but I can't see what it's got to do with-"

He must have come prepared. My question didn't throw him.

"When offered the opportunity of full immersion into cyberspace, a lot of people might want to stay there," he explained matter-of-factly. "Which brings us to the question: what about life support? No, I don't need you to reply to that one.

Just listen to me. The neuroimplant is only a fraction of the entire body of our new technologies. You can't advance the gaming industry by only employing one particular branch of human knowledge. Our work calls for all sorts of cross-disciplinary projects. As an example, we also work with military space forces who supply us with life support systems.

I already knew what he was driving at. Still, I couldn't help asking, "Why me? Millions of gamers will be lining up by your offices as soon as they get wind of this device," my gaze alighted on the microchip.

"They're not right for us, I'm afraid."

"Why not?"

"The risks are too great. As I've already told you, the neuroimplant processes every in-game experience whether it's a whiff of a breeze or a mortal wound. The device is yet to be standardized, and to do that, we need feedback from subjects. Apart from all sorts of risky scenarios, games are full of intricate details which at the moment are a complete mystery to us. Do you have any idea what a wizard feels when controlling the elements?"

"No."

"Neither do we. Will he experience a tickle in his belly or will he drop dead on the spot? You can see I'm not holding anything back from you.

We can't enroll regular game users in our tests. Not even if they volunteer. A volunteer's death or his suffering serious mental damage are bound to become public knowledge. You, however, are perfect volunteer material. Sorry about being so blunt."

"Why perfect? Is it because I'm about to die without next of kin?"

"Exactly."

"So what do I have to do?"

"Just play."

"Playing is brainwork. What about the rest of me?"

"I can't go into details quite yet but let me assure you we'll provide you with the best treatment available. It's actually based on the technologies developed for deep space travel."

"Another experiment?"

He nodded. "Our researchers estimate your body's full recovery period at two years. I'll have to warn you though that some of your organs and even body parts might need to be replaced with biocybernetic prosthetics."

"So what's gonna happen if I survive all that?"

"You'll be able to enjoy life again."

"What, as a cyborg?"

"You shouldn't worry about that. Only a very limited number of people will know about your modifications. There're lots of people around who have a heart implant or a hearing aid — but no one calls them cyborgs! Also, all the surgery will be performed in the so-called background mode. You won't feel a thing, simply because your neuroimplant will be streaming totally different experiences into your brain. Please, don't say no. In your situation this is a very suitable and generous proposition."

"I understand that. I have a request though."

He raised an eyebrow and leaned slightly forward, apparently surprised by my brazenness. "Speak up."

"How many vacancies do you have?"

He paused. "Twenty."

"I know a person that might suit your requirements," I said, then clued him in on Christa's situation.

"You understand, don't you," he said, "that these kinds of decisions are outside my remit. The main selection criterion is the candidate's willingness to volunteer. He or she should understand the risks involved and accept any potential consequences."

"I know. She has nothing to lose."

"We're talking about *your* life now."

"I'd like you to talk to her," I repeated doggedly. "You'll find her address in my nanocomp."

"Don't be so childish!"

"I'm not. Try her. She's a perfect candidate."

No good deed goes unpunished. I didn't yet know how true — albeit cruel — this adage was. But I was about to learn very quickly.

"Are you sure? Aren't you afraid of losing your opportunity?" he glanced at the door as if knowing there was someone patiently hovering behind it, waiting for us to finish this conversation. He leaned over me and mouthed under his breath, "The mere mention of the neuroimplant might put the life of an innocent person in danger. What if she refuses to cooperate? You understand, don't you?"

I weakly shrugged. The medication was wearing off. My lips felt cold. The pain was flooding back. In my situation, it was way too easy to start clutching at straws. Vulnerable is gullible. The whole thing just had to be much more serious and dangerous than the rosy picture he'd just presented me with. It had to be — otherwise the Corporation wouldn't have sent its agents out to scour through every Casualty unit in the city.

Did I even have a choice, anyway?

"Where's the dotted line?"

He promptly shoved a tablet into my

hands.

As I plunged back into the quagmire of agony, I pressed my finger to the biometric scanner window, confirming my decision.

CHAPTER TWO

THE CRYSTAL SPHERE. LOGIN

THE DWARF'S pick struck hard, procuring a cascade of ice fragments that sparked in the torch's light. His breath misted, his beard and mustache already covered with frost.

This was all I managed to take in as I came round.

His pick came down with another powerful swing. Ice crumbled all around me, cascading to the cave's floor and releasing me.

"Finally," the miner grumbled. "Let's have a look. What have we got here?"

A message appeared right in front of my

eyes, startling me.

Neuroimplant: activated

Mind expander (Synaps, basic model): installed

Activation successful

Mnemonic interface downloaded

Alternative start point: set up.

You've received a new ability: Two Worlds. From now on, you'll be able to experience the same range of sensations in cyberspace as in the real world. Courtesy of the neuroimplant, all your skills and reflexes will be identical regardless of the time and place of their initial acquisition.

For your information: all interface types are currently set to 'cyberspace' by default.

The dwarf recoiled, replacing the pick with a battle hammer that surged with pulses of lightning.

"Who is it, Togien?" a voice came from the dark. Judging by the echo, the cave wasn't very big.

"It's all right. It's only a specter. I'll sort him out."

Focusing on me, the dwarf began to incant some kind of spell, his voice grim and low. I couldn't make out the words apart from the final phrase,

"Whoever you are, begone to where you belong!"

Another system message appeared in my mental view, overlapping the cave's interior,

Welcome to the Crystal Sphere!
Please choose your race.

The cave around me became a freeze frame. I watched the tame bolt of lightning entwine the hilt of the dwarf's sword. He was short and stocky, clad in a pair of leather pants and a jacket with sown-on protective links of some dull metal. A pointed helmet was perched on his head.

The dwarf's eyes glared at me from under his bushy eyebrows. His frosted salt-and-pepper beard was plaited and could use a good dose of dye. The metal inlays of his gear too could have done with a polish. His jacket was patched, his helmet dented. He was more than likely a grave robber.

Well, well, well. Did that mean that until I created my character, he could only see me as a ghost? How interesting. Was my arrival in the Crystal Sphere part of some global event? I didn't think so. Most likely, the dwarf couldn't overcome his craving for gold and had decided to check out the cave.

His torch was wedged into a small crevice in the wall. Its flame was static now, fancy swirls of smoke hanging in the air. The torch illuminated a small area covered in large globules of transparent ice entrapping various objects. The picture was reminiscent of some shipwreck flotsam brought into a cave by a turbulent ocean and instantly frozen.

I was curious, of course, but this wasn't the right moment to enjoy the views. I had more important things to take care of.

Oops.

This neuroimplant of theirs was actually quite good! It seemed to be able to recognize my thoughts and react accordingly. The moment I'd thought about creating a character, several translucent images appeared in my view, apparently symbolizing the available races.

Excellent. Mechanically I focused on one of them. Immediately the picture zoomed in and took center stage, acquiring detail.

The mnemonic interface was a pleasure to look at. It was simple and functional. Even though its icons overlapped the general picture around me, they didn't hinder your perception. I quickly discovered, by some basic trial and error, that you could activate icons by swiping them with your eyes. The system was constantly following my gaze, promptly determining if I was focusing on something or other.

A long line of holograms loomed out of the dark. It wasn't for nothing the Crystal Sphere claimed superiority over all other game worlds. Having to choose from hundreds of races many of which were only represented by small fringe groups imported from other game settings wouldn't be at all easy. You could spend weeks just studying their respective properties.

Still, I'd already made my choice. Considering this implant of theirs, I was going to stay human, simply for safety reasons. I still couldn't forget my conversation with the Corporation rep. None of the exotic races could suit me for the simple reason that I had no idea how the neuroimplant would behave in an unhuman body, generating some totally alien perceptions.

I gulped. The dwarf may have been frozen in time — but I wasn't. I was freezing, literally. This was a definite drawback. How could a specter experience physical discomfort?

I had to hurry. I didn't like this icy cave. I had to go out into the warm sunlight.

I was full of projects and hopes. During our last meeting, Mr. Borisov dryly thanked me for recommending Christa to them. She'd agreed to participate. I was going to find her. We had a lot to discuss.

Something had changed around me almost imperceptibly. I noticed a chunk of ice below to my left. It looked as if the dwarf had initially tried to hack it off with his pick but had failed. Now the deep cracks piercing the ice had lit up by a tiny flame glimmering within.

I took a better look. The flame was emitted by a fiery aura enveloping a doubled-up figure inside.

The creature stirred. The light grew slightly brighter, blurring the ice from the inside as it began to melt. The cavity within kept growing, filling with swirling steam.

This player who was about to escape his icy prison — was he also one of us? Did he have a neuroimplant too?

Never mind. Time would tell. Enough stalling! Time for me to get out of here!

So, let's have a look at their choice of human races.

Racial bonus: Determination

You receive two bonus points to add to any characteristic of your choice at your convenience, plus another skill point every five levels.

Not bad at all.

I pressed *Confirm.*

A new choice of character classes followed.

Normally, every class supported two skill development branches: the main one, available to everyone, and an additional one which could only be opened at level 50.

Considering my choice of race, I could pick from among a Warrior, a Wizard, a Hunter, a Light or Dark Knight, a Monk, a Sorcerer, a Rogue — the list went on and on thanks to their account transfer option.

Wait a sec. What was that now? In the midst of all the predictable and expected classes I suddenly noticed a name that struck a familiar note, reminding me of recent events,

A Neuro

I swiped my eyes across the name, activating it.

The Founder Gods, creators of all living beings, used to possess a unique wealth of knowledge, endowing our ancestors with a whole number of long-forgotten abilities.

In bygone days, the Founders visited a great number of the worlds which have since disappeared without a trace. Still, we are reminded of the consequences of their genetic intervention as various nations give occasional birth to a Neuro: a creature whose true potential is

still dormant.

Could you be one of them?

Class bonus: a unique development branch not tied in with the character's specialization, available at level 5.

Would you be up to the challenge?

Accept: Yes/No

It looked like I could forget my habitual choice, a Warrior. The temptation was too great. I also had a gut feeling that this class had appeared on the list for a reason. I was pretty sure that normal players didn't have this option.

In a swipe of my eyes, I accepted.

Please wait. Character generation in progress.

Merging... Scanning...

Character generation complete.

Name: Alexatis

Race: Human

Gender: Male

Class: Neuro

Please confirm or go back to edit your avatar.

He looked the split image of myself: skinny, pale and unshaven. Not the best version of me.

I edited his build here and there, added a

darker hue to his skin and got rid of the stubble. Much better now.

I quite liked the nickname. It sounded unpretentious and similar enough to my own name.

I lingered. It felt like diving from a great height. The moment I pressed the button, my new virtual life would begin.

In the meantime, the melting block of ice had thawed through in the middle, forming a hole that sent a net of cracks in all directions.

Enveloped in steam, surrounded by a weak but already clear fire aura, the creature inside turned out to be... a demon!

Its spidery fingers clutched at the fragile ice, crumbling it, until they found a holdfast. The demon emitted a weak groan as it began to pull itself out of its ice prison. Long rear-facing spines ran the whole length of its forearms. They grew through the demon's grayish olive skin which was covered in asymmetrical black swirls.

Its muscles tensed. The creature eased itself out, peeping its head and shoulders out of the hole in the ice.

The recognition petrified me.

Christa?

Her short ash-blond hair, her fiery gaze, the thin line of her pursed lips — these were features I knew, familiar and yet strangely different. Repulsive.

Glinting with darkness, a supple suit of armor clung to her body, protecting her chest, stomach and hips.

Unlike me, Christa hadn't wasted her time.

I hurried to confirm my character choice. Once again time began to fly by. I jumped to my feet, shivering with cold in my canvas shirt and pants, still in disbelief of her horrible choice, hoping it was a mistake.

"Get out of my way!"

Her fiery aura became more pronounced, outlining a burning name tag,

Christa. Level 1. Demon

I knew why her name hadn't changed. She'd told me she'd had it legally registered.

"Christa, it's me!"

"As if I can't see," her glare faded, acquiring an almost human expression, then burned again, oozing an uncontrollable, impetuous fury. "Out my way!" she hissed, snake-like.

"Hey noobs! You've got a cheek!" the dwarf's amazed voice broke the heavy silence. "How did you get here?"

He never received an answer.

"Alex, step aside."

"No, I won't," I could be stubborn too.

"What were you thinking about, creating this abomina-"

She responded with a lightning attack. The spines on her arms ripped through my shoulder, grazing my throat. My chest seized with agonizing pain. I dropped to my knees. She leaped at the dwarf, her tail lashing him across the face. For a brief moment her body clung to the low ice-covered ceiling, then she darted into the tunnel that oozed a cold draft.

My Life bar faded. My neuroimplant was pumping my brain with sensations of harrowing agony like nothing I'd ever experienced before.

"Don't overact," the dwarf cringed. A crimson scar ran across his cheek. "Gwain, where the hell are you!" he bellowed.

The sounds of scampering footsteps came from the tunnel. "Togien, did you see that?" Another dwarf arrived — a Monk, judging by his gear. "What kind of fire monster was that?"

"A demon," Togien replied, than added, "Give the noob a heal, pronto!"

A healing aura enveloped me. I breathed again. My Life bar quivered and began to grow.

The pain subsided. Still, I'd already learned my first lesson in the world of Crystal Sphere. Its authenticity levels were really off the scale.

"Better now?" the dwarf hid a good-natured smile within his mustache, apparently misunderstanding my stare. "Don't worry. I don't hurt babies. I'm not a grave robber. I'm just a bit down on my luck gear-wise," he stroked his beard mechanically.

"Thanks," I sat up, looking around me.

"How did you get here, anyway... Alexatis? This is miles away from the nearest nursery."

"Must have been a glitch. I've no idea how it happened."

"Have you tried to log out and log back in again?"

I maintained a moody silence. I didn't want to lie to him — and I couldn't tell him the truth.

"Never mind. It's gonna be all right," he said. "You can stay with us if you want. We won't be here long. We just want to check this cave out. I'd like you to meet Gwain. He's my nephew. A real-life nephew, I mean."

This Togien turned out to be a nice guy, after all.

"Thanks for the heal, Gwain," I said.

He beamed. "That's not a problem."

I got the impression that Togien was quite strict with his nephew and didn't mete praise out gladly.

"We level up Archeology, you know," Gwain added. "It may be a secondary profession and all that, but still-" he cut himself short, meeting his uncle's disapproving glare.

"Too much information! Grab your pick and go back to work! Alexatis, you'd better stand aside — better still, wait in the tunnel before one of those ice fragments does you some serious damage! Just meditate or read some guides, or whatever."

I complied. I did have a few things to ponder over.

Togien and Gwain began hacking at the ice, digging for artifacts. Admittedly, they were good at what they did.

I focused on a transparent ice bauble encasing one of the objects, its outlines showing vaguely through the frosty surface.

A Large Block of Ice
Durability: 70/70

The two dwarves must have specialized in Mining. Their picks effortlessly crumbled the fragile crystals. They were giving it their all. I really should keep a safe distance: at level 1, I only had 50 pt. Life. The first large fragment of ice flying my way would be the end of me.

I had no idea where their resurrection point was. I'd been lucky enough to have come across two such friendly individuals. Togien was level 18 and his nephew, 12. Which meant they also hadn't been in the Crystal Sphere long.

The tunnel was damp, water streaking down its walls. The depths of this underground maze exuded subterranean heat.

The tunnel floor was overgrown with soft pale moss. I slumped down onto it, watching the fancy play of light from a torch wedged in a crack by the cave entrance.

My first impressions were sharp and contradictory.

Before, I could never understand why the choice of race was considered a "social act". I'd even gotten into a heated argument with some smartass on the Middle Earth forum about it. My point had been, the reason I'd chosen a Warrior was because I wanted that particular set of abilities, and nothing else!

I might have been wrong, I agree. Everything we hide deep inside our hearts under a fine veneer of social conventions is released into the virtual world. You can't really play a holier-than-thou Paladin if you have a tendency for much lowlier behavior. That's how it happens that by changing chars and adding various alt characters — who might suddenly become our main ones — we look for our *online identity.* Sooner or later, we all find it.

Did that mean I'd known nothing about Christa? Back in the Middle Earth, she'd still been trying to control herself — while here she'd finally lost it, complying with the voice of pain devouring her from inside.

I could change nothing, anyway. Our choices had been made. It was unlikely we'd ever cross paths again. Unless it was in battle.

* * *

I opened my interface, about to distribute the available points, when the earth shuddered, showering me with crumbling rock from the tunnel's ceiling.

A chain of powerful shocks ran through the tunnel, dying in the distance.

The two dwarves ran out of the cave and froze, listening to the far-off rumble of rockfalls. Judging by their alarmed expressions, nothing like this had ever happened here before.

"It has to be the City Guild and its wizards," Togien grumbled. "Let's go back in, Gwain. It seems to be all right now."

They returned to their work. I proceeded with my character research.

Alexatis. Level 1. Neuro.
Life, 50/50
Physical Energy, 37/50
Mental Energy, 50/50
Physical Defense, 2.5 (homespun clothes, 0)

Physical Attack, 2,5 (weapons not equipped)

Mental Defense, 0.5% (abilities not activated)

Mental Attack, 0 (spells not studied)

Mental Energy Regeneration, 2,5 pt./sec (Spirit divided by 2)

Strength, 5

Intellect, 5

Agility, 5

Stamina, 5

Spirit, 5

Main Professions, Not opened

Achievements, None

You have 7 main characteristic points available.

At first, everything seemed simple enough.

Strength was responsible for the amount of damage dealt by Physical Attack, as well as for the weight the char was capable of carrying and the numbers of absorbed incoming damage when parrying.

Intellect was responsible for the amount of Mental Energy as well as the damage dealt by spells. It also affected the char's Learning Skills and the amount of XP (experience) received.

Agility was responsible for the char's

reaction times which affected all of his actions in some way or another.

Stamina determined the amount of Health points that decided the quantity of the char's Life.

Spirit decided the char's resistance to magic attacks, increasing his or her chances of blocking a spell or continuing to cast one while being attacked.

Still, in practice it wasn't that clear-cut and easy. A char's main characteristics were all interrelated. Their interactions could be calculated using special formulas. To give you a rather exaggerated example, every weapon had such characteristics as Weight and Damage. A strong character would have no problem lifting a heavy mace and using it to deal a hit that would strip his or her opponent of (say) 10 HP. But a character who is strong *and* agile would be able to strike twice in the same amount of time dealing double damage — because the high Agility numbers would increase his Attack Speed.

You see my point? My ability branch was still closed. I hadn't been given any tips regarding which particular stats could be vital for a Neuro's successful development. I had a funny feeling it was Intellect — but this was only my conjecture. Which was why I came to the decision to wait until I reached level 5 before distributing any available stat and skill points.

"Alexatis? Mind coming here for a moment?" Togien's bellowing voice disrupted my train of thoughts.

I closed the interface and walked into the cave.

Oh wow. They'd done a good job there, hadn't they? Possibly, with a little help from the earthquake. Tiny ice fragments crunched underfoot, sparkling in the torch light. Not a single block of ice was left — they'd ripped them all apart nice and neat!

"How much weight can you carry?" Togien asked me.

"Sixty pounds."

"That's nothing," he sounded upset. "How big is your inventory?"

I shrugged. "Twenty slots. A standard one."

"I have a proposition for you. What if we give you an extra bag for a hundred slots? We've got too much stuff, you see. We could go all together to Agrion — that's a city on the River Warbler. It's not far from here. We'll give you 1% of the price of what's in the bag. What do you think?"

A newb would have to be a total idiot to refuse this kind of offer. Besides, it didn't look as if the hike to the nearest safe locations was going to be easy, either. The local mobs were definitely more advanced in levels than humble me.

"I'm in."

"Let's load up, then. No, wait," Togien gave my starting clothes a critical look. With a sigh he reached into his stashes, producing a suit of well-worn leather armor. "This is yours. Take a look around and get yourself a weapon," he probably meant the trash items they'd found but which didn't merit the inclusion on their Valuables list.

"Thanks," I hurried to change into my new clothes: a set comprising a leather jacket, pants, gloves and boots with 40% Durability still on them. It fit me well. Judging by their stats, the items didn't have any bonuses but they did raise my Protection to 12 pt. Excellent for starting out!

"Suits you," with another good-humored smile, Togien made some mental calculations. "Thanks don't fill a purse though. We'll subtract the kit's price from your share. Actually, the clothes weigh 12 pounds extra. But it's all right. Gwain will cast a few buffs on you. He needs the practice. Good for both of you."

As the two dwarves continued to sift through their finds, arguing over their potential value and sorting them into several piles, I decided to check out the trash. Lots of curious objects were lying around in the slush — mainly weapons and armor made of some alloy unknown to me. Despite being untouched by rust, their metal had grown dull and brittle.

I reached out for what looked like a decent helmet. It crumbled to dust at my touch. It must have suffered some magic attack.

Trash indeed.

Finally, I had my eye on a sword. Four empty stone slots gaped on its hilt. Its handguard was rather unusual for a sword, formed by several thin masterfully forged strips of metal that completely protected your fingers and the back of your hand. The grip was good. It might take some getting used to but I could already see the design's strongest point: striking it out of your hand wasn't going to be easy. The four empty slots must have been there for a reason. The double-edged blade wasn't too broad. If you took a good look at the fine layer of patina covering it, you could see faint symbols of some mysterious language underneath.

Item received: a Mysterious Sword
Damage: 5
Weight: 2,450
Durability: 15/500
Requires level 1 and 5 pt. Strength.
Class restrictions: none

"I can see you've made your choice?" Gwain glanced at the sword's stats. "Not enough damage. The durability is a bit low too."

"It doesn't weigh much," I argued.

"You're right there," he pointed at a heap of small objects — mainly precious stones and all sorts of weird-looking artifacts. I wouldn't know what to do with them. "Load up. I'm gonna cast two buffs on you: one for Stamina, the other for Strength. Ten minutes both."

"How did you find this cave?" I asked, distributing the items between the slots of the capacious bag they'd given me.

"A quest," Gwain replied brusquely. He raised his hands to cast the spell, apparently unwilling to go into detail. Pale blobs of light escaped the tips of his fingers. For a brief moment they enveloped me, filling me with strength.

"How much mana does it take?" I asked.

"One-third of a full charge. That's all right. I also have elixirs. By the time we get to the city I'll raise you a couple of levels. You'll see."

Who was I to argue?

I decided against equipping my new sword. I put it into my inventory and assigned a quick-access icon to it. Easier that way. I could still whip it out in no time but this way it was safe from prying eyes. Once we got to the city, I'd have to look it up. I'd love to know what kind of trophy I'd gotten. I might even restore its durability which in turn would improve damage. Besides, all those question marks admittedly intrigued me.

"Ready?" Togien gave me a critical look but seemed pleased with the result. "Off we go, then!" he led the way into the tunnel, lighting his path with the torch. "Alexatis, try to keep up. If we come across any mobs, keep your head down. I'll do the tanking. Gwain will heal us."

* * *

Keeping up with them proved not that easy!

Ten minutes later I was already stumbling and falling behind. My physical energy reading was dwindling fast. The extra 25 lbs. of weight were taking their toll. The neuroimplant was adding its two cents, too.

Let me tell you: it had changed the entire gameplay radically. Before, my char could be exhausted and still I hadn't felt a thing. Now my legs shook and started to give under me.

"Gwain!" I called.

"I see," he grumbled. "You're a mana gobbler, you. Wait, I need to sift through the spells."

Being a mule was hard work. Still, I had to grin and bear. It was well worth it.

As we walked, I pondered over my situation.

My character's class was bound to attract attention and raise unwanted questions. Still, at the moment that was the least of my worries. I could always explain it away by having had to import my account from a different game world. However, no one should suspect anything about the mind-shattering authenticity levels I was experiencing. Otherwise I'd be a very easy target. Christa had already taught me this lesson.

So I might need to practice self-control. If the tiniest of wounds made me linger in battle, others were bound to notice it.

Finally Gwain found the spell he'd been looking for. This buff, on top of raising both strength and stamina, would also halve my physical energy losses.

"It took you some time," I walked faster, feeling the energy flow into me.

"My spell book's too thick," he replied, apparently proud of the fact.

"What, at level 12?"

"We're both from Middle Earth, aren't we? We had our accounts transferred from there. We lost our levels but kept all the rest. You have any idea how many scrolls I'd studied there? And this," he grinned, "this girl... do you know her?"

"Yeah."

"You gotta cool it, man. You never know with them. Today she's a princess, tomorrow a demon. Just like in real life," he joked in a clumsy attempt to cheer me up.

Togien didn't join our conversation. Still, he kept his ears pricked.

"What prompted you to level Archeology? Aren't there any mines around here?" I asked simple-heartedly.

"There are, but they're either poor or you need to mop them up first," Gwain replied. "Local mobs have six hours' respawn time. If you do it with two people, there isn't enough time left to mine anything."

"I'm sure they'll fix it soon," Togien said confidently. "They'll be mopping mines up regularly. Then we can talk about resource farming on an industrial scale. First with small groups, but sooner or later big clans will muscle in. Familiar scheme."

"Don't you have clans already?"

"Small ones. They still keep close to cities and starting locations. The Crystal Sphere has incredible territories but its players still need to level up first. Level 45 was the biggest I've seen. And within a week's hike from Agrion you can already come across level-50 mobs. It's a young world, what do you want?"

His words took my breath away. I'd always dreamed of discovering virgin locations. I was so fed up with following in other guys' tracks, doing guidebook quests that had been completed a thousand times before me. I wanted to be a pioneer!

* * *

The long winding tunnel kept forking and branching off. It was riddled with deep crevices: some of them oozing water, others breathing subterranean heat, yet others sweeping you with chilly drafts, freezing you to the bone.

No idea how one could find his way here without a detailed map. Still, Togien strode along without hesitation, taking confident turns every time the tunnel forked.

The two dwarves definitely enjoyed the underground trip. I, however, felt utterly out of my depth.

As if reading my mind, Gwain who walked behind me decided to cheer me up, "It's all right, man. Soon we'll come to the city sewage-" he cut himself short as he stumbled into me, nearly knocking me off my feet.

"Alexatis, what's wrong with you?" he exclaimed. "Keep going!"

I didn't reply. I had a very bad feeling. A whiff of icy cold touched my heart. My breathing seized.

I couldn't keep it to myself. "Togien, wait!"

He turned round. "What is it?"

"You can't go further!"

"Why not?"

"I have a bad feeling about it. Don't laugh! It's true!"

"What's that, an ability you have or something?" Togien asked, hiding a smile. "Or are you pulling my leg? You can't have any abilities, can you? Not at level 1! We still have some walking to do before we can stop for a break," he added sternly.

A shadow darted behind his back. Two swords slashed through his knee ligaments in a treacherous combo. With a yelp, he dropped his battle hammer and slumped to the floor.

Three rogues materialized out of the shadows. Players, levels 16 to 20.

Wheezing, Togien tried to get back to his feet but couldn't. I could clearly see a debuff icon in his tag: both swords were poisoned.

"Finish him off, Mouk! Otherwise we can't collect the loot."

"No, wait. I want to bleed him first. I need some blood for my Alchemy," one of the rogues produced a vial and bent down, filling it with Togien's blood. The other two moved toward me. The tunnel was too narrow, so for the moment they couldn't get to Gwain yet.

Why hadn't he run off while he'd still had

the chance? Rogues were good at ambushing you or assaulting you from the back, but there was no way they could catch up with a dwarf in an underground maze.

"So?" one of the players came closer, playing with his swords. His name tag was recognizably bright red. "Whatcha you gonna do, newb? Will you give us your bag or would you rather we send you to your respawn point?"

The red name tag with a skull icon on it meant he was a PK: a Player Killer. Any city guard's duty was to smoke him on the spot.

"You aren't gonna kill me," I continued to block his way in the hope that Gwain — judging by the bustling sounds behind my back — would finally see his chance and flee.

"Why not?"

"Can't you see my level? This is noob hunting. Go ahead, then. Your PK counter won't like it. This time you won't get off lightly. This won't be a community-work sentence, man."

"Quit being smart," he snapped. Still, he seemed to realize the consequences. At the moment, he was already denied access to the city for the ungrounded murders of other players. But if he as much as touched me, the punishment would be much more severe, stripping him of most of his stats.

"In that case, get out of my way! Hey dwarf,

quit hiding behind the newb! We're gonna get you, anyway!"

"Alexatis, step aside please," Gwain said behind my back, his voice quiet but intense. Was it my imagination or had I heard an empty mana vial clatter to the ground? What was he up to? He couldn't possibly take on three rogues way above his level.

Suddenly Gwain shoved me against the wall. He'd stuck the torch into a crevice in the rock. The hood of his gray cloak covered his head. He'd put his weapons out of sight.

"Give us your bag, monk," said the one called Heilig (I automatically added his name to my KOS list) as he resumed playing with his swords. 'The newb is right. My PK counter doesn't need exercise. This way I can stash away the loot, give myself up to the guards, work a couple days in the stables and start it over with a clean slate."

"You're absolutely right," Gwain mumbled, looking perfectly harmless in his baggy cassock. "Here you are, Sir, take it," he pulled out a fat bag out of his inventory. "Just please don't hurt my uncle. I'm gonna give you his bag, too."

On hearing that, the rogues obediently let him go past the gang's leader. Once he found himself between the three hoods, he bent his back in a deep bow, spreading his arms wide. "Peace be with you..."

A dazzling shimmer enveloped his hands. A blinding light came out of his eyes. A warm healing wave washed over me (because I was neutral to Gwain).

Not so for the PKs! The aura of a blanket debuff turned all three to stone. The one busy collecting blood thumped to the ground, collapsing to one side. The other two stayed on their feet, paralyzed.

Gwain slumped down the wall. Blood soaked his clothes.

"Shitheads!" Togien's roar echoed through the tunnel. He was healed completely. Grabbing his hammer, he took a swing — which was stopped by Gwain's weak outcry,

"You can't finish them off! You know that, don't you?"

Gasping, Togien tried to overcome his fury. "You're right.' He turned to me, "Alexatis, help me, quick!"

"What do you want me to do?"

"Check his bag! Look for a vial with some purple liquid!"

"This one?"

"Yes! Give it here! I'll unclench his teeth and you pour it down his throat! Like this! Good!"

Gwain groaned, stirring weakly. His Life bar began to grow.

Having made sure that he was okay, I

motioned Togien to step aside so that the paralyzed rogues couldn't overhear us.

"Was that a Humble Bow?" I asked.

The dwarf frowned, looking at me unkindly from under his bushy eyebrows. I could understand him. It looked like this account transfer had just played a bad joke with the Crystal Sphere admins.

"How do you know about the Bow?"

"I played in Middle Earth. From what I heard, you couldn't get this ability for love nor money. You have to complete a quest chain issued by the Higher Priests without killing a single mob. That's how they teach Meekness to any potential candidate. Am I right?"

"You should keep your mouth shut about that," Togien said anxiously. "It took Gwain a year to complete it. That's why he lagged behind me level-wise. If anyone hears about his imported ability..."

"You shouldn't worry about me. You'd better worry about these PKs here. They will talk, trust me. You should have given them the bags, really. It was stupid of Gwain to expose himself like that."

"Wait a sec," Togien crouched by the wall, laid his hammer on his lap and logged out. Nothing seemed to have changed. His hands still clutched the weapon's handle. His gaze, however, had become empty and lifeless.

Gwain had already come round. Still, he didn't seem too eager to talk, apparently realizing he'd screwed up.

Now is a good moment to say a few things about that magic ability of his.

When activated, the Humble Bow sucks the life out of the monk who cast it, leaving only 1% — just like the Bleed debuff does — and heals all neutral and friendly characters while paralyzing all enemies within 150 feet for 10 hours with a Stone Curse. Cooldown: 10 days.

Nothing special, you might say? What is so unusual about being able to heal your friends and simultaneously paralyze your enemies once in ten days? Still, the Humble Bow has one truly unique factor. It affects all players *regardless of their levels*.

Now imagine two clans fighting for a new territory, fortress or resource. The battle reaches a critical point; you give it your all, throwing all available forces into the strife; your wizards are out of mana, your warriors barely standing on their feet, and the enemy's high level players are hacking their way through your ranks, about to storm your casters' positions.

At this moment, a humble monk stands in the attackers' way and bends his back in a deep bow. "Peace be with you..."

A blinding light blankets the battlefield.

The monk drops dead. And all around him, your exhausted clanmates arise to their feet and pick up their arms while your enemies freeze like a sea of statues. And nothing can change that!

In all honesty, I didn't envy Gwain at the moment. His unique ability had evaded the Crystal Sphere admins during his account transfer, putting him in constant danger. In this young world troubled by its first turf wars, he wouldn't be able to preserve his neutrality and enjoy undisturbed gameplay. The moment the word got out, everyone would start applying pressure to him, desperate to get a fighter like him into their ranks.

But whoever he joined, others weren't going to stop. They might try to bribe him or simply make his virtual life unbearable. Gwain would lose his freedom, turning into the closely guarded property of a group of influential top-level clan members. If his goal was to make money playing, he would sure do that. Still, I had a funny feeling he was in it for the thrill, just like myself. Gwain craved adventure, not a hedonistic excuse for an existence in some classified citadel vault.

Togien stirred, coming round, and let out a deep breath. "I found it. All three are paying players. They couldn't have played in Middle Earth. They're about seventeen in real life."

"How did you find that out?"

"I paid. There's this online dealer, Arbido."

The recent memory smarted. "I know him. I once ordered some relic gauntlets from him. I needed a full set of armor to complete an instance and I had no time to get them myself."

"Arbido's quite correct. His intel is solid."

"You think these guys don't know about the Humble Bow? They won't be able to put two and two together?"

"I hope not. Middle Earth is closing soon, anyway. They're about to archive all the guides and forums. Just please not a word to anyone. Otherwise others won't leave Gwain alone."

"Sure. I understand that."

"I hope you do. We can be grateful, you know."

Togien has invited you to join his group!

Shit. That was the last thing I needed.

"Hey, Alexatis, what's up? What's there to think about?" he sounded sincerely amazed. "I sent you an invitation, man! We could rush you up to level 5 or even more, how about it? Or are you too conscientious to accept? All right, let us take you to the city, it's a safe zone with newb locations, social quests and whatnot. Do you seriously fancy genociding frogs in the city pond?

Or catching rats in the barn? I don't think so."

He didn't understand anything, did he? His sincere surprise was about to give way to quite understandable suspicion. Problem was, genociding frogs in some slimy pond was the exact thing I needed. It was all because of this neuroimplant I had. I'd no idea what kind of surprises the "hundred percent authenticity" might have in store for me. Small creatures would suit me perfectly well at the moment, allowing me to gingerly feel out my pain threshold and other intricacies of a new combat strategy I still had to work out. And if I joined the group, the dwarves might easily smoke a dozen mobs, rushing me through the first five or six levels (because I'll be receiving my share of XP as a group member). This was gameplay. And once I finally made it to the hypothetical pond, I might be faced not with a harmless frog but with some giant sharp-toothed predator toad.

Still, if I ignored the invitation, Togien might take offence. He might even become suspicious. Normally, no one refuses this kind of offer.

I couldn't help it. It looked like I'd have to play hard. I joined the group and added both dwarves to my friend list.

Togien visibly relaxed. He'd probably already had all sorts of ideas about me.

"Thanks," I said calmly. "What do we do with these guys?"

"Just leave them here. We can't finish them off. If we do, Gwain might lose the ability."

"What, you want them to walk away?"

"Oh no, they won't! They'll get their just desserts, trust me! Come on, let's go now. The city isn't very far."

* * *

The first hour of my new life had elapsed.

The tunnel continued downhill, its interior getting more and more interesting with every turn. Its offshoots were now blocked with massive chunks of stone covered in complex script. I didn't recognize the language. These must have been dungeon entrances.

After our encounter with the rogues, Gwain had clammed up. He hadn't said a word yet.

"One thing I don't understand," Togien said, leading the way, "is how the hell those idiots got here?"

He seemed to be angry with himself, blaming himself for failing to notice the ambush in time.

It was getting considerably warmer. A hot, dry air wafted into my face. The cracks in the tunnel's uneven floor — apparently formed during the recent earthquake — glowed crimson. From time to time, we came across wide fissures which we had to leap across. I looked down one of them and discovered another level below, streaked with slowly flowing lava and studded with the ruins of underground cities. The sight of shadows flitting amid them made your blood freeze.

I shouldn't have worried about Christa. This place was perfect for a demon. Me, I still had some walking to do before I reached safe starting locations.

Mechanically I made screenshots of the dungeons below. This kind of info might come in handy one day.

The exorbitant realism of the experience was beginning to grate on my nerves. It was also causing me considerable discomfort. I'd never had to worry about the size of my gear before — but now that had all changed. The tunnel was so hot I was dripping with sweat. The leather armor was chafing against my body. I should have kept the shirt on. And the bag felt like it weighed a ton.

"Gwain?" Togien said. "What's up, man? Are you asleep or something?"

"Why, is it time already?" the monk said with a start.

"Ten seconds left."

"Sorry, guys. I was away with the fairies," he cast another spell on me, restoring my energy.

"I think the rogues had followed us all the way from the city," Togien mumbled. "They'd been stealthing along, listening in. They knew we'd be back with plenty of loot."

I broke into a cold sweat. The sensation of being watched returned, as if the walls themselves kept an eye on my progress. The feeling washed over me, then disappeared, leaving an itch between my shoulder blades. I must have left the danger behind me.

I celebrated too early. Something touched my face — something light as a feather, gentle and inviting.

With every step I took, this tender, caressing feeling grew stronger. Considering the setting, I had reasons to believe it was fake. What would a friendly creature be doing in subterranean dungeons?

The darkness oozed whispers.

I couldn't make out the words yet. The dwarves didn't seem to notice it. Togien's stocky figure was hovering next to a cave mouth up ahead, illuminated by the flashes of lightning from his charmed hammer.

Should I trust my suddenly acute intuition? And how was I supposed to react to this? Unlike the freezing cold that had assaulted me just before we'd met the rogues, this gentle touch felt good.

"Come here," the darkness whispered. "Come to us..."

"Togien, don't move!"

This time he obeyed instantly and froze, peering into the darkness. "What now?" he asked without turning to me.

"Can you hear whispers?"

"No. All I can hear is the crackling of the rock. And the earth rumbling below," he added.

"Stay where you are!" My gaming experience kicked in. I might be level 1 but I couldn't make newb mistakes.

A taut wave of energy emerged from the cave, filling me with strength.

The Call of the Depths is summoning you

Togien hadn't sensed that, either. Gwain, however, exclaimed in surprise,

"Alex, someone's just cast a buff on you! You've got +10 to Strength for 60 seconds!"

"I shouldn't be so sure. There's something wrong here," I said, reading the system messages. "This is called the Call of the Depths! Heard anything about it?"

Gwain startled. "Shit! It's either a dark caster or an obelisk! Togien, stay away from that cave! We need to check it first!"

"If you say so," Togien shifted his combat stance: now he was holding a shield as well as the hammer. "I need more aggro!"

Gwain raised his hand and drew a golden symbol in the air.

Their plan was simple. The spell increased the level of danger generated by Togien until one of the little monsters sensed it.

I was right. A mob popped out of the cave.

An Imp. Level 3. Mine Digger

The creature was short and ugly, with a large head, pointy ears and a scrawny body covered with wrinkly red skin. He clutched a pick in one hand and a deformed bucket filled with pieces of ore in the other.

On seeing us, the imp froze bug-eyed and open-mouthed, about to scream an alarm.

No chance. Togien reacted promptly, his battle hammer squashing the little bastard into the ground.

Gwain drew another symbol in the air. I watched the unfolding scene without proffering any unwanted advice.

A fine veil enveloped Togien's body. Thus protected, he took a peek into the cave. Immediately he shrank back, forwarding us the resulting screenshots.

The cave's deep mouth was dimly lit by an unsteady, uneven light. A dark obelisk towered atop a small pedestal formed by runs of solidified lava. It was this that was emitting the gentle whispers, soft touches and the Strength-enhancing buffs.

All around it, emaciated figures stooped in small mining shafts: the creatures of many races who had succumbed to the obelisk's charms, becoming forever bound to this place and doomed to mine ore for the powers of Darkness.

Imps scurried among them. I peered at their tags. Those closer to the entrance were workers. Further on, lurking behind the rocks and waves of solidified lava, were imp warriors.

But that wasn't the worst of it. If you peered through the crimson gloom, you could make out the larger outlines of some much more dangerous spawn of the dark.

"Where did they all come from?" Togien sounded puzzled. "We took this very road not two hours ago! There was nobody here!"

"The earthquake?" I suggested.

"Could be. The imps must have crawled out through the cracks in the ground. Even the Dark side needs resources."

"But the obelisk? Surely they don't lug it around with them?" I asked.

"They don't. Ever heard about form and substance? What you see now is the form," Gwain began to explain. "But it's the substance that matters. Inside the obelisk lives a spirit which controls the prisoners. As soon as this place is depleted, the imps will use a special spell to set him free while the prisoners move to another cave. There they'll trap the spirit in another slab of rock to create a new obelisk."

Gwain's eyes glistened with an almost insane glow. What was it with him?

"Can some of them be players?" I asked.

Gwain shrugged. Apparently, he wasn't that interested in the prisoners' fate. It was something else.

"Some may be," he finally replied. "Normally, you can't keep a player prisoner for longer than twenty-four hours. It's against the rules. No one likes wasting time obeying orders. They try to mine as much ore as they can in order to exhaust themselves and then go on to their resurrection point."

"How about their gear?"

"It stays here."

"Do you mind if I ask you why Togien and you don't seem to be affected by the obelisk?"

"Our levels are higher than the spirit's. He can only control those weaker than himself. But over time, his powers will grow."

Togien too looked strangely agitated. He exchanged meaningful glances with his nephew, then turned to me. "Alexatis, I'm gonna ask you to keep quiet about this cave. You shouldn't show your map to anyone. Agreed? We might throw in a few more gold for you for the trouble."

"Why, what's up?"

I could see Togien didn't really want to tell me. Still, he must have failed to come up with a believable excuse because he said,

"Thing is, you know... sooner or later the imps will leave and take the spirit with them. But the rock he's trapped in now, it will stay where it is."

"Is it worth something?"

"It's Smoky Rock. Transformed matter. Obelisk fragments can be sold for a hundred gold apiece, depending on their size. Only a master miner can farm them. But you still need to know which rock the spirit used to inhabit. Because once he's out, the rock will look like any other, you understand?"

"Yeah. I won't tell anyone. I promise."

He seemed to be greatly relieved to hear that.

"You'd better tell me," I went on, "this transformed matter, what's it good for?"

"Alchemists need the dust and the chippings," Gwain replied eagerly. "Smaller fragments can be used to decorate weapons and armor with. Large ones are used to make stat-enhancing runes. There's also crystal armor, very rare. To make it, you need to be a Grand Master — and not in Blacksmithing as you'd think but in Jewelry."

I made a mental note to look into it. "Does that mean we can't go further?"

He shook his head. "Unfortunately not. Gwain and I might have battled through on our own. But not with you, we can't. You need to understand. The weakest imp will smoke you before you know it."

His bad mood was in fact perfectly understandable. The most valuable albeit lightweight part of their loot was in my bag.

"What other options are there?" I asked. "Any Plan B? Any teleports stashed nearby?"

To my disappointment, Togien shook his head. "Teleports! We're less than an hour's walk from the city. Nobody knows about this tunnel, believe it or not. Gwain and I happened to discover a piece of an old map. We couldn't read it so we took it to a local antique dealer. Imagine when instead of buying it he produced the missing part of the map from a box — and on it was the part where the tunnel was marked. Next thing we knew, he issued us a quest to get to the old tomb and bring him any ten items made of cargonite — which is a very rare alloy. The secret of its manufacture is long lost."

So that's what was in their overstuffed inventories!

"Who could have known we'd have an earthquake? Imps are nasty little bastards. The moment there's a crevice in the ground, they pour right out there and then!"

"And how did the rogues get here?" I said, unwittingly touching a sore spot.

"They must have stealthed up to us," Togien gave his nephew the evil eye. "This is what happens when you discuss your plans in a tavern and lay the map on the table for everyone to see!"

"If you hadn't skimped on the room, I wouldn't have had to do so!" Gwain snapped back.

"Enough! Stop aggroing each other!" I shouted.

Both turned to me. "Who do you think you are?"

Shit. I kept forgetting about my level 1. Not a healthy idea arguing with higher-level guys. Still, it was a question of survival. The dwarves had no idea I'd be literally risking my life battling through hordes of imps. How would the neuroimplant react? Would I survive the pain of my injuries? I'd been planning to find that out slowly and gingerly — definitely not by combatting a host of mobs whose levels were five times my own!

Still, I didn't lower my gaze under their glares. "Now. We have two options. Option one is to go back. The frozen torrents of ice in the cave where we first met are there for a reason. It means the water was coming from somewhere. We need to have a good look. There might be some crevice there that might take us up to the surface."

"Waste of time," Togien rejected my suggestion straight off. "By the time we go there and come back, the rogues will recover."

"In that case, option number two. We need to lure the mobs into the tunnel. I want you to rush me a couple of levels, then we might be able to fight our way through."

Judging by Togien's silent sniffing, he liked it.

They had no idea that for me this meant mortal combat — literally.

* * *

"Group of five!" gasping, Togien ran out of the cave and swung round, holding a shield in front of himself.

The imps scurried out along the cave's wall and ceiling. Clever bastards! Three level 5 workers and a couple of warriors. So many! That was one hell of a pull. I had a funny feeling there might be more coming.

One of them lobbed his tin bucket into Gwain's face. The monk ducked just in time. Others attacked Togien. The tunnel was too narrow for all of them to get a good foothold. The warriors began slashing at Togien's shield with their heavy scimitars. They were slightly taller than imp workers: about four foot or so. They fought with abandon — why wouldn't they, considering they received a constant flow of buffs from the obelisk.

The three workers hung overhead like bats, clutching onto the tunnel walls and low ceiling, and kept hacking at Togien's helmet with their picks. Still, they did little damage to his armor's durability considering the level gap.

Togien stayed put, receiving virtually no damage and waiting for his opponents to run out of steam, but the obelisk kept recharging them time after time. We should have retreated further down the tunnel.

Strange things were happening to me. I could still hear the tempting whispers and feel the touch of energy, continuing to receive the buffs to Strength. Still, the call didn't seem to affect my mind. Actually, yes, it did. For a brief moment I experienced a strong desire to pick up the deformed tin bucket and hurry into the cave as if mining ore was my sole purpose in life. The urge disappeared as fast as it had come, leaving a bad taste in my mouth.

Realizing his mistake, Togien changed tactics and slammed his attackers with his shield, knocking them out. They recoiled, shaking their heads, finally allowing him to launch an offensive. His axe whooshed through the air, stripping two of the workers of their lives. He then finished off the two warriors with a few slashing blows.

"Go easy on mana," he said, addressing Gwain. "I'm okay for the moment."

You've received a new level!

A golden shimmer enveloped me.

"Quit stallin'," Gwain gave me a friendly slap on the shoulder. "Let's retreat a little bit. That way the obelisk can't buff the mobs."

So far, so good. I'd gotten a new level. A couple more, and I'd be able to smoke imp workers. That way I'd be less of a liability.

'Any loot?" I cast a meaningful stare at the fallen mobs.

"Sorry Alex, our inventories are packed," Togien said, choosing a place for any new combat.

"I'll just take a look," I said, picking up a scimitar.

Damage, 5
Weight, 5.5
Durability, 7/10
Requires level 3, 10 Strength, 5 Agility

This was classical trash: a low damage weapon, heavy and cumbersome. What about this one?

A Spiked Round Shield
Defense, 4
Weight, 4.5
Durability, 5/10
Requires level 3
+5% to your chances to deal damage while parrying.

I had to take it, no doubt about it. You didn't need a shield to parry — it was a default stat every weapon had. Still, in my situation it was useful. Considering the local authenticity levels, it would be stupid to rely on my leather armor alone. Pain was pain.

"Alexatis! Where the heck are you?"

"Coming."

"I need your help. Can you feel the obelisk's

call?"

"Yeah."

"Think you can define its range?"

I complied. We had to walk back a good fifty feet, all the way round the bend, before fatigue overcame me. My Strength had dropped to its old reading.

"It takes us too long!" Gwain kept casting anxious glances behind us.

My sentiment entirely. As we'd walked back, we'd come across quite a few crevices formed by the unexpected earthquake. I had a sneaky suspicion that imps hadn't been the only creatures of the Dark who'd escaped them.

* * *

"Next group!" Togien sprang out of a bend in the tunnel and swung round, covering himself with his shield.

This time he'd only brought two imp workers. He made quick work of them, then assumed a combat stance. "Get ready!"

Demons! Two of them! Both level 18!

From what I'd heard, imps were nasty greedy creatures standing on the lowest rung of Infernal evolution.

I should have known they were too primitive to control the spirit imprisoned within the obelisk. They weren't the bosses here!

"Behind you!"

I swung round to Gwain's voice. He was right. The ethereal shadow of a lich draped in flowing tatters of clothing peeled off the wall.

Immediately it materialized, its tattered rags a cloak thrown over a rusty suit of armor. The eyeslits of his helmet oozed gloom.

Ancient Lich. Level 3

He didn't attack me. Instead, he raised a bony arm, mouthing a spell. I could hear his blood-curdling whisper, his fingers enveloped in a faint aura.

I had to disrupt the spell!

Mysterious Sword: equipped

This was my mnemonic interface's knee-jerk reaction which gave me a chance to deal a sudden crit.

The sword weighed my hand down. In a lightning motion, I chopped the lich's hand off and shrank back, trying in vain to escape his response attack.

His scream assaulted my eardrums. An invisible force punched my chest, throwing me hard against the rock wall. My vision darkened.

My throat seized up.

Gwain came to my rescue. I knew that monks were expert hand-to-hand fighters but I was yet to see one in action. Even now I wasn't able to see it clearly as the tunnel swam before my eyes.

The aura of his blessing removed the Lich's curses from me. The next thing I heard was the clatter of bones and the clanking of rusty steel as the lich collapsed in a heap under Gwain's devastating assault.

"You freakin' nuts?" Gwain snapped at me, hurrying to return to his position. "You can't do this on your own! Always call us when you need us!"

Very nice. Thanks a bunch, Mr. Borisov. Your idea of an alternative start sucks, if you want to know. Talk about sink or swim. Why did they need to do it?

The demons were pressing upon Togien. He assumed a defensive stance, struggling to fight back against two opponents at once. Parrying with his sword, he was looking for the right moment to counterattack. Gwain kept healing him but still our little group definitely missed a warrior who could deal the damage while Togien was pulling the aggro to himself.

I couldn't help them with that, not yet. Not against level 18 mobs. My hits were little less than mosquito bites for them.

Once I came round a little, I hurried toward the slain lich. Something glinted weakly in the heap of bones and crumbling armor, like a precious stone. It turned out to be the knob of a staff hidden under the lich's tattered cloak.

I grabbed it and checked its stats,

Lethal Wound Staff
Crushing Damage, 5
Dark Magic Damage, 5. Effect: Bleeding, 5 sec
Durability, 9/10
Charges left, 12
Requires: level 2, Intellect 10
Restrictions: Only the undead

Pretty useless for me, wasn't it? I was about to throw it back when my fingers clenched in a spasm. What was that now? I had nothing to do with Dark powers!

My hands were shaking. I tried to fling the staff away from me but I couldn't. My body began to prickle. It felt as if I was the attracting center of some dark, viscous energies flowing toward me from every direction.

One of the demons pushed himself away from Togien's shield, finalizing an attack. The creature clung to the ceiling, growling and emitting an unbearable stench. Then he lunged at me.

Instinctively I raised my hands, trying to block him. I failed to stay on my feet. Still, the demon wasn't interested in me. He grabbed the staff and pulled it out of my hand. His jaws closed around it until it snapped.

A silent crimson flash enveloped the demon. I scampered into the opposite corner, unable to get to my feet or take my eyes away from the scene.

Brown goo gushed from under the demon's armor. He whimpered and collapsed to one side.

Wow.

My dwarven friends didn't waste time. A cleansing aura flashed in the dark, consuming it, as Gwain used yet another one of his abilities. Togien performed a clever combo, stripping the other demon of 30% Life, then attacked him again before he could recover from it. Another scream echoed from the rocky walls, then it was quiet.

I struggled to my feet, disgustedly rubbing my clothes clean from the droplets of nasty goo that had showered everything around.

Experience in our group was distributed equally. The two mobs killed by Togien (who'd also finished off the demon that had snapped the staff with his jaws) had brought me up to level 4.

I ignored the system messages for the time being. I had more important things to do.

"You fucking nuts?" Gwain yelled at me, bug-eyed. "You should know better! What possessed you to pick up the staff?"

"Why not?"

"What's your resistance to magic?"

"Point five percent."

"So? Use your head! It's charged with Dark energy! If you held it for a bit longer, you'd be a fucking zombie by now!"

I didn't reply. I may be an experienced player but I hadn't been allowed the time to look into this new game world. Besides, Gwain wasn't exactly right. This wasn't how it had happened. Firstly, for some unknown reason I'd managed to aggro the demon. Secondly, it didn't look as if it could transform me. The obelisk, too, had been buffing me with Dark energy, but it had failed to control me. Which meant I must have had some resistance to magic — but for some reason, I couldn't see it in my settings.

"Stop it," Togien said sharply. "We'd better think how we're going to get out of here. It looks like we're stuck, doesn't it? If there're demons in the cave, it now makes it an instance. And I don't think we're strong enough to tackle it."

"An instance!" Gwain fumed. "Since when? Two hours ago there was nothing here! We walked through, then the rogues stole after us!"

"An upgrade, maybe?" I offered.

"Possible. It doesn't help us, anyway," Togien grumbled. I told you we should have bought a teleport scroll, didn't I?"

The two were about to have a go at each other again. I had to do something.

"You two are dwarves, aren't you?" I said. "You're second to none when it comes to mining and metalwork. Don't you have some cunning ability that might help us get out?"

Togien stared at me. "You're right!" he slapped his forehead. "Well done! That's smart! The Rescue scroll! I should have thought of it!"

"The Rescue scroll? Never heard of it."

"That's because you've never worked in the mines," Gwain replied. "Miners get buried alive in rockfalls an awful lot. No one wants to hack through the rock for weeks just to get out."

"Will it work? I don't have Mining open yet."

"Doesn't matter. The scroll works for the entire group. The only problem is, we're not buried alive yet."

Togien chuckled. He laid his weapon down and reached for his pick. Then he pointed at a small crevice that branched several feet away from the main tunnel, ending in a dead end.

"Try to get in as far as you can," he said, beaming, apparently pleased as Punch with the solution.

Gwain and I squeezed our way deep into the narrow opening.

Togien took aim, then began hacking at the tunnel wall, puffing and panting. Small rocks showered down. A large crack ran across the wall; then part of the tunnel ceiling collapsed, breaking into large chunks of stone.

"Togien!" Gwain looked seriously worried.

"I'm all right. Light the torch, will you?"

A shaky uneven light illuminated the small space around us. The entrance to the crevice had been blocked solid.

Togien broke the seal on the scroll, opened it and recited a short spell.

The ground rumbled and shook. An invisible force lifted me and jerked me upward.

* * *

The sky was aglow with a fiery sunset.

Peaceful countryside lay all around us. A patrol of three level-100 guards walked unhurriedly along the mud road.

After the stuffy darkness of the tunnel, I felt dizzy. We were sitting by the roadside, gasping. Ignoring us, the patrol sashayed past us toward where the far-off city walls and towers peeped above the horizon.

My Strength buff was still working but I was completely exhausted. It must have had something to do with the fact that this was the neuroimplant's first activation. I might not last very long now before I collapsed with fatigue.

"That's it. Let's move it," the hardy Togien was ready to get going.

"Sorry guys," I said. "I'm afraid I need to log out, now."

"Oh do you? And who's gonna carry your bag to town?"

I scrambled to my feet in the hope I might feel better. As if! If anything, I felt worse. "Sorry. I really need to go. Can't you do anything at all about it?"

"And what are you gonna do with your char, leave him here by the roadside?"

"Is there an inn in this village?"

"As a matter of fact, there is," Togien grumbled. "Ah, fuck it. We'll hire a horse and load it up. We'll give you an advance of five gold. The rest we'll transfer to your account after we close the quest and sell the loot."

"Fine. Thanks. You should deduct the horse hire from my cut."

"We will, don't worry!" Togien swung round and strode toward the village which was only a few hundred feet away. Gwain and I plodded along.

"You shouldn't have touched that staff, man," Gwain misunderstood the reason for my sorry state. "The powers of the Dark never sleep."

I could barely hear him. I'd passed my first trial. I'd earned myself four levels and had lots of new experiences. I'd found new friends and made new enemies.

The only thing I wanted now was get to the inn, rent a room and collapse onto the bed.

CHAPTER THREE

THE CHRYSTAL SPHERE
THE VILLAGE OF HINTERWOOD IN THE VICINITY OF AGRION CITY

A COOL BREEZE rich with the scent of freshly-cut grass burst into the half-open window of my room, awakening me.

A system message flashed before my closed eyes,

You're well-rested.

Effect: Vigor. +2% to XP received. -2% to both Mental and Physical Energy consumption. Duration: 6 hrs.

Indeed, I felt great. Nothing like last night.

I threw the covers back and climbed out of bed. Having washed my face, I walked over to the window. The world outside was still consumed by the early morning twilight. The inn stood at the crossroads outside the city walls surrounded by fields, gardens, meadows and copses of trees.

I was feeling so good. No idea how my mortal body was doing back IRL, but I could safely say I still needed sleep here. Before, I could rarely afford enough rest and struggled to find a few uninterrupted hours of sleep every day. This world made it so much easier. I didn't have to wake up at insane hours to rush to work, oh no. This new life was calling my name. I could finally breathe. New plans, the one grander than the next, were crowding my head.

I was well and truly free. I could go wherever I wanted. I could roam the boundless lands of the Crystal Sphere in order to battle monsters and complete quests. Alternatively, I could settle in a small town, learn a profitable profession and live a happy life.

I'll be honest with you: I'd never even dreamed of anything like it. The neuroimplant made it possible for me to simply swap one world for the other, effacing their boundaries.

That morning, I really believed that all my trials and tribulations were finally over.

My heart beat an uneven rhythm within my chest. My breathing hastened. As I stood there by the window watching the dawn break and sensing the adrenaline pumping through my body, I felt like a prisoner being released from the damp and cramped prison cell of his former life.

Calm down, Alexatis. It's all right to breathe — but not to gasp and choke!

You might find it hard to understand my emotional state. I have nothing to compare it with. For me, cyberspace used to be a temporary refuge where I could escape to for a few hours a day, if that. And now it was my rightful habitat, its incredible authenticity levels harboring a promise of a fulfilling and happy life.

Emotions were getting the better of me. Admittedly, I didn't feel like restraining them.

Someone knocked on the door: a soft, insistent knock.

"Who is it?"

"Alex? May I come in, please?"

I recognized the voice straight away. I didn't have time to say anything, though. The latch on the door turned against my will. The door creaked.

"How's it going? Feeling all right?" a wizard, his ancient back doubled up under the weight of his advanced years, stepped in, leaning heavily on his staff. Suddenly he stood up straight, shaking off the disguise. Mr. Borisov.

"Decided to check on you," he sat down on a stool. "I won't bother you often, don't worry. I just need to clear up a few things. You don't mind a bit of advice, do you?"

I didn't reply.

"As far as Christa is concerned... you shouldn't go around looking for her. You'll only make it harder on yourself," he mechanically crossed his legs.

"Why did you have to make her a demon?"

"Alexis, please. Use your head. Don't try to shift the blame. We're all born innocent angels. But what we grow into is a different question entirely. It depends on lots of factors. Christa made an informed decision. I don't think she'll be happy if you try to meddle and question it."

"But what if she made the wrong choice? What if she overreacted?"

"Time will tell," he said, then hurried to change the subject. "Do you realize now how important sleep is?"

"Yes," I replied calmly. I had neither the desire nor an excuse to antagonize him.

"Sleep is paramount. You need to make sure you don't get carried away playing. You should never deplete your resources. Your brain needs some down time. You might find it difficult at first because you can't log out here. Other players might begin to wonder about your 24/7 virtual presence. You need to keep that in mind."

"There're inns everywhere," I pointed out.

"Still, I suggest you get yourself a tent. It won't cost much. It won't take much place in your inventory, either. But at least it has some Protection stats and a buff to Good Rest. Lots of people use them when they can't leave their char in a safe zone. That would eliminate a lot of questions about your constant presence."

"Thanks. I'll look into it."

"You're not very happy to see me, are you? Why?"

"Nothing personal, Sir. I'm just a bit overwhelmed with it all. Too many things to take in. The authenticity is mind-blowing."

"Right," he said, returning to his wizard's disguise. Groaning, he scrambled back to his feet. "I'm not going to pester you too often, anyway. Enjoy. You've got some leveling to do. Just don't forget to take some proper rest and stay away from demons."

Stepping outside, he turned to me again. "Oh, and talking about leveling. Don't drag it out, okay? Pay special attention to the Neuro's development branch. It doesn't have an ability calculator yet so you need to use your own head. Bad times are coming. A lot will depend on your success. It's not about the Corporation's profits;

it's not even about my own career as you might have imagined."

He handed me a scroll. "Only break the seal in the direst emergency when something goes very badly wrong and it doesn't belong in the gameplay. And one last thing. Try not to think about me. Your neurograms are being monitored."

With this he disappeared, leaving behind an aura of evasive suggestiveness and a yellowed scroll.

What had he been trying to imply? What could have gone "very badly wrong"? Why couldn't he just say?

* * *

This unexpected visit had puzzled me but not enough to dampen my good mood.

I walked downstairs to the inn's common room and headed for the bar. "I'd like to have breakfast and pay for another night."

"Three silver," the innkeeper said disinterestedly, wiping the dishes.

That was all right. He was only an NPC, his Relationship settings neutral by default. You had to complete a quest for him to earn as little as a smile.

I paid and took a table in the far corner. As

I attacked my breakfast of oatmeal porridge — which tasted very good — I started thinking about what I should do next. Should I leave in order to seek adventures? Or should I learn a profession, maybe?

The first option sounded more interesting. I might buy myself a tent and check out the area, at least until I made level 10.

Having finished my breakfast, I walked back to the landlord. Earlier I'd noticed that the local shopkeeper's house was dark and shut up for the night, without a single light in its windows.

"Master Nicholas, why is the shop closed?"

"But that's because of this wretched wyvern, isn't it? She mauled Dimian — he's my son-in-law — just as he was coming back from town with new stock. So he's lying inside dying now. Our new healer, this bastard we took in, turned out to be a total quack! He couldn't heal Dimian so he just ran off like a thief in the night. I did tell our guys not to take him in, didn't I? They should have kicked him out straight away!"

This sounded like the makings of a quest. Low-level location NPCs are normally quite predictable. You should treat them politely and with respect, or they might jack up their prices or simply close their shop to you.

"What a shame," I said. "I'm very sorry.

How come the patrols let the wyvern through?"

"They can't be everywhere, can they? Wyverns are a rare sight in this part of the world. Last time we saw one was a year ago. They don't nest here, you see. They prefer to live high in the mountains. Dimian was unlucky, that's all."

"And what about the wizards? Did you try them?"

"They're all away, just to please! What about you, my good man? You think you could help?"

"I'm not a healer," I said.

"You don't need to be," he leaned closer to me and whispered, "I have an old recipe. It's a potion, so strong it can bring anyone back to life. But it requires some very rare herbs. And fish bile. Me, I can't leave the inn. I could send the kids to get it, I suppose, only it's not safe. Last night the sky over the city was aglow with fires. And before that, we felt the earth shake. Apparently, demons have escaped from their underground dungeons. And early this morning, we saw wolves prowling right by the village gate. Huge ones. So do you think you could do it?"

This was a predicament. Of course I had to help — but on the other hand, neither Fishing nor Herbalism were on my priority list. You had to choose your secondary professions wisely and think about your future — something I as yet didn't know much of.

Unexpectedly, my implanted mind expander helped me out. Reacting to my thoughts with lightning speed, it conducted its own search and delivered the result, displaying it as a prompt in my mental view. Apparently, the Crystal Sphere had no restrictions regarding the number of secondary professions you could have. You could get the initial skill for free from most NPCs. Leveling it up, however, was entirely a question of your own application.

New Quest alert: First Aid

Quest type: Normal

Collect the ingredients necessary to make a healing potion.

Reward: Your Reputation with the inhabitants of Hinterwood will improve considerably. If you complete the quest before dark, the Innkeeper will share the potion recipe with you.

"I'd be happy to help," I said. "Only I've never farmed herbs before. I don't have any fishing experience, either."

"That's not a problem," the innkeeper dove into the back room and returned with a fishing rod, an old bucket, a backpack and an old knife. "Take this piece of bread, too. You should roll small balls of bread between your fingers, put them onto the hook, throw the hook in the water and wait. As soon as the float begins to jump, you should strike very quickly. Put some water in the bucket and place all the fishies you catch in there because I need them alive. Herbs are even easier. You take this knife and cut them about an inch above the root. Then you wrap them in a moist cloth so that they stay fresh and put them in your bag. Easy. Try to do it before sunset, okay? I've marked both the pond and the meadow on your map."

Congratulations! You've learned a new profession: Fishing.

Current level, 1

Congratulations! You've learned a new profession: Herbalism

Current level, 1

* * *

When I came to the pond, I discovered a girl wizard siting there, looking quite upset.

Oblivious to everything around her, she was perched on a hillock, sobbing and wiping her tears, casting occasional glances at a large toad which towered on a huge lily leaf about fifteen feet from the bank.

The sun was shining. A gentle breeze stroked my face. I was rested and well-fed. To me, the whole world answered my mood. Adventures were calling my name.

"Hi," I sent the fishing rod into the grass under a hazelnut tree and walked over to the pond, intending to fill my quest bucket.

"Hi," she replied with a sigh. "Do you see that toad over there? You'd better watch out. It can eat you alive."

"It's not saber-toothed, by any chance?" I asked cheerfully, submerging the bucket under the water.

"You kidding me?"

"Not at all. Why, you have problems with it?"

"You could say that. I lost my staff because of it. The wretched thing killed me twice!"

I checked out their local mob,

A Large Toad. Level, 7

Then I turned round to read the girl's name tag,

Enea. Level 7. Battle Wizard.

She must have read the amazement in my face because she admitted, "I just can't defeat it.

It gets frogs to help it. They bite like hell," she heaved a sigh. "You try it! Go knee deep in the water and you'll see!"

Oh. This was a problem. I could get her staff back, of course. I could see it floating behind the lily leaf, its bejeweled knob glistening. The toad could use a lesson, too. But this wasn't the right thing to do. The girl needed real help, not having her kittens saved from the trees for her.

"Which spells do you use?" I asked.

'I use Ice Arrow. It doesn't work though. It removes 19 pt. Life, and the wretched thing has Regeneration of +20 HP."

"How did you manage to lose your staff?"

"I was out of mana. So I decided to hit the toad on the head."

"I see. Can you cast spells without it?"

"Sure. It takes longer though and uses more mana."

"It's all right. I like your ring."

She tensed up. "You're not getting it!"

"I don't need it, do I? Any stats on it?"

"Sure," Enea stood up tall. "+3 to Loveliness!"

I tried not to crack up. "How long have you been in the game?"

"A week."

Oh. Where do I even start? "All right. What debuffs do you have?"

Judging by her expression, she hadn't understood me. Hadn't she read the New Player's Guide? Not to even mention class guides.

"All right," I said. She merited help, or at least a word of advice. I used to be a newbie too. "A debuff produces a negative effect. A buff, positive. Can you remember that?"

"Yeah."

"Then you should remember one other thing. If you want to level up, just memorizing a spell isn't enough. You can't just receive an ability: you need to know how it works. Can you see my level?"

"It's 4."

"And the toad is level 7. But let me tell you: if I really try, I might be able to kill it."

She took my word for it. "And what about me?" her voice rang with faint hope.

"Especially you! Now let's just think how we can do it. Give me the names of the spells you have."

"Ice Arrow."

"And?"

"Ice. It's a blanket spell but it takes too much mana. I also tried Weakness, but it doesn't affect the toad," she heaved another sigh. "I have another ring, only it's ugly and rusty so I don't wear it. Also, some old woman gave me a scroll for a quest I'd completed. Still, I don't think it'll work. The toad summons frogs, you see. They jump out of the pond and bite me."

"Mind if I take a look at that other ring?"

The ring was awesome. +5 to Intellect! The scroll turned out to be great too — Magic Shackles, perfect for this toad quest. It reduced any enemy's Life by 50% of the mental energy they spent.

"I'd like you to put it on and watch your mana bar," I handed the plain ring back to her.

She obeyed. "My mana's growing!" she exclaimed in surprise.

"That's because your mana is directly related to your Intellect levels."

"Thanks. I'll remember that."

"Take a look at the toad. Can you see its mana bar which looks just like yours?"

"Yeah."

"Your enemy spends energy too whenever they attack you or have to defend themselves. Whether this energy is physical or mental, depends on the mob. You should remember that. Try to use different combinations of the available spells and take every opportunity to improve your stats with buffs, jewelry and stat items. Is that clear?"

"Sort of."

Without betraying my impatience, I made her read the help pages for all the available spells. "How do you want to kill the toad?" I asked her gravely.

She gave it some thought. "I can cast Magic Shackles on it, can't I? Then I'll hit it with Ice Arrow. Then, when it begins to regenerate, it'll keep getting more damage from the debuff, right?"

"Exactly. But it can still summon the frogs."

"That's right," she lost heart again. "What can I do with them? Alexatis? Am I missing something again?"

"The sequence of spells is very important. First you need to cast Ice," I patiently explained. "I know, I know. It'll cost you all your mana but it's worth it. The spell keeps dealing damage time after time, slowing the frogs and preventing them from climbing ashore. Then you can use the scroll to cast Magic Shackles over the toad. In the meantime, your mental energy will restore somewhat. When some of the mobs do climb out, you need to cast Weakness over them, then finish them off with Ice Arrows. It would be good if you found a moment to cast Endurance on yourself: that way you'll have +20 to resistance to physical damage."

"I got it! I got it!" she stroked the rusty ring with respect. She'd definitely changed her opinion of it. "I'll try it now. Could you please stay and wait?"

"Okay," I perched myself on a hillock.

Enea took the upcoming combat in all seriousness. She spent some quality time choosing her position, estimating the distances. Her Ice was quite weak and only worked at a range of about six feet. Was she going to use it randomly?

Oh no, she wasn't. She was doing everything right. She came right up to the water edge. It wasn't easy for her without the staff, so she had to cast a complex spell which demanded quite a bit of time and concentration.

The toad basked in the sun. Suddenly it began to shriek as the lily leaf under it quickly covered with ice. The water around it solidified, glass-like. The toad failed to summon the frogs properly: some of them materialized within the layer of ice, others closer to the surface. All of them got some damage; a few popped their clogs on the spot.

Enea whipped out the scroll and broke the seal. Two new icons appeared in the toad's tag. One of them depicted a symbolic book of spells bound with chains, but the other... it looked like a regular healing spell but was nothing of the kind!

The Magic Shackles produced the desired effect. The toad screamed like a banshee.

Together with Regeneration, it now also received incoming damage, only restoring 10 pt. Health.

In the meantime, the ice covering the lily leaf kept devouring the toad's HP, dealing occasional damage.

A new unsuccessful attempt at Regeneration followed. A furious roar echoed over the location. Someone might have thought these were two buffaloes fighting.

Two groups of low-level players ran out of the undergrowth, attracted by the commotion. They seemed to be leveling up by killing all sorts of insects.

I could hear their surprised voices. Someone was already posting to the chat, sharing their impressions and streaming a video of the scene.

In my opinion, this was nothing extraordinary, but local players seemed to be an impressionable lot. The ring with +3 to Loveliness must have played its role in it, too.

A portal popped open, disgorging a crowd of new onlookers. Apparently, some city wizard had put two and two together and decided to cash in on human curiosity.

At that moment, Ice finished working. With a loud cracking noise, the toad plopped into the water amid swirls of mist, baring its yellowed fangs and creating a powerful swell in its wake.

Enea was high on adrenaline. In the heat of combat, the excess of her life energy began transforming into mana. This must have been some class ability she had. Oblivious of her growing audience, the girl shrank away from the water's edge, drawing fiery runes in the air. Gusts of wind tore at her short tunic as she mouthed something. The toad received a nice whack from Ice Arrow. A half-dead frog who'd had the imprudence to get too close to the girl collapsed awkwardly on its side, its little legs convulsing: a promptly cast Weakness had worked like a dream!

Two more Ice Arrows exploded in a cascade of frozen slush, finishing off more frogs before they could get out of the water. The toad prepared to jump. It only had 10% Life left but that was enough to kill Enea. Well enough.

The onlookers quietened down. Even I began getting nervous. Still, my student hadn't failed her mentor. In a flash of runes and a clap of thunder, her mana dropped to zero but she did it, trapping the toad deep within a large cube of ice.

Wow.

A golden shimmer enveloped Enea. She'd received a new level.

"Cool!" "Well done!" "Awesome!" the happy audience cheered.

Enea turned to the sound. Seeing the crowd surrounding her, she looked sincerely lost.

A huge crystal screen jingled open overhead, materializing high in the azure skies. A banner ran across it,

Video of the Day: Staffless Spell Casting!

The scene of the brief combat we'd just witnessed began unfolding on the screen.

The portal wizard was busy gulping mana by the vial. The simmering veil of the teleport parted, disgorging a group of bards. One of them — a dark-skinned bearded fiddler — was especially picturesque. His white smile seemed to have inspired the crowd, the sounds of a popular song leading everyone into the groove. Within seconds, the pond banks were rocking with an impromptu party.

The video in the sky was already over, replaced by the Screenshot of the Day. It depicted Enea enveloped in the golden shimmer next to the pond' boss: the giant toad trapped within the ice cube.

I was really happy for her. She'd done everything right and deserved her fifteen minutes of fame. But my own fishing trip... it looked like I'd have to delay it somewhat.

You've received an Achievement: Mentor of the Day!

Dear Alexatis, the Crystal Sphere administration is thankful to you for your efforts in promoting the game's principles. We're happy to inform you that we've just credited your account with the sum of 10 (ten) gold as a token of our gratitude.

That was really handy. I could use some startup capital.

"Alexatis, you're awesome! Thank you so much! Thank you!" Enea forced her way out of the crowd and fell upon my neck, screaming with excitement.

I froze. I could feel her heart beat through the fine fabric. The scent of her hair went to my head. Her hot breath burned my cheek.

Neuroimplant, what do you think you're doing to me?

Bringing myself back in check before I could do anything stupid (don't forget that Enea's authenticity settings were vastly inferior to mine) proved not that easy.

"I can't believe I was crying here only an hour ago, not knowing what to do," she laughed happily, oblivious to my state. "Will you stay here for a while?"

"I don't think so. Too much to do. I have a

quest I have to complete till sunset."

"What a shame," she saddened. "Wait! Could we level up together? It's going to be awesome, what do you think? Please!"

I smiled. "You should check your email first. And the PM box. I'm sure you've already got lots of invitations."

"You think?" she momentarily zoned out, checking her inbox. "You're right! It'll take me a whole day just to read through them all!"

"So you see? Enjoy."

"You're going then, are you? Our party is too cool for you? Can't you just stay here and have some fun?"

"Sorry, I really do have too much to do. Would you like me to put you on my friend list?"

"Your friend list? Absolutely!"

* * *

Having bidden my goodbyes to her, I retrieved my bucket and fishing rod, walked to a safe distance from the impromptu party and crouched under a shady shrub, wiping sudden perspiration from my forehead.

The neuroimplant's feedback levels could use some fine-tuning, that's for sure. I'd nearly gone nuts with the hormone overload.

Now was a perfect time to smoke a couple

of mobs.

I opened the map. Most of the area was still covered in the "fog of war", meaning I was yet to explore it. My route from Hinterwood to the pond was the only detailed part of it. The meadow overgrown with the herbs I needed was marked with a question mark and located in the woods nearby.

I switched to global mode. Now I could see a large plain veined with the fine lines of major roads, the outlines of two lakes and a large mountain range about a week's hike away. Besides Agrion, six more cities were scattered all over the continent. Beyond the mountains lay the sea dotted with islands and archipelagoes.

This was only a fraction of the Crystal Sphere. The map was shaped as an old parchment scroll, frayed and yellowed. The fine lines of roads and rivers disappeared within the creases and folds of time.

That much was clear. Those were the areas no one had yet been to.

Good. Enough sitting about. I determined the right direction and set up markers.

I walked unhurriedly, looking around me. It felt like I was on another planet. Never before had cyberspace triggered such an emotionally powerful reaction in me.

The neuroimplant made every twig feel real.

I took in lungfuls of air, listening to the birds singing in the shrubs. The tall grass entangled my legs, hindering my movements.

This was a totally different gameplay. I'd have already been to the meadow and back, having smoked every mob in my way, and now I was *tired,* of all things! My crude and uncomfortable leather armor kept chafing against my body.

In the meantime, the sun had climbed high into the sky. It was getting quite hot. I was thirsty but I had no water on me. From now on, I'd have to be more provident about many things. The first days were bound to be the hardest; after that, I might get the hang of it.

Tree branches crackled, disrupting my thoughts and scaring up a small flock of birds. A rabbit sprang out of the undergrowth and froze, pricking up his ears. A bowstring sang; a clumsily loosed arrow thudded into the ground.

I heard the clanking of metal. Two players ran out of the undergrowth: a hunter and a warrior, both level 10.

"Did you see where he went?" a stifled voice came from behind the warrior's lowered visor. Jesus Christ almighty! The guy was wearing a full suit of steel armor, in this heat! If the game developers wanted to mass-produce their neuroimplant thingies, they had a lot to reconsider.

I pointed in the right direction.

"See ya!" clanking his armor, the warrior hurried after their runaway quarry. The hunter picked up his arrow on the run and followed suit.

* * *

It took me about an hour to get to the spot I'd marked on the map. I lay low in the undergrowth, studying the area.

Nut trees thrived in the shade of towering pines. It was relatively cool here. The air smelled of rotting old leaves.

The brightly sunlit clearing promised no surprises. I could easily discern the herbs I needed: covered in tiny white and yellow blossoms, they were quite conspicuous.

At the center of the opening lay the ruins of some ancient fortification overgrown with dog rose bushes. The air was filled with the chirping of a grasshopper and the rasping of wasps. High above, large dragonflies hovered in the sky.

I kept my eye on the mobs. The level 3 wasps looked like the most dangerous of the lot. Still, there weren't that many of them. I focused on the grasshopper: level 1. A dragonfly: level 2.

Very well, then! Let's do it!

The grasshopper aggroed me first, lunging

at me unexpectedly from a considerable distance. He was the size of a large dog.

I'd already noticed back in the tunnels that my grip on my weapons was correct. That was exactly what a system message had warned me about,

The neuroimplant makes your skills and reactions identical in both worlds regardless of where you acquired them.

Now was the time to check it. The two years' worth of my experience as a warrior should have left their mark.

I dodged the grasshopper's first attack, then hacked at its chitin jaws with all my might. I wanted to somersault over it to perform the coup de grace, but my attempt failed miserably. Luckily, I hadn't broken my neck but I had hit my head against a tree stump nice and hard. I should have known that all my "warrior reactions" had been produced by the prompt manipulation of the game console buttons. Real combat acrobatics lay way beyond my past life's experience.

The mob took its chance and jumped onto my back, sinking its mandibles into my leather jacket.

It was a good job I was alone. I probably

looked a sight. Still, I had no time to ponder over it. I finally shook the creature off my back and jumped to my feet, brandishing my sword. I was soaked in cold sweat. My hits were rare, none of them critical. It took me several minutes to finally smoke the thing. First I poked its eye out, then I happened to chop off a leg, until finally I buried my sword in its belly, my hands shaking. By the time I finished it off, I was all covered in green slime.

Having thus won by a hair's breadth, I staggered back to the nut grove and collapsed to the ground, trying to suppress a bout of nausea.

It took me some time to pull myself together. No idea what I was going to do next. My throat rasped with thirst and the heat. I didn't have much time left to complete the quest. And I still had to get the fish!

How on earth were the neuroimplant developers going to attract billions of users with their contraption? Who would want to experience real pain in game, suffering heat, thirst and exhaustion, hungry and uncomfortable in clumsy clothes and unmanageable armor?

And what about skills? Was I supposed to spend the next few months in training before I could come back here and smoke a couple of dragonflies?

This was crazy. No one was going to agree

to this, let alone pay money for it.

Or could the problem be in my being the first? Was I their guinea pig allowing them to fine-tune their range of potential experiences?

* * *

Stubbornness got the better of me. I wasn't going to leave here empty-handed, period.

I gingerly approached the edge of the opening. I'd learned the grasshopper's lesson well. I was only going to use simple movements. Attack, dodge, recoil. I had to accept the fact that I wasn't some wonder warrior.

I kept a close eye on the mobs. I had about fifty feet to cover to get to the ruins overgrown with dog rose. Halfway to it, I would have to cross the aggro zone of three wasps busy buzzing around some purple-leaf plant unknown to me covered in pink blossoms.

Halfway to the wasps, I could make out some decayed remains lying in the grass: a small bundle of faded clothing gleaming with metal inlays.

How weird. If this was some hapless player, why hadn't he done his corpse run?

I'd have to look into it later.

I peered at the mobs. The longer I focused on them, the more details my mind expander received. Strange. I didn't even know what this device looked like. Was it a separate implant or just part of the neuroimplant itself?

A Wasp. Level 3.

Life, 30/30

Physical attack damage, 10

Additional damage: Venom, 5. Effect: Weakness. Duration: 5 sec. The target affected by the Wasp's neurotoxins can't deal critical damage and slows down, using 25% more Energy for every performed movement. The attacks' effect is cumulative.

Their size was quite intimidating. Their wingspan alone was a good couple of feet.

I might have to aggro them one by one. I just hoped they weren't a pack. The only way to find that out was in action. I had to risk it.

One of the wasps fluttered closer to the edge of the opening. Good.

I sprang out of my hiding place. The wasp saw me and went for me, buzzing. The others stayed put — excellent!

I ran back to safety.

Covering myself with the shield, I stopped at the opening's edge. The wasp had a peculiar way of attacking: it accelerated into some kind of insect cannonball. Now I knew: it was going to first knock me off my feet, then sting me.

Admittedly, I felt anxious. My body froze. It had been a while since I sensed something like this.

I dodged aside, my face barely avoiding an impact with the wasp's tough wings. Just as I'd expected, the wasp found itself in the thick of the undergrowth where it had little space to bank into a sharp turn.

I hacked at its wing, damaging it, and promptly sprang back.

The wasp spun in place, its smooth sharp stinger shaking in synch with the creature's muscle contractions.

Finally it ran out of steam and landed spread-eagled on the ground. I ran up close and took a swing with my sword, chopping through the fine link that connected the wasp's head to its thorax.

You've dealt a critical hit!

I crouched, catching my breath. Not enough to make level 5 yet. Never mind. I was pretty sure I'd make it today — and then I'd be able to finally check out the Neuro's mysterious development branch.

The wasp dropped a Stinger, a Venom Gland and a Small Chitin Plate.

I studied my loot. Chitin was good for armor making. The stinger could make a nice arrowhead. And the venom gland... it deserved looking into.

Venom Gland. Contains a dose of neurotoxin, dealing additional recurring damage. Effects: Weakness, Paralysis. The amount of damage and the duration of the effects depend upon the target's resistance. Does not affect undead species, elementals or golems.

Oh wow. If I put some venom on an arrowhead or my sword blade, potential opponents wouldn't be happy! Still, it wasn't without its drawbacks. Firstly, a wasp didn't have much toxin: a couple of drops at most. Secondly, I had to apply it to my weapons beforehand as I wouldn't be able to do so in the heat of battle.

I placed the precious loot into my inventory.

Time was pressing. It was already early afternoon and I hadn't even farmed the herbs yet.

* * *

I spent the next hour fighting the wasps. I managed to lure them one by one to my hiding place by the nut trees and smoke them all.

They'd only managed to deal me two bites with their mandibles. Most importantly, I'd escaped their toxic stings.

My jacket sleeve had been sliced to shreds, my left arm a bit tender. But most unfortunately, the Mysterious Sword's durability had dropped to critical levels. It might not survive another fight.

I only had the dragonfly left to kill. It was rushing overhead so fast I could barely keep an eye on it.

A Large Green Dragonfly. Level, 2.

No matter how hard I tried to keep the crazy beast in my focus, I hadn't received any additional intel.

Could I be lucky, for a change? NPCs could be non-aggressive, like rabbits or deer who didn't aggro you at all until you actually attacked them.

Having said that... what was wrong with me? This wasn't the era of oral tradition, thank God! I opened the wiki and searched for it.

I'd been right. In the Crystal Sphere, dragonflies were non-aggressive. They were in fact a valuable resource: their wings were used in Alchemy to make levitation potions. Only two dragonfly species were listed as aggressive but those lived deep in the dungeons of the undead and were quite conspicuous, looking like scaled-down copies of bone dragons.

So basically, the place was clear of mobs. I could go through.

Impatient as I was to get to the ruins, collect the herbs and hurry back through the forest to the pond (where with any luck the party was already over), I couldn't just walk past those remains. They begged to be checked out.

Judging by the cloth armor, the dead player must have been a wizard. Then again... I made a mental calculation. Even at the lowest levels, an ice arrow or a fireball can strip one's enemy of 10 HP. It just didn't sum up. No caster in his sane mind would start a hand-to-hand with mobs. Why would he if he could smoke them from a safe distance?

My cheek began to twitch. It was only my second day in the game and already the pressure had begun to show. No wonder, with their authenticity levels.

I had no choice. I pulled out the Mysterious Sword and squeezed the contents of the three venom glands onto the blade. I smeared it around with a twig, making sure the venom covered the blade evenly. Had it been a mistake reducing Enea's suggestion of help to a joke? Now of all times I could use a battle wizard to cover my back.

Never mind. Let's do it! Having completed

my preparations, I stepped over the last wasp's body and headed for the suspicious heap of rain-damaged, sun-bleached rags.

* * *

The sun was blazing, nice and hot. The dragonfly zigzagged overhead. I was bursting with energy.

A heat haze hovered over the ruins. I could see a collapsed doorway and beyond it, some charred ceiling beams and a lone ladder leaned against a wall.

When I reached the center of the opening, I came across a round area covered in withered old grass. This must have been where the wizard had met his fate. Not a single new blade of grass grew there. I'd love to know why.

I crouched and pulled at the end of the threadbare rags. Jesus Christ almighty! The once-expensive robes slid aside, revealing yellowed bones underneath.

Aha. This must have been the clue to a new plot line! When players die, they leave no skeletons behind.

No prompts available. I studied the items without touching anything else. First, a belt with a silver buckle and several quick access slots. Inside them were ten tightly closed vials: three containing Life elixir, three more of mana and four completely unknown to me, their seal wax marked with symbols I couldn't identify.

Now, the staff. It was made of a whole tree root complete with part of the trunk. A simple carved pattern ran along it. The knob of the staff was formed by intertwined roots serving as a setting for a faceted crystal. Much to my disappointment, the stone proved to be cracked.

The Staff of Illusion
Two-handed weapon
Crushing damage, 30
Charges left, 0/20
Durability, 10/250
Requires: Level 7, Intellect, 10

Oh. I was wrong. This hadn't been a wizard but a sorcerer.

I was surprised by the low requirements. Normally, illusion casting only opened at level 50. I could still remember how Christa had been leveling up, desperate to acquire this particular kind of magic.

A good, capacious leather bag with a long strap lay amid the rags, the kind one normally wears over one's shoulder. Its silver buckles had turned black. These remains must have been lying here for years.

You shouldn't touch it. You might regret it,

my inner voice of Caution advised, always ready to support her sister Intuition.

It's true that we only tend to listen to the voice of reason after the fact. No player would walk past unclaimed goodies. If I couldn't use them, I could always sell them. Besides, I was just plain curious.

As soon as I reached out for the bag, the bushes on one side stirred. A triangular green head poked out of the foliage.

My interface flashed red, indicating the mob's high danger levels.

A Praying Mantis. Level 5

The creature's enormous faceted eyes had no pupils. I just couldn't tell what it was looking at. Had it already noticed me?

A rustling sound behind my back made me swing round.

A Praying Mantis. Level 5.

And a third one! This one was prancing in a combat stance with its front legs waving, prepared to attack. I could clearly see the spikes which mantises pierce their prey with once they've struck; they then hold it down with their spiky legs while devouring it. I'd actually witnessed it myself once. Not nice.

I grabbed the bag and the belt and darted for the ruins.

Apparently, the mobs hadn't expected that. I doubted they'd been posted there to guard the wizard's remains. Most likely, they simply found this glade a good place to hunt newbs.

I barged through the dog rose bushes and found myself inside a square structure built with massive blocks of stone blackened by an old fire.

The charred stumps of ceiling beams hung threateningly overhead. The structure had no windows, only arrowslits. The ladder I'd noticed earlier led upstairs. No idea who might have brought it here. Still, it looked solid enough.

Insect wings chattered behind me. One of the mantises sat on the broken wall of the second floor raising clouds of dust, its shadow blotting out the fine sunrays seeking out the gaps between the beams. The creature's triangular head poked through the opening, its antennae twitching. It had noticed me but the opening was too narrow for it to get at me.

Which actually wasn't a problem from a mantis' point of view. Its front claws sank deep into the beam like two serrated sickles, showering me with bits of rotten wood.

Another mantis tried to get to me through a narrow arrowslit. The third one awaited in the doorway. It stood sideways, protecting its head, so all I could see was a sturdy top wing streaked with a veined pattern.

The mobs' actions were well-choreographed. Definitely a pack. And each of them was a whole level above me!

The two realities merged, dissolving into each other. My blood was boiling with adrenaline. My self-preservation instincts had kicked in which wasn't normal for phantom virtual worlds. I was shaking, my nerves like taut strings. My foggy head was ringing.

If I did it now, I could survive in the future as well. But if I broke down, allowing the throat-seizing fear of physical pain to take over me... then I was finished.

My shivering didn't subside. Once again the mantis' leg probed through the arrowslit. My sword reeked with venom. Covering myself with the shield, I crept closer and hacked at its leg as hard as I could. I barely stayed on my feet as the sword went through the chitinous limb with unexpected ease.

The mob squealed. My sword blade glowed with a fiery flourish in a language I didn't know.

A long screeching sound came from above. The mantis on the roof had managed to claw its way through the rotten beams, one of which gave way with a crack. The creature fell right through, knocking the ladder down and crushing a couple of empty crates, sending up clouds of dust.

I barely had time to swing round and parry the blow. The mob's front legs ended in sharp claw-like spikes which it now used to break up my shield with ease, snapping it in two. My left arm went numb. I shrank back to the wall.

The mantis assumed its signature combat stance rocking in place, its front legs raised high in the air. It was about to launch another strike.

My left arm hung listlessly, the fragments of my broken shield still attached to its strap. My Fury counter went off the scale, literally, as a crimson haze clouded my vision.

All my sensations were more than real. My body, smarting from the impact, began to tingle as if I were hooked up to a battery. This felt very similar to what I'd already experienced back in the underground tunnels.

The thought dwindled to nothing like water spilt onto desert sand. The mob approached me sideways, offering its hard top wing to my attack, its triangular head focused on me. It wasn't in a hurry, scurrying confidently toward me on its four hind legs while keeping the two front ones high in the air, ready to lunge at me.

The creature's only weak spot was its segmented belly. I could see it pulsing. The chitin plates protecting it had small gaps between them

— just wide enough for my sword to penetrate.

The tingling stopped. Now I could clearly sense energy coursing through myself. Its source seemed to be located underground: could there be a cellar underneath these ruins?

The symbols covering my sword blade kept glowing weakly. Another mystery.

The mob attacked me first. I'd been waiting for it, watching its every slightest motion in tense apprehension, and still I failed to react in time. The mantis sliced through my armor in an almost imperceptible motion, ripping across it from my left shoulder to the stomach. My body exploded in agony, splashing my face with hot sticky blood.

As I collapsed, I twice managed to bury my sword in its belly.

* * *

The stone floor was cold against my cheek. Something heavy pressed onto me from above.

My body throbbed with pain. I couldn't feel my left arm at all. System messages flashed across my blurred vision but I was unable to focus enough to read them. I could just about concentrate on one thought alone. Groaning, I reached for my belt and pulled out a vial with shaking fingers. I bit through the sealing wax. The content of the vial was tart on my lips.

I gulped it down greedily, choking.

It worked instantly. My vision cleared. My whole body convulsed in a releasing wave of lightheadedness bordering on euphoria. I was alive.

I groped for my sword. The weight pressing down on me turned out to be the dead mantis which hadn't survived two blows to its belly.

There were two more still waiting nearby though. I lay unmoving, listening intently. I could hear a scraping sound very close. This time I wasn't going to wait. I had to act fast, directly and unexpectedly.

My left arm was all right now. Things weren't as bad, after all. The elixirs had worked — and that meant that a whole plethora of little tricks and features peculiar only to cyberspace were going to help me survive.

A triangular head loomed over the mantis' body, its mandibles dripping claret. I played dead, praying I didn't retch with the stench.

The mob must have been sensing blood. Or it could be the scent of the elixir that had attracted it. Not that it mattered, really. I grabbed the sword hilt with both my hands. Now...

Unhesitantly, I buried the poisoned blade between the creature's half-opened jaws. Before it could even squeal, the mantis shuddered and went limp. I'd one-shotted it!

I still had the third one to tackle. I'd heard nothing from it yet: true, the creature had received a helping of neurotoxin from me earlier in the fight.

I scrambled to my feet and cast a look around.

I was feeling okay. The experience had been ghastly, of course. My leather jacket was only good for rags now. The room was covered in my blood. The sight of it made me sick but I tried to suppress the nausea. I might get used to it over time.

Cautiously I approached the doorway and took a peek outside. The third mantis was stirring weakly a few feet away from the entrance. How strange. I'd only grazed him with my sword very lightly.

My mind expander kicked in, responding to my emotion of surprise with a message,

Wasps use their neurotoxin reserves to hunt much bigger insects, paralyzing and devouring them. Using a wasp neurotoxin against other insects gives a +200 bonus to both damage and effect duration.

Aha. That explained why the mantis was in such a bad way. I'd emptied all three venom glands onto my sword blade, and their effects were cumulative, weren't they?

I made a mental note to find out if wasp venom was available in alchemy shops and if it was, how much it cost there. If push came to shove, I could always farm some more. Having some in store for emergencies wouldn't hurt.

As I was thus musing, the last mantis died a quiet death.

A golden shimmer enveloped me, bathing me in warmth.

You've received a new level!

The Neuro development branch has been unblocked!

You have new ability and main characteristic points available!

* * *

Now the clearing was well and truly mob-free. The sun had already begun to set. I didn't bother to meditate: I had too much to do still. I would have to study the new development branch on my return to the inn. You shouldn't take these kinds of steps in a hurry. I couldn't afford to make wrong leveling decisions: unlike other players, I couldn't start anew. Each skill point had to be distributed wisely and only after careful examination of every skill's respective pros and cons.

I found the herbs I needed and cut them with the small and unassuming quest knife I'd been given. Then I walked back to the ruins to search the mantises' bodies.

You've received an item: a Large Chitin Plate. Can be used in making light and comfortable but extremely strong armor.

You've received an item: a Mantis' Spike. Can be used in making traps and arrowheads.

Not bad at all. I ended up having six Large Chitin Plates and three Small ones in addition to twelve Mantis' Spikes.

I had my doubts about their claims of "light and comfortable" armor, though. Either I'd have to look for an armorer who would make a bespoke set for me — which was an admittedly weird demand for cyberspace — or I might even have to make it myself, for which purpose I'd have to level Blacksmithing first (because strangely enough, the Crystal Sphere developers had listed chitin with blacksmithing resources). This was a bit of an overlook on their part, but then again, listing it under Leather Working wouldn't be too appropriate, either.

Right. I was done here. Time to go back to the pond to do a bit of fishing. I still had a quest to close before sunset. I was definitely going to come back here: I was too intrigued by the mysterious symbols covering my sword blade. Also, the sensation of energy coursing through my body had been impressive. There definitely was a dungeon or at least a cellar below these old ruins.

As I was about to leave, I remembered. The staff! I'd taken the sorcerer's belt and his bag, but left his staff behind.

I returned and picked it up, expecting the old bones to disappear with a quest-announcing message. Still, it didn't happen.

Never mind. I might look into it later. The dead sorcerer's notes might shed some light on his death. His bag felt as if it was full of books and scrolls. In any case, I'd had enough surprises for one day. I needed to get somewhere safe first, then I might open it.

It just shows you how fast a 100% authenticity of experience can change a gamer's mentality. I hadn't even noticed it happen. Before, I'd have rummaged through the bag's contents on the spot. Now, however, I was playing it safe — which was the right thing to do even though the temptation was great. I needed some magic abilities really badly. I doubted I could survive such intensity of gameplay as a pure warrior.

Lost in thought, I got back to the pond rather quickly. It had been a long day.

I gave a wink to my old friend the toad sitting back on its lily leaf. I filled the tin bucket with pond water, laid out my fishing gear, rolled a bread ball in my fingers and attached it to the hook, then cast the line into the pond.

The sunset was already glowing crimson. I was sitting on a hillock watching the float quiver as the fish began to bite. Good. Strangely enough, I felt perfectly happy and content.

* * *

Nicholas the innkeeper waited impatiently on the porch. "Have you got it?"

"Sure," I handed him the herbs and the bucketful of fish.

He beamed. "You kept your word! Well done!"

He hurried to give me an already-prepared backpack. It felt heavy. "I'm off to heal Dimian! Your room's been cleaned. Your dinner's already there," he darted off, disappearing down the street.

Quest alert: First Aid! Quest completed!

Your Reputation with the inhabitants of Hinterwood has improved!

Current Reputation status: Friendly.

You've received an item: an Old Scroll.

You've received an item: a Chunk of Dried Meat

You've received an item: a Piece of Bread

You've received an item: a Water Flask.

You've received an item: a Whet Stone

To tell you the truth, I could barely stand on my feet. The day had been too eventful — hectic even. I was falling asleep. I wasn't even that hungry anymore.

Ignoring the food supplies in my bag, I went back to the inn and headed directly upstairs into my room. The dinner was already there. I wolfed it down, peeled my clothes off and climbed into bed, hoping to spend another hour tying up all the most pressing loose ends.

I finally had to check out the Neuro's development branch.

I couldn't keep my eyes open though. The interface windows quivered, floating in my mental view.

I couldn't help it. I was past exhaustion. I just hoped that with time, my body would adapt to the new levels of exertion.

I was asleep before I even knew it.

* * *

About midnight, I was awoken by the dogs' insistent barking outside.

I rolled over in bed and opened my eyes, listening intently to the sounds behind the open window, but it was already quiet.

Could I have dreamt it? Did that mean that I was under the neuroimplant's control at night as well as during daytime?

I drifted off without bothering to get up to close the window.

The wary silence seemed to be pregnant with quiet sounds. The roof joists creaked. A breeze rippled the plain curtains, bringing a whiff of sulfur.

A lithe shadow wrapped in a weak crimson glow slid through the half-open window.

I stared at it breathless, unable to move.

Christa?

She was so repulsively beautiful. The fiery aura did nothing to conceal her naked body; the glow clung to her chest, coursing down her hips, lending her dark olive skin the texture of cracked lava.

What a terrible, torturous dream.

The crimson glow faded. She walked over to me and perched on the bed's edge, then ran her fingers over my chest.

"Christa, don't. Please."

"You've been dreaming about me, haven't you?"

I didn't reply. This may be a nightmare but I still didn't want to discuss her horrendous choice of character.

"Alex, does it really matter to you? Is it the color of my skin? Or maybe," she leaned over to me, "this?"

Her long lithe tail wrapped around my throat several times and slightly constricted, as if strangling me. She was so close I couldn't breathe. The stench of sulfur was gone. Her lips burned my chest.

"We're both free now," she whispered. "You and I, we both have neuroimplants installed. The rest doesn't matter," her hot breath sent an unbearable sweet shiver down my skin.

Some dream!

"Could it be why I agreed to all this?" she whispered. "Because I couldn't stop thinking about you, either?"

My fingers played with her hair. She groaned and pressed her body to mine, shuddering.

* * *

I was screaming, choking on the stench of my own burned flesh.

Someone broke the door down. They were dousing the room with bucketfuls of water, pouring it over the smoldering floor, the burning curtains and the smoking bed.

"We need some elixirs! Fetch them, quick! He's burned all over!"

By now I wasn't screaming anymore. My throat was making croaking noises. The touch of water on my body felt intolerable. Instinctively I tried to sit up but my skin kept bursting, peeling off. I could barely see.

"Quick!" it must have been Nicholas the innkeeper.

"There's been a demon in his room!"

"We should leave him to die! That'll teach him!"

My scorched lips found the vial. The aroma of healing herbs somewhat cleared both my mind and vision. The first thing I saw was bare footprints, scorched black, on the wooden floor.

"Give me another elixir!"

My wounds stank. The room was full of smoke. Still, the pain had already subsided.

"Again!"

I was right: it was Nicholas. A group of armed peasants crowded behind him, one of them a boy barely ten years old, clenching a wooden stake.

After the third elixir, my wounds began to

heal before my very eyes. Soon I was able to scramble to my feet, vacating the wet, burned bed.

"So?" the innkeeper's glare promised me nothing good.

"I thought I had a dream."

"Tell us the truth! Who was here? Whose footprints are these?"

"I'm telling you the truth. I had a bad dream. A nightmare. That's all I know."

"He's possessed by a demon! Impale him! Bury him in the woods and drive a wooden stake through his heart!"

"Shut up!" Nicholas yelled. "This is my inn! I'm the one who decides here! Out now!"

He began driving the villagers out of the room. I used the pause to locate my clothes in the mess created by my rescuers and hurried to put my leather armor on.

"We saw it with our very eyes!" shouts came from the corridor. "The demon stealing up the roof! It climbed into his window!"

Warning! Your Reputation with the inhabitants of Hinterwood has plummeted!

Current Reputation status: Animosity.

Nicholas came back soon, dark as a thundercloud, avoiding my gaze.

"You should go," he finally said.

By then I'd packed all my stuff. I wasn't welcome here anymore which was perfectly understandable. I just couldn't believe it. So it wasn't a dream, after all.

I clenched my teeth, unwilling to make the situation any worse than it already was — especially because I realized that I owed my life to Nicholas' intervention. "I'm very sorry. How much do I owe you?"

"Just go," he waved my question away. "And steer clear of here. Next time they *will* impale you."

I nodded my understanding. I walked downstairs, crossed the common room under the villagers' heavy glares, walked out the door and headed for the village gate. You should never underestimate the dangers of Animosity.

I had no idea where I was supposed to go now. Agrion? Too dangerous. Not even because of my plummeted rep or the rumors — but what if this night's visit wasn't the last one? The sheer thought of it made my blood curdle.

So what now? Should I go and live in the forest?

I was approaching the village gate when I heard a voice behind me.

"Hey, wait!"

A stranger hurried after me — a townsman,

judging by his clothes.

"What now?" I swung round, ready to face anything. "What do you want?"

"Take this," he shoved me a bulky bundle, then hurried to add, "It's a tent. You've been looking for one, right?"

"Dimian?"

He beamed. "That's me! You've saved my life, man. Take this as a token of my gratitude!"

"Thanks but-"

"Just take it! I don't give a damn about what they say in the village. I may keep a shop here for an occasional sale, but I'm a townie myself."

"So you're not worried about the demon, then?"

He grinned. "You're not a demon, are you? I was attacked by a wyvern too. Wasn't my fault, was it?"

"Thanks," I put the tent into my inventory.

"Life is more than just stuff. You should stay away from the local villages though. Rumors spread fast. You'd be surprised what you might learn about yourself. So go directly to the city. Have you got money?"

"Yeah, I have some."

"Then you should be all right, shouldn't you?" he gave me a friendly slap on the shoulder, than added conspiratorially, "This demon chick is quite a looker. I saw her when she was climbing that roof. I couldn't have resisted her myself, may the Gods of Light have mercy on my soul."

With this he walked off, leaving me all alone.

I turned round and headed for the woods, followed by the plaintive wailing of the petrified village dogs.

CHAPTER FOUR

THE CRYSTAL SPHERE
IN THE VICINITY OF AGRION CITY

THE SOUND of horse hooves echoed through the night.

A road patrol rode toward me. The front rider reined in his steed. He had a lighted torch in one hand and a naked sword in the other.

"Are you from Hinterwood? What the hell happened there?"

"A fire," I said, staring at the crackling flames. "They've put it out already."

I was surprisingly calm. You'd think the sight of fire should have freaked me out, reminding me of Christa or even resulting in a full-blown phobia.

Nothing of the kind. It was as if I'd indeed had a bad dream, nothing more. How weird.

The guards headed for the village while I left the road and took a shortcut through the fields.

By the time I reached the nut grove by the ruins, dawn was already breaking. I found a small clearing, read the brief manual and began setting up the tent.

I'd chosen this place for several reasons. Firstly, I needed some space. I had to have a good think. Secondly, the sheer thought of sleeping in bed, however "comfortable", made me doubt the safety of the local inns, taverns, hotels and such.

Thirdly, I still had unfinished business to attend to. I had to study the ruins. Even though the energy boost I'd experienced there hadn't helped me to defeat the mantis, it still intrigued me.

This unusually calm, collected reasoning wasn't at all typical of me. I shrugged. The neuroimplant must have had some kind of stress blocking mechanism installed. This could be the only explanation of my sudden nerve.

The moon dominated the sky. Darkness lurked in the shadows. The forest was living its mysterious night life, filled with creeping and rustling, its tentative silence broken by animal screams. I couldn't yet tell them apart.

I drove the last tent peg into the ground.

Immediately a ten-foot safe zone formed around the tent, glowing a faint green. No mob would be able to trespass it while I was inside resting or meditating. At least that's what the tent manual said.

Players could enter provided they were part of my group. Otherwise, I'd have to send them an invitation to come in. This was how the Crystal Sphere worked. There were restrictions, too: the tent owner couldn't stay inside for longer than twenty-four hours.

You've set up a tent.

The tent has been activated.

Would you like to make it your respawn point?

Absolutely. I shifted my eyes, swiping *Confirm.*

I climbed inside the tent and took a look around. It was rather small and Spartan: a sleeping bag on the floor, a chest, and a little folding table next to the headrest with a small lamp perched on it. Everything a hiker might need. Nicholas' supplies would help me last a few days without venturing into towns or villages.

I had to spend some quality time farming

mobs. I also needed to study the ruins. Then we'd see. I had no idea that by agreeing to have this wretched neuroimplant installed, the good old virtual world would turn into a deadly obstacle course.

The memory of Christa wriggled its way into my thoughts, stinging hard. I could feel emotions seething under the veneer of my composure, as if something wasn't letting them through. A wave of phantom pain surged over my body, turning the already-healed burns crimson.

What if Christa visited me again?

I gasped. My forehead erupted in sweat. I shouldn't be so angry with the neuroimplant developers: having a stress blocking mechanism was vital here. Still, in order to survive, I had to learn to handle any overbearing negative emotions, or at least tolerate them. Also, I shouldn't forget that this was still a game. I was supposed to follow its rules by leveling up, completing quests and acquiring new skills and abilities.

I felt a bit better now. Enough soul searching. Time to do something.

I reached into my inventory for the Mysterious Sword and the whet stone that Nicholas had given me. This offered yet more proof of the fact that cyberspace phenomena worked in their usual way: the moment I touched the sword blade with the whet stone, the weapon's Durability grew 30%.

Although the blade was now free of oxidization, the mysterious runes covering it hadn't become any clearer. They weren't glowing anymore. All I could see was scratch marks covering the metal.

What a shame. I'd have loved to take pictures of them and run a quick image search. Next time I should be prepared whenever the mysterious symbols sprang to life again.

Right. That was my only weapon sorted. It didn't look as if I could raise its Durability beyond 30% with the tools at hand. I couldn't mend the torn jacket, either. I'd have to accept the fact that I looked like a tramp.

Now, the most important.

I gulped some water from the flask and made myself comfortable, then opened my character's development branches.

My interface looked totally different now. The Neuro branch seemed to have taken priority. All the standard combat and magic abilities (which I had initially planned to level up) had turned gray.

In any case, the final choice lay with me.

Neuro Development branch:

Secret Knowledge
Evolution
Power of Reason
Observational Skills
Spell Interception
Intense Training
Insight
Acquisition of Blows and Combos
Unity of Origin
Pain Threshold
Self-Control
Unity of Schools
Reflex Optimization
Synergy
Enhanced Perception

Secret Knowledge:

Eons ago, the Ancient Gods (sometimes also called the Founder Gods) tampered with our ancestors' evolution, endowing them with a number of abilities which are now almost completely extinct. Only occasionally do they resurface in certain individuals known as Neuros.

You're one of them. Both your body and mind harbor a potential yet unlocked.

+1 to Strength
+1 to Intellect
+1% to XP per each invested Ability pt.

Observational Skills:

You're highly perceptive. Whether reading ancient manuscripts or watching other people, you pay attention to every detail, immediately grasping the technique of a combat blow or a spell incantation. You can then enter the knowledge you thus receive into special books or dedicated parchment scrolls for further study.

Warning! The level of the blow or spell you intend to study cannot exceed that of your character.

Each Ability point invested gives +2% to your chances of studying the blow or the spell (regardless of whether the object of your study is an NPC or another player).

Spell Interception

The fact that all spells are recited in the Founders' language combined with your ability to lip read allows you to learn any spell.

Warning! In order to successfully intercept a spell, the caster (observation target) should be located within your direct line of vision. At level 1, your lip-reading range is set at 30 feet.

Each Ability point invested adds 2 ft. to your lip-reading range.

Spell Interception does not preclude other possible ways of spell studying.

Acquisition of Blows and Combos:

You effortlessly memorize new movements while watching combat practice or live combat. Later, this allows you to make a drawing of the blow or even combo technique from memory, recreating both attack and defense maneuvers.

Requires Observational Skills and Intense Training.

Each Ability point invested adds +2% to your chances of studying a blow or a combo.

Unity of Origin:

According to legend, all living beings in the Universe used to have a single ancestor. Some might snicker saying that an orc and a human being can't possibly share ancestry. Still, every legend harbors a grain of truth.

Each Ability point invested adds +2% to your chances of intercepting a spell or learning a new blow typical of other races, regardless of their affiliation (Light vs. Dark).

Unity of Schools:

Some time ago, you chanced upon an ancient book. As you struggled through it, trying to make sense of the faded writings on its crumbling pages, you were surprised to discover the writer's heretic ideas. According to the book's author, all types of magic and sorcery, including elemental and mind control, are firmly rooted in the long-forgotten school of Chaos.

Later, as you watched the effects produced by various schools of magic, your conclusions confirmed the ancient author's ideas. The powers of Chaos had been the foundation of all modern schools and practices.

Each Ability point invested adds +2% to the Range, Strength and Duration of every spell you study, as well as removes all bans and penalties for combining various kinds of magic and sorcery.

Reflex Optimization:

As you watch wildlife species (whose survival depends on their highest levels of ergonomics), you can learn and adopt their energy preservation skills. Your movements become more precise and calculated.

Each Ability point invested gives -2% to your mental and physical energy expenditures in combat.

Evolution:

The activation of this particular characteristic allows you to receive a small but continuous boost to your main stats, depending on the type of your daily activities. These changes will be visible as special boost bars situated opposite their respective characteristics in your character panel. For instance, if you read a lot you might notice the increase of your Intellect boost bar. Once the bar is full, you will receive +1 pt. to its respective characteristic.

The above boost does not cancel traditional characteristic leveling. Neither does it affect your items' bonuses.

Intense Training:

Each spell or blow you study requires constant perfecting. In order to improve your attack and defense skills, you need to practice a lot, creating your own combinations and turning new moves into reflexes.

Ability bonus: your damage, defense, mob control and aura range will improve. This only applies to the physical and magic skills you use on a regular basis, without affecting those you've learned but failed to apply.

Each Ability point invested adds +5% to attack strength.

Pain Threshold:

You learn to control pain. You might have already discovered, by extreme trial and error, that you don't experience pain as long as your Health is above 80%. As your HP dwindle, you start experiencing an increasing pain.

Each Ability point invested raises your pain

threshold 3%. The maximum pain threshold allowed is 50% HP.

Synergy:

Everything in our world is interconnected. You can use various sources of energy, including elements, ancient artifacts and places of power marked by megalithic monuments. As you study them and listen intently to the world around you, you begin to tune in into various energy currents, allowing you to locate their sources and use them to restore your powers and even life.

Starting at level 20, you'll be able to trap and store any excess physical or mental energy within energy crystals.

+5% to your physical and mental energy regeneration speed.

Power of Reason:

A Neuro's intellect affects everything he or she does.

Every 30 pt. Intellect add +3% to both attack and defense and +5% to the XP received for successfully using the blows or spells you've learned from other characters. All such blows or spells will add +3% to your chances of dealing critical damage or, when used in defense, to your chances of reusing the blow or spell with decreased cooldown times and -50% of required energy expenditure.

+10% to your mental energy regeneration speed.

Insight:

You're constantly busy studying everything around you, analyzing the nature of all events and perfecting your abilities and skills. Your goal is to get to the bottom of everything trying to work out how things work instead of mindlessly using them, be it a spell, a blow or a professional skill.

Each Ability point invested gives -3% to cooldown times and energy expenditure required for all types of physical and mental attack, defense and impact.

+2% to profession leveling speed for all farming and manufacturing professions.

Self-Control:

You have a natural 25% resistance to all kinds of magic and mind control. You can successfully resist mental attacks, preserving clarity of mind.

Each Ability point invested adds +2% to your chances of repelling a negative effect or boosting a positive one, be it a spell or your opponent's ability. +2% to your chances of successfully casting a spell when attacked. +3% to mental energy regeneration speed.

On reaching level 5, this ability will allow you to consciously control your mental energy distribution between several recipients — for instance, a magic artifact or an item of gear.

Enhanced Perception:

You learn with remarkable ease. Your outlook isn't limited by racial or class prejudices. You're free from all phobias and superstitions.

As a result, you see and notice a lot compared to others. Your night vision and reduced visibility navigation skills are considerably superior to theirs. At level 20, you will receive a new primary skill, Twilight Vision, which you can consequently level up and improve.

Enhanced Perception allows you to detect danger before others can. It also adds +20% to your chances of seeing a stealthed-up enemy stalking you. Each Ability point invested adds +1 to your Field of Vision Range.

* * *

That got me thinking.

I realized, of course, what kind of decision the game developers were trying to edge me toward. They wanted to use me to study the human mind's reactions to all types of magic as well as its tolerable pain threshold in order to fine-tune feedback.

Still, it was too early to make any decisions about the viability of this particular branch.

Let's presume, for the sake of argument, that I'd chosen it. I ticked the *Follow the Path of the Neuro* box. All the little boxes in my character panel blinked and disappeared, replaced by new ones.

I now had only one development branch left. The two default ones were gone, replaced by two books:

The Book of Spells
The Book of Combat Arts

Was there anything inside them?

You couldn't tell, could you? In order to find out, you had to accept the new branch first.

I didn't have to be a fatalist to realize that my agreement was purely a formality.

Follow the Path of the Neuro: Yes/No?

Yes.

A golden shimmer enveloped me.

You've received a new level!

You have new ability and main characteristic points available!

The Book of Spells has been activated!

The Book of Combat Arts has been activated!

Now the difficult bit.

I began to distribute available stat points, activating each ability at Level 1. That should suffice for the time being.

This was what I had:

Alexatis. Level 6. Neuro

Life, 70/70

Physical Energy, 80/80 (Strength + Secret Knowledge)

Mental Energy, 110/110 (Intellect + Secret Knowledge)

Physical Defense, 15,5 (Leather Armor 12 pt + Agility bonus 3.5)

Physical Attack, 9 (Mysterious Sword, 5 pt. + Strength divided by 2 = 4 pt.)

Mental Defense, 29% (Self-Control + Spirit)

Mental Attack, 0 (requires spell study)

Mental Energy Regeneration, 4,13 pt./sec (Spirit divided by 2 + 0,63 bonus from Synergy, Power of Reason and Self-Control.)

Strength, 7 (+ 1 Secret Knowledge bonus)

Intellect, 10 (+1 Secret Knowledge bonus)

Agility, 7

Stamina, 7

Spirit, 7

Main Professions, Require activation

Achievements, Mentor of the Day (+1 to Fame)

Much to my disappointment, both Books were empty, their pages filled with gray inactive slots. So I was supposed to learn everything from scratch, then. Which meant I had to set out in search of adventure. Alternatively, I could go to Agrion, buy some spell scrolls and visit the local warrior guild in order to watch their training sessions.

I cast a glance over my possessions. There actually was another way to test my freshly-acquired abilities. For the last twenty-four hours, I'd been too busy to check out the contents of the dead sorcerer's bag.

It was heavy. I set it on the floor and sat cross-legged on my sleeping bag, then began undoing all the leather straps and silver buckles.

Contrary to my suspicions, the bag had no traps installed. I focused on the tag,

A sturdy leather bag. Capacity: 50 slots. Made by a Master craftsman. Using it adds +15 lb. to the weight you can carry.

Useful. My inventory had only 20 slots.

What did it have inside?

Three books, some writing tools, a couple of plain-looking rocks, a rusty piece of steel, a small scroll case packed with rolled-up parchments, a piece of dry bread, a chunk of moldy cheese and a half-empty water flask.

The first tome turned out to be an Alchemy manual. I set it aside for the time being. Elixirs were always welcome; every player should have a good stock of them at all times — but personally, I never liked farming herbs or making my own potions. I might give the book a read at some other time.

The second book, bound lovingly in leather, looked quite mysterious.

Illusion Casting. A Sorcerer's Textbook.

My fingerprints tingled when I picked it up. I opened it, breathless, and leafed through it, skimming the pages,

Illusions can't deal damage in combat. Their only purpose is to distract the sorcerer's enemy, allowing you to avoid an attack or strike back when least expected. The easiest way to confuse an unexpected attacker is by recreating a copy of them which works for the majority of aggressive creatures. Still, it might not be enough to fool a player of some experience, be they a wizard or a warrior. In that case, it is advisable to create something dangerous-looking (e.g., a dragon), casting an Aura of Fear on the illusion for a better effect.

Admittedly, illusions were always useful in combat. Still, practicing them could take a lot of time and effort. I leafed through the pages featuring various creatures complete with the calculations of the required level and mana expenditure. The figures were a bit disheartening. If only I could restore the sorcerer's staff!

The third book looked the most used of the three. However, much to my surprise, its frayed yellowed pages turned out to be empty. No trace of ink anywhere!

What was going on? Judging by the recognizable magic symbols on its cover, this too was a Book of Spells. You couldn't confuse them with anything else.

I tried every possible way of activating it, with zero results. The book wasn't protected at all. The records must have disappeared long before I'd gotten hold of it. The pages were covered in damp spots but they bore no trace of blurred ink, as if all the spells had been deleted by some powerful magic. Could this have been the reason for the sorcerer's death?

As I pondered, I opened the scroll case and pulled out the parchments. They were rolled together. None of them was sealed which meant they weren't single-use.

I began sifting through the yellowed sheets. Bingo. I found a Weak Healing Aura and a Minor Shield of Mana.

Excellent. Both spells suited my configuration.

I moved both to the spell tab of my interface. The parchments crumbled to dust, replaced by two icons on the first page of my own Book of Spells. When I clicked them, a prompt appeared; I could also copy them to my quick access panel by dragging them.

You've studied the Weak Healing Aura!

Effect: immediately restores 25 HP.

Requires: level 5, Intellect 10, and 40 pt. Mental Energy.

You've studied a Minor Shield of Mana!

Effect: surrounds the caster or a friendly target with a magic barrier, absorbing 15% incoming damage.

Duration: 5 sec.

Requirements: level 5, Intellect 10, and 40 pt. of Mental Energy.

Feeling much better, I checked the remaining scrolls. Unfortunately, many of them were ruined, some letters blurred by humidity. I only managed to acquire two more spells:

Phantom Warrior. Creates the illusion of an orc warrior.

Duration: 10 sec.

Requirements: level 20, Intellect 25, and 180 pt. of Mental Energy.

The Aura of Fear

Creates a surge of terror either around the illusion of your choice or around the caster.

Range: 10 ft.

Duration: 10 sec

Effect: all creatures of the same level as you or lower feel petrified. They freeze, unable to attack. Creatures whose level is superior to yours lose concentration and slow down.

+30% to your chances of disrupting your enemy's spell

Requirements: Level 30, Intellect 40, and 100 pt. of Mental Energy. Does not affect undead species, elementals or golems.

This Aura seemed like good stuff. What a shame I couldn't use it for a while. I'd have to level up quite a bit and build up on Mental

Energy before I could do that.

Which got me thinking. The Neuro development branch was indeed unique. As long as I leveled hard, mainly to raise my Pain Threshold, I'd be able to live a life of adventure without risking dropping dead from the shock of pain every time I received a serious injury or suffered a virtual death.

I also considered teaming up with other players. Still, this was probably a bit premature. Let me explain: as long as I was under the negative influence of the neuroimplant, experiencing pain and fatigue, I was bound to attract unwanted attention and risk being deleted from the group. No one would tolerate a constantly exhausted, staggering player who wasn't forthcoming with reasons for his erratic behavior.

Intense Training, they said? Under near-combat conditions? Very well.

My mobile respawn point which I'd moved to the tent had already been activated.

That was sorted, then. I had to continue farming mobs in the clearing next to the ruins until I made level 10 at least. After that, I would study the ruins and try to find the entrance to the dungeons below. This was to be my first trial by fire.

I checked the contents of the belt's quick

access slots. I'd already used one of the healing potions during my mantis fight. I had nine left. Four of them were still a mystery to me.

I made snapshots of their magic seals and ran a quick image search. Aha. These were 100% Elemental Resistance potions, one per element. If I didn't use them, I could always sell them.

After some consideration, I kept the two little rocks and the rusty piece of steel. The sorcerer must have had them on him for a reason.

* * *

It was close to midday when I was finally done and could climb out of the tent.

I could see no one. The nut grove was shady and cool. I cast the Minor Shield of Mana on myself and counted till ten.

When its faint haze had disappeared, I glanced at the mental energy indicator. Of the 40 pt. I'd just spent, only 20.65 had restored. I had to level up Intellect ASAP. I remembered Enea's plain ring. Wish I had something like that now!

I tried to cast a combination of two spells. It took me six seconds. Way too much. Even the slowest of mobs would make mincemeat of me in the meantime.

I tried again but lost concentration between

the two spells.

After only a minute's worth of practice, I was already out of mana. I slumped to the ground to meditate, waiting for it to restore.

Welcome to the newb's lifestyle of constant training, followed by the mind-numbing task of farming meager loot. But once things began to work out, you felt really proud of yourself.

About an hour later I realized that I could actually do much more than the Neuro development branch claimed. At one point, I'd managed to cast a series of spells in 4 seconds flat. The spells were actually curt and monosyllabic: I just had to concentrate and stay calm.

Finally, my mana was back up. Now I could test myself in combat. I walked over to the edge of the clearing and looked around.

What a surprise. Instead of the grasshopper, I saw a level 7 locust. The wasps had gone up in levels too, assisted by a fearsome-looking hornet. Oh. I dreaded to even think what my mantises were like.

The locust was already coming at me. I dodged just in time, casting the Shield of Mana, then managed to block its first attack. Not so much luck with its second one though. It didn't hurt yet: I'd only lost 5 hit points.

Fueled by adrenaline, I launched a

response attack, dealing the locust three successive slashing blows to the head. Its wounds gushed greenish goo.

Slowly I retreated toward the nut grove. The monster scurried after me, the tall grass hindering its progress. Why didn't it attempt to fly?

With this unexpected advantage, I tried to outflank it but stopped just in time, seeing the long curved blade attached to its posterior — like a saber of sorts.

This clearing wasn't as easy as it had seemed. It definitely wasn't meant for solo farming. I realized this too late, though. The hornet had seen me. It buzzed past, low above the ground, hitting me with its wake.

Ignoring the still-alive locust, I ran to the side and watched the hornet whose sheer size and stripy brown and yellow coloring made it conspicuous within the undergrowth. Humming, it banked into a turn in order to attack me.

I could use some debuffs now, really.

That's the end of me, the thought flashed through my mind. *I can't run: I might lose my footing in the tall grass and end up exposing my back.*

Once again my sword blade was aglow with the runes syphoning my mental energy.

Enea's face flashed in my mind's eye, her

lips moving.

My inbox dinged. Bad timing.

My lips mouthed a desperate spell. The hornet slowed down in flight, bending its lower body and exposing its stinger, about to impale me, armor and all. My left hand completed the final movement of the spell on its own accord.

An Ice Arrow darted from my fingers, piercing the hornet's wing. The monster spun in place, then dropped to the ground.

Still uncomprehending, I went for it, investing all my remaining strength into the blow. My sword sliced through the hornet's body with the same ease as it had with the mantis, dealing a terrible wound and stripping the creature of 37 hit points. The mysterious symbols covering my sword blade flared up momentarily. Its damage must have increased tenfold.

Then it was all over. I was still shaking, my mental energy dangerously close to zero. Still, the hornet was dead. The wasps were keeping a safe distance and the locust was forcing its way through the grass, leaving a wide trail in its wake.

You've learned a new spell: Ice Arrow!

Enea! Of course! I'd seen her cast the spell, hadn't I? At the time, I hadn't yet known about my Interception ability — but it had worked anyway!

I finished off the locust and returned to the safety of the grove.

I collapsed onto a hillock, gasping. I was alive. I'd made it.

I needed to check the logs and find out whatever had happened to my sword. Could I control the process or was it supposed to just happen sporadically?

Not now. It could wait. I had more important things to do.

I looked through my archive for the video file I needed and opened it in slow motion.

Video of the Day: Staffless Spell Casting!

I focused on Enea's lips moving.

You've learned a new spell: Weakness!

You've learned a new spell: Ice!

Warning! Your Mental Energy levels are too low to cast the spell!

Would you like to move the spells into your Book of Spells?

* * *

Once I'd recovered my breath and calmed down a bit, I opened the message I'd received during combat.

Oh wow.

Your account has been credited with 28 (twenty-eight) gold. Sender: Togien. Thank you for using Crystal Bank.

The dwarf had been true to his word. Should I study Archeology too, maybe? Why not? My 1% of bag contents turned out to be quite a lot.

I sent him a brief thank-you message.

Now the combat logs.

I skimmed their contents which documented a player's every action and its consequences without distracting him or her.

It said nothing about the Mysterious Sword syphoning my energy. I only discovered a few brief mentions,

Your weapon's damage has grown 28 pt.

You've attacked the Hornet! Physical Damage, 5. Mental Energy damage, 28.

That was it. Why had the mental damage grown so dramatically? What could have caused it?

Admittedly, quite a few things had happened in the few brief moments when I'd thought I was about to die my first virtual death.

Firstly, I'd managed to subconsciously think of Enea and copy her Ice Arrow spell without even knowing what I was doing. It was a matter of survival, that's all.

Secondly, I'd lost all my mana. Having said that, Ice Arrow had only taken 10 pt. Prior to that, I'd cast the Minor Healing Aura and the Shield of Mana, that's another 80 pt. down. So I'd had 28 pt. left in total, counting the regeneration — and that was exactly what the hornet had received!

Did that mean that the Mysterious Sword had worked as a conductor of mental energy?

No, that couldn't be. Most likely, it had simply received part of my own stores. That could explain the message about the sword's increased damage.

I should have to look into it. I was pretty sure I could control the process. It was probably the sword itself that had caused it. If only I could find out more about it!

You've received a new quest: The Secret Alloy.

Quest type: Rare

Find Jurg, a master blacksmith who lives in

the foothills of the Azure Mountains. Show him your sword and try to find out more about it.

Reward: varies.

The Azure Mountains? That was a bit of a hike. A lengthy journey like that required thorough preparation.

I opened the map and tried to work out a potential route. I'd have to cross some unexplored lands and locations on my way. I remembered what Togien had said about high-level mobs less than a week's trek from here.

It looked like I'd still have to go to Agrion first: to get some new gear and find out more about the local portal network connecting the big cities. That might considerably simplify the task.

My mana had already restored. Time for me to go back to the clearing to collect the loot and turn my attention to the wasps. I needed to test my freshly-acquired spells.

I lingered a little longer, studying the list of available online services and checking jewelry prices at auction. Everything was quite costly. I spent two gold on a ring with +3 to Intellect. I could get one in town for a fraction of the price but first I needed to get there, while the auction offered instant free delivery.

I also liked a pretty signet ring giving +1 to all main characteristics. Three gold. A bit pricey, but... I read its description. *Restriction: only Combat Wizard.* Shame. Never mind.

My inbox dinged. My Intellect-boosting ring had arrived. I hurried to put it on.

Excellent. Now I had enough mental energy to cast Ice. I opened the interface and distributed the two remaining ability points, investing both into Self-Control. That gave me another 6% to my mana regeneration speed.

Now I was done. Time to do some farming!

The Ice Arrow — which had just saved me from a torturous virtual death — was already sitting in quick access. Thank you, Enea.

Wait up... Alexatis, you're an idiot.

I returned to the auction and scooped the pretty signet ring up without a second thought, then contacted the delivery service.

Please enter the receiver's name.

Enea, Combat Wizard, I laboriously copied her ID from my friend list.

Please enter the sender's name.

I left the box empty. I just hoped she would accept an anonymous gift. I didn't want to explain anything to her.

Please add a message to the receiver.

I typed a smilie: just a regular one, no winks or grins or anything. Just a smile.

Then I clicked *Send.*

* * *

The slain locust had dropped four large chitin plates and a chitin bow — without any arrows but still a pleasant surprise. I was pretty sure I could make arrows myself somehow. Which meant I could hunt now without having to sweat inside my awkward armor chasing after some potential quarry. This could considerably improve my autonomy.

The hornet, however, was a bit of a disappointment. It was a truly dangerous creature and equally useless loot-wise. It dropped a Set of Mandibles (whatever I was supposed to do with them) and a Fragment of a Wing.

Keeping a watchful eye on the wasps, I moved my acquisitions to my inventory. Now that I had an attack spell in my little box of tricks, aggroing mobs became considerably easier. I needed wasp venom in order to successfully defeat the mantises which must have also increased in levels. I just hoped they hadn't turned into something truly horrendous and invincible.

I patiently awaited one of the wasps to leave the others' company, then hit it with an Ice Arrow.

Immediately it aggroed me. Still, its flight was unstable and erroneous, diving into the tall grass, then shooting back up again. I knew that the Crystal Sphere damage system made allowances for its monsters' anatomy. I must have damaged its wing. No need to wait any longer: I had to finish it off.

Here I made my first tactical mistake. Impatient to kill the wounded wasp, I unwittingly crossed the aggro zone of the two others, attracting their attention.

I hurried to cast Weakness over both but it didn't work. In the wasps' tags, small identical shield-shaped icons flashed momentarily, then expired. Both were resistant to the spell. I'd wasted mana for nothing.

This complicated the combat somewhat as two wasps came for me simultaneously from different directions.

I dodged to one side. My sword's blade traced a blurred arc in the air. My right leg exploded with pain. Mechanically I cast a healing aura over myself. One of the mobs disappeared in the grass, critted. The other had stung me and shot back up, banking into a new attack.

I wanted to meet it head-on with an Ice Arrow but the venom debuff had slowed down my reaction times. I was forced to disrupt the spell and stagger back to the safety of the nut grove.

My leg was numb and unresponsive. I was slightly nauseous. Talk about authenticity! I grew weaker with every moment as the neurotoxin spread fast through my body. My HP bar shrank in leaps and bounds as I kept receiving more damage from the venom.

Although the wasp couldn't see me now, it hovered nearby, buzzing its indignation. I was still within its aggro zone. The two wounded ones joined in too.

Suddenly the branches cracked under the wasps' combined weight. My hiding place hadn't been a good one after all.

You've survived your first neurotoxin poisoning!

+2% to Resistance to Neurotoxins

+1% to your chances of ignoring the toxin

-2% to any damage dealt by insects

How cool was that? I hurried to cast another healing aura on myself. Much better! I still had a funny taste in my dry mouth; for the rest, I felt fine.

* * *

I decided not to take any more risks and finished off the wasps right in the grove. I absolutely needed proper combat acrobatics skills for any open-ground fighting. They were an absolute must.

I crouched on the ground gasping, trying to restore. I gulped some water from the flask and waited until my mana was back to normal. Then I rose and collected my loot: the stingers, the chitin plates and the venom glands.

I decided not to leave the clearing until I made at least one level. I had to reconsider my tactics. Apparently, Weakness didn't work on insects — but now I had some of their own neurotoxin.

I smeared some over my sword blade. Time to move it. I was going to stick to the same modus operandi, hiding inside the ruins to prevent the mantises from surrounding me and attacking me all at once.

Where are you, guys?

The runes covering my sword blade came to life with a flash. The symbol closest to the guard was the brightest. The rest barely glowed, and those next to the tip remained dark.

My mental energy indicator quivered as the sword kept syphoning mana which luckily promptly restored.

Suddenly two purple shrubs near to me stirred. The dog rose bushes by the entrance to the ruins swayed simultaneously.

A Venomous Black Praying Mantis. Level, 8
A Venomous Black Praying Mantis. Level, 9
A Venomous Black Praying Mantis. Level, 8

The mobs had cut me off from the old structure and were surrounding me.

They looked unusual. Their purple-black armor was formed by an overlapping pattern of chitin scales. I couldn't see any vulnerable spots in it at all. Also, I was pretty sure they were immune to neurotoxins. They had plenty of it themselves.

The wisest thing now would be to dart for the tent. This little clearing turned out to be way out of my league today. Still, common sense too seemed to have taken a back seat. Losing dangerous amounts of mana, I cast Ice and made a dash for the ruins.

The dog rose leaves turned a wintry silver. The black mantis stopped dead in its tracks in the grip of ice. Swirly patterns of frost ran along its body, its feet frozen solid to the ground.

I invested all my strength into one blow. My sword blade flashed bright, then expired as the runes transformed its accumulated energy into more mental damage.

A crit!

The mantis' triangular head rolled bouncing into the grass while its frozen body remained standing.

I dove into the ruins, panting, my breath misting. The familiar tingling sensation was back. Which meant I couldn't stop halfway. There definitely was a dungeon entrance underneath here somewhere. My mana indicator was growing rapidly, pointing to a source of mental energy below.

I cast another Ice.

I was high on adrenaline, the sensation of mortal danger flooding me and carrying me away.

Everything inside was frozen solid. The heaps of rotting straw, the shattered wooden crates, the mud floor and the old leaves: the contents of the small room had become brittle. I hurried to find the entrance to the dungeon while the cast still held. I had very little time. Another mantis rustled its wings outside, landing onto the second floor of the dilapidated structure.

The floor cracked and sank underfoot. The rotten floorboards gave under my weight. I collapsed into a dark, stale void.

* * *

I landed awkwardly, my feet hitting the floor so hard that I lost my balance and collapsed in a heap.

A spot of light glowed high overhead. It had been a good fifteen foot drop. Judging by the echoing sounds, the dungeon was large. A few paces away from me, I could make out a stone altar which emitted a low rumbling hum, bathing me in a warm wave of growing strength.

An aura made of the tiniest surges of energy coursed the altar's surface, highlighting what looked like the outline of a human hand. It was as if the altar was inviting me to lay my own hand onto it and partake of its power.

My mana indicator was already full. A powerful energy source like this one made you feel invincible.

The mantis' head showed in the hole above. Come on then, buddy, get down here!

It didn't seem to react to my presence. How weird. I attacked it with an Ice Arrow just to wake it up, but missed, causing a shower of ice dust to come tumbling down.

I stepped back into the dark. Now the mantis couldn't see me, blinded by the weak glow of the altar. Let's have a look. What did we have here?

I focused.

An ancient Altar of Chaos

One of the few remaining places of power left after the departure of the Founder Gods. Altars can interact with sorcerers, wizards, mages, druids, shamans and neuros by sharing some of their energy with them.

In order to interact with the Altar, lay your hand on it.

Effect: varies

The ancient power of Chaos can bestow various gifts on its followers, such as raising their levels, granting new abilities or adding new spells to their books.

You can only touch the altar once. Any repeat attempt will be rejected with the following punishment by randomly lowering your characteristics. Still, you can always set off in search of another ancient place of power once you've used this one.

Would you stand up to the challenge?

Yes/ No

Don't touch it! It's mine! barely audible, the voice rustled through the room.

I startled and swung round.

No one.

Was I hearing things?

I looked up. The mantis was still there, staring down the hole and clawing at a broken floorboard which shed flakes of rotten wood.

I stepped a few paces away, waiting in vain for my eyesight to adjust to the viscous darkness. What a shame I wasn't yet entitled to Twilight Vision.

I reached out and felt the wall: it was built with large slabs of stone. I then crouched and touched the floor, finding a gap between two large stone tiles. So this wasn't a natural cave, then, but part of the whole structure. Which meant I just might find a source of light in here.

Slowly I walked along the wall until my hand chanced on a cast-iron torch support. The torch was still in it. Excellent. I just hoped it was in working order.

Still, what was I supposed to light it with? I had no tinderbox on me. All my spells were ice-related.

Wait a sec... That sorcerer outside, he'd definitely been looking for this place. He must have come prepared. What about those plain-looking rocks in his bag? How had he gotten here, anyway? Somehow I doubted he'd intended to access the dungeon via the ruins of the watchtower. I must have been the first person smart enough to fall through the rotten floor from a fifteen-foot height. The dungeon must have had a normal entrance here somewhere.

I produced the two rocks from my inventory and struck them against each other as hard as I could. The impact produced a shower of sparks. Yes! After a few more unsuccessful attempts, I finally managed to light up the torch.

I looked around me at the room illuminated by the uneven flame.

It was huge. My every cautious step echoed from the walls. Flashes of unknown energy flickered at a distance. The stone floor was filthy. Rats squeaked, scurrying through the litter.

I walked along the wall, hoping to come across the exit. No such luck. A few crude columns supported the ceiling. There was less litter here, and it seemed heaped up in places. Could they be human remains?

Steel glistened in the torch's weak light. I was right.

The dungeon seemed to go on forever. I stumbled amid the columns for a while. This seemed to be the final resting place of many an adventure seeker. Their bodies had long turned to dust, their armor and weapons heaps of rusted scrap.

I hurried to return while I could still see the altar's soft glow.

* * *

As soon as I approached the ancient place of power, the same system message popped up again, inviting me to "accept the challenge".

I ignored it, glancing non-committally over it.

There was something fishy about this "altar". The system's promises sounded too good to be true. There had to be a catch. The sheer number of dead bodies set my alarm bells ringing. I immediately thought about the sorcerer's empty book of spells. Could he have lost them all here, then become easy prey for the mantises on his way out?

I re-read the altar's characteristics.

Chaos was the key word, its unpredictable power equally capable of destruction as it was of creation.

Logically thinking, the altar's effects had to be unpredictable too. It could add a new spell to your book but it could also delete it. It could fill you with life — or kill you. Grant you a new level or strip you of your characteristics on the spot.

A faint noise distracted me from my musings. A steel door clanged in the dark, its locks creaking. Footsteps resounded through the dungeon. A faint light appeared at a distance and began to grow, approaching.

I put out the torch and froze.

There were two of them. One walked with a heavy gait, the other scurried along. A warrior and a wizard?

Exactly.

Both seemed quite at home down here. You could tell they'd been here a lot. They didn't even look at the altar, ignoring its defiant glow.

They'd come close enough for me to make out their voices and even recognize some of their gear.

"Max, I just don't get it. What are the techs thinking of? What's with all the wyverns? They're not supposed to be here!"

"See if I care," the warrior grumbled. "Main thing is, we've killed it. You don't mind getting paid for it, do you?"

"No, but did you see how much Life it had?" the wizard pressed on.

"Sure. Almost 10K. Quite a lot. Why, did you expect to see bunny rabbits down here? I thought you'd have gotten used to it by now. Every job is a challenge."

"You don't need to tell me. That's not what I'm talking about. This isn't part of the testing grounds, is it?"

The warrior stopped. "Why?" The torch in his hand cast enough light on both of them now.

"There must be a breach here somewhere. I

could swear this mob has escaped from the testing grounds. Last week we tested a few just like that one for the new continent, remember?"

Breathless, I listened in, studying the strangers. For some reason, I couldn't see their stats. Their name tags were empty, revealing none of their respective levels, races or classes — nothing.

Suddenly the shape of their gear began to distort, transforming. Before I knew it, both were wearing identical gray uniforms. The only difference between them were their shoulder and chest insignia patches.

The distance (they were at least fifteen or twenty feet away from me) and the torch's quivering light prevented me from reading the fine print on the patches. Still, somehow I managed it. It must have been my new Spell Interception ability. This couldn't have been too different from lip reading, after all.

Infosystems Corporation
Defective Mobs Squad

"I shouldn't be too vocal about your breach theory, Mike. Not for the time being."

"Why not? Aren't you going to report the incident?"

"Not yet. Think for yourself: the wyvern was

first sighted just next to Lock 14. I have a tech friend there. I wanna talk to him first. It might have been his error in which case it's up to him to clear up this mess. Otherwise it might look as if I'm pointing a finger at him. Not nice, you know."

The wizard shrugged. "Well, it's up to you. What's going on, anyway? The other day we had an earthquake followed by a demon attack on Agrion. But when I checked the event list, it said nothing about it! The boss is very jittery just lately. What's with shutting half the grounds down? A new experiment, they say. The chief technologist is missing: Jurgen Borne, if you know who I mean. Max? Hello? I'm talking to you! Did you know him?"

The warrior nodded. "He was a good guy," he sighed. "His wife is beyond herself with grief."

The wizard frowned. "How do you know?"

"Thcy're friends with my parents."

"In that case maybe you can tell me what's going on?"

"They seem to be testing some new equipment. Some sort of neuroimplant, or so I heard. But please keep your mouth shut," he hurried to add. "The first test subject was a convicted criminal, from what I heard. Dietrich-something. He lasted less than twenty-four hours."

"Did he go nuts?"

"Oh no, it was worse than that. His identity seems to have disintegrated. Or maybe the neuroimplant just erased it, I don't know. My father said, Jurgen had been against it and even wanted to blow the whistle on the experiments. And then he went missing. So I shouldn't walk around shouting about it if I were you. The top brass have their hands full as it is. I'll report the wyvern myself when the moment is right."

"If you say so," the wizard acquiesced. "I don't need any problems."

Both headed for one of the walls which appeared to be of solid masonry — but the moment the warrior touched it, its surface became fluid, parting to reveal a massive steel door fitted with an electronic lock and a scanner. The door opened, letting the two Defective Mob fighters into an airlock chamber.

* * *

I waited some more, then lit the torch and walked over to the wall.

It was cold and rough to the touch. No sign of the steel door beyond.

I hadn't dreamed it all up, surely? Then again, this was a perfect place to conceal a secret passage connecting this particular location to the corporation's testing grounds.

Oh no, I wasn't touching this Altar of Chaos, not after what I'd just heard. It definitely was here for a reason.

I just couldn't believe it. Then again, why should I? As Dimian had said, it's amazing how rumors propagate. What did I care about the problems at the corporation's testing grounds, anyway?

They were none of my business, period. Did I really have a predecessor who'd gone nuts testing the neuroimplant? I had no idea. Nor did I wish to know. I was fine and that was all that mattered. I had more important things to do than listen to local campfire stories. I had two mantises waiting for me upstairs. And I still had to find the exit from the dungeon.

I gave the altar a wide berth. Someone might say I should have taken the risk but I'd rather do my own leveling, thank you very much. Now the human remains... I actually needed to check them all out. They might drop something useful.

My gaze chanced upon my PM box which I'd moved to the utmost periphery of my interface. Its little envelope-shaped icon was flashing.

Oh wow. Five unread messages? No wonder, considering I'd disabled the audio notification. But who was so insistent in trying to get through to me?

I opened my inbox.

Enea! She must have worked me out, after all. Or was she simply in the mood for a chat?

10.28

Hi Alex. I knew you were cool. Still, you could have added a message.

...

11.00

Hi Alex. Are you all right?

...

12.30

Alexatis,

It's actually bad form to ignore a lady who's on your friend list. If you're busy just let me know. I don't mind.

...

12.40

Alex,

What's up? Where are you? If you need help from a battle wizard, give me your coordinates.

1.10 pm

I can't get through to you. I'm a bit worried. If it's for nothing, I'll survive. Still I believe you need help. I'm coming,

What a predicament!

I glanced at the clock. It was 1.40 pm. Too late to dissuade her. By now, she must have already located my bearings: there was an option allowing you to do it for those on your friend list. I had to find the exit from this wretched dungeon and sort out the mantises before she found me.

The torch cast a small circle of light around me. All I could see on the location map was the altar and a fine line depicting the wall I was now tracing.

I wrote Enea a quick message just in case, warning her about the mantises lurking in the ruins, but it failed to send. The wretched altar! The Corporation had thought of everything. They must have blocked all communications from within the dungeon to make sure a stray player didn't share his accidental discovery with friends.

I came across another disintegrated body. What's with all the stage props? Did the game designers really need so many corpses here? Normally, when a player "dies", he leaves a small bundle of his possessions behind, that's all. Nothing of the kind here. The dungeon's floor was littered with decayed remains, their armor rusted, their clothes long rotten. Could this dungeon be the start of a new plot line, by any chance?

If the truth were known, I couldn't wait to get out of here. There was something not quite right about this place. It wasn't even about the two corporate workers — all they'd done was remind me of the real world outside. The Crystal Sphere settings had already grown on me, to the point where I'd begun to forget the existence of real world problems.

Steel glistened underfoot in the torch's glow. I bent down and picked up a strong-looking round shield with a long spike at its center, trimmed with some metal. It didn't look rusty, its leather straps still quite sturdy. I slid my arm through them.

You've received an item: Sturdy Shield.
Weight, 6.6 lb.
Durability, 70/150
Requires: Level 7, Strength, 5
+5% to your chances of knocking your enemy senseless.

Perfect.

I rummaged through what looked like the remains of an orc warrior and discovered a battle axe with some decent stats. Unfortunately, my level was too low to use it. I threw it into my inventory anyway. I might try and sell it.

I kept walking, checking with the map. Nothing new. The dungeon was enormous.

Gradually the darkness began to subside,

replaced by a crimson glow reflected by the claustrophobically low ceiling. Soon I came across a wide ragged crevice hampering my progress.

Not this now!

I walked warily to the edge.

It felt as if I was looking out of a landing airplane's window. Below lay another underground level, covered in still waves of solidified lava. A fiery river of magma flowed through them. I could make out some ruins covering the lava banks and what looked like mining fields. Countless demonic creatures scurried around them. Judging by the remaining fragments of its architecture, this must once have been a Dwarven city.

The air reeked of sulfur.

Once again the recent earthquake had come to bite me in the backside. Why hadn't anyonc fixed the breaches between locations yet? What had caused it to begin with, anyway? According to what the corporate worker had just said, it had come as a complete surprise to them too. Could it have been a hacking attack?

The fissure was too wide for me to jump across. I had to go looking for a narrower gap.

The bowels of the crevice breathed an intolerable heat. I drank one of the vials from the sorcerer's bag, just to be on the safe side. Thus protected, I walked along the chasm's edge.

Soon the crimson gloom parted, revealing an unfinished bridge arching over the precipice.

I froze, watching a gang of imps drag a multi-ton slab of stone toward the bridge. Their groans echoed from the walls in synch with their efforts. Pulley blocks screeched; leather-wound hoist lines vibrated, growing taut.

At a distance I noticed a bunch of fire scorpions, all levels 16+. The bridge was guarded by several level-10 liches. Further on, I could just make out the outlines of some flying monsters thrashing in the air, their leathery wings rustling.

I couldn't go any further. It looked like I might have to go back to the altar and look for a way up. Shame about the wasted vial.

I needed to search the dead bodies, too. They might drop a levitation scroll or an elixir. If push came to shove, I could make a rope. It was definitely better than trying to fight my way through a bunch of high-level mobs.

Communications were still blocked. I tried to send Enea another message but failed. Once I was out of here, I might need to find a road patrol and report what I'd just seen. That might actually improve my Reputation with Agrion city. They needed to make sure none of these subterranean mobs attacked this low-level nursery, saving newbs from the wrath of the creatures of Inferno.

CHAPTER FIVE

THE DUNGEON IN THE VICINITY OF AGRION CITY

I RETRACED my steps, trying not to stray too far away from my path. The location map was a great help: all I needed to do was follow the thin winding line of my earlier route.

I could already see the altar. Gradually I'd left it all behind: the glow of the subterranean flames, the groaning of the imps, the hissing of the scorpions and the rustling of wings. Still I was on high alert for any eventualities, my sweaty hand wrapped tight around the hilt of my Mysterious Sword. The runes on its blade glowed as the sword siphoned my mental energy.

I kept my sword in quick access, allowing me to equip it at a moment's notice.

I tensed, noticing a new source of glowing light.

I couldn't hear any footsteps. I was approached noiselessly.

Christa. Level 8. Demon

The system message cut me to the quick.

She was clad in the same dark hugging armor she'd wore when we'd first met at the alternative start location, made of skins of some Infernal creatures unknown to me.

A sword hilt peeped from behind her left shoulder. She was holding a vial, clenching it tight.

"Alex, I've been looking for you. I want to apologize. I'm so sorry!" she offered me the potion without explaining its purpose. "It's all gonna be different now. Trust me. Drink this."

Her pupilless gaze oozed darkness. A weak fiery aura coursed her body, as if every level she gained stripped her of her human identity.

No, not really. My mistake. Suddenly everything changed. This was my Christa's gaze — even though she avoided looking me in the eye for some reason.

"Alex, please. This stuff is neutralizing my

shield of fire."

She was a mere pace away from me. I glanced at the vial, then stepped toward her and kissed her.

She recoiled, her face ashen with pallor. "How did you..."

"A fire resistance elixir," I said. "I drank it hoping to cross to the other side. Not that it matters now."

She hissed, her long lithe tail swishing about the floor. The ancient dust began to smolder, belching smoke.

"Christa, what's wrong with you? Have you come to burn me again? Why? Your vial is filled with water."

"How do you know?"

"I'm a Neuro."

She knew what it meant. In a lightning motion, she whipped out her sword.

Sword of Inferno
Damage, 20
Additional fire damage, 10.

"Christa, you didn't answer my question!"

We both froze in a combat stance, sizing each other up.

"Alex, I'm fine! At least now I don't need to suffer in silence! I can deal out pain myself!"

"Excuse me? Am I your enemy? Since when?"

"Ever since you began torturing me!" she spat, lunging at me.

I parried her blow with minimum losses. My shield received a scorch mark, dropping 15 pt. I didn't counterattack. Not yet.

Her glare was ablaze with gloom. "Fight!"

"Why, do you need a real reason to hate me?"

She dashed toward me in a desperate combo, her tail trying to sweep my legs away from under me. Demons didn't seem to have problems with combat acrobatics. I did, but still I managed to recoil, struggling to parry the blows she showered on me. My shield was a sorry sight. It had only 5 pt. Durability left — definitely not enough to survive another attack.

"Christa, wait! Would you like me to contact Support? I can do it! You can still change your race!"

She was gasping. "Why should I?"

The intensity of our experience was identical. I had a split eyebrow. She'd received a lacerated wound to her shoulder where the sharp edge of my shield had grazed it. The wound's edges were on fire.

"Remember when you first suggested we meet in real life? When was it?" she spat.

"I can't remember now," I watched her closely, amazed at her lethal grace.

"Two months ago! I couldn't tell you I was sick. But I couldn't leave you. For two months, my life was hell!"

Did she expect me to apologize? This hadn't been my fault. What a shame it had had to end up like this. "Christa, please. Just go."

"Fight!" she croaked, bursting with hatred. "Or die now!"

Oh no, lady, I'm not your whipping boy. I had to end it now, while the fire defense elixir was still working. Pointless reasoning with her.

I hurried to cast Weakness.

She startled. Her choreographed movements fell out of synch. A debuff icon appeared in her name tag.

The dungeon's floor shuddered.

Enveloped in flames, she froze pointing her Infernal sword at me with her left hand raised, its fingers surging with a fiery aura. Her lips were mouthing something.

With a crashing noise, a giant slab of stone wrested itself out of the dungeon's floor.

And another one.

And again.

Then all three collapsed, raising clouds of dust. I couldn't see anything. A fiery flourish cut thought the haze. I barely had time to raise the shield which disintegrated with the blow, dropping smoldering bits of wood.

We crossed our swords. The fresh holes in the floor seethed, teeming with the undead.

I parried Christa's blow, then chopped the head off a skeleton which had sunk his teeth into my leg while still trying to climb out of the hole. Another one reached out his bony arm, trying to grab my leg. Others (there were at least ten of them) were gradually encircling me.

What now? Was this a speed elevator back to my tent? All of the skeletons were levels 2 and 3; they weren't dealing any serious damage, more like getting in the way. One of them was apparently a caster, his staff shooting off charges of dark energy: clots of darkness veined with crimson and pregnant with debuffs.

I tossed the broken shield aside and kicked the head off another skeleton, grabbing his rusty sword while casting Ice. The area around me filled with frosty statues.

My mental energy bar dropped dangerously low.

Never mind. Thanks to the sorcerer's belt, I still had three more mana vials in quick access slots.

Hatred is a poor guide which had led Christa into making a mistake. The slabs of stone she'd ripped out of the floor turned out to be perfect cover for me. I stepped behind them, dodging the curses addressed at me. Their caster was on his last legs already.

The altar of chaos glowed brighter, throbbing with light. I needed to get closer to it. I could use a source of limitless energy.

Christa kicked off from the rocks and leapt onto me, very nearly knocking me off my feet.

After a lightning exchange of blows, we were circling each other again at arm's length, eyes locked.

My leather jacket had been reduced to smoldering tatters. Her armor too was sliced in a couple of places. The skeletons had crumbled to dust; the dark caster she'd summoned had disintegrated, leaving behind a heap of stinking rags.

I could see Christa wasn't comfortable with my sword which had already left a few deep dents in her own.

Our chances were basically even. The only difference was, she could handle pain while I couldn't. I shouldn't betray my weakness to her. I had to be strong.

I lobbed the useless rusty sword aside, cast a Shield of Mana and attacked her with a slashing blow.

She somersaulted back without even trying to parry it. Was she afraid?

Possible. Still, she wasn't a quitter, I could see that. One of us would have to respawn today.

She momentarily disappeared, consumed by the darkness. She hadn't cast anything, had she? That must have been some ability she had!

She reappeared, backing off toward the altar. She must have sensed its energy. Not good.

A fireball buzzed past me, searing me with its heat. My heat resistance elixir had expired!

Christa increased the distance between us and loosed off several more fireballs. I dodged them with ease, then watched them disappearing in the depths of the tunnels, dripping with flames.

What was she up to? Why did she change the grip on the sword? She was holding it by the blade now. Why was she kneeling?

I cast Ice.

Her shield of fire flared up, absorbing the spell.

Christa closed her hands tight around the blade, cutting them. Her lips mouthed something as her dark blood began to trickle down the infernal weapon. Its metal hissed as if attacked by acid. The Altar of Chaos erupted with an unbearable light.

You've learned a new spell: Sacrifice

She threw her head back and screamed, burying the hilt of her sword into the floor like it were soft wax. The tunnel's walls and ceiling shuddered. A wave of dark energy rippled through it, expanding. It passed right through me without hurting me, just leaving a faint numbness behind.

The heaps of rotten clothes littering the floor shifted. Piles of rusty armor began to clatter.

The numerous dead bodies surrounding the altar came back to life — sort of. The worst thing about them — apart from the fact that they'd been lying here accumulating darkness all that time — was that they'd kept their levels, too!

Christa pulled the sword's hilt out of the stone and scampered aside, staggering, all the while casting another spell. She wasn't the one who controlled the undead. On the contrary, she'd pulled their aggro to herself but promptly managed to cast a spell allowing her to escape their range.

They surrounded me. I struggled to discern what they had once used to be. Oh wow. They had all sorts here.

My Mysterious Sword arced through the air, dissecting their shriveled flesh.

An axe sank into my back. The agony! A blinding flash of light exploded on the edge of my field of vision. Still, I had no time to look around.

I gulped another Health elixir and began hacking my way through the thick circle of the undead, trying to get to the altar.

I almost made it.

I could barely move with exhaustion when Christa stepped in my way. She didn't look too good. Her fiery aura had paled, her black armor falling apart.

"We aren't finished yet!" she hissed.

Without saying a word, I lunged at her, wasting my last strength on this attack. I had no elixirs left. My Life had dropped to 30%.

"Leave my guy alone, you bitch!" Enea's voice rang through the air, followed by a barrage of ice arrows.

Christa stopped in her tracks in disbelief. Her shield absorbed the last dose of damage, then expired.

"*Your* guy?" her glare burned a hole in me. "That was quick. You don't lose much time, do you? Very well, then. Enjoy!"

She darted away, leaving the two of us surrounded by the high-level undead.

* * *

"Hold on!" a stifled voice came from the lowered visor of a knight's helmet.

Enea had brought reinforcements!

Zander, a level 45 Paladin, has invited you to join his group!

Mechanically my gaze swiped the virtual button, accepting the invitation.

"Step back, both of you!"

A healing aura enveloped me. Simultaneously a bright flash of Light magic scorched the first ranks of the undead, allowing us to take a breather.

Enea cast Ice, all the while supporting me.

"I'm fine now," I managed. "Thanks." Not a good moment to ask her how on earth she'd gotten here.

"On my signal!" the Paladin snapped. "Follow me, no aggroing, no loot picking, nothing! The exit is near!"

"No, wait," my voice broke, breathless. "How did you get here?"

"Ever heard of teleport scrolls? We set it to your last known coordinates," Zander replied.

He wasted no time hacking a path through the crowd of zombies. Paladins were used to handling the undead; besides, his level 45 was way out of their league. It was a pleasure watching him. Even the altar's glow had faded in the light of his Righteous Anger and Cleansing Aura.

With a whoosh, his sword of moon silver

arced through the air, slicing through the zombies' timeworn armor.

I watched his murderous solo closely, trying to memorize his every move and blow. Having realized how many strong enemies we were against, Enea had gone quiet, trying to go easy on mana.

"Why is he helping you?" I asked her.

"Em, how can I say... you see... basically, he's rushing me," she admitted shyly, taking cover behind me from the hail of shriveled flesh flying from the Paladin's sword.

"Are you paying to play?!"

"No way! You think I'm nuts? But I did receive five gold from the admins for that frog video, so I gave it to him. I had to find you, didn't I?"

During our whispered exchange, Zander kept hacking through, adding two levels to each of us. "Keep going! Don't lag!"

"No — you stop," I said.

He looked back at us. "What's up?"

"We can't get through there," I told him about the chasm and the Infernal city below.

"Everything to please!" he spat. "Never mind. I'll call in a few guys in a moment."

"You can't. There's no signal here. See for yourself if you don't believe me. How much do you charge?"

"Ten gold."

"Listen to me. You've got five from Enea already. I'll send you another five once the communications are back up. That's the extent of it. Deal?"

"Don't you two want to level up?"

"We do. But we'd rather do that on our own."

"Any ideas how to get out of here?"

"Look," I pointed at the light high overhead.

"Will do," Zander slapped my shoulder. "Wanna earn a few gold?"

"How?"

"Have you filmed the demonic city?"

"Sure."

"Will you send me the video? I help people level up — and an Infernal city is a rare find, trust me. What level are the mobs there?"

"Ten to thirty."

"Perfect!" he cheered up. "I'll give you a hundred gold for the tape. I don't need the map. I know where the entrance is. But I might need your video in order to lay the route. Consider this gig a free bonus. The teleport scroll is on me too. What do you think?"

I nodded. "It's a deal."

All this time, Enea had been listening in. Still, she didn't say anything.

"Excellent," Zander summed up. "Now all

we have left to do is get out of here. I could mop up the bridge, I suppose, but it might take too much time. I have a levitation potion. I'll use it to climb up. Then I'll pull you out with a rope."

"Sounds good. Keep in mind there're two venomous mantises in the ruins," I warned him.

"I'll sort them out," he cast a long look around at the scorched ground, apparently seeing no immediate danger for the two of us. All the zombies were dead. "I won't be a moment."

He gulped the elixir and began floating toward the hole in the ceiling.

"Alex," Enea gave me a warm smile, sincere and carefree. "Alex, I've saved your life!" she emitted a tiny shriek of delight. "Can you imagine?"

Infected by her joy, I smiled back despite my aching jaw and busted lips. "You're awesome."

"You're not angry with me, are you? And that girl, what's her name... Christa... the demon..."

"I'll tell you later. It's a long story."

A length of rope fell at our feet, unraveling.

"Enea, hold on to me. Put your arms around me, like this. Zander, we're ready! Pull!"

* * *

Outside, the sun was already setting. I'd noticed

that the day was shorter here than in the real world.

"Zander, thanks. You've really helped us out."

He coiled up the rope and packed it into his inventory. His bag must have been full of useful goodies for every occasion.

"Likewise. The video?"

"Sure."

The in-game network worked fine up here, as if nothing had happened. I sent Zander the panorama of the ancient dwarven city. Immediately, a hundred gold dropped into my account.

"I'll see you around?" Zander said, impatient to leave. He must have already been busy making new plans.

"Yeah. We can manage on our own now. Can I ask you just one last question? Teleport scrolls, can they really be set to selected coordinates?"

"Sure."

"And what if I don't know the coordinates but have them marked on the map?"

"Then you need to see a cartographer," Zander explained. "He'll calculate them for you. Just don't tell him you need it to teleport or he'll charge you an arm and a leg. One other thing: teleport scrolls come in three types. Some are preset to particular locations. It's cities usually. Others only work within your line of vision. Perfect for combat. And the third type only work within the operating radius. They're the ones you need. Just keep in mind there's always the risk of a stupid death if you miscalculate and get yourself ported inside a cliff or a tree. So I suggest you choose barren locations when using them. Right, I'm off. Too many things to do. If you need anything, PM me."

In the whoosh of a teleport, he disappeared.

All this time Enea had been curiously studying the dead mantises (the one which I'd smoked and the two others that had apparently been slaughtered by Zander). "Are we supposed to walk to the city?"

I hadn't even thought about it!

She glanced at me and burst out laughing, hiding her face in her hands. "Are you always so serious? Relax! Do you mind if I leave my avatar in your tent for the night? In the morning, we'll think of something. You do need to go to the city, don't you? Surely you aren't going to wear these rags?"

I smiled back. She already knew about my tent! "Fine, then, let's go. We can have a quiet candlelit evening and a talk. Just let me pick up the loot."

"Can't it wait till tomorrow?"

"I don't think so. The mantises will disappear soon."

I frisked the bodies.

You've received the Shell of a Black Praying Mantis. It can be used for making light scaly armor.

The Shell looked sturdy but supple. It must have been a rare item indeed.

You've received a Venom Gland of a Black Praying Mantis. Contains a dose of neurotoxin, effective against large animals, dealing 10 pt. Damage and paralyzing the victim for 5 sec.

In total, I collected three Shells and three Venom Glands. "Good. Let's go now. It's not very far."

Less than five minutes later, Enea and I had reached the tent.

I turned on the light, placed the folding table in the middle and lay out the bread, meat and cheese. "Tuck in!"

"Why?" she raised a surprised eyebrow. "What's with all the buffing up? It's nighttime already. Aren't you going to log out?"

"Oh, no. I have too many things to do."

"Well, I'm tired. I'd love to go to bed. And I need a proper meal. Mind if I crash out here?"

"Be my guest."

"All right then," she gave me a peck on the cheek. "See you in the morning?"

"See ya."

She logged out, leaving behind her sleeping avatar and the faint scent of her perfume.

Our authenticity levels were drastically different. We might just as well have been living in two parallel worlds. No idea how I was going to get around this problem.

I needed some sleep too. I had a quick bite, then lay on the ground next to her. Still, I kept tossing and turning for hours, thinking about Christa and the recent changes in her.

I awoke before sunrise, fresh and well-rested. Trying not to disturb Enea (which was stupid of course because her avatar couldn't sense my presence) I crawled out of the tent and reached into my inventory for the orc warrior's battle axe. My current level allowed me to use it now.

Interestingly, my respective Intellect, Strength and Agility boost bars had grown considerably. So apparently, my Evolution ability had lived up to its promises.

Very well. I was ready to level up further. Now I could turn my attention to Intense Training and reflex optimization. My brief encounter with Christa had highlighted my vulnerabilities. Combat acrobatics definitely were my weakest spot. So that's what I should practice first.

* * *

Breakfall. Block. A quick Minor Heal. I finished with a run across the beam.

The tall stumps of wind-broken pine trees served me as practice dummies. I somersaulted, positioning myself behind an imaginary adversary's back, and performed a combo against two more attackers. The video I'd made back in the dungeon had helped me a lot. I'd kept watching it until I thought I could repeat some of the Paladin's moves. Now all I had to do was practice them.

I fully intended to capitalize on all my class abilities, both combat and magic ones. A Neuro shouldn't limit him or herself to one particular practice. I had to mix and match the two in order to be able to tackle the biggest variety of potential enemies.

Which meant I would have to be able to improvise. At least this way my agonizing struggle to register Christa's every lip movement hadn't been in vain.

I went back to my starting position, sword

slung behind my back in a crude DIY scabbard. I made some "targets" out of rocks and set them up on the edge of my training circuit.

I didn't have much mana at the moment. Potions could be the answer but I decided against having to rely on them during practice.

I ran along the beam, trying to keep my balance, sword at the ready. Another breakfall. An attacking combo, a block, a turn, a spell!

Breathless, I fluffed the spell and had to start all over again.

Let's do it!

The beam. The somersault. A figure-of-eight slashing blow against two attackers. Parry. Another spell.

A fireball escaped my left hand and went whooshing toward its target, landing a few feet short and setting the grass on fire.

I followed it up with an ice arrow. This time I didn't miss, extinguishing the fire before it had had the chance to spread.

I gasped, sweating like a pig. My homespun shirt and pants didn't restrict my movements at the moment, but once I put armor on, the same routine would be a challenge.

Enough. I was out of mana. Time to take a break.

* * *

The sun was already high when I resumed my starting position. It was getting hot.

Out of the corner of my eye, I noticed the tent flap sway. Enea crawled out and froze, amazed by the sight.

A combo. A spell!

A fireball hit the "target", sending fragments of rock flying everywhere.

"Wow. What class are you?" she demanded, fingering a strand of hair.

I ran a shirt sleeve across my sweaty forehead. "Hi there. You look great. Had a nice break?"

Mr. Borisov had warned me about the potential danger of even mentioning the neuroimplant to anyone. No, I didn't want to drag Enea into this.

"No way," she flashed me a shy smile. "I forgot to put my Loveliness ring on. Am I still pretty?"

"What kind of question is that?" I said, wiping my dripping face. "Of course you are!"

She looked over my makeshift assault course. "Is your char custom-made? With an odor generator and everything?"

"What do you mean?"

"You look sort of drawn," she said, her eyes

fixed on me. "And you need a shave. You don't smell of roses either, if you'll excuse my French. You smell like... like a *man*."

She burst out laughing. "Look, he's blushing! Never mind! Fancy a run to the pond? I'll murder that frog and we can have a swim!"

I took a deep breath. My hormones were in overdrive. I know what I'd like to murder. Pointless though. Our authenticity levels were too far apart. Never mind. I might need to practice self-control, that's all. I still had to answer her questions. I had to explain Christa to her somehow, as well as my own hybrid class.

A noise disrupted the awkward pause: the rattle of armor and the thudding of hooves trampling the undergrowth.

Not good. I whipped out my sword and stepped forward, protecting Enea.

Let's just hope they're not demons.

With a cracking sound, the nut trees parted, letting out a cavalcade of level-50 warriors clad in mithril. They reined in their horses, earth and moss flying from under their hooves.

I checked their name tags.

NPC mercenaries. All but one, that is. Their leader was a player.

The stranger looked a bit out of place among them. His horse didn't wear armor. His saddle was tall and comfortable, definitely not meant for mounted combat. He had no weapons, either. What a weird avatar.

Two of the mercs jumped off their steeds and crossed their outstretched arms, helping the aging gentleman to dismount.

Enea heaved a sigh. "Shit."

I was about to ask her whether she knew the guy but he beat me to it.

He gave me a look filled with contemptuous indifference. "Put your weapon down."

"What's going on?"

"Shut him up. Just don't kill him. Enea, where are you supposed to be now?"

The shaft of a spear took my legs from under me. They effortlessly disarmed me, then gave me a smack in the mouth. Blood trickled down my lips. Two of the mercs held me tight by my shoulders. I tried to struggle free but failed.

Enea was shaking — not with fear but rather with indignation. "Dad? What do you think you're doing? Leave Alex alone!"

"Why should I? You should be meeting our business partners now, not having fun with peasants!"

She turned pale. "Don't you dare insult my friends! I'm a grown-up now, in case you didn't notice!"

"I did. That's why you have

responsibilities," he replied coldly.

His avatar didn't have a level. How interesting. Did that mean he could enter the Crystal Sphere without even creating a char of his own, just by kicking open some secret "door" known only to him and instantly receiving a squad of mercs and information about his daughter's whereabouts?

"Log out, now!" he snapped. "You've got a car waiting. You have five minutes to get ready!"

"I'm not coming," she said in a soft voice. I forced my head round to take a look. Her avatar was fading, disappearing into thin air.

Then she was gone.

Her father didn't seem to be bothered by the fact that all this was a blatant violation of player's rights. He gave me another look of contempt. "If ever I learn you're still around, I'll find you in real life. Then you'll regret it. She's not for the likes of you, remember. Give him his weapon back. Let's go!"

A merc stuck my sword into the ground. Others helped the man into the saddle. Then they were gone.

I wiped away the blood and picked up my sword. Then I hurled a fireball at a rock target.

It didn't make me feel any better.

* * *

I spent the next week practicing and farming wasps and locusts.

Enea had never been back. I'd tried to contact her a few times only to receive a system message,

We're sorry. The character you're trying to contact is currently offline.

I'd earned three levels. My combat acrobatic skills had improved considerably. My makeshift obstacle course had become a breeze, every move and blow practiced to perfection. I'd stopped hitting my head on tree stumps. I could cast a spell no matter how breathless I was. These days I killed a mantis with one blow.

My nightmare had returned. I dreamed of being rushed somewhere on a gurney, the life support machines bleeping desperately by my pillow. I'd awake drenched in sweat.

On the eighth day, I'd had enough. No good sitting on my backside. I had to move on.

It was about time I visited the city, sold all the loot I'd amassed and gotten myself some new gear. Enough looking like a tramp!

CHAPTER SIX

THE CRYSTAL SPHERE STARTING LOCATIONS

PREDICTABLY, Agrion City turned out to be a run-of-the-mill provincial medieval town.

Only the central street was paved. The moment you turned off it, you entered a rambling maze of rather unseemly lanes.

The place was buzzing with players. Their gear and name tags made them easy to identify. The local NPCs walked unhurriedly around. They had their own lives and agendas.

The guards at the city gate gave me a suspicious look but let me through. Judging by snippets of other players' conversations, they were still busy rectifying the consequences of the recent surprise event. They'd already restored the houses which had suffered from the earthquake and were now mopping up the city dungeons of all the undead that had broken through. That meant lots of one-off Reputation quests and even small plot lines for beginning players.

Enea was tagged as *Offline.* I just hoped she might be back one day so we could finally talk. Still, I wasn't going to lose any sleep over it.

I was looking at a dangerous and adventurous journey. I absolutely had to get to the Azure Mountains and complete the quest by solving the mystery of my sword. I still had a lot of training to do before I could tackle this. I'd already realized, from previous practice, that I had to keep my left arm free for casting spells and whipping out vials, meaning I could only use it to hold a shield in the direst of circumstances.

Which also meant I needed to concentrate on clothes, armor, spare weapons, elixirs and jewelry.

The market was located in the city's main square. I wasn't impressed. The place was small, about twenty stalls at the most. Their prices were reasonable but the choice was rather poor, targeting beginners. Lots of statless items under level 10. And although I'd come across some level 12+ weapons and armor, I was forced to reject everything that was even remotely heavy or cumbersome. You could say I had special needs, I suppose.

For me, the choice of gear was paramount. My armor had to be light and offer additional stats. I browsed through loot displays but found nothing. A hundred and twenty gold doesn't go far, you know. I had to spend it wisely.

Had Dimian already been back to town?

I peered at the shop signs lining the square,

Juguld the Jeweler
Scrolls and Manuscripts For Sale
Agrion's Best: Potions and Elixirs
Khorg's Armory
Pret-a-Porter
Scribe and Cartography Services
Dimian's Emporium

If I wanted NPC vendors to offer me their best items at their best prices, I had to complete their quests first. In that respect, Dimian was my best bet. Despite the recent Hinterwood developments, our relationship was quite friendly.

* * *

"Alexatis! What a nice surprise!" Dimian seemed sincerely happy to see me. "So you decided to come to the city, after all? I wondered when you might drop by to see me. You look much stronger now!" he announced, studying my battered leather armor.

Before, I'd never bothered to ask myself if NPCs held their own opinion on players. Were they self-aware at all, or did they just follow a fixed set of computer commands? You couldn't really tell by the way he behaved. As I'd already noticed back at Hinterwood, his speech patterns could be quite elaborate.

"Morning, Dimian," I replied politely. "You're right, my gear could use an upgrade. So I immediately thought about you."

"You did the right thing," he nodded, stroking his short beard. "I'm not some greedy market dealer. I might not hold as much stock as some of them do but this is all quality stuff made by Master craftsmen. No second-hand items here! No rusty swords with blood spots! Come over here," he pushed open a small inconspicuous door in the wall.

Honestly, I was speechless. This must have been a special stash reserved for VIP customers. The choice was quite decent: all the items were one of a kind. Speaking about the importance of one's Reputation with NPCs! It could work wonders, apparently. I just wished his goods were more affordable.

My eye chanced on a set of undergarments made of some smooth fabric, soft and lightweight, lined with an unpretentious embroidered pattern. 18 gold.

I checked its stats,

A homespun undershirt made by a Master craftsman.

Durability, 100/100

Armor, 1

Weight, 1 lb.

Bonus: +5 to HP when equipped.

Homespun underpants made by a Master craftsman

Durability, 100/100

Armor, 1

Weight, 1 lb.

Bonus: +5 to HP when equipped.

Currently, my Stamina was 10 which meant I had 100 HP. If I equipped these two items, it would make it 110.

I tried both on. The items were comfortable; but most importantly, you could wear them under light armor.

Eighteen gold for a set of undies! The mind boggles. Still, I couldn't help it. The items were both useful and comfortable.

"You've got some good stock here," I said. "I'm gonna buy this shirt and the pants."

He looked pleased. "You seem to appreciate comfort wear."

You bet I did. Now at least the armor wouldn't grate against my skin. Plus, at my current authenticity levels, extra HP meant a higher pain threshold. Also, the fact that the bonus was measured in per cent rather than in points, meant that it would grow exponentially as I continued to level up.

The doorbell dinged. Dimian hurried to meet a new customer. "Have a look around," he told me. "I'll be back soon."

I used this opportunity to compare his prices with the auction. I ran a quick search until I found a similar set of underwear.

Fifty gold for an item with identical stats! What was the difference, then?

A Homespun Undershirt. Class: Relic.

Aha. So someone must have worked out the ancient item's secret and learned to produce similar ones. What could I say? A master like that deserved all the respect he could earn.

It took me over an hour to study all the items exhibited in Dimian's back room.

I'd discovered an excellent set of leather armor. Another 50 gold for a pair of pants, a jacket, some boots, gauntlets and a helmet. Made by a Master craftsman, each item had a bonus to one of the main characteristics. It was fashioned with care and attention to detail, with no stat overlapping. It fit me well, too. Equipping the full set gave you +10% to each item's Durability.

Dimian returned. When he heard how much money I intended to part with, he couldn't have been more pleased.

I shelled out 68 gold, then changed into my new clothes on the spot.

"You look awesome!" he commended.

Your Reputation with Dimian has improved!
Current Reputation status: Respect
Next Reputation status: Selfless Friendship

Business out of the way, we got talking.

"Dimian, you seem to travel a lot, right?"

"You could say that."

"You ever been to the Azure Mountains, by any chance?"

"Oh, no. Never been that far. That part of the world isn't yet explored. Some big city merchants wanted to start a trade route. They set off with lots of goods and an armed escort to match but they failed to battle through the wilderness. In my opinion, it might take an army to do that."

"Who were they going to trade with?"

"What do you mean, who with? With the dwarves, of course! The local foothills are inhabited by the Dark Elves, and everything above that belongs to the dwarves. They sell ore and jewels really cheaply. We could offer them everything they need. But you can't do much business using teleports, can you? You need a safe trade route. Still, it might take a while."

"Who's in control of teleports, then? Wizards?"

"Sure. Only they charge you a king's ransom. Their services aren't very reliable, either. Think for yourself: a top arch mage can only cast a seven-second portal. Can you imagine the number of wizards needed to teleport a whole caravan — goods, guards and all? Don't even go there."

"Can't you use portal scrolls?" I tested the ground.

Dimian shook his head. "I'm not sure. Scrolls can be tricky. At long range, they aren't too accurate for what they cost. You need to really know the area. Without a good map, you risk losing your stock or even your life."

"But in theory, is it possible?"

"It is," he threw me a squinted look. "Why are you so interested?"

Now I had an idea. Let's see if my current Reputation was enough to talk him into a risky enterprise. "And what if someone laid the route, marked the coordinates, struck a deal with the dwarves and prepared a loading area?"

Dimian heaved a sigh. "I'd pay any money to someone brave enough to do that. The guild charges me more than the dwarven jewels are worth! If only I could do it on my own!" his eyes lit up. "Now is the time to cash in, when there're no trade routes laid yet!"

"I might try. Problem is, I have no scrolls. You would need two for a return journey."

"Are you serious? Or is all this a joke? Where are you supposed to get the coordinates from? The guild keeps them under lock and key."

"I have a quest to see one of the dwarven masters. Complete with a marker on the map. And I do know that a good cartographer can calculate a place's coordinates by its marker. Then all you need to do is enter them into the scroll."

The blood drained from his face. I was worried he might faint right in front of me. There was some serious inner struggle going on inside the man.

"It's so risky," he finally mumbled. "But the potential... oh my."

He gave me a sharp look. "You mix with demons," he pointed out.

"I could say the same about you," I replied. "You mix with wyverns."

"You're right!" he emitted a nervous chuckle, then grew broody again. "A scroll for that kind of distance is gonna cost at least fifty gold."

"Now think about all the profits," I upped the ante. "It's my risk and your money. What would you say to that?"

He frowned, pondering over it. "Arright," he finally wheezed. "If you make it there and back, you won't regret it. If you bring me some jewels and set up a route, even if it's good enough for one mounted traveler alone, I'll make it worth your while. Mark my words. And if you die..."

"Don't speak too soon," I stopped him. "Now we need to get some scrolls and visit a cartographer."

"Cool it. I think I've got some," he headed to a dusty old chest in a far corner. "Here, look. I've got three even. Nobody buys them. They're too expensive."

"I was also told that if the cartographer finds out it's for a teleport, he'll hike the price."

"He will. And it's none of his business, anyway. So what do you suggest?"

"I have an idea. I'll see him myself and get the coordinates. Then I'll come back here and we'll enter them together. Deal?"

"Deal!"

New quest alert: Trade Route

Quest type: Rare

Find out the coordinates of a location situated in the Azure Mountains, then explore the route using a teleportation scroll and bring some jewels back to Dimian.

Reward:

1. ???? gold, depending on the number of jewels you manage to procure from the dwarves.

2. A considerable increase in your Reputation with Dimian.

* * *

Much to my surprise, the cartographer turned out to be a player. His name was Vichoralius, of all things.

"Hi," he seemed happy to see a customer. "I have a recent update of the city dungeons and the catacomb atlas complete with a bosses guide. Only three gold for all the information you'll ever need!"

"Not interested," I slumped into a soft chair. I was actually happy he wasn't an NPC. Now I knew exactly what to say to him. "I need a navigator."

He didn't reply.

I feigned disappointment. "You're not my man, then."

"Bots are illegal," he mumbled.

I shrugged. "They are. But I have a quest. I need to get there double quick, preferably using existing roads.

"Sorry. I've only just opened this shop. I don't want any problems. Why won't you download one online?"

I winced. "As you wish. In this case, can you at least help me calculate the coordinates? I'll need to enter them into the navigator, won't I?"

"Easy. What have you got?"

I opened the map of the continent in my mental view, most of it still clouded in the fog of war apart from a small area around Agrion. A question mark glowed by the map's western edge. I took a screenshot of the map.

Vichoralius cast me a quizzical stare.

"No, I'm not a nutcase," I answered his unasked question. "I'm gonna take it easy. I'll do it in my own time, leveling up when I can and switching over to the bot whenever it's safe. I can't be online 24/7, can I?"

"Whatever. It's ten gold."

"You don't think that's a bit over the top?"

"It's not. I could have offered you a discount provided you gave me a copy of your map once you were back. The problem is, no one has ever made it back from the Azures. So it is what it is. Happy with that?"

Grudgingly I parted with ten gold coins. My Inbox blinked, reporting an incoming message.

"These are the coordinates," he said. "If you do get there, keep your route under wraps, will you? I'll take you to a big cartographer from the capital. He offers good money for this sort of thing."

"Really? Isn't there some legal app to document the route? Some kind of map-making module?"

"Sure. You can't use it though. In order to install it, you need to receive the Pioneer achievement first. It's awarded to those who discover a new location or frequently travel long distances."

"Never mind. Thanks, anyway. This is good enough."

I wanted Vichoralius to remember me as a newb adventure seeker, reckless and arrogant. This was the best way to prevent rumors from spreading.

* * *

"So? Did you get the coordinates?" Dimian asked, consumed by anxiety.

"I told you I would."

"Let's do it, then!" he lay out three teleportation scrolls on the desk. "If you explore the area and make an agreement with the dwarves, you won't regret it."

Yeah, right. A fair deal indeed. He was risking his scrolls but it was my head on the block.

All this had happened too fast. On my way to the city earlier that morning, I hadn't even dreamed of any such rapid developments. Still, it was more fun this way.

"Come on, enter the coordinates," I told him. "Your handwriting is nicer than mine."

Dimian sat at the desk and pulled the inkstand closer. He anxiously chewed his lip as he scraped the quill over the parchment, entering the numbers.

"That's it," he finally said. "I set the second scroll to a nice safe spot in my back yard. The third one I've left blank, just in case. You should keep it for any eventual emergencies. I can see your bag is big enough," he rose and opened the chest, producing three small boxes, locked and tied up with string.

"What's this?"

"It's Spectral Dust. It's used in ore treatment in order to change its properties. From what I heard, the Azure dwarves pay good money for it. You can swap it with them for some jewels."

"Which ones?"

"I've got a list. I asked our master jewelers to make it for me."

That was quick. Then again, I shouldn't Have been surprised. Quests like this one were arranged long beforehand. This way one could jump into action straight away.

If the truth were known, I was much more interested in my sword and the mystery it was supposed to harbor. Meeting Master Jurg was my priority. Then I might get around to doing some trading with dwarves if I had the chance.

I remembered Zander's warning about coordinate-armed teleport scrolls. Apparently, they looked different. They weren't sealed. Which made me wonder how I was supposed to activate them.

I studied the old parchment.

Aha! A prompt popped up,

Teleport Scroll

A guild-produced magic item

In order to activate the scroll, touch the

coordinates entered into the text.

"Ready now? Let's go to the back yard," Dimian demanded, impatient.

"Okay."

I just hoped these scrolls were foolproof. The coordinates I'd received from the cartographer were two-dimensional. They didn't take altitude into account. That was quite risky, considering I was going to port to a mountainous area.

Game developers aren't that stupid, I tried to reassure myself. *Otherwise Enea and Zander wouldn't have been able to port to the dungeon, would they?*

* * *

The teleport popped close. The world span around me, twisting into a tight colorful spiral.

I was falling. My heart missed a beat. Had I been wrong? What if the scrolls weren't foolproof, after all?

A fat tree branch cushioned my fall. I kept tumbling some more until I landed on my shoulder. I lay motionless, my eyes squeezed tight, my heart about to explode.

I'd survived.

Congratulations!

You've discovered a new location: the Azure Mountains!

You've received an Achievement: Pioneer. +5% to the XP received when discovering new locations and setting new routes (including sea routes).

I tried to move. I seemed all right. No bones broken.

I opened my eyes a little. I was lying under an enormous pine tree next to a towering cliff. It looked like Dimian had been right. Loading a horse wasn't even an option. Still, scrolls seemed to offer some protection, after all. Judging by the ravaged undergrowth covering the fissures in the cliff, I must have landed on a small platform at the top of the cliff but failed to stay put, tumbling all the way down.

My fall hadn't been that big. The pine tree had cushioned it, too. It could have been worse. I was shaken but unhurt.

I rose, brushed the pine needles from my clothes and listened.

The air was cool and fresh. River rapids roared nearby. Mountains towered everywhere I turned. Their slopes were covered with a mix of forests: the deep green of conifers forming irregular spots in the golden crimson of deciduous growth. The autumnal sun hung low and weak in the sky.

This was virginal wilderness in its original glory.

Right in front of me, the small rocky platform ended in a steep drop. I could make out a trail snaking through the tall withered grass. Which meant this was an inhabited area.

I opened the map. Aha! The cartography bot (I had indeed downloaded it earlier) seemed to work just fine, displaying the area relief in every detail complete with the map grid. The question mark was gone. If I followed the trail uphill it would take me to a cave next to which stood Master Jung's smithy.

How cool was that?

From overhead came a faint sound, like a suppressed sniffing.

Slowly I looked up at a low pine branch hanging above my head where a lynx lay skulking, ready to spring onto me.

Its eyes glowed yellow. Muscles bulged under its spotted coat.

I wouldn't have time to whip out my sword. A spell? That would be futile, too.

My hesitation was quite understandable:

Mountain Lynx. Level 18. A Pet.

Level wise, one blow from the beast's powerful paw was enough to send me back to my respawn point. The fact that this was a pet was encouraging though. The lynx had an owner, and the said owner was bound to be somewhere nearby.

The footsteps of two people echoed behind my back, soft and weightless.

"Sarah? Get down, now!" a girl's clear voice called. "What do you think you're doing, pestering newbs?"

The lynx obediently dropped to the ground and sashayed past me.

I turned round.

Two young Drow girls studied me shamelessly, smirking. Ashen gray skin, fair hair, reddish doe eyes. Complex tattoo designs ran from their temples to their cheekbones. Light armor hugged their graceful bodies. These two were lethal, however pretty.

Liori. Level 21. Warrior

Kimberly. Level 21. Warrior.

"Hi," I offered in a friendly voice.

"Hi," Kimberly dug her fingers into her pet's thick fluffy nape. The lynx kept a watchful eye on me. "We saw you drop from the cliff," she suppressed a smile. "Where are you going?"

"I'm looking for Master Jurg," I said.

Liori laughed. "You are, are you? In that case, join the queue. We've come to see him first."

I warmed up to their friendly attitude.

"You can come with us," Kimberly offered. "It's not very far."

She set the lynx free. The beast trotted along the trail, sniffing the air.

"So how do you find the mountains?" Kimberly asked. "Where are you from?"

"Agrion. I like it here. It's really nice."

We went on, talking. Judging by their behavior, the place was safe.

"Why are they called Azure Mountains?" I asked.

"Wait till it gets dark, then you'll see," Liori replied mysteriously.

The trail continued uphill, skirting larger rocks. Soon we entered a sparse woodland overgrown with pine trees, beyond which lay a steep weathered gorge.

The trail narrowed, growing steeper. A new bend took us into a large open area in front of a cave.

A squat log house calked with moss stood next to it, surrounded by equally sturdy outhouses.

A dwarf walked out of the smithy, wiping

his hands on a cloth and squinting in the bright sunlight. He gave us a good-natured grin as if he'd known the girls for quite a while.

"Morning, Master Jurg!"

"Morning, Liori! Hello there, Kimberly!"

He ignored me entirely as if I wasn't even there. What a character.

Never mind. I could wait. Sarah the lynx stretched out on the ground next to me, offering her body to the sun as she awaited her owner.

"What can I do for you today?"

"Kim would like you to make her a piece of jewelry," Liori replied. "Do you think you could do it? She has a sketch."

"Let's have a look," the dwarf opened the scroll. "Aha. This might need some very special stones. Have you got them?"

The girls exchanged disappointed glances. It didn't look as if they'd thought about it. Which meant they might receive a quest to go and procure some.

I was right. Kimberly tilted her head to one side, listening to the dwarf.

"Not a problem," she said confidently. "We'll be right back!"

The girls bade their goodbyes and left.

The dwarf turned round and returned to his smithy without as much as a glance in my direction.

Never mind. No one had said it was going to be easy.

* * *

I knocked on the door. Having received no answer, I pushed it and entered.

The room was hot. Master Jurg placed the girl's drawing into a carved box and turned to me. "What do you want?"

Dwarves are grumpy. They don't like strangers. Still, once you get to know them, you don't regret it.

"From what I heard, Master Jurg, you're an expert in your-"

He raised a quizzical eyebrow. "Cut the crap. Just spit it out."

That wasn't how NPCs were supposed to talk!

Having received no answer, Master Jurg lost all interest in me. He began rearranging some steel armor parts on his worktable.

Suddenly he cussed and snatched his hand away. He must have cut it on the edge of a steel breastplate that was lying there awaiting repair.

That wasn't possible! He could feel pain, just like myself!

I thought about the two corporate workers' conversation back in the dungeon. Had they said

"Jurgen"? It had sure sounded like it. Could they have fitted the whistleblowing technologist with a neuroimplant and locked him up in the game?

"So what do you have to say for yourself? Speak up. I have work to do."

"I have this piece of antique gear. Would you care to take a look?"

"Can't see why not. Where is it?" he seemed to have thawed a little. "What's your name? Have you traveled far?"

"I'm Alexatis of Agrion upon Warbler. Do you know it?"

"Never heard of it," he replied. "It's been a while since lowlanders showed up here."

This was weird. His name tag was identical to that of an NPC. My quest too had sent me to see "Master Jurg". Or was it just another sick experiment I wasn't supposed to know about?

I shouldn't overcomplicate it, anyway. This could have been a mannerism the game designers endowed him with, making him snatch his hand away every time he cut it.

"Here," I unsheathed the sword and laid it on his worktop.

"A cargonite alloy!" he murmured in surprise, having barely looked at it. "Antique indeed. How did you manage to lay your hands on it?"

"I got it in a dungeon not far from Agrion."

"What, on your own?"

I nodded.

"Bullshit," he cast me a disapproving look. "You're not up to those kinds of feats yet. The secret of the alloy is long lost. The items can't be evaluated in gold. There might be some ancient stashes left but they're all guarded by the Founder Gods' servants: the fire-spitting golems."

"No golems in there. It was a cave like any other."

"Then you must have followed in somebody else's tracks," he added grudgingly.

"I wanted to ask you if you had some runes for me. Do you think you could repair the sword? To improve its Durability and Damage?"

"You're not worthy of it!" he snapped, glaring at me. "You're too weak to own a fine weapon like this!"

Here we go again. What about my quest? Logically, he was obliged to tell me about the sword and ask me if I could procure more cargonite items. Instead, he lost all interest in me again.

Your Reputation with Master Jurg has suffered.

Current Reputation status: Mistrust

What a shame. How on earth had cargonite

items ended up in that cave, anyway? Probably, through water currents. I remembered the frozen waves of ice in the cave. Could it have been an old spring?

This uncooperative and paranoid NPC threatened to sabotage my two quests. Just when I was desperate for some positive Reputation with the dwarves, too. But how was I supposed to rectify the situation?

Could I try and trade with him, maybe? Wonder if some Spectral Dust could pique his interest?

I picked up my sword and resheathed it. "You don't happen to have anything for sale, by any chance?"

"I might," he replied non-committedly.

A vending interface opened in my mental view. Good. I checked the items available to me.

Two plain spiked maces, fifty gold each! A rusty dagger, a hundred!

He was something, really. If it went on like that, I wasn't going to do much trade, that's for sure. I had to do something ASAP otherwise I could forget jewels. I'd hate to go back to Dimian empty-handed.

Should I try and offer him some chitin for a start? I hadn't noticed any insects here yet: the mountain climate must have been too cold for them. Would he be interested in an unusual crafting material like that?

I dragged one of the Small Chitin Plates into the interface window.

A penny a dozen? He had to be kidding me!

I tried to offer him a Stinger from a wasp. It changed nothing. Same price.

Never mind. I wasn't going to sell them to him, anyway. I might need them myself for arrowheads. Let's try it again.

I reached into my inventory and produced some of the mantises' loot.

At the sight of a black scaly shell Master Jurg turned pale. "Where did you get this from?"

"I won it in battle."

"Don't you lie to me!" his eyes glinted. "You can't have killed a hydra! You wouldn't have been able to get anywhere near the Toxic Moors!"

"Sorry, Master, but I'm telling you the truth. This isn't a hydra's skin. This is the shell of an insect I killed in battle."

"Let me have a look at it."

"Help yourself."

He fingered the scales, studying their overlapping design, and even tried to pull a few off, testing them every way he could. With a sigh, he returned the shell to me.

"You're right. This isn't from a hydra. But it looks almost identical. It's probably just as good. How much of it can an insect drop?"

"What you've just seen, Master."

"Don't *master* me! I might have a proposition to make to you."

Your Reputation with Master Jurg has improved.

Current Reputation status: Interest

Your reputation with the Azure Mountain Dwarves had improved.

Current Reputation status: Indifference

"I want you to listen closely," he said. "I have an order I can't finish. It's very important. Do you think you could bring me ten skins like this one?"

"This isn't a skin. This is-"

"Shut up. I'm not interested. A skin, a shell, a scale — I don't give a shit what you call it as long as it works. Think you can do it? I'll make it worth your while. I'll build you a set of armor like you've never seen before! It'll make you stronger and protect you from the enemy. *And* it'll last forever!"

New quest alert: An Unfinished Job

Bring Master Jurg 10 Shells of Black Praying Mantises

Deadline: 48 hrs.

Optional: Bring Master Jurg 10 more Shells of Black Praying Mantises so he can make you a new set of armor.

Deadline: none

Reward I: a set of light scaly armor made by a Master craftsman.

Reward II: your Reputation with both Master Jurg and the Azure Mountain Dwarves will improve considerably.

Unhesitantly, I accepted the quest. I knew of a perfect place to farm mantises. Also, if my Reputation improved, he just might tell me more about my sword.

Besides, I was curious about this new set or armor he'd just promised me.

"Agreed," I said. "I can give you four shells now so that you can start your work. The rest I'll bring the day after tomorrow."

"Can't you do it sooner?"

It was amazing how his attitude had changed.

"Sorry, but I can't. I have an urgent assignment from a vendor. He asked me if I could swap some Spectral Dust for jewels for him. He even gave me a list. Maybe you could direct me to the nearest dwarven settlement, that way I don't need to lose time looking for it?"

"I can. But it's not a settlement you need.

They won't let a stranger in, anyway. They have special trading posts. One is just round the Twin Watch Ravine. You've got long legs so you should get there in two hours tops. I'm gonna mark the route on your map now."

"Thanks."

"Make sure you come back soon! And bring me the remaining shells. Go now, chop chop!" he unceremoniously pushed me toward the door. "Go and get your jewels before it gets dark! You'll see two statues on your way: a dwarf and a Dark Elf. The ravine is just past them. I'll send them word to let them know you're coming."

* * *

Autumnal nightfall comes early in the mountains.

I ran along the trail, my legs already shaking with fatigue. Night was fast approaching. I feared I might not be able to make it before darkness fell.

I just didn't care about the surrounding vistas anymore. They slid past without touching my heart. The 100% authenticity levels forced all my attention to the road underfoot to make sure I didn't stumble or break my neck.

By the time I got to the gorge, it was almost dark. I stopped to catch my breath. Two rocky statues guarded the entrance: one tall, the other squat. Just as Master Jurg had told me.

Glimpses of light flickered at a distance. Torches?

One last push. Let's do it!

To my relief, the gorge turned out to be quite shallow. Soon I saw a brightly lit clearing crowded with stalls and surrounded with what looked like one-story warehouses. The square around the bonfire in the middle was empty. The stalls were unmanned. The dwarves must have already left to round their day off with some quality drinking.

I ran up closer, then stopped, looking around myself. They should have guards posted here, surely?

My interface pinged with an incoming message. In the dark, the PM window glowed especially bright. Who was that now?

I opened the message.

Alexatis, I'm back online. I really have to see you. We need to talk.

Enea

I hurried to type a brief reply,

Not now. I'm out on a quest. I'll PM you as soon as I'm back.

A door creaked. Two dwarves walked out of a building. They saw me; still, neither of them looked worried. Unhurriedly they walked toward me.

"You Alexatis?"

"That's right!"

"Jurg told us about you," one of the two chuckled. "You may have long legs but you can't run fast, that's for sure. You're late."

"What do you want me to do? Wait till next morning?"

"Depends on what you've got. What are you selling?"

"Spectral Dust," I said. "I'll swap it for some jewels from this list."

The dwarves exchanged glances. "It's not jewels we're missing," one of them glanced over the list. "Question is, do you have enough Dust?"

They were quick, weren't they? I hadn't even had the chance to check out prices yet. Let's just hope they weren't taking me for a ride.

I pulled out one of Dimian's three carved boxes. I didn't want to start big. "How about this?"

They craned their necks for a look. In combination with their short stocky frames, it gave the impression that they were highly agitated. Was Spectral Dust so valuable here?

"Come with me," one of them boomed. "I

need to open the shop."

'No, you'd better come with *me*," the other one protested.

Both clenched their fists, frowning, about to go for each other's beards.

"Gentlemen, please," I said. "No good raising your voices. Others might hear you. Is that what you want?"

It worked.

"Very well," the smaller one admitted his defeat. "Today is your turn. But next time I'm buying up all of his stock!"

"Deal. Come on, Alexatis. My name's Mychior, by the way. He is Azamaul."

Two name tags materialized over their heads, glowing in the dark.

Your reputation with the dwarves of the Twin Watch Ravine has improved!

Current Reputation status: Interest

"Do you think you could bring more Spectral Dust?" Azamaul asked, trotting after me.

"I could," I replied confidently. I still had two more boxes that the other one didn't know about. And it looked like I might get rid of them tonight, too.

The log house was hot like a furnace inside. A burning fireplace in the corner belched flames. Massive squat dwarven furniture cast long shadows across the floor.

The two offered me a seat at a sturdy table. Mychior scurried into a backroom, then returned dragging a large bag behind him. Between Azamaul and himself, they hauled it onto the table.

"Here," Mychior said. "Are you going to count the stones?"

I stopped my jaw from dropping just in time. "Did you check it against the list?" I asked gravely.

"Sure. Jurg sent us a messenger pigeon to let us know you were coming."

I focused my stare on the bag.

A Bagful of Jewels. Capacity, 250. Weight, 55 lbs. Takes 1 inventory slot if unopened.

Warning! Once opened, the contents of the bag will require 250 inventory slots.

I just hoped they hadn't stuffed it with bricks. I couldn't even open and check it. My inventory was way too small to accommodate everything.

"Well, if you did, then it should be all right," I placed the box of Dust on the table, trying to prevent my hands from shaking. Fifty-five pounds of jewels for a couple handfuls of

Spectral Dust! No one would believe me!

In one smooth motion, Mychior secreted the box within his garb. "Would you like to stay for the night?"

"Oh no, I can't. I have to get back."

"When can we expect you next?"

"In a few days. I'll have to see Master Jurg first, then I'll come here. Question: how much Dust would you like to buy?"

"Did you hear that?" Azamaul shook a finger at Mychior. "It's my turn now! Whatever you can bring, we'll buy it."

"You sure you have enough jewels?"

"Plenty," Mychior assured me. "If push comes to shove, we can always pay you in gold. Or some rare metals. I'm not going to lie to you: we need Dust to make some truly amazing alloys. So we're a bit desperate. We'll buy it in bulk, whatever you can bring."

* * *

The teleport popped again. Reality began spinning, twisting itself into another colorful spiral.

Dimian's back yard was dark. The windows of his house were brightly lit, though. He was wide awake. I could see him pacing the room, restless with worry.

I knocked on the door.

Heavy footsteps resounded from within. The door bolt clanged. The hinges creaked.

"Alexatis! You're back! Glory be to the Gods of Light! Come on, tell me!"

"Mind if I come in?"

"Of course! Sorry! Come in, please! Are you hungry?"

He was doing his best to behave like a hospitable host but I could see he was all nerves, despite his being an NPC.

"Don't bother, I'll eat at the inn," I said, watching his clumsy attempts to throw together a meal. "Well, it's all sorted! I've been to the Azure Mountains. I've done some trade with the dwarves and made an agreement to come back."

"Have you got the jewels?"

"Here," I pulled the heavy bag out of my inventory and hauled it onto the table. I couldn't wait to see what was inside, either.

I opened it.

You should have seen it. Rough jewels, large and colorful, tumbled onto the table, glittering in the candlelight and scattering all over the floor.

Dimian rushed to pick them up, delirious. The game programmers had done a great job modeling a greedy vendor's behavior.

Having collected them all, he walked

around the table several times in disbelief, unable to drag his gaze away from the huge pile of jewels.

"Do they have more?" his Adam's apple twitched as he gulped.

"Keep your hair on. They do. They're waiting for us."

"How much Spectral Dust do they want?"

"As much as we can bring. They'll take it all."

For a moment, I thought he might faint. He didn't. On the contrary, he stood tall and proud, trying to bring his emotions under control. "Can we take a horse?"

"Easy. I've found a good landing site. Perfectly flat and close to the road. No cliffs or trees around."

"Any robbers?"

"That I couldn't tell you. It was dark when I went to see the dwarves. They won't talk, if that's what you mean."

Dimian forced his eyes away from the jewels. "You've done me a great service, Alexatis! Really!"

He walked over to a wrought iron chest and opened a giant padlock. Grunting with the effort, he lifted the lid. "Here, take it," he handed me a hefty pouch.

You've received 3,000 gold!
Trade Route: Quest completed!

Your Reputation with Dimian has improved!
Current Reputation status: Selfless Friendship

Your Reputation with the citizens of Agrion has improved!
Current Reputation status: Wary Curiosity

You've received a new level!
You have new ability and main characteristic points available!

"Alexatis, I have to get ready for the trip. I might need a couple of days. Please stay in touch."

New quest alert: Trading Mission
Quest type: Rare
In two days' time, come to see Dimian and accompany him to the dwarves' trade post.
Reward: varies. ???? gold, depending on Dimian's profits.

Warning! Completing this quest may considerably affect your Reputation with the Merchants Guild.

Right. What had my Reputation with the Merchants Guild got to do with it? I wasn't a vendor, was I? I really should check the in-game forums about this. Also, my reward: had it been adequate? Three grand is a king's ransom for a newb. But was it on a par with the job?

I accepted the quest. Dimian's face cleared. He stood up straight. "Where are you going to stay the night? I have a spare room."

"It's all right. I'll go to the inn. I don't want to inconvenience you."

"Just please don't disappear!"

"Don't worry, I won't. I need some rest and a good night's sleep. I might do some sightseeing while I'm in town."

"Very well, then. I suggest you go to the Golden Carp. The owner is a relative of mine. I'll send him word in a minute."

He didn't want to lose me from sight, did he? Never mind. It was his problem. I still had Jurg's quest to complete. I already had one teleport scroll; now I could afford to buy another one. I might indeed stay at the Golden Carp, grab a couple of hours of sleep and be back at the ruins by dawn. I had my mantises to farm!

* * *

I checked into the inn (which, to be fair to

Dimian, was indeed quite decent), had a nice big meal and walked upstairs to my room. I didn't go to bed, though. I still had some important business to attend to. The thing was, I didn't want to buy another teleport scroll. It was a rare and expensive commodity. I didn't want people to start talking behind my back.

I sat down at the table and reached into my inventory for the sorcerer's parchments and writing tools. I spread one of the scrolls on the table and gave it a closer look. It seemed quite ordinary.

Time to test my unique class abilities.

If I could intercept spells by lip-reading them, could I copy a scroll too?

I pored over each character. It didn't take me long: the spell was quite short. I didn't understand the words written in the ancient tongue of the Founder Gods. Still, it just might work — provided my current level was up to it.

Let's wait and see.

I meticulously copied every stroke and flourish, then double-checked it. It looked more or less identical, apart from my poor calligraphy skills.

Now, the coordinates.

I opened up my map and looked for the clearing where I used to practice, then entered its coordinates into the magic item I was creating.

We were all set!

I packed my stuff and left the room door locked from the inside.

I was anxious. My fingertips began to tingle. This was a good sign. I touched the coordinates.

Nothing happened.

What a crying shame. I perched myself on the edge of the bed and got thinking, staring at the scroll I'd just made. What was the difference? Why would one scroll work, crumbling to dust on activation, and another one wouldn't?

I decided to look for the answers at the in-game forum. It took me quite some time to peruse it. Apparently, all spell scrolls were produced by scribes who then took them to the Wizards Guild.

For what, exactly?

Similarly, spell scrolls were available either from scribes themselves or from the Wizards Guild shops.

I dug some more,

I've chosen the profession of Scribe. But whenever I try to copy a scroll, they don't work. Any ideas?

Don't be such a noob! Just take your scribbles to the Wizards Guild and they'll charge them for you.

Thanks for the tip! Turned out it wasn't cheap! But at least they work now.

So that's what it was, then!

Teleportation spells were only available to wizards of at least level 30. I was level 12.

Wouldn't it be easier to just hike to the nut grove?

No way. I was a Neuro. I had all those unique abilities begging to be learned and used.

My current level didn't allow me to either cast or intercept a Teleportation spell. Still, anyone could use a scroll regardless of his or her level. All I had to do was charge the scroll using mental energy.

I opened another forum search and entered *"how to charge a magic scroll".*

Every city branch of the Wizards Guild has a source of power a wizard can use to charge scrolls, charms and other items requiring an independent energy supply.

Can't we do it ourselves?

You can, provided you have enough mana. In order to charge an item, you need to clench it in your hand. The process will begin automatically. If you run out of mana before the item is charged, you've done it for nothing. Personally, I always keep a few vials at hand to boost mana regeneration times.

Teleport scrolls:
Small range (within direct line of vision): 300 pt. Mental Energy
Medium range: 1,000 pt. Mental Energy
Long range: 5,000 pt. Mental Energy
Extra-long range (intercontinental travel): 10,000 pt. Mental Energy

Another tip for you guys: you can also charge scrolls as a group. But if one of you loses concentration or runs out of mana, you can forget it.

Now the picture was pretty clear, with one exception. What was the required mana transfer rate?

I might have to find that out by trial and error. At the moment, my Intellect was at 12 which meant I had 120 pt. mana with regeneration times 4.34 pt. per sec (Spirit divided by 2 plus the 0.84 pt. from Power of Reason, Synergy and Self-Control with the 3 ability points I'd already invested in it).

Enough calculations. Time to try it out. I wasn't risking a lot: in the worst-case scenario, the scroll would fail to charge, that's all.

I sat on a chair, rolled the scroll up and closed my left hand tight around it.

The familiar tingling sensation was back. My mental energy bar quivered and began to plummet. When it was 1/3 down, its rapid fall began to slow up until it finally stopped completely, hovering at 15% without going up or down.

Excellent. My mana regeneration rate seemed to be adequate. Still, I had another five minutes of mana pumping.

At first, it went very well. Then my head began to spin. After a minute, my Physical Energy bar began to shrink slowly but surely. Soon I felt exhausted. Then it went from bad to worse: after two minutes, my Life bar started sagging. HP began to dwindle, moving toward the critical 77% of my pain threshold.

My head began to ache. Then my muscles. Still, I only had 30 seconds left.

I could do it. Not for the sake of the fifty gold, you understand, but simply to test my own limits.

The muscle pain grew, turning into spasms. My teeth throbbed. I couldn't think straight.

Twenty seconds.

Ten.

You've created a magic item: a Medium-Range Teleportation Scroll!

All three indicators soared back up. I slumped into the chair, feeling absolutely broken. It felt like I'd been crushed by a sledge hammer.

This had been an extreme and scary experience. I didn't envy wizards who had to charge up to fifty scrolls a day. Then again, they didn't have neuroimplants.

Slowly I was coming round, trying to take stock of what had just happened. What could I compare the process of creating a magic item with?

In my case, I could liken it to an unequal combat, fast and brutal, that burned one's strength, life and mana.

All the battles I'd ever been in had been a walk in the park compared to this exhausting and acute experience.

I needed to level up ASAP. I had my Mysterious Sword to sort out. I also needed to complete the quest Master Jurg had issued me. I could sure use the armor he'd promised me!

I rose and paced the room, grabbed a drink of water, then sat back at the table and laid out more blank scrolls. I took one and began copying a new teleportation scroll.

No, I wasn't a masochist. I'd just realized

that the proximity of the Altar of Chaos meant an almost instant Mental Energy regeneration. There, I could safely charge magic items.

Having filled in five more scrolls, I glanced at the clock. 3 a.m. The next few days promised to be very busy. I'd have to make do with two hours of sleep. I still had to get some mantis shells, give them to Master Jurg and pay another visit to the dwarves before Dimian could find more Spectral Dust.

* * *

It was 5.30 a.m. when I finally got to the ruins.

I decided against setting up the tent. I had plenty of time to do so. The local mobs had two-hour respawn times. I had to do some farming first.

I left the cover of the nut grove feeling quite optimistic.

Three hornets hovered nearby. Two locusts lay low in the tall grass. The ruins appeared unchanged.

Funny I hadn't seen any wasps yet. Was it because of my new level? Had they become too insignificant for me?

This area must have been 100% adaptive, which wasn't common for starting locations. Normally, mobs couldn't grow more than a few levels so if you wanted to continue leveling, you had to move on to less explored parts of the world.

As I thus pondered, I killed the hornets without much difficulty and headed for the ruins. I already had a nice strong rope stashed away in my inventory. I had to climb down and try to charge the scrolls standing next to the Altar of Chaos.

The three Black Mantises had to appear at any moment. I ignored the locusts, giving their aggro zone a wide berth.

Nothing happened. I waited some more. The dog rose bushes didn't move. The morning breeze was the only thing that stirred its foliage.

Where were they?

I took another step, approaching the roses, and cast a close look around me.

The top floor of the ruins looked different now, its once-gray stonework a rusty red. I couldn't quite see what it was. It could be that the moss covering it had faded in the sun. Or...

The wall shifted. I startled. A disgusting creature clung to the wall. It arched its body, twitching its spindly legs in the air.

A Giant Venomous Millipede
Level 12
Life, 90/90

The ground heaved underfoot. A brown pincer emerged from below, dropping dry clumps of earth.

A Mole Cricket
Level 12
Life, 90/90

The bushes toppled, uprooted. A scary-looking mob escaped its underground lair and charged at me. Still, the week's worth of training had served me well. I promptly dodged the cricket's attack, then cast Weakness over it. My Mysterious Sword sliced deep through its chitinous armor, aiming for the only vulnerable spot where its massive pincer connected to its leg.

The cricket screeched. I leaped aside, casting Ice over the millipede. It stopped moving, frozen solid to the stonework. My arsenal of combat spells may have been small but I'd practiced it to knee-jerk perfection.

As the injured cricket span in place, I loosed off two ice arrows at it, gulped down a vial of mana and even managed to hurl a fireball at the motionless millipede. As I'd perused the forums last night, I'd learned that the contrast of two opposing elements (like Fire and Ice) could lead to some interesting effects causing additional damage.

I was eternally grateful to the wizard who'd shared that bit of intel. The millipede disintegrated, dropping fragments of chitin. I attacked it again with a powerful coup de grace (which I'd learned by replaying the video of the paladin's solo).

You've received a new level!

I was so upset I didn't even bother to check the loot. I entered the ruins through the collapsed doorway and slumped onto a crate, deep in thought.

The Black Mantises were gone! This was one hell of a disappointment. I should have realized that the location was adaptive. It must have had something to do with the dungeon which apparently was one of the Corporation workers' entrance points. Unwilling to expose the fact to the players, they must have placed both the ruins and the dungeon entrance deep in the heart of a difficult location with randomized mobs high enough in levels to discourage any stray adventure seekers.

What a bummer. With my level 13, I had no chance of fighting more mantises.

Never mind. Where else I could find them?

I opened the Wiki. As it turned out,

venomous Black Mantises were very rare. Their natural habitat was the Toxic Moors in the south — just like the hydras mentioned by Master Jurg.

It looked like my quest had just fallen through.

Oh no. I didn't want to even think about it. I had to get a grip.

I tried to pull myself together. Soon I was able to think straight again.

It looked like I'd found a solution.

If the location was adaptive, all I had to do was bring another player here whose levels were low enough. A level 7 or 8 player would trigger the scripts I needed, tricking the system into generating more black mantises.

Okay, but a player like that was bound to start asking questions, wondering why I wanted to collect his loot and what made it so valuable. I could always try to bribe them into silence, of course, but that was too iffy. Besides, I didn't have much time.

Who did I trust enough to share my secret with?

Enea! She was back, wasn't she?

I opened my friend list. She was online, excellent! We could meet up in a small village nearby, provided she agreed to help me.

I typed a quick message,

Hi. I'm back. Need your help. Can we talk?

She replied almost straight away,

Absolutely.

What level are you now?

9. Same as I was before. What difference does that make?

I'll explain when I see you.

You want us to meet? Where?

The village of Warblerford. There's an inn there, right next to the ford across the River Warbler. When can you come?

I'm not far from there now.

Excellent. I'm on my way.

See ya.

CHAPTER SEVEN

THE VILLAGE OF WARBLERFORD IN THE VICINITY OF AGRION CITY

IT TOOK ME about twenty minutes to get to Warblerford.

The small village was bustling with life. It boasted the only fording place on the River Warbler for miles. Several guards were posted there, next to some stacks of logs and a small impromptu market. It looked like they were going to build a bridge there.

The tavern was packed with players as well as NPCs. All the tables were taken. Enea waited by the bar, casting frequent glances at the door.

Today she looked sort of... different? Her blonde hair was done up into two funny pigtails which made her look like a baby squirrel about to take on the world.

She waved her hand to me, then whispered something to the landlord who leaned toward her, listening. He nodded his understanding and stepped aside.

I elbowed my way through the crowd of angry warriors demanding separate tables for themselves — apparently, in order to celebrate a successful instance completion. All of them sported the logo of the Raven clan on their armor.

"Hi," I said to Enea. "You look cool."

"Thanks. It's just to put me in the mood. I'm so fed up with looking serious. This is my *'I don't give a damn'* hair."

She took me by the hand and led me into a small inconspicuous passage behind the bar.

Voices merged into the background. We entered a spacious room whose modern café-like interior clashed with the medieval atmosphere. Soft music was playing. Most of the tables were empty, apart from one taken by two level 30 wizards talking unhurriedly over their meal.

I pulled a chair out for her.

"Aren't you mad at me?" Enea asked, looking embarrassed.

"No," I said honestly.

"Why not?" her gaze focused, her eyes locking with mine, inquiring and slightly guilty.

"You can't be responsible for another

person's actions," I blurted out. The whole Christa experience was still fresh and smarting. I wasn't seeking Enea's sympathy, oh no. It had simply given me a new prospective, that's all.

"Alex, that was my *father*! He treated you like trash!"

"That's all right. I can live with that. D'you wanna talk about him?"

"Not really," she said. "I need to talk about *me*."

"Can I order you something?"

"No, thanks. I've already eaten," a tear glistened in the corner of her eye.

"Would you like an ice-cream?"

She nodded, wiping her eyes inconspicuously.

They brought in our order. I wasn't hungry. I had too many things to do. Still, I could see she needed to get it off her chest. The mantises could wait.

"The reason why he was so mad was because I'd escaped from home," she said. "I needed some space."

"Why here? I thought you weren't into computer games?"

"I'm not. I'm a real-world girl," she cast me a cheerless smile. "That's exactly why I wanted to try it. I needed to test myself. I wanted to start from scratch, to try something I had no idea how to do. Without daddy's bank account to bail me out, if you know what I mean. I needed to know if I was worth anything at all."

"And?"

"Honestly, I didn't like it that much at first. I would have probably spent some more time by that pond and just logged out for good. But then it got better," she took a bite of her ice-cream. "It tastes really good!"

"D'you think you're gonna stay?"

"I will. I've had a falling-out with Dad. It's about time I take a hiatus from him. Our relationship is too much like business. You know his favorite expression? *'Big business demands big sacrifices'.* Can you imagine he wanted to take it out on you in real life? I told him to forget it. I said, if he didn't stop controlling my every move I'd leave him. Who does he think I am? I'm almost twenty-five, for crying out loud! He treats me like I'm a stupid little girl: *'don't touch this, don't go there, my business is our livelihood'*, that sort of thing. As if people aren't making money playing games! You really not angry with him?"

"I'm not. Just forget it. I need your help."

She perked up. "No way! Tell me."

I gave her a summary of the last few days.

She eyes lit up. "Can I have a look at your contract, please?"

I laughed. "NPCs don't issue contracts! It's

just a quest I received from Dimian. You can have a look if you want," I forwarded her a screenshot.

She frowned, poring over it. "It's worded all wrong," she finally concluded. "But it's all right. I know how to fix it. Just make sure you don't give him the coordinates!" her words betrayed steely business acumen at the first mention of money. She may have been a newb wizard but she definitely wasn't new to money making. I wouldn't want to close any deals with her. The girl was a financial shark in the making.

"How can I *not* give him the coordinates?" I asked, curious about her train of thought.

She gave me a cute smile. "According to the quest, you're taking on the obligation to 'explore the route'. It says nothing about the coordinates becoming his property."

"But that's not fair, is it? He counts on my giving them to him."

"On the contrary, it's great! When the guild finds out about his new business, they'll destroy him. They might even torture the coordinates out of him. And that way he's none the wiser! I'm pretty sure I can explain this to him."

"So how is he going to trade with the dwarves, then?"

"You two are going to do it together! I'll sort out the paperwork. Dimian will buy teleport scrolls from you. You'll be entering the coordinates into them yourself, then inviting him to join your group for an agreed percentage."

She didn't waste time, did she?

"You can't make deals with NPCs," I said. "I don't think the admins will even allow it. This is a quest. It has certain rules..."

"We should try," she insisted. "Otherwise all you might get is a few more handfuls of gold, and even that at his discretion. You have any idea what kind of profits he might be looking at?"

I shrugged. I wasn't born yesterday but math had never been my forte.

"Alexatis, I could try and sort it all out for you if you let me. Can we go see Dimian together?"

"And what if he refuses to change the quest's rules? Like, totally?"

"Then you should refuse to help him. Make him sweat for a day or two. You think he can take it?"

"Enea, he's a *toon*! He's part of a computer program!"

"We'll see."

I suppressed a smile. "All right. Let's go and see him. Actually, this wasn't why I wanted to see you."

"Really?" she leaned forward, curious.

"I have another iron in the fire. And I can't do it without your help, either."

I told her about the mantises.

"Wait," she looked me in the eye, breathless, "does that mean we're together now?" She paused, embarrassed. "I mean, we're *leveling* together?"

"We are. But not as a group. Not yet. Also, you won't do much leveling today, I'm afraid. Loot is more important. I'll make it up to you, I promise. Let me explain. The location is adaptive. The player's own level determines the levels of the mobs it generates."

"I see. If I enter the clearing, I'll see wasps and mantises. And if you do the same, you'll have to fight hornets, mole crickets and other nasties."

"Exactly. All you need to do is trigger the mob generator. Whatever you do, don't touch them. Otherwise you might make another level yourself and that's the end of it. Then I'll have to find somebody else to do it, someone we don't even know. And I really don't look forward to doing that."

"So what are we waiting for?" she hurried to finish her ice-cream. "We can talk as we walk."

* * *

It was almost midday already. As previously agreed, Enea entered the location first. I had a very vague idea of where the adaptive area began: there were no prompts or apps to download, nothing. Which was why we set up camp deep in the woods. I stayed by the tent, using the chat to monitor her progress.

"I can see a dragonfly. Is that okay?"

"Excellent," I drove the last peg into the ground and climbed inside the tent. Once there, I reconfigured my interface, allowing Enea to move her respawn point to the tent.

"Alex, what am I supposed to do now?"

"Just be quiet. I'm coming!"

I had no idea how the game engine would react to my arrival. I was a bit worried it might trigger the generation of the millipede and other monsters. But it seemed okay. The wasps and the hornet were already there, their name tags gray. Which meant I received no XP for smoking them, seeing as their levels were not up to mine.

It looked like my plan had worked after all.

I shot them all down with Ice Arrows and hurried over to the ruins. Time was at a premium.

The dog rose bushes stirred.

A Venomous Black Praying Mantis. Level, 8
A Venomous Black Praying Mantis. Level, 8
A Venomous Black Praying Mantis. Level, 8

Glory be to the Gods of Light! I felt better

already. It looked like I might complete the quest, provided I acted fast.

It took me less than a minute to smoke them all. I picked up their shells and hurried back to Enea who was watching my escapades from the safety of the nut grove.

"I have an idea!" she pointed at a tall lone pine tree. "I want you to climb it and watch."

"Why?"

"To save you a two-hour wait!" she seemed to be quick on the uptake. "What's gonna happen to the mobs' bodies if I leave the location?"

"They'll disappear."

"Exactly! So if I re-enter the location, they'll be obliged to regenerate again, right?"

"Of course! Which means we won't have to wait till they respawn! What a clever girl!"

I climbed the tree as high as I could. From there, I could see the clearing and the wasps' bodies lying in the trampled grass.

Enea retreated toward the woods. Yes! The wasps' bodies blinked and disappeared.

"Enea, could you please mark the place where the location ends? Just break off a branch and stick it in the ground. Or whatever."

"Got it. There's a tree stump here and a massive dry root lying on the ground. I've marked it down on the map. Here, I'm sending it to you. Would you like me to wait a bit?"

"No," I said, watching the clearing closely. "You can go back in now."

The moment she stepped over the invisible boundary, the wasps reappeared. "Excellent! Don't move! I'm coming!"

* * *

I kept farming mantises almost until dark.

Enea kept me on my toes. She didn't seem to enjoy lounging around. As I worked, we used the voice chat to communicate. I told her about the teleport scrolls and shared some tips I'd gleaned from the forums. During brief intervals in the farming process, I shared two new spells with her, the Fireball (her current level allowed her to copy it to her book of spells) and the Wall of Flames.

"Enough for today!" I announced when the sun began to dip below the horizon.

"How many?" Enea asked who'd spent the last few hours doing Fireball target practice.

"Twenty-seven mantis shells!"

"Oh wow! You've got enough and then some! What now?"

"I'm going to go down to the dungeon and charge the scrolls. Then I'll port to see Master Jurg."

"Can I come with you? Please!"

"Absolutely. Aren't you afraid of teleporting?"

"No idea. I've never done it before."

Now Enea was impatience itself. I found her cheerful spontaneity quite infectious. She was a happy soul, delighted at the sight of many things that I had long been taking for granted.

Darkness descended quickly. We walked over to the ruins. I lit up two torches, then tied a rope to a rusty steel lamp mounted on a wall.

"Can I climb first?"

"No, you can't. You aren't going in there. Wait for me here. I won't be long."

"Please don't."

This time the dungeon harbored no nasty surprises. The reason why I hadn't allowed Enea to come with me was because I was afraid that charging up the scrolls might be a problem. I didn't want her to watch my Life and Strength dwindle to near nothing. That might trigger a new round of questions I wouldn't be able to answer without disclosing the existence of the neuroimplant.

The Altar of Chaos hadn't let me down. The process of mana regeneration took split seconds here. After only a few minutes, all the scrolls were already charged up.

I climbed back up the rope, untied it and stashed it away. "Are you ready?"

She nodded.

"Give me your hand. Hold on tight!"

The teleport scroll crumbled to dust.

* * *

Darkness enveloped us. The snow-covered summits around us were edged with a cold emerald-blue glow, heralding the Moon's imminent arrival.

A skyful of stars loomed overhead.

Enea tilted her head up and froze breathless, absorbing the scenery. I too stood quite smitten. This is why they were called the Azure Mountains!

The air was fresh, cold and clear.

Rapids roared nearby. It felt as if we were alone in the whole universe.

Night had swallowed the mountain slopes, the aura etching their outlines growing ever brighter and more intense until it began to opalesce.

"That's something you don't see in town," Enea mouthed. "All you have there are commercial modules. Never the stars..." she squeezed my hand.

The howling of many wolves sliced through the silence, echoing off the slopes. It sounded as if several packs were stealing up on us from every direction.

"Do we have far to walk?"

"Not at all."

"I can't see very much," she sounded insecure.

"It's not a problem. I have Twilight Vision now, don't forget. It's available from level 12. Don't let go of my hand. There should be a trail here somewhere."

"How about the wolves?"

"They're probably too far away. But you should watch out anyway, just in case."

We walked in pitch darkness edged with the azure aura. Nothing was aggroing us: I must have been right in saying there were no mobs nearby. Still, the very silence gave you goosebumps, especially when disturbed by a distant growl or the snapping of a twig.

Eventually, the trail turned. The roaring of the rapids gradually died away. It was marginally lighter here. Finally, we saw the welcoming twinkle of light in Master Jurg's windows.

"Whew," Enea stopped to catch her breath. "Is it so beautiful everywhere here?"

"*Here?* In the virtual world, you mean?"

"Yeah. In the Crystal Sphere."

"Oh, yes. I haven't been everywhere yet, though. But it must be equally awesome everywhere you go."

"I can't believe it. I don't think I'll be able to sleep tonight. Who would have thought that a bunch of holograms and tactile sensors could be so believable! Can you feel the difference in temperature? It's impressive!"

"It's fall in the mountains, what do you want? You'd better get used to it. No comfy aircon controls here. It's supposed to be realistic. Having said that, there's always the environment generator."

"Oh, no," she said, shrugging off the chill. "This is a unique experience."

"Mind if I ask you? How come you don't have any gaming experience? Didn't you play at all when you were little?"

"I did. I played Economy Strategies since I was three. That's when they decided I was big enough to study business."

Ouch. That was tough. Those bastards had stripped the girl of her childhood. Then again, who was I to judge? What if this Crystal Sphere gig was only a hiatus for her, a temporary break from a predictable lifelong routine?

"Come on now, let's get to Master Jurg's before he goes to bed," I said. "I don't feel like spending another night in the tent."

Soon the smithy loomed out of the darkness, surrounded by the squat outhouses. The lamp over its front door swayed in the growing wind.

Master Jurg was still awake. I glimpsed his outline through the window.

I knocked confidently. Footsteps approached the door; the bolt rattled.

"Alexatis! Come in! I didn't know what to think! You're not alone, I see."

"Hi, I'm Enea. I'm traveling with him."

"Well then, welcome, the two of you!" he let us both in, locked the door behind us, then swung toward me. "Have you got it?"

"Well, what do you think? Of course I do! I've got more than we originally agreed on."

"Excellent!" he said. "Enea, come in here."

He pushed a door open and walked in. We followed. "This is our guest room. Make yourself comfortable. I need to talk to your boyfriend first. He'll be with you soon enough."

Enea and I exchanged glances. She struggled to suppress a smile, which looked utterly cute. Even Master Jurg couldn't take his eyes off her.

"Or whatever," he finally boomed, looking embarrassed. "This is the room, anyway. Alexatis, drop your stuff in here but be quick. I'll be outside waiting for you."

He closed the door behind himself.

Enea giggled. "*My boyfriend*! I love it! And what if he's right?" he looked me in the eye but immediately turned away. "I'm sorry," she said, her voice filled with sadness. "This dwarf is so funny. I need to log out now."

"I'm gonna stay. I still have this quest to complete. See you in the morning?"

She nodded. "I might be back about nine a.m. Or even before that. Remember what you promised?"

"Sure. You've got some leveling to do, lady. We'll try to rush you to level 15 if we can. At least."

She nodded, then disappeared. This time she didn't leave her avatar behind. So lifelike only a moment ago, she just vanished into thin air as if she'd never existed.

I waited for a while, then walked out of the room to close the quest.

* * *

Master Jurg was in the smithy, waiting for me.

I located him by the constant ringing of his hammer. He was working a red-hot strip of steel, flattening its edges with fast heavy strokes.

"Here, Master," I said, laying my day's loot on the table. "Twenty-seven shells."

He wasn't in a hurry to check them. He finished his work first and wiped his hands on a cloth. Only then did he walk over to the table, gave the shells a closer look, then nodded. He didn't seem surprised with the sheer amount of it. Still, his gaze betrayed concern.

What was wrong with him? Was he upset about something?

"I need to finish the order by morning," he said.

"Does that mean you'll have to work through the night?"

He heaved a sigh. "I wish. There's an important ingredient missing. It's a good job you left me a few, this way I could at least get the feel of it. Problem is, it's not exactly the same as hydra's skin."

This sounded like the precursor to a new quest. I waited patiently for him to continue. The initial plot line seemed to have grown new branches. "Can I help?"

"You?" He looked me over, doubt in his stare. "You might... The problem is, you might not want to. In order to alter a shell's substance, I need some Spectral Dust. You must have heard about it. So you can imagine how valuable it is in my line of work."

"I can, yeah."

"I had some, but I went a bit over the top with it. Had I been using it to alter hydra skin, I'd have had enough. But mantis shells require larger quantities. You sold some Spectral Dust last night at the Twin Watch Ravine, didn't you? You also promised them to bring some more."

"I might go back there in a couple of days."

"Any chance you might have some on you?" his voice rang with hope.

I didn't play hard to get. "Actually I do."

It looked like I might complete another quest without even leaving his smithy!

"Alexatis, I need to finish this order by the morning. They're coming to collect it. My reputation's at stake. I can't explain it to you now, but if I fail to deliver, I'll be washed up."

"I have some on me. How much do you need?"

He gave me a long searching look. "A lot. At least two handfuls. The problem is, I can't pay at the moment. I'm a bit down on my luck, you see. I have neither gold nor jewels."

New quest alert: Selfless Aid

Master Jurg needs two handfuls of Spectral Dust.

Reward: your Reputation with Master Jurg will improve considerably. He might make it up to you in the nearest future.

This wasn't an easy choice. I hadn't opened Dimian's boxes so I had no idea how much Dust there was inside. I had a good idea of its market price, though.

Jurg kept catching my eye.

Ah, whatever. You couldn't earn all the money in the world. At the moment, XP and Reputation were key. Besides, I really wanted to help him. He was a good man — never mind he was only an NPC.

"Here," I laid the two plain boxes on the table next to the shells. "You think it's enough?"

With a reserved nod, he finally averted his gaze.

You've passed the test!

Congratulations! You've received a new level!

Quest alert: Selfless Aid! Quest completed!

Your Reputation with Master Jurg has improved!

Current Reputation status: Respect

Quest alert: An Unfinished Job! Quest completed!

Congratulations! You've received a new level!

Your Reputation with Master Jurg has improved!

Current Reputation status: Friendship

Come back in the morning to claim your reward.

"I'm going to work through the night," he said. "You've really helped me out. Come with me now," he suddenly added. "We need to talk. Mind your head. The beam is low."

Without uttering a word, I followed him through a doorway. I had nowhere to hurry to, anyway. Dimian didn't expect me back until tomorrow night. Besides, I was curious. What did he want to tell me? Why such a rush? What's with the test I'd supposedly passed?

He took me to a typically dwarven squat room with a fireplace, crowded with massive furniture.

"That sword you showed me last night. Is it with you?"

"Yes, Master."

"Mind if I take another look?"

"Here, Master. Take it."

"I told you to drop the *master*!" he took the sword from me, laid it on the table and ran a finger along the blood groove, mumbling something. Then he turned back to me,

"Would you like to leave it in my safekeeping?"

"No, I wouldn't," I replied adamantly even though his question had caught me unawares.

"It's gonna kill you."

A shiver ran down my spine. "Why do you say that?"

"You're too weak. Too weak, too inexperienced. I could safeguard it for you. Once you get stronger, I would give it back to you."

"No. Sorry. It's saved my life quite a few times already."

"Saved your life! You don't know what danger is yet!"

"I'd like to find out more about the runes."

"You're obstinate, aren't you? Well, suit yourself. I'll tell you if you so wish."

He opened a cupboard and produced a weird-looking contraption caked in a mass of wax. It consisted of an old candle stuck in a holder and a magnifying glass secured on a makeshift support in front of it.

Master Jurg lit the candle and mounted the contraption on his head. Once again he leaned over the sword and began studying its hilt and guard.

Finally he let out a gasp. "I knew it. Alexatis? Here, take the sword. Close your hand tight. Like this, good. Now!"

He took a swing and tried to punch me in the face.

Mechanically I dodged the blow, toppling a chair, and was about to strike back at him when I cast a glance at the sword in my hand. It was ablaze with fiery runes.

"How did you know that would happen?"

"I read about it in some old book," Master Jurg removed the magnifying glass from its support and handed it to me. "Look at the hilt. Let me shine a light on it for you."

The moment I let go of the sword, the runes faded — but my mental energy indicator soared as if I'd just gulped a vialful of mana.

I peered through the magnifying glass. The sword's entire hilt was covered in a multitude of barely perceptible little spikes.

Did that mean that every time I closed my hand around it, they dug into my skin?

"This is a combination of some powerful magic and ancient technologies," Master Jurg confirmed my suspicions. From his dwarven point of view, this must have sounded perfectly normal. Dwarves were famous for their knack with mechanisms. They were the only ones who could build golems as well as all sorts of clever mechanical thingies.

"The sword becomes part of you," Jurg explained confidently. "It's more than just an arm extension. The first few runes are easy to understand. They must mean the first few digits: one to five. Don't you think they look like an energy indicator?"

I nodded. I didn't know what to say.

Jurg was a player, definitely. Neither his behavior nor his train of thought fitted the NPC mold. But even if he indeed was the missing technologist — the Corporation's unlucky whistleblower — it still didn't mean I could get to the truth. His neuroimplant must have controlled his behavior, preventing him from remembering his past but unable to completely suppress his identity.

"Now look here, on either side of the blade," he went on. "After those five, the symbols are split into two rows. They also become smaller. Did you notice that certain symbols don't glow at all?"

He was right. I checked the video of myself holding the sword. Indeed, four long inscriptions ran along the blade, two on either side. Each of them had a different number of active symbols glowing.

Of the first five bigger runes, only the first one glowed. The other four remained dimmed. If he was right about them being some sort of an energy indicator, it might mean that my resources weren't enough to activate the sword to its full capacity.

"So? Did you manage to work it out?" Jurg asked me.

"I think I don't have enough mana."

"Exactly! Which is why the sword only deals a small amount of additional mental damage without revealing its true potential."

"What kind of potential is that?"

"Don't you know yet?"

"Not really."

"Each one of these lines," he announced confidently, "is an ancient spell! They serve as powerful debuffs," his use of gaming terms confirmed my idea of him being an ex-player. "But in order for them to work, you should have at least 3,000 points mana!"

"*How much*? That's 300 pt. Intellect!"

"Exactly," he nodded. "How much do you have now?"

"Twelve."

"Well, there's room for improvement, I suppose," he attempted a clumsy joke. "But seriously, I do suggest you leave it with me for the time being. Otherwise one day it might end up sucking you dry. All of you — Life, Strength, everything."

"You mean, if one day I face an enemy much stronger than myself?"

"That's right. No one's immune to this sort of thing. Ancient items harbor a great power but in weak hands, they can be treacherous! So what do you think? Will you leave it with me?"

"No. Thanks, anyway. Still, I'd really love to know more about it. You don't happen to know someone who could read the runes?"

"You're something else, Alexatis, you really

are. Talk about obstinate," he made a helpless gesture, accepting the fact. "There're some ruins at the other end of the continent. If you give me the map, I'll mark them down for you. According to legends, that's where some very powerful wizards used to live. Apparently, they still remembered the rule of the Founder Gods."

"What happened to them?"

"To whom, the gods? No idea. But it was an artifact like this one," he cast a meaningful stare at the sword, "that became the wizards' undoing. One day their citadel simply crumbled to dust, aged by millennia within a split second. From what I heard, its ruins harbored many an ancient scroll. Apparently, the citadel used to house the biggest and oldest library in our world. I suggest you check it out. If you fail to find anything, you can talk to the prospectors who flock there from everywhere."

"What exactly do you want me to look for? What should I pay attention to?"

"Rune interpretation. Ancient maps."

"Why maps?"

"I told you before, the secret of the cargonite alloy is lost. But there must have been some foundries or smithies where they made it! You need to look for them — or their ruins, rather."

He took the magnifying glass from me, put

out the candle and replaced the makeshift device in the cupboard.

Quest update alert: The Secret Alloy!

Locate the ruins of the wizards' citadel, then try to find out everything you can about the ancient runic symbols.

Find any old maps of the continent and explore the locations that could have harbored the Founder Gods' smithies.

Deadline: none

Reward: any information you can unearth about the runes might help you find out more about the sword's properties, increase its damage, restore its durability, or add [????] effects to the blows dealt with it.

Any information you acquire regarding the secrets of the lost cargonite alloy can be used by Master Jurg in order to build items every bit as good as their ancient prototypes.

"You can go to your room now," he told me. "In the morning, I want to see you and Enea in my smithy."

* * *

I had a great night's sleep and awoke late, when

the sun had already risen over the mountains.

I climbed out of bed and had a quick wash and a bite to eat, then walked outside. The air was still frosty, the cliffs' shady sides glistening with ice crystals. A hammer rang incessantly, disturbing the windless silence. It looked like Master Jurg had indeed worked through the night.

The door behind me creaked.

I turned round. "Hi."

Enea flashed me a dimpled smile. "It's cold!" she said with a light shudder. "I should have put something warmer on."

She was wearing the same short tunic. If she didn't want to catch a cold, she needed to have the environment generator in her room set to comfort mode. I could almost see her spread in her seat, surrounded by high-density holograms.

"We need to see Master Jurg," I said. "He wants to talk to us both."

"Alexatis!" she was in a good mood today, all bright-eyed and bushy-tailed. Last night's sadness was completely gone. "Are you aware that if a lady looks good, you need to acknowledge the fact?"

She was poking fun at me again! Still, she was right. She looked utterly awesome: intelligent, young, beautiful and happy. Problem was, I wasn't too quick on the uptake — which was only too understandable.

She laughed. "It's all right. Don't sweat it," she took me by the hand and pulled me toward the smithy. "We'll pick up your reward and go straight back, right? I have my leveling to do! I'd like to try Wall of Fire! Can't you help me sort out the ability calculator? I tried it last night, thinking how I could create a development branch, but it turned out sort of clumsy."

"Of course I can," I said. "It's not that difficult, provided you decide on your objectives first. What would you like to specialize in?"

I pushed the door of the smithy open, stepped aside and froze in my tracks.

"Ah, come in, you two! Great to see you!" Master Jurg couldn't have been more welcoming. He seemed to be in a good mood too — maybe because completing the old order was a big load off his mind. "Here, I want you to try them on!"

A couple of crude wooden mannequins stood side by side, sporting two unique sets of gear.

Two?

One for me — did that mean the other one was for Enea?

Don't get me wrong, I didn't feel bad about him using extra mantis shells. It just didn't feel right. What Master Jurg had just done contradicted the very nature of NPCs. They never did anything for nothing, let alone make gifts without good reason. In order to simply attract their attention — most of them, anyway, — you needed to complete a quest first.

"So, what do you think? Do you like them? Don't just stand there, try them on!" the dwarf rubbed his hands, concealing a smile in his fat mustache, apparently enjoying the effect.

"No way!" Enea walked around the mannequin, admiring the peculiar craftsmanship. The material seemed to flow in folds like the finest of fabrics, its glowing scales preserving the strength of the mantises' natural armor. "Is this for me?"

"For you to enjoy and for your enemies to-"

Enea leaned down and threw her arms around Master Jurg's stocky dwarven frame. She gave him a peck on the cheek. "Jurg, you're the best dwarf ever!"

The stern blacksmith was lost for words. He turned crimson, losing his cool.

This must have been much more than her Loveliness ring working. The dwarf was just too human — fatherly even. And he was indeed a great master of his craft. This job was exactly something the missing technologist Jurgen Borne might have done.

Could this be a human being trapped inside an NPC?

No one would tell me that. Not here, not now, anyway.

Having recovered from my stupor, I peered at the two suits' stats. So this was what Master Jurg must have used most of my selfless offering of Spectral Dust on!

A Scaly Tunic. A Unique item made by a Master craftsman. One of a kind.

Durability, 1000/1000

Weight, 9 lb.

Protection, 75

Effect 1: +50% to resistance to cold when equipped

Effect II: +3 to Stamina when equipped. +2% to full Mental Energy regeneration

Restrictions: Only Human. Only Combat Wizard

Soft Scaly Hood. A Unique item made by a Master craftsman. One of a kind.

Durability, 500/500

Weight, 4.5 lb.

Protection, 20

Effect: +1 to Intellect when equipped.

Restrictions: Only Human. Only Combat Wizard

Soft Scaly Gauntlets. A Unique item made by a Master craftsman. One of a kind.

Durability, 500/500

Weight, 4.5 lb.

Protection, 20

Effect: +2 to Loveliness when equipped. +5% to staffless spell casting times.

Restrictions: Only Human. Only Combat Wizard.

Elegant Scaly High Boots. A Unique item made by a Master craftsman. One of a kind.

Durability, 500/500

Weight, 5.5 lb.

Protection, 30.

Effect: +5% to Speed when equipped. +1 to Agility when equipped.

Restrictions: Only Human. Only Combat Wizard.

Equipping the entire kit gives +5% to the wearer's chance of receiving an additional Blindness effect to his or her attacking spells.

The second kit (apparently meant for me) wasn't as elegant but had much higher protection stats.

I touched the armor. Seamless, it wasn't going to chafe against my skin. It looked like

Master Jurg understood the discomfort of 100% authenticity.

I peered at my armor's stats,

A Scaly Breastplate. A Unique item made by a Master craftsman. One of a kind.

Light armor. Durability, 1000/1000

Weight, 9 lb.

Protection, 120

+10% to Elemental defense when equipped.

+5% to current Intellect level when equipped

+5% to current Health level when equipped.

Restrictions: Only Human. Only Neuro.

An Open Scaly Helmet. A Unique item made by a Master craftsman. One of a kind.

Light armor. Durability, 500/500

Weight, 4.5 lb.

Protection, 20

Effect: +5% to mana regeneration rate when equipped

Restrictions: Only Human. Only Neuro.

Scaly Gauntlets with Bracers. A Unique item made by a Master craftsman. One of a kind.

Light Armor. Durability 500/500

Weight, 4.5 lbs.

Protection, 20

+5% to spell casting times when equipped

Restrictions: Only Human. Only Neuro.

Scaly Pants. A Unique item made by a Master craftsman. One of a kind.

Light Armor. Durability 500/500

Weight, 6.5 lb.

Protection, 30

+5% to current Strength level when equipped

Restrictions: Only Human. Only Neuro.

Scaly High Boots. A Unique item made by a Master craftsman. One of a kind.

Light Armor. Durability 500/500

Weight, 4.5 lb.

Protection, 20

+5% to Speed when equipped. +1 to Agility when equipped.

Restrictions: Only Human. Only Neuro.

Equipping the entire kit gives the wearer +5% to the power of attack, +5% to his or her chances of dealing a critical hit, and +5% to his or her chances of stunning the enemy with a blow.

Enea had already changed into her new armor. The black material had a deep purple sheen to it which highlighted her own beauty. Her eyes sparkled.

I changed into mine, too. The scaly armor

hugged my body, repeating its every curve and move. There was also a scabbard for my sword behind my left shoulder.

The gauntlets and bracers, the pants and the boots felt like a second skin. They didn't hinder movement whatsoever. The entire kit was virtually weightless.

I couldn't have even dreamed of this degree of comfort and protection. "Thank you so much, Master!"

He looked at us, proud of his work. "Be worthy of wearing it," he said, brushing away a furtive tear. "Take good care of yourselves. May the Gods of Light be with you! Now go. If you manage to get more shells, bring them to me. I can always use them."

Enea quietened down. The mischievous glint in her eyes disappeared, replaced by sad pensiveness.

"Go now. You don't have much time," Master Jurg turned his back to us, once again behaving like a typical grumpy NPC.

"Alex," Enea whispered to me, "is he all right?"

"Let's go now," I nudged her toward the door. "I think he needs some space. He's been working all night. He must be really tired."

"If you say so. You sure he won't mind?"

"I know he won't."

We walked outside. The autumnal sun hung low, weak and tepid.

Enea seemed overwhelmed by all the sudden developments.

"What do you want to do now?" I asked her. "Shall we port back and rush you for a bit? Then later we can go and see Dimian."

"I'd rather we saw him first. You never know, he might be a hard negotiator. In which case we might need a bit of time."

"Are you still going on about it? That's against the rules, you know. I've already accepted the quest."

"Don't worry. I'll give it a try, that's all. Your quest conditions aren't going to change. Your reward might become less ambiguous, that's all. I know, I know this isn't real life. It's slightly different here. But I've already looked into it. Dimian wasn't correct with you."

"Or really? How exactly wasn't he correct?"

"I'll tell you later. No good you getting upset now."

"Very well."

Pointless trying to talk her out of it. Besides, I was curious. Would she manage to pull it off?

"Now you can join my group," I said. "I'm sending you an invite."

* * *

The streets of Agrion were busy, mainly with newbs levels 1 and 2. It looked like the Crystal Sphere had just entered a new phase in its popularity.

Admittedly, we — or rather our unique bespoke gear — attracted stares, some admiring, others jealous. Some even sized us up with contempt, probably thinking we'd paid for the privilege of owning it.

"It's time we move on," I said, opening the door to Dimian's Emporium.

"Meaning?" Enea asked, looking around herself with curiosity.

"We're too conspicuous. Today we'll rush you a bit, then we'll have to continue leveling in some unexplored locations."

She nodded, all the while studying the place. I could see she wasn't impressed by what the shop had to offer.

"His stock isn't that special, is it?" she mouthed to me.

Dimian motioned a shop assistant to replace him at the counter and hurried to greet us. "Alexatis! Look at you! Who is this beautiful lady?"

"Enea, this is Dimian, our trade partner. Dimian, this is Enea. From now on, she will represent me in all our negotiations."

Dimian choked. "Alexatis! I thought we had an agreement! Have you changed your mind?"

"No, not at all. We're setting off tomorrow as planned. Still, we need to get a few details out of the way."

Dimian regained his cool surprisingly quickly. "Very well. What exactly do you want to discuss?"

Enea flashed him a cute smile. "Is there anywhere we could talk in private? Like a conference room?"

"A *what*?" Dimian looked lost. "Alexatis, is she from the Guild?!"

He pushed open the familiar door into his special-stock room.

"Alex," Enea said, "I don't need you. You can wait here."

She followed Dimian into the storeroom and closed the door shut behind herself.

* * *

After about ten minutes, Dimian emerged from "the conference room" red as a lobster.

"Thank you very much, Alexatis!" he glared at me. "Why didn't you just bring a demon to my shop? Ten freakin' percent! Did you hear that? She twisted me around her little finger and tied it in a knot! And now she wants it in writing sealed with my signature!"

Enea walked out after him, looking pleased like a cat who'd gotten the canary. "Dimian, we're saving you from a certain death. You and your '*Impossible!*' Please."

She leaned closer to his ear and whispered, "Imagine Guild representatives knocking on your door — what are you going to say to them?"

"I don't know!" he grabbed his head with both hands, all but belching smoke out of his ears.

"Well, in that case you'll send them to see Alex. It'll all be in the scroll we're about to sign. You tell them that Alexatis pressurized you into this deal, as simple as that. What could you do? You're only a humble vendor, aren't you?"

"They're going to ask me why I hadn't turned to the Guild for protection."

"Because you didn't know, did you?" smiling, Enea continued instructing him. "What if Alexatis lied to you? What if he was going to port you into some unknown location and rob you there? Turning to the Guild leaders in that situation would mean putting their lives in jeopardy. But seeing as everything had worked out well, you were obliged to pay Alexatis his share. Because you had to comply with the contract!"

"They'll want to know the coordinates. They might try to torture them out of me."

"Exactly! You don't know the coordinates, do you? You're not even sure if Alexatis would ever take you on a repeat lengthy journey like that again. Which means it's not your fault. You haven't broken any Guild rules. As far as I understand, one-off deals are not subject to guild taxes, are they?"

"They're not," Dimian's voice rang with the first glints of understanding. He began to cheer up.

"You see? They don't have a leg to stand on!"

"You don't know them! The Guild love harassing people."

"That may well be, but by then you'll be a rich man, won't you? You might have more trading capital than some of their Council members! I wonder if it might just open the door into their big boys circle? Or even secure you a place on the Guild Council? What do you think?"

Dimian turned blue in the face with what looked like an agonizing inner struggle.

"Very well," he finally said. "Where's this contract of yours? Let's sign it."

* * *

Once we got that out of the way, we spent a quality afternoon leveling up by the nut grove. Later that night, however, I had a very unexpected visitor.

I had just come back to the Golden Carp, had a nice big meal and was lying in bed reading the Illusion Casting Textbook when I heard an insistent knock on the door.

I put the book away, got up and lifted the latch, then stepped aside. "Come in."

"Hi Alex," Mr. Borisov closed the door shut behind himself. He perched himself on a rickety stool and cast me an angry upward look. "What are you playing at?"

I sat down too. "Meaning?"

"A player can only enter into contractual agreements with other players! You and this girl of yours, have you decided to create a precedent? Are you aware that you've forced our programmers to modify the code ASAP?!"

"To modify what exactly? Or should I say, *whom*? Dimian, maybe?"

"Very funny! You knew you couldn't do that, didn't you? Or did you think you could get away with it?"

"Didn't you say I needed to level up? That '*a lot would depend on my success*'? Your words, not mine. And this is exactly what I'm doing. Trading with dwarves offers an excellent opportunity. Gear means too much to me. I need much more comfort and protection compared to regular players. I do whatever I can — and I'm forced to rely on money whenever I can't!"

"You're doing a great job, I agree. Which is why we're going to overlook this little liberty you've taken — but just this once! You should keep this deal under wraps. We don't want any more players haggling with NPCs over quest conditions!"

"I'll keep that in mind. You *are* aware of the fact that there's nothing in the rules that prevents players from striking deals with NPCs, aren't you? How about mercenaries? You can enter into a contract with them, can't you? Negotiate contract terms and everything?"

"Don't you get fresh with me!"

"Why, what happened? All we're going to do is visit the dwarves a couple of times, big deal."

"Alex, you really should stay away from Enea. Her father is a very wealthy man. And he isn't happy about your relationship to put it very mildly."

"Enea is my *friend*. Can't you see?"

"I can. He can't."

"Why, is he really such a big shot?"

He waved my question away. "Nothing we

can't handle. But you, please stop asking for trouble. Things are getting too complicated too quickly. You're becoming the epicenter of some very rapid developments."

"Let me guess. Could it have something to do with me trying to survive? You dumped a blind kitten in the water to see if it sinks or swims?"

"Yes, I suppose you could say that. Okay. Go your own way. Just remember you've still got a lot of swimming to do. No more special treatment for you. Rules are rules. You'll have to stick to them like everybody else."

CHAPTER EIGHT

CRYSTAL SPHERE. THE AZURE MOUNTAINS.
THE VICINITY OF THE TWIN WATCH RAVINE

"GOSH, IT'S beautiful here! I've never seen anything like it!" Enea looked around herself, excited. The last time we'd been here, night had concealed the rich autumnal crimson of the slopes.

Having calmed down the horse, Dimian was now busy rearranging his cart's harness, casting anxious glances at the split in one of the wooden wheels. It was a good job we'd taken a few spares.

"Alexatis, help me!" he croaked, trying to lift the loaded cart. Apparently, jacks hadn't been invented here yet. Did he want to bust his gut?

I looked around myself until I found a fat branch broken off by the wind and pushed it under the axle, lifting the cart even with this makeshift lever. My muscles seized with the effort.

"Change the wheel, quick!" I shouted at Dimian.

He hurried to obey. "Got it!"

Phew. I'd very nearly had my own gut busted. He must have bought up all the local stocks of Spectral Dust!

"Are we going, then?" I asked.

Dimian kept casting wary looks around. "This place must be teeming with dangerous beasts."

I'd already worked out that the local locations were quite safe — not at all adaptive. "It's all right," I said. "Enea and I can handle them. You'd better stay out of harm's way."

He climbed atop his loaded cart, laid a strung crossbow upon a wrought-iron chest next to himself, and seized the reins.

We set off. I walked in front, leading the way, prepared to pull any potential mobs' aggro to myself if necessary. As previously agreed, Enea hovered about a dozen paces behind, keeping the caster's habitual distance.

Endlessly snaking uphill, these mountain

roads weren't easy. Unused to the effort, the poor horse struggled to pull the heavily loaded cart. We'd come across lots of fragments of single-standing ancient cliffs collapsed by time: perfect places to set an ambush. Most Crystal Sphere races — including dwarves and Dark Elves — had the class of Robber, which was why we had to keep our eyes peeled.

The first hour on the road had passed quickly as we enjoyed the sunshine and the walk. Soon, however, the weather began to change. A wind had risen; clouds coated the sky, spitting a miserable cold drizzle.

Visibility dropped rapidly as the numerous gorges and ravines so common on woody mountain slopes began oozing a hazy fog.

Dimian quietened down. I could quite understand him: he was both scared and out of his depth here. On flat terrain, one could note danger a mile away — but here every turn of the road harbored unknown dangers.

The bundles and bales holding his stocks were soaking wet, rain trickling down the chests. Even the cart wheels stopped creaking, so damp was everything. The wind wailed overhead, bringing heavy thunderclouds our way, while here below it was deadly quiet as if time stood still.

Finally, the familiar ravine loomed out of

the mist. Once we cleared it, the dwarven trade post was only a stone throw's away.

The horse was struggling, exhausted. The road underfoot had changed again: the dirt ruts marked with wilted grass gave way to a washboard-like surface of rock.

Fog swirled around the cliffs which towered on both sides of us. The statues cut in stone still guarded the entrance to the ravine.

Last time I hadn't had a chance to take a good look at them, so now I studied them curiously.

To one side stood a Dark Elf, his face cracked; to the other, a stocky dwarf. According to Master Jurg, the two statues marked a safe passage, symbolizing peace between the two races which used to be at war with each other. Still, one couldn't be too sure.

Dimian's lips were moving. He was probably mouthing some protective spells when an arrow whizzed through the air, piercing one of his chests.

I couldn't see the archer through the curtain of rain. But it had to be a Dark Elf. Their eyesight was way superior to ours. His arrow had just brushed the chest, barely sinking in.

Petrified, Dimian tried to climb under the cart.

"Where do you think you're going?" I

snapped at him. "Get back! Take cover behind the shield and keep driving!"

Although we'd discussed emergency measures in the case of a surprise attack, he must have forgotten all of it. He climbed back onto the bales and cowered behind a wicker shield with an archer's slit cut in it.

I didn't like the shooter's style. Warning shots weren't how robbers would do it.

"Enea, come here, quick! Grab your shield and take cover! Watch the entrance to the ravine! Be ready to alert me if necessary!"

"Alexatis, where are you going?"

"They're behind us! The one in front is a decoy! Dimian, keep your eyes peeled!"

There were three of us. Our enemies must have been more numerous. I looked around me, searching for their positions. Two groups of cliffs stood behind us at an equal distance from the road. The range was too big for an archer, which meant our enemies were stealthing up on us.

Another arrow whizzed past, embedding itself into a bale. One more, and I'd be able to calculate the archer's approximate range. But not now.

I opened the battle chat and sent Enea a quick set of instructions. She grasped everything straight away. Clever girl.

I repeated my order out loud for Dimian,

not trusting the chat as I had no idea how NPCs were supposed to interact with the in-game network.

"Hold the reins tight and make sure the horse doesn't bolt!"

"He won't. He's barely alive, poor nag."

Enea gestured to us, letting us know she was ready.

I stepped a few paces away from the cart and drew my sword. The runes covering its blade glowed defiantly. Players weren't supposed to aggro each other — or were they? Neither a market trader shaking with fear nor a girl wizard cowering behind a wicker shield could be seen as potential threat. Me, however, I was a different beast entirely. None of the robbers would appreciate being sent to their respawn points while their comrades were sharing out the loot. Which was part of my plan. The robbers were obliged to try and get rid of me first before turning their undivided attention to Enea and Dimian.

The rain lashed against my scaly armor. This was an advantage for us and a definite disadvantage for the thugs — although they didn't yet know it. Stealth works great in fine weather. I'd once managed to locate an enemy rogue by a maple leaf which had drifted off a tree and clung momentarily to his armor before continuing its descent.

I could see them! The rain treacherously outlined the vague shapes of five assailants. Had the distance been bigger, I might have failed to notice them; but the moment they drew nearer, my Enhanced Perception ability kicked in, adding 20% to my chances of seeing a stealthed-up enemy.

Pretending I was looking innocuously around, I took a screenshot and forwarded it to Enea, making sure it included the corner of the cart to help her get her bearings.

Still, I'd underestimated them. The robbers split up, three of them continuing toward me while two more headed for the cart.

"Enea, do it!"

I think I actually shouted it out loud. Dimian jumped, mechanically firing his crossbow. The bolt shot between the two rogues and thudded into a boulder, splitting it in two.

Enea followed with her magic. I knew how much she liked the element of Fire, but in this situation she had to use Ice, considering the weather.

She got them both!

If you haven't seen the effects of an ice spell cast in rainy weather, you've missed a lot. The spell permeates everything, turning raindrops into sharp crystals and freezing all water-drenched objects solid, temporarily reducing them to fragile dummies devoid of Durability.

Enea had invested all of her mana into the blow. She hurried to open a vial, restoring her stocks, then attacked again.

The ground and air itself around the cart filled with feathery patterns of fern frost. The five rogue stalkers froze temporarily in their stealthing poses, their armor ice-bound, their swords covered in floral ice swirls.

Their levels were equal to mine but they were at a definite disadvantage. Their combat tactics were based solely on a surprise effect allowing them to deal one decisive critical hit.

Ringing through the air, ice crystals showered to the ground as I sent the first robber back to his respawn point. I slashed through the second one's forearm, then somersaulted toward the third one who looked completely lost, cussing and trying to strip away the ice covering his face.

He proved to be a hardened fighter. Parrying my blow, he rapidly brandished two short swords, forcing me to dodge them. The two others were already hurrying to his aid. I shouldn't hold my breath for an easy win. Another arrow shot past, brushing the ice-bound land but bouncing off it.

Not bleeding any longer, the wounded

robber dropped an empty vial to the ground and rejoined the rogues.

I switched to defense, trying to keep them at a safe distance. My longer sword gave me a distinct advantage. Enea's spells had already expired. The repeated Ice damage had shrunk their life bars but very slightly.

They surrounded me. Now it was four against one.

I'd managed to draw them away from the cart. The Dark Elves were taller than myself but their rogue stance made them look awkward. Their half-crouched bodies made them appear as if they were constantly stealing up on you, clenching a knife in each hand.

I invested all my strength into the blow I'd learned from Zander. My sword traced a fiery arc in the air. Two of the rogues recoiled just in time; a third one had his throat slashed — this one had his respawn point waiting for him. But the fourth one expertly dodged the blow, catching me unawares and burying both his knives in my back.

For a split second, the agonizing pain paralyzed me. I staggered but remained standing. My scaly armor absorbed most of the incoming damage — and still I lost half my life. This must have been a crit. I didn't even get the chance to down the vial which had been promptly knocked from my hand.

Now three of the rogues were left on their feet. I was bleeding profusely, the deep wounds in my back hindering my movements. Still, my constant practice sessions finally paid off. I rolled over to one side, increasing the distance, and cast a Minor Healing Aura. Its crystalline shimmer enveloped me, dulling the pain somewhat.

Having lost another group member, the rogues were now furious, aggroing me mob-like.

Enea jumped at her chance. Roaring, a fireball escaped the gloomy drizzle and exploded, searing me with its flames. A rogue screamed as his clothes began to smolder, his life bar shrinking rapidly.

I lunged at him with my sword and finished him off, then swung round, parrying two more blows. Everything was happening much faster than words could convey. Now the rogues, skillful to begin with, had nothing to lose. Blood streaked down my armor, my left arm growing weak from several knife wounds.

The rogues had no idea that their every blow, apart from depleting my HP, also caused excruciating pain, disrupting my concentration and stripping my movements of any accuracy.

I couldn't even see the cart in the blinding rain. I'd told Enea to stay with Dimian whatever happened, but now she disobeyed me, sending yet another fireball sizzling through the air, leaving behind a trail of evaporating moisture.

Her magic attack distracted my enemies, allowing me to down a health elixir. The empty vial clattered onto the rocks. I hurried to cast Ice.

That slowed the rogues down again. Cussing, they began shaking off the iridescent layer of frost. Dripping with aura, my Mysterious Sword drew a deadly sequence of blows through the air. Another rogue down. The last of the Dark Elves lost it and ran for his life.

I could barely stand on my feet.

My wounds were still bleeding. My life bar quivered in place without either shrinking or growing.

Enea appeared out of the rain and ran toward me, her eyes filled with worry, fear and fury.

I gave her a hug. She clung to me, shuddering. This was her first PvP fight. You don't forget that sort of thing in a hurry.

"I don't have enough mana," she was still living the minute-long fight. "I just keep losing it! I really need to level up," she looked me in the eye. "Do you think there'll be more of them next time?"

I didn't want to lie to her. "There will be. Players never forgive defeat. Besides, rumors about the precious goods we're delivering will spread fast."

"Then we'll need a convoy of warriors and wizards as our escort."

"We'll think about it once we're back. You all right?"

"The archer is still there," Enea said, suddenly all shivery again.

"We'll sort him out. Why are you shaking? Are you soaked?"

"I'm all right. It's probably nerves. How can we locate the archer?"

"Just watch his arrows fly."

She was still clinging to me, locking my stare with her trusting gaze. These few brief moments felt like an eternity. The rain pelted down even harder.

"Hey you two, quit your lovey dovey," this was Dimian, finally brave enough to leave the safety of his cart.

Reluctantly I released Enea from my embrace. "Go check on your horse," I told him. "We won't be long."

"Alex, we can't get too close to the ravine," Enea said. "Elves never miss."

She must have spent last night perusing the Wiki.

"I know. We aren't going to risk it," I walked over to the cart and crouched, studying the arrows. There were more of them now; some had sunk well into the ground. They were nicely grouped, considering the gusty wind: the archer definitely knew his job.

"How are we supposed to get closer to him, then?" Dimian asked, fidgeting.

I did a quick estimate of the arrows' trajectory. My Enhanced Perception ability proved a big help, focusing my stare on a small rock ledge a little higher and to the left of the dwarf statue.

"We'll use fireballs," I told Enea. "On my signal. Are you ready?"

She nodded, confirming the reception of the approximate aiming point I'd forwarded to her.

Three pairs of fireballs headed for the rocks. Unlike arrows, fireballs don't need ballistics: they just keep whizzing on in a straight line until they meet with an obstacle.

Explosions rumbled in the distance.

Our mental energy levels were restoring slowly. We didn't want to waste vials unless absolutely necessary.

"Two more, now!"

Flames flared up again, leaving murky trails in the fireballs' roaring wake. More rumbling noises reached us from the cliffs.

No return fire. Nothing.

"Do you think we might have got him?" Enea asked, peering into the distance.

"We scared him, that's for sure. I don't think he'd want to confront two wizards!"

"How do we know that?"

"I'll activate the Mana Shield and go first. You two follow quietly behind. If the archer exposes himself, I want you to attack him with more fireballs."

"Okay. Just watch out, please."

* * *

The archer was gone.

I walked unhurriedly, keeping my eyes peeled. Only two of the robbers seemed to have survived — even though I wasn't so sure about the archer anymore. A clumsy makeshift parapet of rocks piled on top of each other betrayed his position, blackened and gaping from the direct hits of at least three fireballs.

Enea caught up with me. "Alex, I really, really want to start leveling. I need more mana and new spells. I want... I want everything to go up in flames around me whenever I cast a spell!"

I smiled. "You do realize, don't you, that in that case, mobs will become stronger too?"

"You don't understand! I think I got hooked. I can't get enough of this."

"How about real life? I thought you had responsibilities there?"

"I'm working on it."

Shaped as an arch built of reddish blocks of granite, the ancient entrance to the ravine stood out dramatically against the gray limestone used for the two statues.

Dimian and Enea lingered, admiring them. Tufts of moss peeked out of the cracks in the limestone; ivy entwined the Dark Elf's legs as if reminding us of his race's ancient affinity with the boundless woodlands.

Here, the road was much better. Its rippled surface smoothed out somewhat. Soon we could see the squat buildings of the dwarven trade post.

We'd made it!

Next time it wouldn't be so easy. The rogues weren't going to forget their defeat in a hurry. My PK counter had four kills on it; Enea's had one, which meant that she had indeed smoked the archer with her fireball. Only one robber had escaped.

Still, the kill numbers glowed yellow which meant that we'd been defending ourselves. No penalties involved.

You might ask what the other players were doing here at all. The answer was simple: the world of Crystal Sphere was densely populated with plenty of starting locations scattered all over its map. A player's initial location after their first login depended mainly on their racial choice.

But the uninhabited lands, that was different again. The game developers used them to separate the large populated regions, thus priming their future world for wars as well as great geographical discoveries which would allow the players to lay new trade routes to gain access to the overseas goods they so desperately needed.

Dwarves poured out of the storehouses to stare at us, exchanging whispered comments,

"Just look at their armor! It has to be Jurg's work!"

"No way! Can you imagine how many hydra skins he'd need to make it?"

"The girl is pretty. Just look at her!"

"A whole cartload of Spectral Dust? It can't be!"

"Why would you care? Azamaul and Mychior are buying it all up!"

"Oh really? Do you think they have enough gold and precious stones?"

"In that case, what are we waiting for? I'm the first in line!"

Enea and I led the horse by its reins without showing any reaction to their furtive conversations. Dimian perched himself on top of all his bales, chests and crates, soaked to the bone but looking utterly contented.

I really appreciated Master Jurg's help. Without his armor, I'd surely have been stuck now at some unfamiliar respawn point, gearless and surrounded by strangers of an unknown race.

* * *

We drove the cart under a lean-to.

The dwarves surrounded us, each demanding over the others' heads,

"Do you have Spectral Dust in all those crates and boxes?"

"What's your asking price?"

"Are you bringing more if there isn't enough to go round?"

Unhurriedly Dimian climbed down from his loaded cart. He produced a scrap of parchment from his bag and used his dagger to pin it to the tethering post.

"Read it," he said. "It's two gold a gram. I've also made a precious stone conversion chart in case you need it."

The dwarves grew agitated — but not because of the price. They seemed quite happy to pay — but they didn't look as if they'd expected so much to arrive. Fingering their beards, they engaged in another series of whispered exchanges.

Both Mychior and Azamaul promptly arrived, followed by a bunch of apprentices loaded with crates.

Enea and I exchanged glances. She elbowed me, "What did I say to you? No one's gonna believe it in real life!"

I had nothing to say to that. Two gold per gram of Spectral Dust? The mind boggles. I knew Dimian wouldn't play it small but he'd really invested his all into this trip. Had I not made him sign the contract, he might have paid me five grand at the most. And this was at least twenty times that!

In the meantime, all the dwarves had studied the announcement and scurried back to their storehouses, rain-drenched, without as much as questioning the price.

Between themselves, Mychior and Azamaul only managed to buy one-third of the cartload. A long line formed in their wake. The large stack of cratefuls of gold and bagfuls of precious stones next to Dimian kept growing.

How on earth were we going to transport it all back?

The Dust was selling fast. Before paying, each of the dwarves would whisper something to Dimian who'd nod and make some notes on a piece of parchment.

In less than an hour, the cart was empty.

"Who's going to load us up?" Dimian demanded, pale and restless.

"The cart won't take it," I pointed out.

"We aren't going to go anywhere, are we?"

That made sense. We could use a scroll to port back home. But first we had to load the cart.

Enea was as cool as a cucumber. The trip's resounding success didn't seem to have impressed her in the slightest. That was understandable. According to Mr. Borisov, she was used to handling much bigger sums on a daily basis. Her heart craved adventure, not the boring drudgery of trading operations.

"Let's do it together," I told Dimian when all the dwarves had gone back to their storehouses, apparently not interested in helping us. Funny people. "We'll load up the crates first and heap all the bags on top."

It took us a good hour to load the cart with our treasures. In the end, it all fit but the cart looked as if it was about to disintegrate. No way the horse could even budge it.

"We need to go back now," Dimian kept urging me.

"Wait a sec," I drew Enea aside and gave her one of the teleport scrolls I'd made earlier. "The moment we leave, touch the coordinates to port out. We can't take you. The cart is falling apart as it is."

"Okay," she seemed happy we could finally go back. "You two be careful!"

Dimian had already climbed onto the cart. I followed suit. "Off we go!"

* * *

The impact dumbfounded me. In the rattling of wood and ripping of fabric, the cart fell apart. Dimian cried out. The horse neighed, petrified.

Talk about a crash landing. The port scroll had returned us to Dimian's backyard. Still, he had his work cut out for him now to collect all the gold and precious stones lying scattered in the dirt. The horse was dashing around, trampling them further into the ground.

"Quiet now!" Dimian grabbed the reins, calming the animal, then led him to the manger.

Another teleport popped open. Enea struggled to conceal a smile on seeing all the mess.

"Alexatis," Dimian said, tethering the horse, "could you help me here?"

"I don't think so. You can do it yourself. No offence, man. I still have Enea to take back. You can transfer my cut to my Crystal Bank account."

"Never mind. I'll have to ask my workers then. Just please don't disappear! The dwarves are expecting me back."

"I'll see you in a couple of days. Then we can talk."

We bade our goodbyes and left him alone with his fabulous treasure.

"You don't look too happy, do you?" I asked Enea.

"I'm just tired. Sorry."

"Now you'll probably make Agrion's Top 10 of the most successful players."

"Alex, please. I've had enough of that stuff in real life. I wanted to escape it. Remember the toad by the pond? That was really cool!"

"Cheer up. This world is about adventure, not daily grind, I assure you. You gonna log out now?"

"I am. I'm too tired. I've been stuck in the capsule all day."

"Will I see you tomorrow?"

"Sure. I just need some sleep. Shall we have lunch together?"

"Agreed. PM me as soon as you log back in. I'll probably be in the inn."

"Do you ever log out?"

"I have too many things to do, I'm afraid. We can talk about it tomorrow. Give me your bank account number so I can send you your half."

"I don't need it. Forget about it. I insist."

"Why?"

"I still don't know whether I'll stay," she admitted. "It looks cool but I have mixed feelings about it all. Not easy to choose."

"Choose what? The virtual world? Over the real one?"

She nodded, gave me a peck on the cheek, then disappeared.

* * *

Dimian sent fifty-seven thousand gold to my in-game account. Later that night, I realized I had to give my nearest future some thought.

Quest alert: Trade Route! Quest completed!

You've received a new level!

You've received 57,000 gold coins!

You've received 100 pt. to Popularity! Current Popularity: 100 pt. (Gentleman of Fortune)

A map update available: Real Estate Atlas! (provided by Crystal Bank)

I opened the updated map of the continent. Now that my solvency had dramatically improved, I discovered a few very interesting locations marked on it. If our little Spectral Dust gig continued in the same vein, my lifestyle just might change very soon. Virtual gold was still gold. Not that I was going to buy myself new skills or levels, oh no. Both Enea and I were going to do our own leveling, for fear of losing interest in the game.

Still, considering my authenticity levels, was I supposed to sleep rough or knock about from one inn to the next, forced to answer uncomfortable questions about my char's class?

Should I buy my own place, maybe?

Not really. That might provide me with a roof over my head; maybe some illusion of stability even; but that was the extent of it. I shouldn't forget that I was constantly under the Corporation's scrutiny. I was their test subject, wasn't I? If the truth were known, one day they might decide they didn't need me anymore. Or even worse, they might get rid of me as an unwanted witness. You never knew.

Mr. Borisov's visit last night worried me a lot.

How could I secure myself from any potential threat?

I could see one possible way out. I had to become a major player in the game — a force to be reckoned with. I had to work out a plan aiming to increase my Popularity. That way, they wouldn't be able to get rid of me on the sly.

Let's have a look, then. What could I do in

order to gain consistent but comfortable levels of Popularity? Fifteen minutes of fame didn't suit me: it had to be something permanent.

As I pondered over it, studying the map, I couldn't help thinking about Enea.

Would she too choose to stay in the Crystal Sphere?

Impossible to tell. Her ties with the real world were way too strong. A family business was a serious thing.

I had to concentrate on my current problems. I needed to come up with a couple of out-of-the-box actions that might secure my future.

I opened the Real Estate Atlas.

It was basically a collection of screenshots that offered some idea of certain areas in far-off locations which might trigger any upcoming clan wars.

Securing any real estate in a world about to become a new home for billions of users was a serious claim to fame indeed.

I kept leafing through the atlas till midnight and bookmarked a few quite interesting — and affordable — places.

The future was calling my name. A few more trips to the Azure Mountains, then I could start considering a totally new level of freedom.

* * *

An insistent tapping on the door awoke me in the morning.

What were they like? Couldn't a man get some sleep? Enea wasn't to arrive for our lunch date until midday. And it wasn't even six o'clock yet!

The knocking repeated, the initial tapping now replaced by desperate banging on the door.

I got up, splashed some water on my face, then hurried to equip my gear, keeping the sword close at hand. I lifted the latch and stepped back. "Come in!"

The door swung open, letting in Dimian, pallid and agitated. He was babbling something as if unable to speak.

"Sit yourself here! And calm down!" I pulled out a chair and forced him to sit at the table, then shut the door. "Is the money stolen? Someone robbed your house? Was it burned down? Say something, for crissakes!"

"Alexatis, please help! I beg you in the name of the Gods of Light! Woe is me! I was greedy and stupid!"

I handed him a glass of water. "Can you tell me what happened?"

His hands were shaking so much he spilt half the glass over the table. "Where's Enea?" he finally asked once he'd got his breath back.

"She'll be here later."

"Tell her to come. Now."

"Why, did you get a visit from the Guild?"

"Ouch! Don't say that! No, everything's fine with them. I offered a few handfuls of gold to the right people so the Guild isn't a problem."

"What is, then?"

"We were going to make another trip in a week's time."

"That's right. I remember. It's still valid. I'll hire a convoy of merc guards so you shouldn't worry about that."

His hunched shoulders shook. He dissolved into sobbing. "Woe is me! Call Enea now, please!"

"Quiet!" I grabbed his lapels and gave him a good shake, trying to bring him back to his senses. "Tell me exactly what happened! Now! We're not waiting for her!"

He nodded. "It's the Spectral Dust..." his voice broke. He was gasping, unable to speak. I'd never seen a hysterical NPC before. "I thought this would be a one-off. One trip, that was it... Remember the parchment Enea made me sign? That's when I decided to take the biggest cart and load it up with as much Dust as I could."

I was beginning to understand. "How much did you promise to bring them the next time?"

"Two cartfuls."

"How much do you think you can raise?"

"None! None at all!" he groaned, crumpling an embroidered handkerchief in his hands. "I've bought it all up already!"

"What were you thinking when you promised more to the dwarves?"

"Greed clouded my judgment! I thought I might be able to get more within a week. There's none available! And the prices!" he shrieked. "It used to be two coppers a gram, and now they want a gold piece! And even so it'll take them a month to deliver it!"

"Relax. Have some wine. I'm sure I'll think of something."

His gaze filled with desperate hope. Obediently he drank some wine, spilling most of it.

I sat opposite him and opened the auction.

All the Spectral Dust was gone. The price had already soared to three gold a gram. Okay. Let's check the in-game newsfeed.

Holy cow! Rumors of a trader buying up the Spectral Dust had spread like wildfire. Instances were packed solid with promptly-made groups busy purging dungeons. Specter farming was the thing — but still the admins, although suitably impressed by this sudden surge of interest, refused to reduce Specters' six-hour respawn times point blank. According to them, the dungeon-generating servers would go into overload otherwise.

I made a quick estimation of how much Dust could one farm in a week. Not much. A couple of crates if one was lucky. But a couple of "cartloads"? You could forget it. Besides, we'd have to sell it at a loss, considering the dwarves were offering us two gold a gram.

Very well, then. I PM'd Enea. We had to come up with a solution.

By now, Dimian was drinking wine from the bottle. I took it from him. The drink was supposed to have been therapeutic.

A few minutes later, Enea arrived. She gave me a peck on the cheek, then attacked Dimian,

"Where did you learn your business practices? What were you thinking of? You should have been buying Dust in small batches, constantly monitoring the prices! You've collapsed the market! It'll take vendors at least a month to realize their mistake! They'll keep prices high hoping to get their money back for something no one even needs here! But you can forget two copper a gram, that I can guarantee!"

Dimian maintained a grim silence.

"Please don't," I finally said. "Enough. He knows it already."

"Enough? I haven't even started yet!"

"There's no point in arguing," I said. "I

actually have an idea."

Both fell silent.

"Speak up," Dimian croaked, his eyes glinting with hope. "Don't drag it out!"

Enea sat at the table, apparently skeptical of any economic miracles. "Let's define our objectives first," she said. "We want to keep our word given to the dwarves, right? In that case, we'll have to work at a loss but at least we'll save our reputation with our partners. Another very important thing is to keep our trade route secret."

"You're right!" I announced as I'd made a final decision. "With one little correction: we aren't going to work at a loss. It's pretty obvious that we can't buy so much Spectral Dust. Which means we need to farm it."

"What, two cartloads?" Enea asked, incredulous.

"Yep."

Dimian leaned closer, his breath reeking of alcohol. "How are we going to do that?"

"*You* aren't doing anything. You're going home now."

He sobered up. "Excuse me?"

"You heard. The source of Spectral Dust is a secret. All you can do is wait and keep your mouth shut."

"I can't wait! I'll die of worry!"

I shrugged. "I'll get the Dust. But my cut

might change."

"Does that mean we'll have to sign another piece of parchment?"

"Absolutely. Enea will explain its new terms to you later. One thing I promise: I'll get the Dust and take your caravan to the dwarves. All you need do is stand behind the counter and sell it while watching the dwarves line up in front of your stall."

"What, no costs? Not even a copper a gram?"

"Exactly. Good enough?"

"I'll be going, then," he scooped up his hat as if afraid I might change my mind. "When can I expect to hear from you?"

"We'll meet at your place in a week's time. Don't say a word to anyone. Get the carts and the horses ready. If someone comes to you offering Spectral Dust, just tell them you don't need it anymore. Don't mention the Azure Mountains to anyone. Understood?"

"Yeah..."

"Excellent. Off you go, then."

* * *

"Alex? What's all this about?" Enea asked, alarmed. "You sure you're okay? How are you going to get that kind of amount? Are you going to hire some mercs? Not a good idea, trust me," she hurried to add. "For two reasons. Firstly, they'll report our trade route to the guild. And secondly, it's just pointless, can't you see? There's a waiting list to enter dungeons! The servers are about to crash!"

She didn't seem to see a way out of this. I, however, knew how to do it. Provided we were prepared to take a risk. A crazy, desperate risk which would put everything we'd gained on the line.

"We're going to create a clan. And then-"

Her eyes glistened. "A clan? Oh wow! Do you mean it? You're too cool for words, you know that? A clan of our own! What shall we call it? Oh, sorry. I didn't mean to interrupt you. What did you say? We create a clan and then what?" she asked, breathless.

"And we buy the derelict castle on the Toxic Moors!"

"No way!" her gaze lit up with excitement. "A clan and a castle?"

"A *derelict* castle," I said. "Complete with imps, specters and all sorts of undead monsters for us to purge. For what it is, it's a bargain."

"What's a bargain?"

"They want a down payment of fifty grand."

"But that's all you have!"

"It is. The rest I can pay back to Crystal

Bank within a year."

"Crystal Bank! Their interest rates are outrageous. Still, if it all works out with the dwarves, we might just make it. Now," she grew serious, "what's the catch? Where are you going to get two cartfuls of Dust? We only have a week! Even if you do buy the castle and throw together a hundred-strong group, you still won't be able to farm that much."

"We don't really need to kill specters, do we? What we'll need is some weapons and gear plus two craftsmen: a Master in Alchemy and another one in Mining."

I told her what I knew about dark obelisks and transformed matter.

"Smoky Rock?" Enea asked, pensive, while perusing some online information.

"Exactly. I've been wondering how I might use it. I need some for a quest I received. It's about my sword. So I thought, I might have some to spare. It's a valuable resource. You look it up later. So I was researching its potential uses but found very little. Apparently, all you can do with it is sell it to jewelers. But I also discovered something else. When you break up a dark obelisk into fragments, the crumbling Spectral Dust is the biggest danger. If you inhale too much of it, you might turn into an undead yourself."

"How cool is that?" Enea exclaimed. "Yes, I see now! If there're plenty of imps there, there must be lots of obelisks too! Lots of obelisks mean plenty of Smoky Rock! Can you imagine?" she asked, her imagination going into overload. "Those gloomy ancient halls... cobwebs everywhere... and a thick layer of Spectral Dust covering the floors!"

"Not sure about the floors."

"Then we'll definitely need some wizards and warriors."

"No, we won't. All we'll need is a small group of mercs plus some weapons and gear."

"Can you prove it?" she held her breath, expecting me to wow her with another surprise.

"Dark obelisks enslave spirits. By destroying them, we liberate the NPCs trapped inside them. I have a funny feeling they'll be more than happy to help us purge the castle."

"Wait a moment," Enea did another online search. "Found it. A clan application. Requires a minimum of five members and a registered name. A clan has a year to acquire a castle, either by buying or conquering it. Currently they're running castle promotion offers, excellent. That'll save us a few gold. Ah, there it is! *'Non-Player Characters can join a clan provided their numbers don't exceed those of the players — unless they're hired to defend the clan's citadel."* Brilliant. It means we *can* use NPCs to help us purge the castle..." her voice tailed away. "But what about the two craftsmen we're supposed to find?"

"I know a Master in Mining," I said. "But a Master Alchemist capable of turning Smoky Rock to Spectral Dust... we'll just have to find one."

"Okay," Enea agreed, cheering up. "I can do that. May I?"

I frowned.

"Alexatis, what is it? You think I don't understand what's at stake? You're risking your own life! If you fail to pay, they'll find you in real life. Which is why I'm joining your clan!" she announced. "And I demand to be present at all of the clan's negotiations! I might be a newb but I'm no spring chicken in business..."

"Is that your decision?"

"Absolutely."

"That's it, then. We won't discuss it anymore."

She breathed a sigh of relief. "You're something, Alex, you really are. I was really afraid of this conversation. Never mind. We don't have much time. We should apply today. I'll start filling in the form while you should start thinking of a name."

I could literally feel her adrenaline rising.

"The Black Mantises," I replied without hesitation.

"Awesome. Why Mantises?"

"Just an idea. Firstly, because Rion Castle stands right in the heart of the Toxic Moors inhabited by hydras and Black Mantises. And secondly," I cast a meaningful glance at my scaly armor, "in future, this gear may become our clan's signature feature. We'll have plenty of source materials right on our doorstep!"

"Excellent," she said, already busy online. "We need at least three more players."

"Two I already know. We'll talk to them in a minute. They're dwarves. One of them is a Master Miner even though he keeps his achievements under wraps for the moment. The fifth... no idea. Know of someone?"

She heaved a sigh. "No."

I pondered for a while. Once again, things were happening too fast. Only last night a clan and a castle had felt like an impossible dream — and now I was filling in the application form!

"Then we'll have to invite anyone, the first person we see," I said.

"You can't do that, either," Enea replied. "The five clan members listed in the application make up the Clan Council and have the right of vote. You as the clan founder have two votes, by the way. I shouldn't invite those two dwarves, either," she added confidently. "They need to have a trial period."

"So what do we do?"

"There're two types of applications," she replied. "The other one is for those who buy a castle at the same time as registering a clan. In which case, you only need two members: the founder and the treasurer. This is a simplified option for those Crystal Sphere investors who aren't prepared to share their power."

"Excellent. Perfect in our case. Sign us up."

"The application is accepted. They'll review it within an hour. Now the castle. Why do you want to buy it? Why not conquer it? Is it because time is an issue?"

"Lots of reasons. Firstly, if you buy it, they give you the castle's coordinates. Which means we can teleport there. Secondly, I don't think we're strong enough to conquer it."

"They don't give you much time to claim it, though. We have twenty-four hours to get to the donjon and activate the safe respawn point in the main hall."

"I know. That's why we need the mercs. As far as I understand, the castle ruins are absolutely packed with the undead. We'll need a paladin. How about Zander? Better the devil you know."

She nodded. "Good idea. I've filled in the castle application. Should I send it off?"

"Please do."

Once again I had this funny feeling as if I was standing on a cliff edge, about to jump into the void.

"The application is accepted. Now you can contact your dwarves. We'll speak to them first before contacting Zander. Now, a Master Alchemist... that might take some doing. I don't think we can find a good one among the players. How about an NPC?"

"How about having lunch first?"

She gave me a sly smile. "I love it when men keep their word. Oh, come on, I'm only joking!" she burst into happy laughter. "You don't need to take everything so seriously!"

I laughed too, then took her by the hand. "Off we go, then!"

CHAPTER NINE

YOUR CLAN application has been approved! Congratulations! You've created a clan: The Black Mantises. Your Popularity among Crystal Sphere denizens has grown!

You've received Achievement: Clan Founder.
+ 1,000 to Popularity
+1 to all Reputations

Your castle purchase application has been approved by the Crystal Bank!

Your bank account has been debited with 50,000 gold coins.

Warning! You have 24 hours (in-game time) to claim your clan's citadel!

RION CASTLE was situated about three weeks' journey from Agrion. It stood on a long rocky plateau surrounded by a never-ending maze of marshes and treacherous bog mires.

The few available images betrayed the ancient castle's deplorable condition. Still, it must have suffered most of the damage during some recent attack. Its numerously breached walls bore silent witness to that: this wasn't the damage of time but rather the result of some well-coordinated fighting.

Someone knocked on the door.

"Come in," I said.

"Hi there," Zander entered the room alone. "Why did you want to see me?"

"I need to hire a group of mercs."

"How many?" he cast a curious glance at the holographic images but chose not to say anything. Still, I could see he'd recognized them: he didn't look too surprised neither did he ask me which castle it was or where it was located.

"Five. Preferably the same level as you."

"For how long?"

"Two or three days. I bought this castle, you see, and now I need to claim it. But it's packed with the undead."

"Do I understand correctly that these are the Toxic Moors?" now he peered at the 3D map image with some interest.

"Have you been there before?"

"Not really. Still, it's quite doable. All mobs are level thirty-plus," he said as he promptly researched the location online. "I do hope you have the coordinates to teleport there."

"I do, which is why I don't want to call up an army. But I do need your services in order to purge it before deadline. You think you could throw a group together?"

"I most definitely can."

"How much?" Enea butted in.

"A grand per day plus a percentage of any loot we farm outside of the donjon walls. Whatever we manage to farm inside is rightfully yours."

"Deal. Enea will make out a contract in a minute."

"Excellent. I'll need a couple of hours to get it up and running. When are you planning to depart?"

"Later in the afternoon, I think. I need to talk to a few more players."

"It's up to you," Zander said, scrutinizing the images of the castle and taking in the details of the future campaign. "Have you already checked the coordinates against the map? Where are you planning to port to, exactly?"

"Here," I marked a small access point on a small rocky island where the castle's barbican stood. "We'll have to start purging right from the front of the bridge all the way to the central dungeons."

"I see. What's this, an old road?" he pointed at a gray line snaking deep into the moors.

"Apparently. Still, I've no idea whether it's usable. So we'll have to port both in and out. A castle of this caliber is obliged to have a stationary portal. The admins have promised us a safe respawn point in one of the starting locations, but I'd rather we used tents."

"Good idea. Very wise, considering all the legends about Rion Castle. There're no safe respawn points on the moors no matter what anybody says. You can forget it. Now inside, it's a different story. There's bound to be a place of power in the donjon's main hall, complete with a respawn point."

"How do you know all this? What legends do you mean? Tell me. I had no time for any research."

He grinned his understanding. "An impulse buy?"

"You could say that. It happened too quickly."

He didn't look surprised. "Every ancient castle has its own place of power and an associated respawn point. Rion Castle... the legends are legion, each scarier than the next. I'm afraid, we'll have to sort fact from fiction as we go. The only thing I can tell you is that the castle was built during the Founders era. For centuries it served as a citadel to the Order of the Disciples."

"Never heard of them!" Enea announced.

"The Disciples used to worship the Founder Gods. There're very few surviving mentions of them. I know because I earn my living by seeking out rare artifacts," Zander chuckled. "Rion's actually on my list of *'places to check out'*, but I never thought I might be going there so soon. That's why my quote is reasonable. I'm just curious."

"The castle must have fallen to an enemy invasion," I pointed at the tell-tale pattern of breached walls. "Do your sources have anything to say about that?"

"They do and they don't," Zander replied. "Some claim that after the Founders' departure, the Crystal Sphere split into two camps — basically, into the forces of Light and Dark. The Order of the Disciples united all the warriors and wizards who'd refused to accept the new order. The Disciples and their followers preserved an armed neutrality while continuing to study the Founders' legacy."

"So I suppose the new religions weren't happy with them?" Enea asked.

"Not at all," Zander replied. "This was actually the only precedent in the entire history of the Crystal Sphere when both sides united against a common enemy. As Rion Castle was considered impregnable at the time, they decided to storm it on three fronts: from the moors, by air and under the ground. So the castle fell. Each and every one of the Disciples died in the process, which led to the loss of all the knowledge they'd amassed. Gradually, the castle ruins started swarming with the undead — as is often the case."

"What, did no one really try to get to it?" I asked in disbelief.

"Oh yes, they did," Zander grinned. "Quite a few, in fact. Still, even a well-prepared group can't tackle the Toxic Moors on its own. Which is why I'm quite happy to accept your invitation."

"I think I'm going to add a non-disclosure clause to the agreement," Enea reacted instantly, "about keeping the castle's layout, its coordinates and the maps of the surrounding area secret."

Zander nodded. "Fair enough. In that case, I'd like to have the right to buy up any artifacts of my choice."

"Provided they're not part of the castle's infrastructure," Enea immediately offered an amendment.

"If you say so."

Someone knocked on the door again. I hurried to unbolt it.

Togien barged into the room. "Phew! I thought I'd be too late!"

He nodded to Zander as if he'd known him for ages. Then he stared at me in amazement. "You haven't wasted your time, have you? Level 18! That's quick!"

"Togien, I'd like you to meet Enea."

He grinned, recognizing her too. "Sure! The staffless spell stunt! I watched it in the inn, it was absolutely packed!"

"Right. I'm off to get this show on the road," Zander said. "Don't expect me back soon. I need at least a couple of hours."

I gave him a hearty handshake and saw him to the door, then locked it. "Togien? Why are you here alone?"

"Gwain's busy right now. He's got a quest-" Togien faltered, unsure whether he could go on.

I understood his reservations. This was what I'd said in my message to him,

There's an opportunity to farm some Smoky Rock. We need a Master Miner.

"It's all right," I said. "We have no secrets from each other. Take a seat," I pointed at a spare stool. "So you're a Master Miner who prefers to keep his achievements under wraps?"

"Possible. But you did promise, didn't you, that you were going to keep Smoky Rock a secret?"

"And I kept my word. No one knows about that particular obelisk. I've discovered another source. Do you think you could break up a couple more obelisks for us?"

"You bet I can!"

"Can you do it on your own? Or do you need a few apprentices, maybe?"

"Nah. Can I have the details, please?"

"Enea will clue you in in a moment. You can discuss your terms with her, too. I might need to pop out to do a few things. You don't happen to know a Master Alchemist you can trust, do you?"

"Someone I can trust?" his voice tensed up. "No, I don't think so."

Did I detect some anxiety in his tone? Or even animosity? "Mind telling us about him?"

"About whom?"

"The alchemist."

"Alexatis, you're scaring me. Are you a mind reader now?"

"Togien, please. We don't have the time. If you know of someone, tell me!"

"Yeah," he grumbled. "I suppose you could say I know him. That mad scientist bastard! The crazy genius!" his cheeks exploded in blotches of crimson. "Gwain and I, we ordered some Strength elixirs from him. A hundred, to be precise!"

"And?"

"And he made explosives instead! Ruined all the ingredients we'd given him! He said he'd been so sorry seeing us picking at the rock and gulping elixirs by the dozen when all we needed to do was blow it up. Can you imagine? And he acted so offended when I taught his sorry ass a lesson! He even filed a complaint with my guild."

"And the explosives, did they work?"

"Do I look stupid enough to try? I know the rules! No firearms or explosives in the mines with the exception of magic bombs. You blow something up once and they'll disable your account for good. Oh no, sir, thank you very much!"

"Can I have his contacts, please?"

"You can, but I shouldn't hold your breath. The guy is trouble. Don't say I didn't warn you."

My interface flashed with an incoming PM message. "Never mind," I gave Enea a wink. "Enjoy yourselves. I'm off now. The clock is ticking."

* * *

The alchemists' quarter was small but quite conspicuous. A huge iridescent magic dome towered over it. Cast by the neighboring Wizards' Guild, it protected all other city inhabitants from the obnoxious stench of the cooking potions and elixirs.

The air here was heavy, that's for sure. Each profession has its drawbacks.

It didn't take me long to locate the house I'd been looking for. With a powerful popping sound, an attic window spewed out a cloud of blue smoke. The neighboring window panes disintegrated, showering the pavement with cascades of broken glass. The air turned blue with cussing and angry voices,

"How many times do we need to tell you? The bedroom is for sleeping! The shed is for working! Go and test your concoctions there!"

My Master Alchemist looked quite eccentric. His clothes were covered in burn marks and ragged holes, his hair disheveled. His eyes weeping (from the toxic smoke rather than remorse), he turned to face his landlord.

I checked his name tag,

Platinus. Level 9. Sorcerer.

"Step aside, Master Gorn, Sir!" he exclaimed, addressing the landlord. "I'm on the brink of a major breakthrough! All I need is a tad more Blood of a Dragon! Don't cringe! I'll pay you as soon as..."

"I think I might call the guards this time!"

"Be my guest! Science has always been fettered by ignoramuses like you, sir! You'd rather have lead turned into gold, wouldn't you?"

"Not necessarily. Normal gold will do nicely. Problem is, you don't have it. You never will! Right, I've had enough. I'm evicting you. I'm confiscating all your pots and vials to pay what you owe me!"

The landlord seemed to mean it. He might have actually called the guards. It was time for me to interfere.

"Platinus?" I said. "Mind stepping aside, please? Need to talk."

"I've got nothing to talk to you about!" reaching into his pocket, Platinus swung round, about to hurl some stinky vial into my face. Clever bastard. Always prepared. Apparently, life wasn't easy for him here.

I stopped his hand in mid-swing, grabbing his wrist tight while whispering in his ear, "I have an offer to make to you."

"I don't care!" he spewed, trying to wriggle himself free.

I pushed him through the open doorway. The room was still filled with smoke, its walls and floor splattered with Blood of a Dragon. The vial must have exploded because he'd miscalculated the ingredients.

"I need to talk to you," I repeated. "Are you indeed a Master Alchemist?"

"So what if I am?" he stared at me defiantly. "What's that got to do with you?"

"I might have a job for you. You're gonna like it. It pays well, too."

He sort of slackened, allowing me to snatch back the initiative, "You're not leveling Sorcery, are you? I can see you prefer to invest everything into your profession instead."

"Sure. Problem is, I have to live with these nincompoops! The fact that they don't let me do my research in real life isn't enough for them! Here they start it all over again!"

I had no time to listen to his tales of woe. "Have you heard of Smoky Rock?"

"I might have," he slumped onto a stool, his head hung low.

"Mind telling me about it?"

"What's this, a job interview? Don't you think you're going too far?"

"Please don't make me angry. Just answer the question. I would also like to see your achievements. You'd better show them to me if you don't want to spend the night in the cooler. How much do you owe your landlord?"

"Twenty-five gold," he spat out. "Plus damaged property."

"That can be arranged. So what can you say about Smoky Rock?"

"It's a rare ingredient. Transformed matter. It can be farmed from rocks previously inhabited by a Dark Obelisk spirit."

"What can you make with it?"

He perked up. "Some very special stuff. If you mix some Spectral Dust with the root of Crumbly Moss and add ten drops of Specklewort juice, you can make a Potion of Stealthed Entry, allowing you to penetrate walls. I haven't quite fine-tuned it yet, though. I gave some to a rogue guy to try free of charge but he wasn't very happy. He very nearly killed me afterwards."

"Why, didn't it work?"

"It did, but only halfway. He got stuck in the wall."

"What's Spectral Dust got to do with it?" I asked in a deadpan voice, struggling to wipe a smile off my face. "My question was about Smoky Rock!"

"I dissolve it in the juice of Mountain Vine which partially neutralizes the power of the Dark Obelisk and creates a sediment of Spectral Dust. Easy. Only why would you waste such an expensive resource to make Spectral Dust?"

"That's none of your business. Sorry to be so rude but at least I'm being honest with you. This Vine juice, is it hard to procure?"

"Not really. I used to have a whole pitcher of it but I wasted it all on Disintegration Potions. Please understand: I'm not one of those run-of-the-mill bunglers! I'm an artist! I create new formulas! I had my Disintegration Potion patented with the admins. I meant to use it to make bombs but no one seems to be interested."

"What kind of bombs?"

"Well, the vial explodes on impact, nullifying the enemy armor's Durability. Still, no one seems to care. They said to me, *Why would we want to ruin good gear?*"

"Makes sense. So can I see your achievements?"

"Be my guest," he sent me the information I needed.

Oh wow. He was a Master Alchemist all right!

"I'm calling up a raid on the Toxic Moors," I said. "Would you like to join us? I can see you're not exactly welcome in town."

"The Toxic Moors? Cool! They're packed with rare ingredients! What do you want me to do there?"

"At a certain point, I might need you to

turn some Smoky Rock into Spectral Dust."

"Is that it? Not a problem. My Disintegration Potions will do the job nicely."

"You sure?"

"Ninety percent sure," he admitted. "They should work. The Vine juice is better, I agree. Will I be allowed to do some research on the way?"

"Absolutely. Whatever herbs we come across are all yours. If we smoke a mob, you'll get all the Alchemy-related loot. On one condition. I want you to take as many Disintegration Potions with you as you can. How many do you have?"

"I might still have a few," he said. "About a dozen, give or take. I need to check the shed. I'm pretty sure I have some in one of the drawers. The problem is, I don't think my landlord will let me in. Didn't you hear he wants to confiscate everything?"

I PM'd Enea:

Everything all right?

I've made an agreement with Togien. He's in.

Good. Could you please research prices for Mountain Vine juice and see if it's readily available?

OK. How's the alchemist, is he sound?

Sort of. Perfect for the job though. I'll be back soon.

I'm waiting.

I turned to Platinus. "So what do you think? Will you join us?"

He looked around himself, taking in the gutted room. "Yes," he nodded vigorously. "I've had enough of this boring town!"

* * *

We put Platinus up in the Golden Carp Inn.

"You should stay in your room," I told him. "Make a list of everything you need and PM it to Enea. Here's her address. We're leaving in an hour. Try to stay out of harm's way. Think you can manage that?"

"I might have a nap," he reassured me. "I don't need a list. I carry everything I need on me."

He threw his sorcerer's robe open.

Oh wow. The guy was smart, you had to give him that. His robe's lining secreted a multitude of little pockets filled with all kinds of vials and chemicals. This was one highly explosive geezer.

"How old are you? In real life, I mean," I asked him.

"I'm thirty-seven."

"You're funny, you know that? You should be leveling Sorcery."

"Who are you calling funny?" Platinus sounded offended. "If you absolutely must know, I have a doctorate in chemistry! I used to do all sorts of research in real life!"

"Used to? What happened, then?"

"They fired me. I'm out of work."

"Why?"

"They installed a new-generation neuro computer to replace me. According to them, it's more efficient and less problematic. And everywhere I turn, it's the same! We're being evicted from the real world! By machines! That's why I decided to go virtual! I thought that here my skills might be in demand! As if!"

I seemed to have touched on a sore subject. "Leave it, man. I might need a clan alchemist soon. Full time. If you can prove yourself, the job's yours."

He perked up. His eyes glinted with hope. "Will I be able to do some research?"

I hesitated. Wasn't I jumping the gun, promising things to all and sundry?

"You will," I replied earnestly. "We'll set up a lab for you, too. But first we need to purge the castle and get some Spectral Dust. The rest, at the moment, is academic."

"Alexatis, I promise I won't let you down! I've had this town up to here!" he made a slashing gesture across his throat.

"Okay. We'll see what you can do. Now try to get some rest and please don't leave the room."

My intercom icon flashed.

"You gonna take long?" Enea asked. "I've got the vine juice. Zander contacted me. He's put a group together. I've drafted a contract for them, provisionally for two days with the possibility of extension. Our bank account is virtually empty."

"I'm coming. Could you please buy a stack of parchment sheets and some ink?"

"Not a problem."

All this had been quite enough for one day. And it wasn't over yet! In just an hour, we were going to port to the Toxic Moors: to face the unknown, not to even mention level-30 mobs.

* * *

When I returned to my room, I discovered there — apart from Enea and Togien — also a stranger: an unpleasant-looking sleazy guy who gave me very bad vibes.

"Sir Alexatis!" he sprang from his stool and hurried to shake my hand. "Congratulations on creating a clan, sir!"

"Thanks," I said warily. "Do I know you?"

Enea watched me with a foxy smile. Togien frowned, suppressing a smirk.

"News spreads fast here!" the stranger announced. "We have received official information about the upcoming Rion Castle raid! You only have twenty-three hours left to complete it, don't you?"

That was one stupid question. Who was this smartass, after all? And what was he doing in my room?

"Miss Enea allowed me to wait for you here. I'm Sciatant."

Was I supposed to know his name? "Have we met before?"

"Not yet. I'm from Crystal Daily News. I have an offer to make you."

"Which is?"

"I'd like to accompany you. First we can run a quick story from the town's central square as you and your fellow clan members port to the heart of the Toxic Moors! I'm sure it'll make the headlines! Then we continue with a series of..."

There you have it. The first signs of our future popularity. "Absolutely not," I said.

He couldn't believe his ears. "You surely don't mean it! We're talking fifteen hundred grand! And free publicity for your clan! You won't even have to do anything! I'll just do a bit of filming, that's all!"

"Absolutely not," I repeated politely but firmly.

"But that'll make you famous!" he just couldn't see my point. "Your clan is the second in Agrion! We're obliged to report a story of this caliber!"

"Sorry but you're wasting my time."

I wasn't yet prepared to prance around in front of cameras surrounded by crowds of curious onlookers. And he could forget filming the castle! As far as I was concerned, everything pertaining to the raid was classified information. Posting an online video wouldn't be wise to say the least. Besides, we still didn't know if the whole thing would be a success.

"If you leave me your contact information, Sir Sciatant," Enea helpfully butted in, "I can promise you a string of stories about the clan. At the moment, I'm afraid we really don't have much time. We have too many things to do."

"If you wish," he said, disappointed. "You've no idea what kind of opportunity you're missing."

Enea paused, thinking, then offered, "We have a counter proposition to make. You can't go with us but we can film everything ourselves, of course. Alexatis will then choose what in his opinion can be made public. Not as good as live coverage, I agree, but at least your channel will have exclusive rights to it."

"Good idea!" Sciatant announced unhesitantly.

"I'll get back to you in a couple of days. See you then," gentle but resolute, she led him to the door.

Having closed it behind him, she turned to me,

"I bet he's gone to the main square now, to post his paparazzi. By the way, Zander doesn't want to make his group public, either. I've spoken to the innkeeper. We can port from his back yard."

I heaved a sigh of relief. "Clever girl. Are you ready?"

"You bet!" she was fidgeting, impatient. "You can't imagine how awesome everything is here!"

"Please don't mind me," Togien concealed a good-natured smile in his mustache.

"We don't. Still, it's time to get off your ass, man," I said, doing a quick mental check of our readiness. "Let's move it!"

* * *

We met up with Zander's mercs in the backyard next to the Golden Carp's stables.

"Great job getting rid of the reporters," Zander gave me a friendly slap on the shoulder. "I'd like you to meet my friends."

Two warriors and two wizards — all of them level 35 as luck would have it — hovered nearby.

"Tylor," a mithril-clad gray-haired warrior bowed his head. I'd better get used to this kind of treatment now. Had he come across me earlier in the street, he wouldn't have even looked my way. Still, now I was a clan leader and his employer which was a whole new ball game.

I shook his sturdy hand.

"Virgil," the other warrior introduced himself.

I tried to work them out. Zander was their tank: this much was clear. He had a higher level and more appropriate gear. He would be the one who'd pull aggro to himself, allowing the two warriors to deal damage. They looked like a well-knit team. The men's faces didn't betray any anxiety.

The wizards were tall, clad in long robes girded with wide leather belts. Both were dark-faced, their chiseled features betraying their kinship. I didn't know this race. They must have imported it.

"My brother and I are from the Talgaim people. My name's Rodrigo. He's Iskandar."

I introduced Enea, Togien and Platinus.

"Excellent," Zander turned to me. "You can create a group now. We've already agreed on our percentages of XP and loot."

By then, I had everything up and running. In a few quick clicks, the group was created.

"Now the main thing," Zander began. "I'll do the tanking and aura casting. My range is sixty feet. I want you to keep this in mind and stay within it. Togien, when we approach the castle I want you to join Tylor and Virgil. The three of you will deal close-combat damage. Enea, you can join Rodrigo and Iskandar and cast long-range spells. Close combat is not your thing. Understood?"

Enea nodded.

"Now you," Zander turned to Platinus. "Just keep your head down, okay? Stay behind the wizards and sit tight. If the going gets really tough, Tylor and Virgil will also do some tanking. The three of us will form a triangle, the others will take cover inside. In this scenario, Alexatis and Togien will have to deal what damage they can, choosing appropriate targets. Enea, you too can cast whatever spells you have. Rodrigo will control mobs and cast debuffs. Iskandar will do the healing when necessary. Platinus, same tactic: just freeze and pretend you're not even there. Questions?"

"And if the going doesn't get too tough, what am I supposed to do?" I asked.

He turned to me. "Alexatis, you're a clan leader. Until we find a safe respawn point and bind to it, you're our most important asset. Don't argue. It's my group's reputation at stake. If we lose you, it'll be a mark of dishonor for the entire Mercenary Guild."

"I'm not going to hide behind any wizard's back!" I protested.

"I'm afraid you'll have to. You can't engage until absolutely necessary."

"All right," I reluctantly agreed. "I suppose I could join Enea and cast long-range spells."

"Can you do that?" Zander sounded sincerely surprised.

"I can. Didn't you see my class?"

"I did. I saw it when I first met you. Is it imported?"

"It is. I can switch between wizard and warrior no problem," I fed him a heavily edited version of truth to explain away my multi polyvalence.

"Very well, then," Zander agreed. "You can join the wizards then. Any more questions?"

Platinus seemed to be about to say something but reconsidered.

"Excellent. Let's do it! May the Gods of Light be with us!"

* * *

THE CRYSTAL SPHERE
THE VICINITY OF RION CASTLE

With a splash, the earth gave underfoot, squishing, sucking me into the treacherous quagmire.

I began to sink. The murky swamp water filled my field of vision, overlapped with system messages,

Congratulations! You've discovered a new region: The Toxic Moors!

You've received Achievement: A Celebrated Pioneer! Your map-making app is now available in full detail mode.

Warning! You've received 15 pt. Damage!

I thrashed desperately upwards, aiming for a bleak gleam of light overhead.

Finally, my head surfaced. The thick bog parted. The midday sun blinded me. I heard Enea cry out. Somewhere nearby, Togien cussed.

Something wrapped itself around my leg and was pulling me back into the deep, drowning me yet again.

I couldn't reach out for my sword. Nor could I cast a spell. Noxious bubbles of swamp gas shot up past me through the water.

The air struggled to escape my lungs. My hand chanced on some slimy object; I grabbed at it for dear life, trying to hinder my descent, then attempted to resurface again.

Yes! The unknown monster had let go of my leg. After a few powerful strokes, I finally saw the blurred sphere of the sun gleaming overhead.

Come on, Alexatis, do it!

I resurfaced, gasping, and spread my arms wide across the thick heaving layer of morass.

The heady smell of wild rosemary hung in the air over a moss-covered islet surrounded by what looked like a thick growth of giant ferns and horsetails.

"Give me your hand!" Zander reached out to me from a hillock encircled by blackened driftwood.

"Thanks!"

The breeze bore a nauseating whiff of hydrogen sulfide. I could see Togien who'd already climbed out onto some driftwood and was looking around himself. Quiet and scared, Enea grabbed at the broken trunk of a dried-out young tree a couple dozen feet away from me.

Iskandar hovered in the air overhead, surrounded by the bubble of his Levitation aura.

His robes weren't even soiled. He reached out in the direction of the bog, his hands sending jets of air into the water which was now seething, bringing more rotting driftwood to its dark surface.

"It's too deep!" said Iskandar, grunting with the effort. "Rodrigo, give me a hand, man, or I might not make it!"

The other wizard — soaked and covered in sludge — joined in. Together they cast Levitation spells, rescuing the warriors who too were sinking into the quagmire.

Zander and I got to the safety of the islet. It was firm and relatively dry, overgrown with sedges and studded with the occasional sickly little tree.

Enea was quite close to us. Her initial fear was already gone; she looked around herself in curiosity.

"Where's Platinus? Anyone seen him?"

"I'm here," a voice said.

"Where? Show us!"

Water ran from under my armor. I grabbed at a piece of driftwood and thrust another one toward Enea, helping her to climb onto the island.

"Platinus! What do you think you're doing?"

"I told you I'm here," he finally climbed out of the muck — disheveled and soaking wet but looking utterly pleased with himself. He scrambled to his knees and waved to us while pulling at a lump of knotty root bulging with nodules. "This is Noxious Weed!" he announced, triumphant. "I heard about it but I've never seen it before!"

Zander shook his head, watching Platinus' reckless excitement.

Tylor and Virgil stood on the opposite banks of the island, each about sixty feet away from us. Those teleport scrolls weren't exactly accurate, were they?

"We've missed," Zander told us after consulting his map. "No idea how this could have happened."

"How far is the castle?" Enea asked.

I opened my map and compared our current location with the castle's coordinates I'd entered into the scroll. Then I checked it against the logs.

We'd missed indeed! The castle's coordinates we'd received upon purchase were correct. Still, it looked like some unknown force had pushed us way off target.

"It's possible that the castle's magic defenses are still functioning," Zander said.

"It definitely looks that way," I agreed. "This is what the logs say: *an unexpected teleport error occurred.*"

"So where *is* the castle, then?" Enea wondered.

"A couple of miles from here."

"A couple miles of quagmire," Togien grumbled from his comfortable seat of driftwood. "How long will it take us to get there?"

"Alexatis, you don't happen to have any more teleport scrolls, do you?" Zander asked.

"I do. But I don't think it's a good idea. A couple of miles isn't that much of a hike. But if this *'unexpected teleport error'* kicks in again, we might end up miles from here. Provided the castle's magic defenses indeed keep deflecting all incoming teleports, then it's not worth the risk."

"You have a point there," Zander agreed, watching the warriors prod their way onto the island through the quagmire, probing their paths with long poles. "Iskandar, Rodrigo! Can you levitate them here?"

"We can't use the vials quite yet," one of the wizards replied. "Need to meditate for a bit."

"Okay, in your own time. Tylor, Virgil, don't risk it! Stay where you are and wait for the Levitation Aura to arrive! Platinus, lie down and try to crawl toward us! Whatever you do, don't try to stand up! You'll sink!"

"In a moment! I'll just pick some of these roots! They're sitting quite deep! I'll pull them out and be with you straight away!"

Zander frowned. "This guy is trouble. Absolutely uncontrollable."

"He's not in trouble yet, is he?" Togien took Platinus' side. "There don't seem to be any mobs around here."

Togien had been lucky enough not to port into the bog. His clothes were dry — but falling on top of all that driftwood must have hurt, that's for sure.

"Wretched leech!" Virgil slapped his steel gauntlet on his armor. "It's sucking on me!"

"It's all right," Zander told him. "I'm going to cast a cleansing spell in a minute. That'll take care of all the petty mobs."

He turned to me, still waiting for the wizards to restore their mana. "We'd better start thinking about an access route. Logically, a direct path would be the best, wouldn't it?"

"Not really," I forwarded him the data from my own detailed map. Apparently, the map-making app seemed to work well in conjunction with my Enhanced Perception ability. "Can you see those dotted lines?"

"What about them? They seem to lead to the castle. Why, what are they?"

"I think they might be old passageways across the bog."

"We should check them out," Zander said, cheering up. "In a moment we'll regroup, then we'll investigate."

The air shattered with Platinus' desperate screaming.

"Hydras!" Tylor yelled.

I whipped out my sword and swung in the direction of the growling sounds, shielding Enea with my body.

"Rodrigo, control them!" Zander's shouted command was drowned out by the hydras' roaring.

The nearest monster resurfaced within a dozen feet from the island.

It looked a sight, I tell you! The creature was lithe, aggressive and incredibly strong. It had six legs, a powerful body and twelve heads, their jaws exuding Acid Mist.

Common Swamp Hydra. Level 35, my interface reported.

Common, yeah right. Its skin was an olive color and scale-free. Not that it made our job any easier.

Thoughts began flashing through my head. At the moment, we were scattered. We couldn't make a formation. Our wizards were exposed, and Platinus was basically without any protection at all.

"Enea!" I shouted. "We're casting Ice,

together! Now!"

The spell failed to deal much damage to the hydra. If anything, our attack infuriated it. The spell had only slowed it down for a few seconds. The monster craned its necks; then its heads assaulted us all at once — but recoiled from a promptly cast Sanctuary as Zander placed it in the hydra's way, saving us from a sure respawn.

"Help me! Heeeelp!" Platinus' desperate screaming echoed over the quagmire.

A barrage of driftwood behind our backs shifted, sliding toward the water's edge as one of the hydras attempted to climb ashore.

We were separated and surrounded. The acid-green whiffs of the hydras' toxic breath hadn't reached us yet in the safety of our little Sanctuary bubble which repelled all mobs, momentarily protecting us from their powerful debuffs.

Momentarily being the operative word.

Zander wasn't going to last forever. Besides, his abilities were geared more toward the powers of the Dark, and these were Elemental mobs. Not all of Zander's tricks were going to work. A lot would depend on his quick thinking and his knowledge of his own class.

My mana bar plummeted, followed by my Physical Energy indicator. My Life began to dwindle rapidly. The runic symbols covering my sword began to glow, filling with light.

Exactly as Master Jurg had predicted!

I gulped a mana vial. Enea stared at me in confusion as my face seized with agonizing pain.

She didn't hesitate long. A promptly cast Healing Aura breathed life back into me.

Zander was busy giving orders in the combat chat,

"Iskandar, cast Levitation over the warriors! Rodrigo, cast Subzero!"

Enea was restoring her Mental Energy. She didn't look scared anymore. If anything, she looked about in awed excitement.

Her dreams were coming true. The entire space around our little island was seething with magic attacks.

The Sanctuary still held. Two Levitation Auras lifted Tylor and Vigil over the bog, followed by a blanket attack with Subzero.

Platinus stopped screaming.

Part of the bog had frozen solid. A powerful frigid wind arose, lashing our faces with sharp flakes of snow.

Platinus was frozen in. His face was covered in a crystalline crust of ice. The spell hadn't dealt him any damage but you shouldn't forget this world's lifelike laws of physics: caught in the water, Platinus was now being squashed by a thick layer of ice.

"Enea, heal him!" Zander snapped as he cast Fury over himself and dashed toward the motionless hydra, pulling aggro to himself. The other mobs were already breaking through the ice, demonstrating their impressive resistance to Elements.

Platinus was free. A puddle of molten ice formed around him. The moment he got out, Rodrigo cast another Subzero.

Togien whipped out his charmed battle hammer entwined with lightning and lunged onto the nearest hydra, giving me a quick nod *en passant*.

Both Tylor and Virgil descended onto the ice-bound bog.

Zander's Fury was generating indecent amounts of aggro. The mobs ignored the warriors entirely, stretching their necks toward Zander and oblivious to everything else.

This wasn't the crunch moment yet but still, the situation didn't look as grim as it had but a few moments ago.

Then again, *every* moment could decide the battle's eventual outcome.

Zander's two-handed sword kept arcing through the air as he launched combo after precise combo, chopping their heads off, with Togien, Virgil and Tylor close at hand. Still, the mobs' regeneration times and their resistance to damage were dreadful. Their necks kept sprouting new heads where the old ones had just been, their powerful feet breaking through the ice, their long necks reaching out in every which way, allowing them to attack several targets at once.

Critted, Virgil dropped to one knee. A Wall of Fire whooshed past him, melting the ice, immediately followed by another Subzero as our wizards went into overdrive, casting spells in rapid succession.

A powerful blow threw Togien a good thirty feet through the air. He jumped to his feet and hurried to change his weapon. His hammer had proved useless against the hydras' thick skin. Crushing blows couldn't do much against them: you needed something to deal slashing damage.

Tylor was almost done, having stripped his mob of 80% hp. Still, he could only do so much against a creature that regenerated non-stop.

"Alex!" Enea shouted. "The Shackles!"

We hurried to cast more debuffs over the monsters. The well-practiced spell worked like a dream, its damage consuming 50% of their regeneration.

Iskandar and Rodrigo had incinerated one of the hydras and were now gulping elixirs, having lost all of their Mental Energy.

Zander was in full control of the situation.

His decisions were fast and fearless. When he noticed the icons of the Magic Shackles that Enea and I had cast on the mobs, he used the situation by casting a Healing Hand, restoring life and strength of all the raid members. Then he surrounded himself with the Shield of Light and cast another Fury on himself, increasing his aggro until four hydras lunged onto him all at once.

Twelve heads each! His defenses couldn't absorb so much damage, surely!

My sword dripped with energy: the shortest of the four lines of symbols was completely full and glowing with fire.

I might just as well use it. I was dying to find out what kind of debuff those ancient symbols could inflict. I darted to the warriors' aid, dropping to Enea as I ran,

"Keep healing me!"

I hadn't made it halfway when I noticed Platinus, lost and forgotten. He'd already crawled out of the bog and was now stealing toward one of the mobs, holding something in his hands that resembled a crudely made wooden box.

Before I could react, he hurled the item right under the hydra's belly.

A deafening blast followed.

A roaring column of fire mixed with ice and muck shot toward the skies. The blast wave hurled us to the ground. The hydra (which had had about 20% HP left) had been blown to pieces.

* * *

Time seemed to have frozen. Platinus' actions had attracted the admins' attention. For the first time in my life, I was witnessing a player being stripped of his levels. A murky brown aura enveloped him as if his body was streaming with mud.

His name tag blinked and expired. Then it reappeared,

Platinus. Level 7. Sorcerer.

Level 7! He used to be level 9.

A crystal screen appeared in the sky above the bog, sporting a fiery message,

Platinus the Sorcerer has been degraded 2 levels as a warning for using prohibited (i.e., unpatented) explosives. Any repeat offense will result in his account being terminated.

Enjoy the game!

WITH A FLASH, time accelerated back.

Platinus didn't seem to care. He shrugged the warning off, apparently not upset about losing two levels, then whipped a vial out from his enormous stocks and hurled it at another hydra.

A Loss of Durability debuff icon appeared in its tag.

He'd used a Disintegration Potion this time.

Zander jumped to his feet — but by killing the hydra, Platinus had already pulled the aggro of all the remaining mobs to himself. Three of the hydras left Zander alone and swung round, darting toward our hapless alchemist who fumbled through his tangled robes, trying to reach for another vial.

Damn. The man was toast.

The Subzero spell had already expired. The ice rapidly melted. The snowstorm had stopped, revealing the sun.

Splashing through the melting slush, the hydras charged at Platinus, their outstretched heads tense, their mouths gaping. Tufts of moss flew everywhere. The hydras' guttural hissing, the foul clouds of acid breath and their thunderous but swift gait left no doubt about the doomed alchemist's fate.

Virgil and Tylor attempted to step into the monsters' way and even managed to deal some minor damage — but the hydras flung them aside, concentrating their blind fury on Platinus alone.

He screamed, realizing what he'd just done, and ran for his life — sort of. Immediately he stumbled over a piece of rotten wood and bellyflopped into the shallow bog, but continued scrambling on.

Zander and I arrived at the scene almost simultaneously. While the wizards were casting debuff after a desperate debuff, trying to slow the hydras down, Zander lunged at the mobs from the side in a well-calculated move. He then activated a string of abilities which maxed out his physical damage. In a splash of blinding light, his two-handed sword sliced through one of the hydras, severing its spine and chopping off its lower body complete with its back legs and tail.

I attacked another one, using the same trick by jumping onto it from the side. The fact that Platinus had pulled its aggro to himself allowed me to invest all my strength into the blow.

A heart-rending scream deafened me. The runes on my sword blade flashed brightly, then expired. My mana indicator plummeted to zero.

Although I'd failed to smoke the monster, I'd dealt it a vicious wound despite the level gap. Still screaming, the hydra turned to me. It had stopped regenerating. A weird icon appeared in its tag, resembling a broken swirl.

Its movements became sluggish. Its strong

supple skin started to burst before my very eyes, oozing blood. Its necks stooped. That gave Zander enough time to hurry toward us and deal it one more powerful final blow.

I couldn't unclench my sword hand. Virtually every bar and indicator in my interface glowed a big fat zero. Finally, thanks to Zander's auras and Enea's non-stop healing, I managed to move my hand in order to sheath my sword, freeing myself from its destructive power.

Immediately all my stat bars quivered and began to fill. I staggered away from the fallen hydra and grabbed at a dry branch, taking in the panorama of battle overlapped by the flickering of system messages.

Platinus had only one enemy left — but by now, Virgil, Tylor and Togien were already on the scene, helping him. Togien grabbed Platinus by the scruff of the neck and dragged him away, allowing the two warriors to pull the aggro to themselves, forcing the last hydra to defend itself.

Too weak to resist, it didn't last long.

Enea walked over to me. "You all right?" she said, touching my shoulder.

Good question. I forced a smile. She shook her head, then cast another Minor Heal.

Zander wiped his sword clean from the toxic slime, then turned to us. "Alexatis, you shouldn't have done that. It wasn't worth the risk."

"I know. But I need Platinus."

"You really think he can be any good after his level drop?"

"Hopefully, it didn't affect his profession," I said, expecting Zander to ask me about my sword. Still, he seemed to avoid the subject.

"This I doubt," he said. "If the truth were known, it's professional skills that the admins really should cut. That would teach some of us to fool around with explosives!"

Finally, all group members came together. Platinus had to be dragged by his armpits. He was white as a sheet.

"Why did you have to interfere, for fuck's sake?" Zander attacked him. "You have any idea you could have caused a wipe? The situation was perfectly under control! I was pulling the aggro so that the others could do their jobs!"

"I thought... I thought..." Platinus managed, his erratic panting pregnant with the first angry notes. "I thought they were going to kill you!"

Zander bent down and whispered something into his ear. Platinus turned even paler.

"Next time that's what I'm going to do, understood?" Zander finished his phrase out loud. "Now just pray to the Gods of Light that

Alexatis doesn't expel you from the group."

"Why? In case you didn't notice, I was saving the raid! You were attacked by four hydras!"

"Nothing I couldn't have managed on my own," Zander repeated calmly. "Their levels were inferior to mine. But you — you very nearly let everybody down. Another prank like that, and I'll take the law into my own hands."

I decided it was time to put my foot down. "Very well," I said. "Lesson learned. Platinus, how's your profession doing?"

"It's okay," he mumbled.

"We have five minutes to meditate and collect the loot!" Zander concluded.

* * *

The bog was still heaving. Patches of dark water gaped in its moss-blanketed surface, releasing putrid bubbles of bog gas amid the floating bodies of frogs, toads and water snakes stunned by the explosion.

Expertly using his knife, Rodrigo skinned the hydras. I could see that his main profession wasn't his only forte.

"Why would you ruin something like this?" he complained.

Platinus pricked up his ears. "Are you

talking to me?"

"Who do you think?" Rodrigo said as one of the skins fell apart in his hands like a piece of rotten cloth, completely devoid of Durability. "You can't make armor with it now, can you? What was that stuff you threw at it?"

"Just some Disintegration Potion," Platinus grumbled. "Why are you all so mad at me? You need skins? How about all the frogs lying about? They're gonna make some fine armor! Never mind a wart or two."

"Very funny," Rodrigo suppressed an angry glare.

It looked like everybody had a problem with Platinus. I wasn't too happy with him, either. I took him aside and read him the riot act.

He pouted his lips. "I can see that joining you wasn't a good idea."

"Yes, it was. Problem is, you're too absorbed in your own craft to learn the game's ropes. Let's do it this way. I'll do my best to set up a lab for you as promised. You can do what the hell you want there in your spare time, I'm not going to interfere. But in battle, you follow orders without questioning them. Understood?"

He perked up. "Absolutely."

"Have you got any explosives left?"

He heaved a sigh. "I might."

"I want you to throw them in the bog. Now."

Reluctantly he reached into his robes, pulled out two more wooden boxes and dropped them in the quagmire. They sank straight away.

"Much better," I said. "Next time you want to make a bomb, I suggest you discuss it with our wizards first."

This unexpected hydra encounter had just shown us how perilous the Toxic Moors in fact were. They'd caught us with our pants down. The teleport hadn't been exactly a success, either. We really had to make sure it never happened again.

I needed to talk to Zander. But first, I perched myself on a piece of wood next to Enea. "You okay?"

"I'm fine!" the battle adrenaline was still coursing through her veins. "I got four levels! I'm not going to distribute my stat points though. Not quite yet. Think you can help me with that?"

"Sure, in a moment. I haven't even read my own system messages yet. We need to decide on our route first, then we can look into it as we get under way. Okay?"

"Okay," she nodded. "Did you see how the wizards scorched that hydra?" her eyes lit up. "The ashes sure went flying! D'you think I'd be able to do something like that one day?"

"By the time we get to Rion Castle, we might have learned a lot, all of us. Can I ask you to keep an eye on Platinus, please? I need to have a word with Zander."

"Don't worry, I'll find a way to cheer him up. What are you all like, attacking him? He meant well!"

* * *

I took Zander aside.

He seemed to be in a good mood. True, the whole operation had been a bit of a disaster but that had nothing to do with him. The main thing was, we were still alive.

"I doubt the old passageways have survived," he said.

"Let's go and have a look, then. Somehow I don't think they were made of straw," I said.

"Where did you see them, made of straw?" Zander demanded. "There's nothing like that on my map!"

"Just an ability I have," I said. "Plus I have a map-making app."

"You don't want to tell me you've got Pioneer?" he asked, incredulous.

"Actually, I have. I just happened to discover a new location."

"I wonder if it was you that made the merchants' guild nuts? From what I heard, someone had managed to travel to the Azure Mountains and back. Everybody seems to be crazy about Spectral Dust at the moment."

I ignored the question, steering the conversation back to its original subject, "We seem to be quite close to the first mark on my map."

"I got the message. It's none of my business," Zander chose a young tree and used it to make two long poles. "Watch your step. Rodrigo, I want you to have your Levitation ready in case we start to sink."

We began to prod our way through the bog. Time was an issue but there wasn't much we could do about it. I just hoped that the teleport error wasn't too random. Otherwise, why would the mysterious marks on my map start so close to our current location, leading directly to the castle?

"Why can't we just use Levitation?" I asked. "Can't Rodrigo and Iskandar keep the spell going?"

"Theoretically speaking, yeah," Zander replied. "Problem is, you can't do much fighting with the Levitation aura all around you. It blocks most abilities and disrupts your coordination. Which is why we'll only revert to Levitation when everything else fails."

My pole struck a hard surface below. "Aha," I said, "I think I've found something. Could it be rock?"

"I don't think so," Zander replied, measuring the bog in front with his own pole. "The depth is the same everywhere. About a foot deep."

"One of the passageways?" I suggested.

"A secret path, more likely. Look how narrow it is," he poked the surface with his pole, demonstrating the width of the path. "A couple feet, if that. It also tends to meander. Unless it's marked on the map, you'll never get through it."

"True. We seem to be in luck."

"That's what you say. It doesn't offer much room for combat maneuver. I think it's a trap."

"Not for someone who can cast Subzero," I pointed out. "It serves two purposes. By freezing the bog, it offers you a hard foothold while also controlling the attacking mobs."

He didn't reply. Instead, he checked his map. "We should be able to make it before sunset. All right, let's move it! We're wasting our time."

* * *

The thick canopy of bog vegetation exuded a heavy heat. Gingerly we inched toward Rion Castle. The secret path (which must have been laid by the Disciples themselves) continued to meander, frequently heading away from the castle, taking us back to where we'd come from. Still, we didn't seem to have any other option. The narrow strip of solid ground underwater must have been built with magic — and it seemed to be our only access route toward the rocky island on which the castle stood.

You could forget shortcuts: the moment you stepped off the path, you would sink into the treacherous quagmire.

Tylor walked first, feeling the way with his pole and checking the path against the constantly updated map which I kept forwarding him.

Zander followed, focused and tireless as usual in the face of any potential surprises, casting occasional cleansing and healing auras over us to protect the raid from all the petty mobs: insects and such. They could do a nasty job on a lone unprepared traveler, could even kill you if you weren't careful. The shaded greenery swarmed with mosquitoes as big as my fist. Enea kept scorching them with fireballs.

Rodrigo and Iskandar made up the center of our small formation, followed by a crestfallen Platinus still upset by what he considered our "overreaction" to his valorous deed.

Enea and I followed him, with Virgil and Togien bringing up the rear. We communicated via the group chat.

Good job, Enea, thanks, Rodrigo posted.

What for? she replied.

For showing us how effective some underrated spells can be.

What, the Magic Shackles? As if you didn't know!

We did. Still, we mostly have to deal with the undead. Regeneration isn't their thing. Also, the Shackles are pretty useless against dark casters which is another reason we don't use them a lot. As you probably know, each wizard tends to have a hand-picked set of spells while leaving all others to gather dust. Which isn't a good thing to do really.

Enea looked pleased to hear that. Still, Rodrigo had a point. It wouldn't be a bad idea to create a particular set of spells for each of the game's regions and their respective mobs: those which had worked against the undead were pretty useless against an Elemental.

I kept an eye on their exchange.

Iskandar and I could share a few of our own

spells with you. You seem to like Fire. We have some rare scrolls you might find interesting.

Cool. Still, my mana isn't up to much yet.

Then you should focus on your abilities.

I know. I haven't quite yet worked out how they affect each other. Too technical for me. I spent all last night reading up on them, but it's pure math! You need to remember which abilities have to be leveled first, which ones they affect or interact with, and which ones can wait... it's just too technical for me.

Mind if I explain?

Absolutely!

She cast me a furtive glance. True, I'd promised to help her but until now, I hadn't had the chance to even check out the standard combat wizard development branches. Rodrigo's offer was extremely convenient for both of us. Both he and Iskandar seemed to like Enea which was only logical. Firstly, she'd helped them out in battle, showing some quick thinking and considerable courage. Secondly, she had this thing about her... some personal magnetism, should I say. She had this natural enthusiasm and curiosity which allowed her to enjoy things that veteran gamers like myself had long ceased to notice.

I PM'd her,

You need to listen to what they have to say. Just remember that your current gear offers you some decent physical defense. So you need to concentrate on mental damage, looking for abilities that decrease casting times as well as mana expenditure. Also, you might need to improve your regeneration rate.

She nodded, then engaged in an animated discussion with the two wizards.

I really needed to check out all the system messages I'd received in the heat of battle. My surprise hydra encounter had brought me up 3 levels. Normal: newbs could expect to receive generous helpings of XP, especially as group members. Still, it wasn't going to last forever. Very soon, I might need to sweat every new bit of char development.

I began distributing new stat and ability points with a focus on Intellect, attack strength and mental energy regeneration rate.

This is what I finally had,

Alexatis. Level 21. Neuro

Life, 172.5/172.5 (Stamina, 150 + Gear, 22.5)

Physical Energy, 105/105 (Strength, 90 + current abilities and the gear bonus, 15)

Mental Energy, 198/198 (Intellect, 150 + current abilities and the gear bonus, 48)

Physical Defense, 215 (Scaly Armor, 210 + Agility bonus, 5)

Physical Attack, 42 (Mysterious Sword at 30% Durability, 15 pt. + Strength, 5 + the gear bonus, 2 + Intense Training, 6 + character level, 20)

Mental Defense, 39% (Self-Control + Spirit + the gear bonus)

Elemental Defense, 15% (Spirit and the Scaly Breastplate)

Mental Attack, 52 (spells studied, 30 + Unity of Schools, 2 + character level, 20)

Mental Energy Regeneration, 4,34 pt./sec (Spirit divided by 2 + 0,84 bonus from Synergy, Power of Reason and Self-Control)

Strength, 10.5 (Secret Knowledge, 9+1 + the gear bonus, 0.5)

Intellect, 19.8 (Secret Knowledge, 15+1 + the gear bonus, 0.8 + the ring, 3)

Agility, 10 (the gear bonus, 9+1)

Stamina, 16.5 (15 + the underwear kit bonus, 1.5)

Spirit, 10

Main Professions, Require activation

Achievements:
Celebrated Pioneer (a map-making app available)
Clan Founder (+ 1,000 to Popularity, +1 to all Reputations)

All in all, I had nothing to complain about. I invested 2 ability points into Intense Training to bring up physical damage, then added 4 more to Pain Threshold. This way I wouldn't experience any negative effects until my Health dropped to 62% — not bad at all.

I invested another couple of previously saved points into Self-Control. For two reasons. Firstly, this increased my mana regeneration rate 6%. Secondly, I could now finally control my mental energy distribution between several recipients. And this was vital considering my sword's peculiar behavior whenever death threatened me.

I picked up the sword. A new icon lit up in my interface: *Energy Distribution.* I set up a provision to share 10% of my mana with the sword, just to try it out. I just hoped it would be enough to protect me from any surprise attacks.

Once I reached level 30 (which was soon), I would finally have access to more abilities. I was curious. Until now, I'd had lamentably little time to study new spells and blows. Once I claimed my clan's castle, I really should spend some quality time looking into it all.

Last but not least, the mysterious blow that had allowed me to wound the remaining hydra. The damage caused by it was mind-blowing.

I scrolled through the battle logs, looking for the right message,

04.23. You've activated an ancient curse: Mortal Allegiance. Affects all enemies regardless of their race, class, or level, whenever they receive damage from the Mysterious Sword. Any creature whose level is lower than yours receives a Skin of Stone buff, becoming your ally for the duration of 2 minutes.

Whenever your enemy's level is higher than yours, they will receive additional recurring damage from the Curse of Stone, losing strength and life. Both the amount and duration of damage depend on the target's resistance.

04.24. You've attacked a Hydra!
Physical Damage: 80 (critical hit)
Mental damage: 200

Effect: Mortal Allegiance

This was one hell of a variable spell. In all my years spent playing, I'd never seen anything like it!

I activated the battle video and began scrolling through it until I found what I was looking for, then stopped it and zoomed in on the scene.

The nine fiery symbols on my sword's blade formed a short phrase: two words inscribed in the long-forgotten language.

Suddenly I knew it. Let's suppose that the two words were in fact the name of the spell. Considering that I knew how to pronounce the Founders' spells, I should actually be able to compare the symbols to the sounds they were supposed to signify. This way I might work out the letters of the Founders' alphabet!

I should look through the scrolls and check for identical symbols. With any luck, I might be able to compile the complete alphabet and a small glossary of a few dozen basic words whose meaning was clear from the way the spells were pronounced — such as Weakness, for instance.

I opened the book and began comparing the symbols.

The first rune in the word Weakness was identical to the one on my sword.

Knowing that "weakness" sounded like *"twalgue"* in the Founders' language, the first rune must have stood for the letter "t".

New quest alert: The Mystery of the Ancient Manuscripts!

Quest type: Unique

Try to compile the Founders' alphabet, then translate at least one page of any of their ancient books.

Deadline: none

Reward: access to unique knowledge unavailable to others.

Oh wow. I hadn't expected that at all.

I accepted the quest. How was it possible that no one had ever thought of comparing the known pronunciation of the ancient words with the symbols of the language? Every crumb of ancient knowledge these books might harbor was infinitely more valuable than any amount of gold or precious stones!

Actually, I shouldn't forget that at the moment, I was the only person in the Crystal Sphere who could call it his home. All the others had come here for a bit of fun and adventure. Why would they be interested in poring laboriously over some research which might take decades?

"Penny for your thoughts," Enea's voice brought me back to reality.

"I've been checking the logs," I said. "I was trying to find out what made the sword syphon my health and mana."

Anxiety glistened in her gaze. "I don't think keeping this sword is a good idea."

"It's all right. Nothing drastic has happened."

"That's what you say. Wish you could have seen yourself then."

I chose to drop the subject for the time being. "The hydra probably thought the same. How's *your* progress? Did you get the chance to use the wizards' advice?"

"Oh!" she gasped, impatient to share the news. "It's so simple! Much easier than I thought! Rodrigo and Iskandar explain everything so clearly! They've helped me to distribute my ability points. Plus, I've also learned four new spells! Guess how much mana I have now?"

I raised a quizzical eyebrow. "Tell me."

"Two hundred and fifty!"

"And Intellect?"

"Twenty-five!"

"No way! Do you imply your IQ is higher than mine?"

"Very funny. And do you know it's all thanks to those two old rings? The rusty one I received for my first quest and the one you gave me later."

"I'm very happy to hear that. And what about the spells?"

"I have Lightning and Minor Teleportation," she began proudly, "which transports you several feet within your range of vision. Also, a five-second Levitation, Ice Spear, Inferno, Muteness and Fiery Guard."

I knew them all. Not bad for level 20 — all apart from the latter, that is. Fiery Guard was still a bit out of her league. This spell summoned a fire elemental who could momentarily protect the summoner from physical attacks. Casting it took 7 seconds and 230 pt. mana. I'd say it was only worth using starting at level 50-plus.

Inferno dealt blanket fire damage over 200 square feet. This was a powerful and very effective spell you could use against a numerous enemy. Muteness was a highly useful debuff which disrupted an enemy spell while preventing the enemy caster from repeating it for the duration of several seconds. Lightning dealt more damage and was more accurate compared to Ice Arrow or fireballs while Ice Spear was more destructive. Both Levitation and Teleportation were pretty self-explanatory.

"Can I copy them later?" I asked her.

"Absolutely!"

Tylor who walked first stopped and raised a warning hand.

I checked the map. Here, the line signifying the ancient path was broken. No wonder Tylor's pole kept sinking into the bog over and over again.

"Leave it," I told him, then ran a quick map update. We had barely an hour's hike left to the chain of small islands which encircled Rion Castle. We were obliged to get there before sunset, exactly as Zander had promised. Which left us just over twenty-four hours to take over the castle.

Zander cast a wary glance around. "Do you think it's a trap? Or just natural damage?"

"A trap for an idle traveler," I said.

"Meaning?"

"Meaning there're two stone platforms underwater on both sides of the broken path. Can you see those two small squares on the map?"

"And? What do you think they're for?"

"The gap between them and the path is quite big," I said. "The idle traveler might turn back thinking he couldn't go any further. But someone in the know might simply activate one of these two platforms."

My fingertips began to tingle. There must have been a source of magic energy around here somewhere.

"Alternatively, he might have built a raft," Zander pointed at a thick wall of some bamboo-like plants which lined the path. "Simple."

"And sail it right into a trap," I said.

"You wanna bet? How about two gold?"

"If you want."

"A bet?" being a dwarf, Togien didn't miss a trick whenever gold was mentioned. "Five gold on Alexatis!"

Zander grinned. 'Anybody else?"

"Count me in!" Iskandar perked up. I'd had no idea he had a gambling streak. "Ten gold on Zander's theory!"

"Enea?"

"Ten on Alexatis!"

"Twenty on Zander," Virgil boomed. "Just look at all the vines. We can build a raft in no time!"

"Just promise me you aren't going to board it," I told them. "We'll just push it out and see what happens. Okay?"

This time no one argued with me.

* * *

It didn't take us long to throw together the most basic of rafts. With the help of Togien's axe and a few handy spells, we cut an armful of hard bamboo-like stems, then bound them together with vines. We didn't care much about the quality: no one was going to board it, anyway.

For a more convincing effect, Togien used a few more sticks to fashion a rather ungainly-looking scarecrow, mounted it at the center of the raft and clad it in strips of moss and algae.

Virgil took careful aim with his crossbow, constantly consulting the map, then loosed off a bolt with a double length of string tied to it.

The bolt sank into a tree trunk about a hundred feet away from us where the secret underwater path was supposed to resume.

"All done," Virgil checked the string, then tied the raft to it and pulled, causing the fragile structure to float across the stretch of water.

We watched, tense and silent, weapons at the ready. Our wizards too were on full alert.

The raft was about thirty feet away when the water heaved on both sides — but contrary to our expectations, it didn't release any abysmal monsters.

The bog inhabitants, whatever they were, chose not to expose themselves. Swiftly they swam underwater, causing the raft to rock on the flat waves.

"Keep pulling," Zander said softly.

A few more feet, and the raft was almost halfway through. The creatures had disappeared back into the depths without ever noticing us.

Then I heard a weird sound. Disturbed by the arrival of the invisible monsters, the murky water began swirling, faster and faster, forming a gigantic whirlpool.

"Virgil, watch out!"

He let go of the string and stepped back. The raft was caught in the whirlpool and began to circle it, accelerating. The vines binding it snapped. The scarecrow dropped into the water. The raft fell apart. Its remains were sucked rapidly deep underwater.

Immediately the whirlpool disappeared. The bog calmed down as if nothing had ever happened here.

"Holy cow," Togien commented, then turned to me, "You think we might be able to levitate over it?"

I decided to continue with my research. "Rodrigo?" I turned to the wizard. "Mind casting a quick one?"

"One won't be enough," Rodrigo replied. "If you want to make an Air Bridge, Iskandar will have to help me."

"Try it."

Zander chose not to interfere.

Two Levitation Auras formed over the bog, their presence betrayed by a faint haze in the air.

The whirlwind arrived unnoticed. The

heavy air stirred, shuffling the foliage and swaying the thick clumps of bamboo. The fat ferns heaved.

Both auras rippled. The two wizards broke the spell before they could renew it. The whirlwind promptly stopped.

Zander frowned. "We can't go any further."

"How about the two platforms?"

"Too risky. The place is a trap. We need to make another raft, go back and try to find a safe detour."

"What, on a raft?" I pointed at the thick vegetation lining the path. "Can you imagine how long it'll take for us to hack through these?"

"Then you'd better tell us why you're the only person who has both the path and the platforms marked on his map? Why can't *we* see them?"

"Why, is it a problem?"

"Not really but..."

"It's pretty simple," I said. "Maps don't show underwater objects, right?"

Zander nodded. "Right."

"This was exactly what the Disciples counted on. If you didn't have the right map, you had no business being here."

"Logical. Does that mean you have their map?"

"No, I don't. Still, my Enhanced Perception

ability allows me to see underwater objects at sufficiently shallow depths."

"Which means you don't know the purpose of those platforms?"

"I suppose one of us might need to stand on it."

"Stand on which one? And what do you think might happen?"

"No idea. It's a fifty-fifty chance."

This wasn't an easy choice. Once we'd ported here, our resurrection point had been automatically moved to the center of the bog. Not the safest of locations if you asked me. These moors weren't called Toxic for nothing.

"So what's stopping you?" Enea asked, then added softly, "Are you choosing a team member we can afford to lose?"

"I'm trying to think of something," I replied.

We were surrounded by quagmire. "Not even a rock heavy enough to imitate a human body's weight!" I complained.

"It wouldn't help," Platinus elbowed his way to me. "If it's a magical trap, weight can't trigger it. Actually, I could make a rock out of water. Still, it won't have the aura typical of a living being."

"That's something we can cast," Rodrigo hurried to add. "Good idea! You're not just a pretty face!"

Platinus beamed. All that time since the hydras encounter, he must have felt like a fifth wheel. Cheering up, he reached for one of his homebrew concoctions, its vial sporting a skull and crossbones. More explosives?

"Hey, don't forget you can have your account blocked!" I warned him.

"That's all right. This stuff is perfectly legal."

"What is it?"

"This is a Stone Golem Extract. A very rare ingredient. If you pour it into the water..."

Unexpectedly he pulled out the stopper and threw the contents of the vial into the bog. "Cast Levitation, quick!"

The wizards barely made it. An impressive-looking boulder hung in the air, supported by Rodrigo as Iskandar hurried to cast some spells unknown to me.

I focused on the man-made boulder. It actually had a tag!

A Minor Spirit of a Warrior.

A magic trap.

Exudes a fake aura serving to distract the enemy from their target.

"Alexatis, which one?" Rodrigo asked me.

"Let's try the one on the right."

"Everyone step back, now!" Zander ordered, ready to protect us with a Shield of Light.

Created by Platinus and "personified" by Iskandar, the boulder floated through the air, controlled by Rodrigo.

"All done!" he reported. "Would you like me to lower it?"

"Go ahead!"

The boulder dropped with a splash. On depressing the platform, it disappeared.

"This is a teleport," Iskandar commented confidently.

"A teleport? Where to?" Enea demanded. "Directly to the castle?"

"I don't think so," I replied. "Why would you build a secret path, damage it, create all sorts of traps just to port you to the castle?" as I was speaking, I jumped onto the platform to my left.

"Alex, don't!" Enea screamed.

A screeching sound drowned out her voice. The stone surface quivered, unmoved by my weight. The bog, however, bubbled with gas as something massive began resurfacing from its depths.

A new line appeared on my map, filling the gap in the path.

The murky water seethed, rising up, then crashing down in two big waves.

"Zander, I want my money," I said. "You've

lost."

He shook his head, incredulous at my recklessness.

The bog was still seething as the missing part of the path rose from the depths.

Rodrigo gave Platinus a friendly slap on the shoulder. "Great job! I never thought I'd live to see a rock made out of water!"

Platinus beamed. "Nothing special, really. What a shame I don't have enough Extract otherwise I could have built you a stone bridge all the way to the castle!"

I leaped back onto the path. The sun had already begun to decline. We couldn't afford even a well-deserved break.

* * *

As we approached Rion Castle, the landscape began to change.

The bog began to peter out. The first cliffs arose from the water, breaking it into separate streams. Here, vegetation was more diverse with occasional copses of conifers and deciduous trees adding to the horsetails and ferns.

Giant orchids thrived in their shade. Sunlit mossy clearings were strewn with crimson clumps of bog berries. Here too, the air was permeated by the scent of wild rosemary.

To an ignorant city dweller like myself this confusing blend of climate zones looked quite acceptable. Platinus, however, kept complaining, mumbling the plants' names under his breath and bemoaning the game developers' ignorance.

"Please stop it. Just accept it," Enea told him, unable to take her eyes off all the stunning flora.

The secret path built by the ancient Order of Disciples entered a rocky outcrop — then ended.

A scattering of small isles lay before us. We couldn't see the castle yet, mainly due to a heavy fog floating over the shallow waters. A generous sun heated the moors, drawing moisture upwards in hovering sheets of haze clouding the hollows.

Humidity was at 100%. The air was close. Visibility had dropped dramatically. We kept walking, constantly expecting an attack.

"This is another line of the castle's natural defenses," Zander motioned us to stop. "Let's take a break."

He'd chosen the place well. Judging by the squat fortifications of piled-up rocks, this small islet must have already served as a camping place at some point in the past. A few sharpened stakes, dark with time, were stuck into the ground. But most importantly, a rather noticeable breeze was blowing the effluvia of the bog away.

"What kind of wood can survive millennia?" Platinus touched the stakes in disbelief, then pointed at the thick fog supposedly concealing the walls of Rion Castle. "Did you see that? What's that, a siege tower?"

I peered through the haze. Indeed, a tall siege tower rose nearby on its giant wooden wheels, its listing multi-tiered log structure still quite solid.

"The siege of Rion lasted a very long time," Zander replied. "Unfortunately, very few first-hand accounts have survived. From what I know, the two armies surrounding the castle had built their siege machines deep in the local woods, deforesting them, then dragged them to the front line."

"You seem to do a lot of reading," Togien commented.

"I've compiled a list of places people would like to visit," he replied calmly. "I'm a group guide, don't forget. In my line of work, there's no such thing as too much information."

Togien shrank, fingering his beard. "Sorry, man. I didn't mean to offend you."

"You can't," Zander looked around. "Alexatis? We need to talk."

He took me aside. "We should take a

break," he said. "Everyone's been at their game consoles all day. This looks like a good place to set up camp. The moors have been the easy part. Now it might get tough."

"Oh really? The castle is almost within reach."

"Exactly. Which is where the problems start. You shouldn't think that it was the castle walls that kept the enemy out for so long. The castle approaches are swarming with mobs. These tents can serve us as safe respawn points. It's not for nothing one of the armies camped out here. This place should be relatively safe."

His arguments convinced me. "Okay. Let's set up tents and take a break. Thirty minutes?"

"An hour."

"Do you suggest we walk to the castle in the dark?"

"When the sun sets, the fog will thin out. It'll be much easier, trust me. All we need do is get to the barbican. After that, it's plain sailing."

"Okay. Let's set up tents and take an hour's break. You have a point. This isn't going to be an easy night."

* * *

All the others had logged out, leaving me alone in the camp.

Setting up tents had been a great idea. We'd managed to move our respective respawn points over to them. Once everyone was back — which was in less than an hour — things would really get rolling.

Me, I had nowhere to go. Should I grab some sleep? But how much sleep can one get in an hour? So instead, I decided to investigate the island while I still could.

The old fortifications proved to harbor nothing of interest. The siege tower, however, seemed to be calling my name.

I wondered if the ladders inside were still in one piece. The attackers must have treated the wood with special magic-enhanced alchemical formulas.

It wouldn't be a bad idea to climb up and check out our surroundings while the dying daylight allowed.

* * *

The inside of the tower was bathed in gloom. Tiny shafts of light poured in through the cracks between the withered and darkened planks of the outer cladding. Just as I thought, the wood was still strong.

I began climbing the ladders, stopping at each "landing" for a breather. I could already see that no one had set foot here ever since the legendary battles. An iron-bound battering ram dangled from some rusty chains on the tower's "ground floor". On the next level, a ballista was mounted against a horizontal firing slit, its horse-hair torsion still intact. The walls were lined with arrow stands, many still holding the heavy arrows with flat steel arrowheads, big enough to serve as spears to some mythical giants.

The following two landings contained nothing of interest. They must have served to house the warriors themselves. Question: considering the area's rugged nature, how had the besiegers expected to drag this behemoth structure to the castle walls?

I found my answer on the fourth floor littered with magic stones, dark and cracked, set in rusty metal rims. I focused on one of them,

A Big Stone of Levitation
Charges, 0
Destroyed and unfit for purpose

Finally, I climbed to the top landing which must have served as the launch platform for the troops.

The vista took my breath away. The ribbons of mist lay far below; the treetops didn't hinder the view. Rion Castle stood before me in all its glory.

The ancient citadel had been built on an oblong island, taking advantage of its natural defenses. The castle's impregnable walls seemed to be at one with the precipitous cliffs they rose upon.

Even from where I stood I could clearly see the castle's three main defense levels. The lower circle of walls bordered the quagmires. I could make out the barbican — the tower which served as the castle's outpost — rising on a separate little isle quite close to our camp. A drawbridge, lowered and partially destroyed, hung on its massive chains, still connecting the barbican to the castle's sole gate.

The second defense level was located on a small plateau encircled by high walls that perched on the edge of a yawning chasm. I counted ten towers, also partially destroyed, which must have suffered disastrous ballista fire. The second-level gate lay in ruins, the road leading to it buried under large fragments of crumbled walls.

The castle's impregnable donjon rose defiantly over all this demolition. It was fashioned from several peaked cliffs which the workers had shaped into a single architectural ensemble. Arrow-slit defense galleries lined its walls, connecting the many small fortified platforms built at several levels. Giant weather-worn statues flanked the tall vaulting windows of inner halls which adorned the precipitous walls way above the reach of even the longest of siege ladders.

I was speechless. What kind of battles must have erupted here in the past if even the citadel itself had been well-nigh obliterated? My imagination offered me scenes of charging hordes as the powers of the Dark escaped their underground dwellings while magic-controlled harpies and wyverns attacked the castle from the air.

Now Rion Castle lay here fallen, its cliffs overgrown with ivy, its majestic glory shrouded in the dust of time, the vines sinking their air roots into the furrowed faces of the ancient statues.

I took a good look, trying to memorize the view. Suddenly I realized that whenever I concentrated on a detail, it would zoom into focus: this was my Enhanced Perception ability kicking in.

A movement caught my attention. I peered in its direction, focusing.

What had initially seemed to be swirls of dust raised by the wind began acquiring shape and detail. Now I could see warriors clad in flaking armor ramble around the castle, climbing its towers and walls, disappearing, then materializing again.

An Ash Guard. Level 18
An Ash Guard. Level 16
A Warrior of the Dark. Level 20
A Disciple's Ghost. Level 22

Oh. We had our job cut out for us. Still, I wasn't going to turn back. Rion Castle had already ensnared my imagination.

The ancient citadel was beckoning me, as if begging me to save it from oblivion, promising to become our clan's faithful stronghold.

A sudden noise disturbed my thoughts.

Enea climbed out onto the platform and froze in awe. "Alex, this is incredible!"

I couldn't agree with her more. "I didn't expect you so early," I said.

"And you, did you log out at all?"

"I just wanted to have a look at the castle. It was worth it, don't you think?"

"It's a bit high. My head is spinning," she took me by the hand and led me to the edge of the platform bristling with the broken planks of the old drawbridge. "What an amazing, wonderful world. I never thought that virtual reality could be so consuming! It draws me in like a whirligig," she leaned forward, peering into the distance.

A sliver of wood was caught in her tangled

hair. I reached out to remove it — but my hand froze halfway.

A Black Mantis.

A tiny little creature, a carbon copy of its grown-up counterpart, was lurking in her hair.

Enea stood on the very edge of the shaky, treacherous platform. I didn't want to give her a start. Her every abrupt movement could become her last.

The mantis stirred, raising its front legs menacingly as it turned its little head, watching me.

"Enea will you please step back from the edge?"

"Don't worry. It's all right. I'm holding tight."

"Enea, please. Those planks are completely rotten."

"If you wish," she said, stepping back. Then, turning to me, she asked, "Are you so jumpy because of the castle?"

"Not really. You've got a black mantis in your hair. Don't worry, I'll kill it now."

"Don't you dare! He's so tiny and helpless, don't you understand?"

"But it's venomous!"

"Wait a sec... I've received some messages... oh. I don't understand any of it. What is *a pet*?"

I couldn't believe my ears. How was it

possible?

The tiny mantis still stood rampant in his combat stance, watching my every movement. Only now he had a tag!

A Black Praying Mantis. Level 1. A Pet.

The last word kept flashing.

"Alex, they want me to decide! I need to press *Yes* or *No*!"

"Can you read me the message?"

"*You've been kind to a helpless creature. A Toxic Moors dweller, this Black Mantis is lonely and grateful for your generosity. Would you like to accept him as your pet?*"

"Enea, it's up to you to decide," I hurried to explain. "It's a very rare offer. Quick, make up your mind. A pet is a creature which will follow you everywhere. When it grows up, it will protect you. But at the moment, you'll have to take care of it. You'll have to feed it, raise it and level it..."

"Of course! I remember reading about it," she offered the mantis her hand. The tiny beast climbed over to her index finger. "He's so *cute*! What does he feed on, do you know?"

"Not the slightest idea. What I do know is that you need to give him a name first. Once that's done, he'll be yours for good."

Enea studied the tiny creature. "A name?"

I too decided to take a closer look at the little beast. He reacted straight away, raising his front legs and swaying, defending his new owner.

"Angry, aren't we?" I said.

"And fearless," Enea added, enthralled. "Do you think it's a boy or a girl?"

"It has to be a male," I said. "An alpha male, most likely."

"I know! I'm gonna call him Alpha!" she exclaimed.

The creature's tag blinked, refreshing.

Alpha. A Black Praying Mantis. Level 1. A Pet.

* * *

Back in the camp, the other raid members were duly impressed by Enea's pet.

Contrary to what you'd think, the tiny black mantis refused to be unsummoned by his new owner. He was constantly with her, snug and comfy within her tresses and definitely not going anywhere. He only left the safety of his new abode whenever Enea offered him her hand; then he'd crawl over onto her index finger where he'd immediately assume his combat stance, swaying and turning his watchful head around.

"This is a good sign," Zander prophesized.

"It looks like this place approves of what we're doing. He can become the clan's mascot when he grows up."

"We'll see," Togien grumbled, studying the screenshots I'd made. "He's cool, I agree. Maybe now the big mantises will stop aggroing us. Still, we have enough problems without them as it is."

"It's all right," Zander replied. "I've fought both Ash Guards and Warriors of the Dark in the past. Their levels are okay. Nothing to sweat about."

"Maybe not," Rodrigo added. "Still you shouldn't forget their nasty habit of creeping up on you. They always materialize behind the warriors' backs when least expected, trying to get to the wizards."

"I know."

Zander explained our new formation to us. Now both Virgil and Tylor were to flank Iskandar and Rodrigo, protecting them. Togien was to cover Platinus. Enea and I were to work together. Zander would be our point man, walking a dozen paces in front of the rest. His Fury ability generated so much aggro that the enemy would simply ignore us. Sounded easy enough.

We didn't break camp. This had now become our new respawn zone. We wanted to leave Platinus there "to do the housekeeping" but he refused point blank.

"I'm not staying behind!"

"Promise to obey orders?" Zander asked him sternly.

"Yes, yes! I remember! Enough!"

'Very well, then. Everybody ready? Off we go!" he headed for the trail that led to Rion Castle.

Sticking to our new formation rules, we followed him at a safe distance.

* * *

The first surprises awaited us as soon as the rocky trail connecting the little islands dove into the murky bog water.

Night was falling fast. By the time we'd set off, the setting sun had already touched the treetops. Five minutes later, the shady path was submerged in deep twilight.

Zander lit a torch.

Wisps of fog lingered over the quagmire. The ruins of the barbican were about a hundred paces away. The weird whispering sounds we'd first believed to have been the rustling of foliage had now grown louder, revealing themselves as wistful sighs and moans.

Zander stopped.

In the unsteady light of the torch, the surface of the bog looked leaden. It was rippling

— even though the air was perfectly still.

Apprehensive, Zander stuck the torch into the ground. His hand closed around the hilt of his longsword, its moonsilver blade dripping a faint aura.

The fog thickened. The whispers grew louder.

With a splash, the water stirred, sending circles throughout the bog. The clatter of steel disrupted the chilly silence. The fog parted, disgorging dozens of armor-clad figures. Water poured out of their empty eye sockets, the rusty steel streaked by silt and mud.

Their stumbling slowness was a decoy. Suddenly they lunged at Zander all at once!

His two-handed sword drew a fiery arc in the air, splitting a dozen attackers in two. Not a pleasant sight: caught in the mud, the warriors' legs remained standing while their torsos collapsed into the water.

Zander retreated a couple of paces and hurried to cast an Expulsion. Its brilliant cleansing aura swept the enemy away, only to be replaced by new warriors.

"More spells!"

Iskandar, Rodrigo and Enea took turns casting Inferno non-stop. The fiery spell torched the bog, evaporating it and scorching the overhanging tree branches. And yet still more and more warriors materialized out of the flames, burning as they ran toward the shore.

Tylor, Virgil, Togien and I parried their attacks shoulder to shoulder, not letting them get to the wizards. Protected by the Shield of Light, Zander fought the enemy in the thick of the flames — but their numbers didn't drop.

"Wretched place!" Zander took a few more steps back. "I'm pretty sure it stopped thousands during the siege of Rion!"

"What do we do?" I shouted, fighting off the undead.

Judging by the incessant clanking of vials hitting the ground, our wizards were giving it their all. Several dozens of burning figures were already outflanking us. Platinus cried out in fear.

Suddenly Zander buried his sword in the ground and dropped to one knee. "All freeze!"

Cold white flames engulfed his hands closed around the hilt of his sword.

The rapid sounds of a new spell made the enemy recoil.

A bright dot of light grew over the quagmire. The magic flames had already expired, not yet replaced by darkness, allowing us to see the real state of affairs: the stretch of bog between the two islands was heaped with dead bodies.

The battle that had raged here millennia

ago must have created some powerful pockets of Dark energy.

A resonant bell-like sound rolled over the Toxic Moors.

The light hit the thick mass of long-dead bodies, slicing through them, then exploded in a cascade of crystal chiming.

I'd thought Zander would cast another Expulsion. Instead, he'd recited a Liberation, completely exhausting himself in the process.

Flashes of light darted to the sky, expiring in its depths.

The bog had completely boiled away, its bed packed with a thick layer of rusty armor. This time, however, the dead steel harbored nothing inside.

Water warbled, running back into the bog.

I turned round.

Pressing shaking fingers to her pale lips, Enea watched as the heaped-up armor disappeared underwater.

Clinging to her hair, the tiny mantis swayed in his combat stance.

* * *

None of us spoke.

Squelching, the rising bog formed a new quagmire between the two islands. The ruins of the barbican seemed almost within reach but the dark waters glowed threateningly at us.

Rodrigo and Iskandar cast two Levitation Auras.

Zander and I were the first to climb the opposite bank. He stuck his torch into a crack in the ancient stonework. An unsteady light shone on the flat bank. Night had already fallen. A waning moon had risen in the sky strewn with stars.

Virgil's figure loomed out of the dark, followed by Enea. Both walked above the water in the safe embrace of the Levitation Aura.

While we waited for the others to cross, she whispered, "You think it's gonna get worse? Even scarier?"

"I don't know," I replied earnestly.

As we talked, the two wizards had also arrived. Now three torches were casting their uneven light on the barbican walls.

"Over here," Zander pointed at a wide breach hole.

Inside, the barbican lay in ruins. Huge piles of collapsed masonry hindered our progress. One of them, shallower than the others, led to the barbican's next floor.

A few minutes later, we finally climbed out into weak moonlight.

The nightly calls of moor creatures reached

us from across the water. A high-pitched howl resonated through the air, followed by the sounds of heavy wading through the water.

The moat was wide. The drawbridge across it lay askew, its rusty chains taut like wires. The bridge's decking had collapsed in places, exposing darkened log trestles beneath.

Zander stopped, listening in and casting wary glances below. His anxiety was understandable: he'd already used up his two most powerful abilities in order to release the slain warriors' souls. If I wasn't mistaken, both had a sixty-minute cooldown. We simply didn't have the time.

"I'll go first," I said.

"But-" Zander attempted to interfere.

"Just do as I say."

Decisively I stepped onto the bridge's treacherous decking. As clan leader and the castle's new owner, I had to be the first to walk through the gate. Otherwise Rion Castle itself might refuse to accept me.

The waters of the moat lay calm below.

The logs creaked dangerously. The runes on my sword blade glowed weakly. Ever since my hydra battle, I'd had to keep an eye on my mental energy readings. Still, the new Self-Control effect seemed to be working well.

Finally, the gate. The entrance to the castle

was a death trap. It was shaped as a long tunnel lined with arrowslits high overhead, allowing defenders to shoot the enemy at close range. The tunnel's ceiling was studded with square holes meant to pour boiling oil over the attackers' heads.

Dust swirled up into the air.

Three Ash Guards appeared out of nowhere, surrounding us. Their armor was caked in rust, their blank faces blurred.

They didn't aggro us, just kept circling around. Instinctively I stepped forward and walked right through one of them.

With a disappointed groan, the clouds of ash floated to the ground.

The narrow tunnel ended. I walked out into the moonlight.

For millennia, no human being had set foot here.

The lower yard was the biggest. It still preserved traces of an ancient settlement. I could make out the cobbled surface of streets and the foundations of burned houses.

Everywhere amid the ruins, more ashen swirls arose.

You shall not pass, the silent walls whispered.

The donjon's empty arrowslits watched me warily from above, guarding a Rion Castle still cocooned in oblivion.

* * *

"Good decision," Zander stepped next to me. "Had somebody else entered the castle first, I don't think we'd have made it this far."

He must have understood that my activation of the location had also secured the group's superiority in levels.

"Did you see the guards turn to dust?" I asked him.

"Sure. Still, I shouldn't count too much on your right of entry," he said, watching the ashen swirls regroup. "You've got to prove it first. This is peanuts. When we get to the donjon's main hall, that's when the fun will really begin. There, they aren't going to budge."

The enemy numbers grew as the arrowslits of collapsed towers kept spewing new clouds of ash.

Both Rodrigo and Iskandar were remarkably impassive. Enea's hands were enveloped in magic auras: she had both Fire and Ice ready. Still, I doubted either would affect Ash Guards. Platinus clenched a vial in his hand, his face pale.

As previously agreed, Tylor, Virgil and Togien were covering the wizards.

The Ash Guards were getting closer, their approach slow but imminent. They were legion.

"What are we waiting for?" I asked.

Zander grinned. "We're waiting for a spell to be cast. Trust me, we know what we're doing."

Rodrigo and Iskandar began incanting an impossibly long spell.

The swirls of dust began taking shape, materializing as warriors. Their serried ranks were about to lunge upon us, trampling us into the ground.

The familiar sad howl reached us from afar.

The moonlight faded. I glanced up. To my surprise, the sky was already overcast. Thunderclouds hung low overhead.

The two wizards gasped in unison, spewing out the last word of the extended spell.

With a flash, lightning forked down, colliding with the earth. A clap of thunder followed. The skies opened up, pelting us with torrential rain.

Surges of interference ran over the guards' figures. The magic-drenched rain turned ash into torrents of sticky mud which ran down the slopes toward the gaping holes in the walls and gushed down into the moat.

A new bolt of lightning illuminated the castle ruins. The rain stopped. The clouds parted. Water burbled in the silence.

Unharmed by the magic rain, a couple of dozen dark warriors charged upon us again.

Two new spells sped from Enea's hands: Fire burned away the darkness while Ice slowed down the enemy approach.

Virgil and Tylor defended the two exhausted wizards. Zander and I fought shoulder to shoulder. Togien's hammer surged with lightning, dealing incredible damage.

Platinus hurled one of his vials at the enemy. Two of the Dark warriors disappeared in a flash while Platinus himself was embraced by a golden shimmer. He'd received a new level!

"Keep fighting! Get to the second gate!" Zander shouted, casting a Heavenly Shield over us.

* * *

We took a brief break.

We'd purged the lower yard. Its ground had already begun to dry out after the magic-induced rain, swirling with the newly respawned clouds of ash.

"Alex," Enea said, breathing on her hands to warm them, "are they always going to fight us?"

"Not at all," I said. "Once I claim the castle, all the undead should disappear."

"Are you sure?"

"Rion Castle will enter a new stage in its development," Zander agreed with me. "Its dead past will finally bury its dead."

"I do hope so," Enea said, only partially convinced.

"You'll see how beautiful it'll be once we've restored it," I tried to cheer her up.

The night was still young but we'd already advanced quite a bit. A small natural plateau lay behind the broken second gate. In years gone by, it must have housed the smithies, armories, the warriors' training grounds and the wizards' tower. If whatever information I'd received when buying the castle was correct, the plateau's rocky depths were veined with numerous water wells and riddled with caves which served as food storage. The entrance to the larger cellars — which we still had to purge — lay below the donjon itself.

Pointless worrying about it yet. First we'd have to take the donjon's main hall and claim the castle.

Time was an issue. We had to step it up.

Zander met my gaze and nodded. "The break is over," he commanded. "Off we go!"

* * *

The castle's second level met me with a resounding silence. I had a bad feeling about it.

I took a look around. Gray quarrystone walls towered to my both sides in the moonlight, roofless and gaping with charred arrowslits: the evidence of the fires that had once raged here. The place must have born witness to desperate battles assisted by the most powerful of magic. The fire-swept paving stones were vitrified in places, their murky surface glossy with tiny bubbles of air trapped inside.

Zander had caught up with me. "This silence is bad news. Allow me to go first this time."

A wide street led uphill toward a demolished gate. Beyond it lay the castle's third level. Even from where we stood we could see that both gate halves had been ripped off their hinges, the portcullis breached.

Something was about to happen. The air itself felt electrified. I sensed the familiar tingling sensation in my fingertips.

Soft popping sounds echoed around us like the activation of teleports. Several phantom figures stepped in our way.

A Disciple's Ghost. Level 30

A Disciple's Ghost. Level 30
A Disciple's Ghost. Level 30

"Serry ranks! Regroup!" Zander promptly cast a Heavenly Shield over us, rightly expecting a powerful mental attack. The undead wizards' first assault failed, deflected by our radiant dome.

They disappeared, only to materialize further away.

By then, we'd regrouped again, Zander, Virgil and Tylor forming a triangle around the rest of us.

After more popping of teleports and another magic attack, Tylor cried out in pain.

They'd breached our defenses! Tylor had crumbled under pressure. His avatar rippled, then disappeared, leaving behind a small cloth bundle containing his stuff.

The Disciples' triumphant laughter echoed from the castle walls.

Now they attacked us non-stop. Zander lunged toward one of them, slicing the enemy sideways. Immediately his life bar shrank halfway from the devastating return damage.

With more popping sounds, two of the Disciples materialized within our group's serried ranks.

Togien and Iskandar fell under their merciless blows. Everything had happened so quickly I'd barely had time to draw my own sword. Mechanically I lashed out at one of the two ghosts before he had the chance to port out. With a deafening shriek, the creature banked into a steep turn in the air, then lunged at me.

A blow. A flash of agonizing pain. My sword traced an arc in the air, followed by the creature's fading scream.

I staggered. My life was deep in the red. Enea was busy healing me. Rodrigo was casting some elaborate spell, his face twisted with the effort. I was frozen on the spot, too weak to avert my gaze from his lips mouthing the spell.

You've studied the Spell of Absolute Negation!

Requires level 37 and 500 pt. Mental Energy.

Cooldown: 12 hrs.

When cast, all spells cast by enemy wizards within the spell's range revert against them, disrupting their casting and decreasing their resistance to magic by 50%.

The world crumbled. Pain clouded my mind. My legs slackened but I couldn't afford to collapse.

Zander shouted something. The ghost's outline dissolved in the air — but it wasn't porting. It was decomposing!

Rodrigo had managed to cast Absolute Negation, then sank to the ground as the outline of the other ghost fell apart in the air.

Zander's sword kept drawing patterns of complex combos.

Sounds started to return.

"I got him!" Zander's voice faded into the cotton-wool silence, followed by Enea's whisper,

"Alex, stay with me... please... wake up..."

She was actually screaming as she poured a healing elixir down my throat. She was completely out of mana.

Platinus had another elixir ready.

"I'm okay," I didn't recognize my own voice. "You'd better help Rodrigo. I'm fine."

The same unnatural silence shrouded the ruins. Still, the tingling sensation in my fingertips was already gone.

* * *

We'd lost three group members.

Togien, Iskandar and Tylor had been sent back to their respawn points. Zander's life bar barely glowed. He refused an elixir and cast a healing aura on all of us instead.

Enea helped me back to my feet.

Zander walked over to me. "How did you do

that?" he asked, locking his gaze with mine.

"How did I do what?"

"You killed a Disciple's Ghost with two blows, disrupting his teleport."

"I just parried his attack, that's all."

"Could it be your sword, then?"

"Possible. It's made of some ancient cargonite alloy. Apparently, ghosts can't stand the touch of it."

Zander nodded, seemingly happy with my explanation. I made a mental note to ask him if he knew anything about the mysterious alloy.

Virgil was sitting on the ground shaking his head. He was in a state. His health wasn't in a hurry to restore.

Holding onto the wall, Rodrigo scrambled to his feet.

"Are we going back?" Enea asked once she'd made sure I was okay. She and Platinus were the only two group members who hadn't been wounded in this brief melee.

"No, why?"

"We've lost three players!"

"That's not a problem," Zander replied, taking stock of the situation. "All group members have spare gear sets in their tents. The path has been purged. They can use a walk. Give them ten minutes. We really should wait for them here before advancing any further."

"Not a healthy idea," I said. "We don't know the ghosts' respawn times. If they reappear, we might regret it. We need to keep going and activate the next location."

"And who might be waiting for us there?" Zander snapped. "You didn't think about that, did you?"

"But Zander, staying here is much more dangerous! There're only three ghosts which might mean that they used to be the strongest wizards among the castle's defenders. Can Iskandar cast Absolute Negation?"

"He can't," Rodrigo replied. "His level's not high enough."

"Which means that if they reappear we have nothing to defend ourselves with. The ghosts were strong enough to breach the Heavenly Shield! If we stay here, we're all gonna die, it's as simple as that!"

Reluctantly Zander agreed. "I'll send the guys a message and tell them to move it. The ghosts might respawn soon, you're right. In which case we're toast. So let's do it this way. We simply walk through the gate and wait right there. We aren't going anywhere near the donjon, okay?"

I nodded. "Fair enough."

* * *

I was the first to walk through the crumbling gate of the castle's third and highest defense level.

Then I froze, recognizing a familiar figure.

Christa. Level 21. Demon.

Level 21! She hadn't wasted her time. Leathery wings were folded behind her back. Her eyes glowed. A fiery aura was coursing her body.

Her ability to fly probably opened at level 30. I suppose that was the good news.

Blocking our approach to the donjon, rusty ranks of high-level undead bristled with flaking weapons. Groups of Dark casters lurked behind their backs.

"I heard you and your new girlfriend bought the castle?" Christa's voice rang with hatred. "Very well. Try and claim it if you can!"

The tip of her infernal sword drew an arc in the air, pointing at Enea. "I challenge you!"

Cut into the cliffs, the chiseled precipitous outline of the castle towered in the night behind her.

Silence fell, disrupted only by the occasional rattling of metal as the undead shuffled their feet. They must have been NPCs controlled by some powerful Dark spell. A group of trolls nearby was my biggest concern, their massive bodies reeking with decay.

We were but few compared to their dozens. This was against all the rules. But this was how cyberspace thrived these days: feeding on human emotion. These infernal hordes had been drawn here by Christa's hateful fury.

Pointless reasoning with her. Words wouldn't break the chain of fatal events. Christa would stop at nothing to feed the anger devouring her from inside. I dreaded to even think how much she'd charged for her soul in order to gain control over these top-level NPCs.

"Enea, you don't have to-" I began.

"It's all right. I'll manage," her voice tinged with strange new notes. "We can't leave this unanswered!"

Zander frowned. He zoned out momentarily, checking the in-game network, then addressed Christa,

"You didn't file the castle application. Which means you have no right to be here. Back off!"

"So what if I didn't? I'm here, aren't I? What are *you* gonna do about it, *mercenary?* File a ticket with the admins?" she snarled in disdain.

I noticed a pale and agitated Platinus sneak a couple of vials to Enea. Iskandar offered her some whispered advice; she nodded inconspicuously.

"I challenge you!" Christa's voice shattered into a thousand echoes.

"I heard you the first time," fearlessly Enea stepped forward, motioning to me not to interfere.

The moon rose from behind the donjon, its dull greenish light brushing the scales of Enea's unique armor. Now she had a staff in her hands — the one I'd salvaged by the pond all that time ago. It was topped with a modest-sized precious stone. The opposite end of the staff was sharp and pointy.

Enea raised the large hood of her cloak, both to protect her pet and to activate the full-kit bonus which offered +5% to her chances of receiving an additional Blindness effect to her attacking spells.

Breaking the duel code, Christa lunged forward, her every movement sleek and lethal. My breathing seized as her infernal sword drew a complex combo in the air. Enea, however, dodged the blow with an effortless ease. Her staff top flashed as she cast a spell, sending a flurry of snowflakes into the air. Then her outline disappeared in the popping of a teleport only to reappear a good fifteen feet away from Christa.

Another spell! A magic Ice Spear glistened in the moonlight; Christa's Fiery Shield umbrellaed out, deflecting the spell. Fragments of ice flew everywhere, consumed by clouds of boiling steam.

"Aren't you going to stay and fight?" Christa bellowed.

A circular wave of darkness swept through the gloom. Reaching Enea, it crashed into the raid buff Zander had cast earlier and transformed into a response blow of cleansing light.

The discordant wailing of the undead echoed from the ancient walls as they'd also received their share of damage. Still, the demonic spell binding them didn't allow them to disperse.

Enea used the opportunity to port again and reappeared next to Christa, surrounded by a halo of razor-sharp ice flakes.

"Your hatred will kill you one day," Enea breathed out, casting a new attacking spell.

"Your stupidity will kill you earlier!"

In a lightning exchange of blows, both recoiled. Christa's shoulder was seized by ice. Enea's cheekbone dripped blood onto her tunic.

In the deafening silence that followed, the gate creaked, letting in Togien, Iskandar and Tylor. They'd already picked up their stuff and equipped their gear.

"What the hell's going on here?" Togien boomed in disbelief.

"Quiet!" Platinus hissed at him, then murmured under his breath, craning his neck for a better look, "The vial... Throw it *now*..."

From behind the safety of the Mana Shield, Enea kept parrying the incoming blows with her staff, receiving minimal damage while waiting for a chance to cast another spell. I shuddered. I don't think I'd ever been so anxious in my entire life. No idea what kind of abilities the neuroimplant developers had endowed Christa with, but now she was acting like a warrior. And a wizard has virtually no chances against a warrior in close combat.

Time slowed down around me. The emotional strain must have triggered my mind expander into action. I saw the infernal blade trace an arc through the air and watched Enea dodge aside, throwing her head back as she recoiled. A strand of her hair floated to the ground, severed by the sharp demonic steel.

Christa stepped closer, exiting the slashing blow. They now stood face to face. Gripping tightly onto the scales of Enea's armor, the baby mantis swayed in his combat stance, trying to protect his owner. But he wasn't up to it yet.

Apparently, that wasn't what he thought. Alpha the Mantis threw his tiny front leg in the air. A small spike full of neurotoxin sank into Christa's eyelid.

She didn't even feel it. Still, the venom had disrupted the choreographed precision of her movements. Temporarily blinded by the piercing pain, she failed to complete the combo. With a shriek, Christa sprang back.

Enea jumped at her chance and increased the distance using another short-range teleport she'd learned from Rodrigo and Iskandar.

Sheets of foggy haze swirled around us. The castle's inner yard was rather messy, littered with rusty weapons, rotting rags and piles of collapsed masonry mixed with the heaping deposits of sand and clay brought here by torrential rain.

The combat grew ever more desperate.

A few Ice Arrows finally removed Christa's Fiery Shield, dealing her some minor damage but unable to stop her lightning strike.

Enea cried out. A fierce slashing blow of Christa's sword had sliced through her staff and part of the tunic, leaving a bleeding wound in her shoulder.

Mechanically I went for my sword.

Zander lay a firm hand on my shoulder, "Don't."

For a brief moment, Enea lost concentration. Immediately Christa dealt a merciless coup de grace while ignoring the desperate spell Enea was attempting to cast.

A dull slurping sound filled the air. Enveloped by a Levitation Aura, a massive chunk of stone forced its way out of the mud and flew into the air.

Christa's sword struck sparks against the rock, throwing the unseemly flagstone out of her way until it hit the donjon wall and shattered.

Enea sank her staff's sharp end into Christa's thigh and recoiled again, breaking the distance and gulping a quick mana elixir.

Bellowing curses, Christa dropped to one knee. Grinding her teeth, she forced the broken staff out of her bleeding wound and lunged at Enea, limping.

Two more attack spells met her. An Ice Spear and a fireball hit the demoness simultaneously.

Christa staggered. She must have counted on a quick and easy victory. Well, she couldn't have been more wrong. Her life bar hovered dangerously in the red, her tag sporting a Blindness icon compliments of Enea's full-gear bonus.

The undead lunged forward. They picked up her collapsing body and dragged it closer to the donjon entrance, then closed their ranks again.

"Let me go!" a furious shriek came from where she lay. "I'm not finished here yet!"

Oh. It looked like Christa wasn't the one running this show.

"Regroup!" Zander stepped forward, readying himself to fight a losing battle.

I supported the staggering Enea. She could barely breathe, shivery after having given her all in combat.

"I did it," she kept whispering.

The murmuring voices of the dark wizards rustled in the distance, followed by a growing rumbling noise. The black mouth of a portal opened in front of the donjon entrance and swallowed the undead.

Zander lowered his sword and turned to us. "What the hell was that?"

"No idea. Look!" I pointed at the peaked cliffs which formed the castle's main tower.

Where only a moment ago the moonlight had played with the donjon's vaulted windows, darkness reigned.

Rodrigo frowned. "Did they teleport to the upper halls?"

"We'll soon find out," I said, heading decisively for the tower.

* * *

Enea and I stepped together into the ground-floor main hall.

Echoes filled the vast vaulted space. Everywhere you turned you were confronted with the dust-buried evidence of desperate fighting which had raged here millennia ago.

A circle at least 30 feet in diameter stood out clearly on the floor.

The walls lit up, lined with a multitude of tiny flames welcoming our arrival.

The circle's edge shimmered blue. A column of emerald light lit up at the far end of the hall.

Congratulations! You've activated the castle's stationary teleport!

Congratulations! You've activated the castle's safe respawn zone!

Congratulations! You've claimed ownership of Rion Castle!

You've received a new level!

New quest alert: Purge

Quest type: unique

Before dawn breaks, you need to purge the donjon of the spawn of the dark.

Reward: By succeeding, you'll remove the ancient curse cast on the castle by enemy wizards. The castle control interface will be unblocked.

Enea gave me a quizzical look. "Does that

mean we're done here?"

"Not really," I copied the messages into the group chat and added as I listened to the trolls' heavy gait thundering overhead, "Zander, I'm extending your contract. We've got to move our respawn points."

"Agreed," he too listened intently to the sound of heavy footsteps reverberating through the walls. "No one's logging out! We have six hours left till daybreak!"

"If he only knew we have five days left to farm two cartfuls of Spectral Dust," Enea whispered.

"Hey, look what I've found!" Platinus scooped through the dust coating the floor and pulled out a staff topped with a crimson stone. "Enea, what do you think? Can you use it instead of your old one?"

She smiled. "I can try."

Her fingers touched the darkened wood. A tiny speck of light glistened inside the magic stone.

"Alexatis, mind coming here for a sec?" Zander brushed the dust off the wall, revealing some symbols. "This looks like a door. I can push my knife into the crack. Still, I can't open it."

"Watch out," Enea warned him. "Can't you see all the magic seals?"

The symbols looked familiar. Some of them

were identical to the runes on my sword blade.

"This is probably the entrance to a vault," I said. "I'm pretty sure there's something of great value inside."

"Think we can open it?" Zander asked.

A new message appeared in my interface:

Quest update alert: The Mystery of the Ancient Manuscripts!

Translate the inscription in order to gain access to the secret vaults of Rion Castle.

"We're wasting our time."

I couldn't shake off the thought that Christa's arrival had been no coincidence. Most likely, her motives had just happened to suit some much more powerful entity. Somebody — or something — unwilling to see Rion Castle regain its old freedom and glory.

The trolls' footsteps resounded overhead.

We faced a long and grueling night.

END OF BOOK ONE

THE MC'S STATS AS OF THE SECOND BOOK'S END:

Alexatis. Level 21. Neuro

Life, 172.5/172.5 (Stamina, 150 + Gear, 22.5)

Physical Energy, 105/105 (Strength, 90 + current abilities and the gear bonus, 15)

Mental Energy, 198/198 (Intellect, 150 + current abilities and the gear bonus, 48)

Physical Defense, 215 (Scaly Armor, 210 + Agility bonus, 5)

Physical Attack, 42 (Mysterious Sword at 30% Durability, 15 pt. + Strength, 5 + the gear bonus, 2 + Intense Training, 6 + character level, 20)

Mental Defense, 39% (Self-Control + Spirit + the gear bonus)

Elemental Defense, 15% (Spirit and the Scaly Breastplate)

Mental Attack, 52 (spells studied, 30 + Unity

of Schools, 2 + character level, 20)

Mental Energy Regeneration, 4,34 pt./sec (Spirit divided by 2 + 0,84 bonus from Synergy, Power of Reason and Self-Control)

Strength, 10.5 (Secret Knowledge, 9+1 + the gear bonus, 0.5)

Intellect, 19.8 (Secret Knowledge, 15+1 + the gear bonus, 0.8 + the ring, 3)

Agility, 10 (the gear bonus, 9+1)

Stamina, 16.5 (15 + the underwear kit bonus, 1.5)

Spirit, 10

Main Professions, Require activation

Achievements:
Celebrated Pioneer (a map-making app available)

Clan Founder (+ 1,000 to Popularity, +1 to all Reputations)

The Neuro Development Branch:

Secret Knowledge:

Eons ago, the Ancient Gods (sometimes also called the Founder Gods) tampered with our ancestors' evolution, endowing them with a number of abilities which are now almost completely extinct. Only occasionally do they resurface in certain individuals known as Neuros.

You're one of them. Both your body and mind harbor a potential yet unlocked.

+1 to Strength

+1 to Intellect

+1% to XP per each invested Ability pt.

Observational Skills:

You're highly perceptive. Whether reading ancient manuscripts or watching other people, you pay attention to every detail, immediately grasping the technique of a combat blow or a spell incantation. You can then enter the knowledge you thus receive into special books or dedicated parchment scrolls for further study.

Warning! The level of the blow or spell you intend to study cannot exceed that of your character.

Each Ability point invested gives +2% to your chances of studying the blow or the spell (regardless of whether the object of your study is an NPC or another player).

Spell Interception:

The fact that all spells are recited in the Founders' language combined with your ability to lip read allows you to learn any spell.

Warning! In order to successfully intercept a spell, the caster (observation target) should be located within your direct line of vision. At level 1, your lip-reading range is set at 30 feet.

Each Ability point invested adds 2 ft. to your lip-reading range.

Spell Interception does not preclude other possible ways of spell studying.

Acquisition of Blows and Combos:

You effortlessly memorize new movements while watching combat practice or live combat. Later, this allows you to make a drawing of the blow or even combo technique from memory, recreating both attack and defense maneuvers.

Requires Observational Skills and Intense Training.

Each Ability point invested adds +2% to your chances of studying a blow or a combo.

Unity of Origin:

According to legend, all living beings in the Universe used to have a single ancestor. Some might snicker saying that an orc and a human being can't possibly share ancestry. Still, every legend harbors a grain of truth.

Each Ability point invested adds +2% to your chances of intercepting a spell or learning a new blow typical of other races, regardless of their affiliation (Light vs. Dark).

Unity of Schools:

Some time ago, you chanced upon an ancient book. As you struggled through it, trying to make sense of the faded writings on its crumbling pages, you were surprised to discover the writer's heretic ideas. According to the book's author, all types of magic and sorcery, including elemental and mind control, are firmly rooted in the long-forgotten school of Chaos.

Later, as you watched the effects produced by various schools of magic, your conclusions confirmed the ancient author's ideas. The powers of Chaos had been the foundation of all modern schools and practices.

Each Ability point invested adds +2% to the Range, Strength and Duration of every spell you study, as well as removes all bans and penalties for combining various kinds of magic and sorcery.

Reflex Optimization:

As you watch wildlife species (whose

survival depends on their highest levels of ergonomics), you can learn and adopt their energy preservation skills. Your movements become more precise and calculated.

Each Ability point invested gives -2% to your mental and physical energy expenditures in combat.

Evolution:

The activation of this particular characteristic allows you to receive a small but continuous boost to your main stats, depending on the type of your daily activities. These changes will be visible as special boost bars situated opposite their respective characteristics in your character panel. For instance, if you read a lot you might notice the increase of your Intellect boost bar. Once the bar is full, you will receive +1 pt. to its respective characteristic.

The above boost does not cancel traditional characteristic leveling. Neither does it affect your items' bonuses.

Intense Training:

Each spell or blow you study requires constant perfecting. In order to improve your attack and defense skills, you need to practice a lot, creating your own combinations and turning new moves into reflexes.

Ability bonus: your damage, defense, mob control and aura range will improve. This only applies to the physical and magic skills you use on a regular basis, without affecting those you've learned but failed to apply.

Each Ability point invested adds +5% to attack strength.

Pain Threshold:

You learn to control pain. You might have already discovered, by extreme trial and error, that you don't experience pain as long as your Health is above 80%. As your HP dwindle, you start experiencing an increasing pain.

Each Ability point invested raises your pain threshold 3%. The maximum pain threshold allowed is 50% HP.

Synergy:

Everything in our world is interconnected. You can use various sources of energy, including elements, ancient artifacts and places of power marked by megalithic monuments. As you study them and listen intently to the world around you, you begin to tune in into various energy currents, allowing you to locate their sources and use them to restore your powers and even life.

Starting at level 20, you'll be able to trap and store any excess physical or mental energy within energy crystals.

+5% to your physical and mental energy regeneration speed.

Power of Reason:

A Neuro's intellect affects everything he or she does.

Every 30 pt. Intellect add +3% to both attack and defense and +5% to the XP received for successfully using the blows or spells you've learned from other characters. All such blows or spells will add +3% to your chances of dealing critical damage or, when used in defense, to your chances of reusing the blow or spell with decreased cooldown times and -50% of required energy expenditure.

+10% to your mental energy regeneration speed.

Insight:

You're constantly busy studying everything around you, analyzing the nature of all events and perfecting your abilities and skills. Your goal is to get to the bottom of everything trying to work out how things work instead of mindlessly using them, be it a spell, a blow or a professional skill.

Each Ability point invested gives -3% to cooldown times and energy expenditure required for all types of physical and mental attack, defense and impact.

+2% to profession leveling speed for all farming and manufacturing professions.

Self-Control:

You have a natural 25% resistance to all kinds of magic and mind control. You can successfully resist mental attacks, preserving clarity of mind.

Each Ability point invested adds +2% to your chances of repelling a negative effect or boosting a positive one, be it a spell or your opponent's ability. +2% to your chances of successfully casting a spell when attacked. +3% to mental energy regeneration speed.

On reaching level 5, this ability will allow you to consciously control your mental energy distribution between several recipients — for instance, a magic artifact or an item of gear.

Enhanced Perception:

You learn with remarkable ease. Your outlook isn't limited by racial or class prejudices. You're free from all phobias and superstitions.

As a result, you see and notice a lot compared to others. Your night vision and reduced visibility navigation skills are considerably superior to theirs. At level 20, you will receive a new primary skill, Twilight Vision, which you can consequently level up and improve.

Enhanced Perception allows you to detect danger before others can. It also adds +20% to your chances of seeing a stealthed-up enemy stalking you. Each Ability point invested adds +1 to your Field of Vision Range.

ABOUT THE AUTHOR

Andrei Livadny is a popular Russian science fiction author. Born on May 27 1969 in the city of Pskov, he was an avid reader from an early age. But it was the Russian translation of Robert A. Heinlein's *The Orphans of the Sky* that decided his choice of future occupation. The story has become a pivotal moment in the boy's life, leaving a lasting impression on him.

Andrei wrote his first book at the age of eight. Since then, he's never stopped working on new books. His passion for science fiction has gradually become his career.

In 1998, Andrei debuted in Russia's leading publishing house EKSMO with his novella *The Island of Hope*. Since then, he has penned over 90 books that have enjoyed a total of 153 editions.

Andrei has created several unique worlds, each unlike the previous. He wrote *A History of Our Galaxy* with humanity itself as a protagonist. This sixty-book series creates a history of our future civilization and its contacts with alien races, forming a convincing and logical picture of humanity's development for two millennia from now.

Besides hard science fiction, Andrei Livadny also works in cyberpunk genres which allow him to focus on human relationships and raise questions about artificial intelligence and identity uploading, describing cyberspace as humanity's future environment.

The English translation of *A History of Our Galaxy* will be available shortly.

Thank you for reading *The Crystal Sphere!*
If you like what you've read, check out other sci fi, fantasy and LitRPG novels published by Magic Dome Books:

***An NPC's Path* LitRPG series by Pavel Kornev:**
The Dead Rogue

***Level Up* series by Dan Sugralinov:**
Re-Start

***The Way of the Shaman* LitRPG series by Vasily Mahanenko:**
Survival Quest
The Kartoss Gambit
The Secret of the Dark Forest
The Phantom Castle
The Karmadont Chess Set
Shaman's Revenge
Clans War

***Dark Paladin* LitRPG series by Vasily Mahanenko:**
The Beginning
The Quest
Restart

***Galactogon* LitRPG series by Vasily Mahanenko:**
Start the Game!

***The Bard from Barliona* LitRPG series by Eugenia Dmitrieva and Vasily Mahanenko:**
The Renegades

***The Neuro* LitRPG series by Andrei Livadny:**
The Curse of Rion Castle
The Reapers

***Phantom Server* LitRPG series by Andrei Livadny:**

Edge of Reality
The Outlaw
Black Sun

***Reality Benders* LitRPG series by Michael Atamanov:**

Countdown
External Threat

***The Dark Herbalist* LitRPG series by Michael Atamanov:**

Video Game Plotline Tester
Stay on the Wing
A Trap for the Potentate

***Perimeter Defense* LitRPG series by Michael Atamanov:**

Sector Eight
Beyond Death
New Contract
A Game with No Rules

***Mirror World* LitRPG series by Alexey Osadchuk:**

Project Daily Grind
The Citadel
The Way of the Outcast
The Twilight Obelisk

***AlterGame* LitRPG series by Andrew Novak:**

The First Player
On the Lost Continent
God Mode

***Citadel World* series by Kir Lukovkin:**

The URANUS Code
The Secret of Atlantis

***The Expansion (The History of the Galaxy)* series by A. Livadny:**
Blind Punch
The Shadow of Earth

Point Apocalypse *(a near-future action thriller)* **by Alex Bobl**

***The Sublime Electricity* series by Pavel Kornev**
The Illustrious
The Heartless
The Fallen
The Dormant

You're in Game!
(LitRPG Stories from Bestselling Authors)

You're in Game-2!
(More LitRPG stories set in your favorite worlds)

***The Game Master* series by A. Bobl and A. Levitsky:**
The Lag

***The Naked Demon* by Sherrie L.**
(a paranormal romance)

More books and series are coming out soon!

In order to have new books of the series translated faster, we need your help and support! Please consider leaving a review or spread the word by recommending *The Crystal Sphere* to your friends and posting the link on social media. The more people buy the book, the sooner we'll be able to make new translations available.

Thank you!

Till next time

www.ingramcontent.com/pod-product-compliance
Lightning Source LLC
Chambersburg PA
CBHW060758030726
47503CB00002B/295

9788088231233